Also available from

# NORA ROBERTS

### *COLD NIGHTS, WARM HEARTS*
Sometimes the gift you need most
is the one closest to your heart

### *LOVE AND OTHER STARS*
Forbidden fruit and irresistible secrets reveal themselves

### *THE BRIGHTEST OF STARS*
Their love shines brightest on the darkest of nights

### *ALL MY STARS*
A cosmic trio: bounty hunters, jewel thieves
and memory loss

### *SUMMER ALL ALONG*
A captivating Calhoun tale of charm, faith
and rich family history

### *THE DARKEST OF NIGHTS*
The darkest of nights are rife with desire and danger

For a full list of titles by Nora Roberts
please visit www.noraroberts.com.

T0359187

# NORA ROBERTS

## Enchant My Heart

Published by
Mills & Boon
An imprint of Harlequin Enterprises (Australia) Pty Limited
(ABN 47 001 180 918), a subsidiary of HarperCollins
Publishers Australia Pty Limited (ABN 36 009 913 517)
Level 19, 201 Elizabeth Street
SYDNEY NSW 2000
AUSTRALIA

® and ™ (apart from those relating to FSC®) are trademarks of Harlequin
Enterprises (Australia) Pty Limited or its corporate affiliates. Trademarks indicated
with ® are registered in Australia, New Zealand and in other countries.
Contact admin_legal@Harlequin.ca for details.

Printed and bound in Australia by McPherson's Printing Group

# CONTENTS

# Charmed

To everyone who believes in happy endings.

# *Prologue*

Magic exists. Who can doubt it, when there are rainbows and wildflowers, the music of the wind and the silence of the stars? Anyone who has loved has been touched by magic. It is such a simple and such an extraordinary part of the lives we live.

There are those who have been given more, who have been chosen to carry on a legacy handed down through endless ages. Their forebears were Merlin the enchanter, Ninian the sorceress, the faerie princess Rhiannon, the Wegewarte of Germany and the jinns of Arabia. Through their blood ran the power of Finn of the Celts, the ambitious Morgan le Fay, and others whose names were whispered only in shadows and in secret.

When the world was young and magic as common as a raindrop, faeries danced in the deep forests, and—sometimes for mischief, sometimes for love—mixed with mortals.

And they do still.

Her bloodline was old. Her power was ancient. Even as a child she had understood, had been taught, that such gifts were not without price. The loving parents who treasured her could not lower the cost, or pay it themselves, but could only love, instruct and watch the young girl grow to womanhood. They could only stand and hope as she experienced the pains and the joys of that most fascinating of journeys.

And, because she felt more than others, because her gift demanded that she feel more, she learned to court peace.

As a woman, she preferred a quiet life, and was often alone without the pain of loneliness.

As a witch, she accepted her gift, and never forgot the responsibility it entailed.

Perhaps she yearned, as mortals and others have yearned since the beginning, for a true and abiding love. For she knew better than most that there was no power, no enchantment, no sorcery, greater than the gift of an open and accepting heart.

# Chapter 1

When she saw the little girl peek through the fairy roses, Anastasia had no idea the child would change her life. She'd been humming to herself, as she often did when she gardened, enjoying the scent and the feel of earth. The warm September sun was golden, and the gentle whoosh of the sea on the rocks below her sloping yard was a lovely background to the buzzing of bees and the piping of birdsong. Her long gray cat was stretched out beside her, his tail twitching in time with some feline dream.

A butterfly landed soundlessly on her hand, and she stroked the edge of its pale blue wings with a fingertip. As it fluttered off, she heard the rustling. Glancing over, she saw a small face peeping through the hedge of fairy roses.

Ana's smile came quickly, naturally. The face was charming, with its little pointed chin and its pert nose, its big blue eyes mirroring the color of the sky. A pixie cap of glossy brown hair completed the picture.

The girl smiled back, those summer-sky eyes full of curiosity and mischief.

"Hello," Ana said, as if she always found little girls in her rosebushes.

"Hi." The girl's voice was bright, and a little breathless. "Can you catch butterflies? I never got to pet one like that before."

"I suppose. But it seems rude to try unless one invites you." She brushed the hair from her brow with her forearm and sat back on her heels. Ana had noticed a moving van unloading the day before, and she concluded she was meeting one of her new neighbors. "Have you moved into the house next door?"

"Uh-huh. We're going to live here now. I like it, 'cause I get to look right out my bedroom window and see the water. I saw a seal, too. In Indiana you only see them in the zoo. Can I come over?"

"Of course you can." Ana set her garden spade aside as the girl stepped through the rosebushes. In her arms was a wriggling puppy. "And who do we have here?"

"This is Daisy." The child pressed a loving kiss to the top of the puppy's head. "She's a golden retriever. I got to pick her out myself right before we left Indiana. She got to fly in the plane with us, and we were hardly scared at all. I have to take good care of her and give her food and water and brush her and everything, 'cause she's my responsibility."

"She's very beautiful," Ana said soberly. And very heavy, she imagined, for a little girl of five or six. She held out her arms. "May I?"

"Do you like dogs?" The little girl kept chattering as she passed Daisy over. "I do. I like dogs and cats and everything. Even the hamsters Billy Walker has. Someday I'm going to have a horse, too. We'll have to see about that. That's what my daddy says. We'll have to see about that."

Utterly charmed, Ana stroked the puppy as she sniffed and licked at her. The child was as sweet as sunshine. "I'm very fond of dogs and cats and everything," Ana told her. "My cousin has horses. Two big ones and a brand-new baby."

"Really?" The child squatted down and began to pet the sleeping cat. "Can I see them?"

"He doesn't live far, so perhaps one day. We'll have to ask your parents."

"My mommy went to heaven. She's an angel now."

Ana's heart broke a little. Reaching out, she touched the shiny hair and opened herself. There was no pain here, and that was a relief. The memories were good ones. At the touch, the child looked up and smiled.

"I'm Jessica," she said. "But you can call me Jessie."

"I'm Anastasia." Because it was too much to resist, Ana bent down and kissed the pert nose. "But you can call me Ana."

Introductions over, Jessie settled down to bombard Ana with questions, filtering information about herself through the bright chatter. She'd just had a birthday and was six. She would be starting first grade in her brand-new school on Tuesday. Her favorite color was purple, and she hated lima beans more than anything.

Could Ana show her how to plant flowers? Did her cat have a name? Did she have any little girls? Why not?

So they sat in the sunshine, a bright pixie of a girl in pink rompers and a woman with garden dirt smearing her shorts and her lightly tanned legs, while Quigley the cat ignored the playful attentions of Daisy the dog.

Ana's long, wheat-colored hair was tied carelessly back, and the occasional wisp worked free of the band to dance in the wind around her face. She wore no cosmetics. Her fragile, heartbreaking beauty was as natural as her power, a combination of Celtic bones, smoky eyes, the wide, poetically sculptured Donovan mouth—and something more nebulous. Her face was the mirror of a giving heart.

The pup marched over to sniff at the herbs in her rockery. Ana laughed at something Jessica said.

"Jessie!" The voice swept over the hedge of roses, deeply

male, and touched with exasperation and concern. "Jessica Alice Sawyer!"

"Uh-oh. He used my whole name." But Jessie's eyes were twinkling as she jumped to her feet. There was obviously little fear of reprisals.

"Over here! Daddy, I'm right over here with Ana! Come and see!"

A moment later, there was a man towering over the fairy roses. No gift was needed to detect waves of frustration, relief and annoyance. Ana blinked once, surprised that this rough-and-ready male was the father of the little sprite currently bouncing beside her.

Maybe it was the day or two's growth of beard that made him look so dangerous, she thought. But she doubted it. Beneath that dusky shadow was a sharp-featured face of planes and angles, a full mouth set in grim lines. Only the eyes were like his daughter's, a clear, brilliant blue, marred now by an expression of impatience. The sun brought out glints of red in his dark, tousled hair as he dragged a hand through it.

From her perch on the ground, he looked enormous. Athletically fit and disconcertingly strong, in a ripped T-shirt and faded jeans sprung at the seams.

He cast one long, annoyed and unmistakably distrustful glance at Ana before giving his attention to his daughter.

"Jessica. Didn't I tell you to stay in the yard?"

"I guess." She smiled winningly. "Daisy and I heard Ana singing, and when we looked, she had this butterfly right on her hand. And she said we could come over. She has a cat, see? And her cousin has horses, and her other cousin has a cat *and* a dog."

Obviously used to Jessie's rambling, her father waited it out. "When I tell you to stay in the yard, and then you're not there, I'm going to worry."

It was a simple statement, made in even tones. Ana had to respect the fact that the man didn't have to raise his voice or spout ultimatums to get his point across. She felt every bit as chastened as Jessie.

"I'm sorry, Daddy," Jessie murmured over a pouting lower lip.

"I should apologize, Mr. Sawyer." Ana rose to lay a hand on Jessie's shoulder. After all, it looked as if they were in this together. "I did invite her over, and I was enjoying her company so much that it didn't occur to me that you wouldn't be able to see where she was."

He said nothing for a moment, just stared at her with those water-clear eyes until she had to fight the urge to squirm. When he flicked his gaze down to his daughter again, Ana realized she'd been holding her breath.

"You should take Daisy over and feed her."

"Okay." Jessie hauled the reluctant pup into her arms, then stopped when her father inclined his head.

"And thank Mrs...?"

"Miss," Ana supplied. "Donovan. Anastasia Donovan."

"Thank Miss Donovan for putting up with you."

"Thank you for putting up with me, Ana," Jessie said with singsong politeness, sending Ana a conspirator's grin. "Can I come back?"

"I hope you will."

As she stepped through the bushes, Jessie offered her father a sunny smile. "I didn't mean to make you worry, Daddy. Honest."

He bent down and tweaked her nose. "Brat." Ana heard the wealth of love behind the exasperation.

With a giggle, Jessie ran across the yard, the puppy wriggling in her arms. Ana's smile faded the moment those cool blue eyes turned back to her.

"She's an absolutely delightful child," Ana began, amazed that she had to wipe damp palms on her shorts. "I do apologize for not making certain you knew where she was, but I hope you'll let her come back to visit me again."

"It wasn't your responsibility." His voice was cool, neither friendly nor unfriendly. Ana had the uncomfortable certainty that she was being weighed, from the top of her head to the bottom of her grass-stained sneakers. "Jessie is naturally curious and friendly. Sometimes too much of both. It doesn't occur to her that there are people in the world who might take advantage of that."

Equally cool now, Ana inclined her head. "Point taken, Mr. Sawyer. Though I can assure you I rarely gobble up young girls for breakfast."

He smiled, a slow curving of the lips that erased the harshness from his face and replaced it with a devastating appeal. "You certainly don't fit my perception of an ogre, Miss Donovan. Now I'll have to apologize for being so abrupt. She gave me a scare. I hadn't even unpacked yet, and I'd lost her."

"Misplaced." Ana tried another cautious smile. She looked beyond him to the two-story redwood house next door, with its wide band of windows and its curvy deck. Though she was content in her privacy, she was glad it hadn't remained empty long. "It's nice to have a child nearby, especially one as entertaining as Jessie. I hope you'll let her come back."

"I often wonder if I *let* her do anything." He flicked a finger over a tiny pink rose. "Unless you replace these with a ten-foot wall, she'll be back." And at least he'd know where to look if she disappeared again. "Don't be afraid to send her home when she overstays her welcome." He tucked his hands in his pockets. "I'd better go make sure she doesn't feed Daisy our dinner."

"Mr. Sawyer?" Ana said as he turned away. "Enjoy Monterey."

"Thanks." His long strides carried him over the lawn, onto the deck and into the house.

Ana stood where she was for another moment. She couldn't remember the last time the air here had sizzled with so much energy. Letting out a long breath, she bent to pick up her gardening tools, while Quigley wound himself around her legs.

She certainly couldn't remember the last time her palms had gone damp just because a man had looked at her.

Then again, she couldn't recall ever being looked at in quite that way before. Looked at, looked into, looked through, all at once. A very neat trick, she mused as she carried the tools into her greenhouse.

An intriguing pair, father and daughter. Gazing through the sparkling glass wall of the greenhouse, she studied the house centered in the next yard. As their closest neighbor, she thought, it was only natural that she should wonder about them. Ana was also wise enough—and had learned through painful experience—to be careful not to let her wondering lead to any involvement beyond a natural friendliness.

There were precious few who could accept what was not of the common world. The price of her gift was a vulnerable heart that had already suffered miserably at the cold hand of rejection.

But she didn't dwell on that. In fact, as she thought of the man, and of the child, she smiled. What would he have done, she wondered with a little laugh, if she had told him that, while she wasn't an ogre—no, indeed—she was most definitely a witch.

In the sunny and painfully disorganized kitchen, Boone Sawyer dug through a packing box until he unearthed a skillet. He knew the move to California had been a good one—he'd convinced himself of that—but he'd certainly underestimated the time, the trouble and the general inconvenience of packing up a home and plopping it down somewhere else.

What to take, what to leave behind. Hiring movers, having his car shipped, transporting the puppy that Jessie had fallen in love with. Justifying his decision to her worried grandparents, school registration—school shopping. Lord, was he

going to have to repeat that nightmare every fall for the next
eleven years?

At least the worst was behind him. He hoped. All he had
to do now was unpack, find a place for everything and make
a home out of a strange house.

Jessie was happy. That was, and always had been, the most
important thing. Then again, he mused as he browned some
beef for chili, Jessie was happy anywhere. Her sunny disposi-
tion and her remarkable capacity to make friends were both a
blessing and a bafflement. It was astonishing to Boone that a
child who had lost her mother at the tender age of two could
be unaffected, so resilient, so completely normal.

And he knew that if not for Jessie he would surely have
gone quietly mad after Alice's death.

He didn't often think of Alice now, and that fact sometimes brought him a rush of guilt. He had loved her—God,
he had loved her—and the child they'd made together was a
living, breathing testament to that love. But he'd been without
her now longer than he'd been with her. Though he had tried
to hang on to the grief, as a kind of proof of that love, it had
faded under the demands and pressures of day-to-day living.

Alice was gone, Jessie was not. It was because of both of
them that he'd made the difficult decision to move to Monterey. In Indiana, in the home he and Alice had bought while
she was carrying Jessie, there had been too many ties to the
past. Both his parents and Alice's had been a ten-minute drive
away. As the only grandchild on both sides, Jessie had been
the center of attention, and the object of subtle competition.

For himself, Boone had wearied of the constant advice, the
gentle—and not-so-gentle—criticism of his parenting. And,
of course, the matchmaking. The child needs a mother. A man
needs a wife. His mother had decided to make it her life's work
to find the perfect woman to fit both bills.

Because that had begun to infuriate him, and because he'd

realized how easy it would be to stay in the house and wallow in the memories it held, he'd chosen to move.

He could work anywhere. Monterey had been the final choice because of the climate, the life-style, the schools. And, he could admit privately, because some internal voice had told him this was the place. For both of them.

He liked being able to look out of the window and see the water, or those fascinatingly sculptured cypress trees. He certainly liked the fact that he wasn't crowded in by neighbors. It was Alice who had enjoyed being surrounded by people. He also appreciated the fact that the distance from the road was enough to muffle the sound of traffic.

It just felt right. Jessie was already making her mark. True, it had given him a moment of gut-clutching fear when he'd looked outside and hadn't seen her anywhere. But he should have known she would find someone to talk to, someone to charm.

And the woman.

Frowning, Boone settled the top on the skillet to let the chili simmer. That had been odd, he thought as he poured a cup of coffee to take out on the deck. He'd looked down at her and known instantly that Jessie was safe. There had been nothing but kindness in those smoky eyes. It was his reaction, his very personal, very basic reaction, that had tightened his muscles and roughened his voice.

Desire. Very swift, very painful, and totally inappropriate. He hadn't felt that kind of response to a woman since... He grinned to himself. Since never. With Alice it had been a quiet kind of rightness, a sweet and inevitable coming together that he would always treasure.

This had been like being dragged by an undertow when you were fighting to get to shore.

Well, it had been a long time, he reminded himself as he watched a gull glide toward the water. A healthy reaction to a beautiful woman was easily justified and explained. And beautiful she'd been, in a calm, classic manner that was the direct opposite of his violent response to her. He couldn't help but resent it. He didn't have the time or inclination for any kind of reaction to any kind of woman.

There was Jessie to think of.

Reaching in his pocket, he took out a cigarette, lit it, hardly aware he was staring across the lawn at the hedge of delicate roses.

Anastasia, he thought. The name certainly suited her. It was old-fashioned, elegant, unusual.

"Daddy!"

Boone jolted, as guilty as a teenager caught smoking in the boys' room by the high school principal. He cleared his throat and gave his pouting daughter a sheepish grin.

"Give your old man a break, Jess. I'm down to half a pack a day."

She folded her arms. "They're bad for you. They make your lungs dirty."

"I know." He tamped the cigarette out, unable to take even a last drag when those wise little eyes were judging him. "I'm giving them up. Really."

She smiled—it was a disconcertingly adult sure-you-are smile—and he jammed his hands in his pockets. "Give me a break, Warden," he said in a passable James Cagney imitation. "You ain't putting me in solitary for snitching one drag."

Giggling, already forgiving him for the lapse, she came over to hug him. "You're silly."

"Yeah." He cupped his hands under her elbows and lifted her up for a hearty kiss. "And you're short."

"One day I'm going to be big as you." She wrapped her legs around his waist and leaned back until she was upside down. It was one of her favorite pastimes.

"Fat chance." He held her steady as her hair brushed the deck. "I'm always going to be bigger." He pulled her up again, lifting her high and making her squeal with laughter. "And smarter, and stronger." He rubbed the stubble of his beard against her while she wriggled and shrieked. "And better-looking."

"And ticklish!" she shouted in triumph, digging her fingers into his ribs.

She had him there. He collapsed on the bench with her. "Okay, okay! Uncle!" He caught his breath, and caught her close. "You'll always be trickier."

Pink-cheeked, bright-eyed, she bounced on his lap. "I like our new house."

"Yeah?" He smoothed her hair, as always enjoying the texture of it under his palm. "Me too."

"After dinner, can we go down to the beach and look for seals?"

"Sure."

"Daisy, too?"

"Daisy, too." Already experienced with puddles on the rug and chewed-up socks, he glanced around. "Where is she?"

"She's taking a nap." Jessie rested her head against her father's chest. "She was very tired."

"I bet. It's been a big day." Smiling, he kissed the top of Jessie's head, felt her yawn and settle.

"My favorite day. I got to meet Ana." Because her eyes were heavy, she closed them, lulled by the beating of her father's heart. "She's nice. She's going to show me how to plant flowers."

"Hmm."

"She knows all their names." Jessie yawned again, and when she spoke again her voice was thick with sleep. "Daisy licked her face and she didn't even mind. She just laughed. It sounded pretty when she did. Like a fairy," Jessie murmured as she drifted off.

Boone smiled again. His daughter's imagination. His gift to her, he liked to think. He held her gently while she slept.

* * *

Restless, Ana thought as she strolled along the rocky beach at twilight. She simply wasn't able to stay inside, working with her plants and herbs, when she was dogged by this feeling of restlessness.

The breeze would blow it out of her, she decided, lifting her face to the moist wind. A nice long walk and she'd find that contentment again, that peace that was as much a part of her as breathing.

Under different circumstances she would have called one of her cousins and suggested a night out. But she imagined Morgana was cozily settled in with Nash for the evening. And at this stage of her pregnancy, she needed rest. Sebastian wasn't back from his honeymoon yet.

Still, it had never bothered her to be alone. She enjoyed the solitude of the long, curved beach, the sound of water against rock, the laughing of the gulls.

Just as she had enjoyed the sound of the child's laughter, and the man's, drifting to her that afternoon. It had been a good sound, one she didn't have to be a part of to appreciate.

Now, as the sun melted, spilling color over the western sky, she felt the restlessness fading. How could she be anything but content to be here, alone, watching the magic of a day at rest?

She climbed up to stand on a driftwood log, close enough to the water that the spray cooled her face and dampened her shirt. Absently she took a stone out of her pocket, rubbing it between her fingers as she watched the sun drop into the flaming sea.

The stone warmed in her hand. Ana looked down at the small, waterlike gem, its pearly sheen glinting dully in the lowering light. Moonstone, she thought, amused at herself. Moon magic. A protection for the night traveler, an aid to self-analysis. And, of course, a talisman, often used to promote love.

Which was she looking for tonight?

Even as she laughed at herself and slipped the stone back into her pocket, she heard her name called.

There was Jessie, racing down the beach with the fat puppy nipping at her heels. And her father, walking several yards behind, as if reluctant to close the distance. Ana took a moment to wonder if the child's natural exuberance made the man appear all the more aloof.

She stepped down from the log and, because it was natural, even automatic, caught Jessie up in a swing and a hug. "Hello again, sunshine. Are you and Daisy out hunting for fairy shells?"

Jessie's eyes widened. "Fairy shells? What do they look like?"

"Just as you'd suppose. Sunset or sunrise—that's the only time to find them."

"My daddy says fairies live in the forest, and usually hide because people don't always know how to treat them."

"Quite right." She laughed and set the girl on her feet. "But they like the water, too, and the hills."

"I'd like to meet one, but Daddy says they hardly ever talk to people like they used to 'cause nobody really believes in them but kids."

"That's because children are very close to magic." She looked up as she spoke. Boone had reached them, and the sun setting at his back cast shadows over his face that were both dangerous and appealing. "We were discussing fairies," she told him.

"I heard." He laid a hand on Jessie's shoulder. Though the gesture was subtle, the meaning was crystal-clear. *Mine.*

"Ana says there are fairy shells on the beach, and you can only find them at sunrise or sunset. Can you write a story about them?"

"Who knows?" His smile was soft and loving for his daughter. When his gaze snapped back to hers, Ana felt a shudder down her spine. "We've interrupted your walk."

"No." Exasperated, Ana shrugged. She understood that he meant she had interrupted theirs. "I was just taking a moment to watch the water before I went in. It's getting chilly."

"We had chili for dinner," Jessie said, grinning at her own joke. "And it was *hot!* Will you help me look for fairy shells?"

"Sometime, maybe." When her father wasn't around to stare holes through her. "But it's getting too dark now, and I have to go in." She flicked a finger down Jessie's nose. "Good night." She gave a cool nod to her father.

Boone watched Ana walk away. She might not have gotten chilled so quickly, he thought, if she'd worn something to cover her legs. Her smooth, shapely legs. He let out a long, impatient breath.

"Come on, Jess. Race you back."

# Chapter 2

"I'd like to meet him."

Ana glanced up from the dried petals she was arranging for potpourri and frowned at Morgana. "Who?"

"The father of this little girl you're so enchanted with." More fatigued than she cared to admit, Morgana stroked her hand in a circular motion over her very round belly. "You're just chock-full of information on the girl, and very suspiciously lacking when it comes to Papa."

"Because he doesn't interest me as much," Ana said lightly. To a bowl filled with fragrant leaves and petals she added lemon for zest and balsam for health. She knew very well how weary Morgana was. "He's every bit as standoffish as Jessie is friendly. If it wasn't obvious that he's devoted to her, I'd probably dislike him instead of being merely ambivalent."

"Is he attractive?"

Ana lifted a brow. "As compared to?"

"A toad." Morgana laughed and leaned forward. "Come on, Ana. Give."

"Well, he isn't ugly." Setting the bowl aside, she began to

look through the cupboard for the right oil to mix through the potpourri. "I guess you'd say he has that hollow-cheeked, dangerous look. Athletic build. Not like a weight lifter." She frowned, trying to decide between two oils. "More like a...a long-distance runner, I suppose. Rangy, and intimidatingly fit."

Grinning, Morgana cupped her chin in her hands. "More."

"This from a married woman about to give birth to twins?"

"You bet."

Ana laughed, chose an oil of rose to add elegance. "Well, if I have to say something nice, he does have wonderful eyes. Very clear, very blue. When they look at Jessie, they're gorgeous. When they look at me, suspicious."

"What in the world for?"

"I haven't a clue."

Morgana shook her head and rolled her eyes. "Anastasia, surely you've wondered enough to find out. All you'd have to do is peek."

With a deft and expert hand, Ana added drops of fragrant oil to the mixture in the bowl. "You know I don't like to intrude."

"Oh, really."

"And if I was curious," she added, fighting a smile at Morgana's frustration, "I don't believe I'd care to see what was rolling around inside Mr. Sawyer's heart. I have a feeling it would be very uncomfortable to be linked with him, even for a few minutes."

"You're the empath," Morgana said with a shrug. "If Sebastian was back, he'd find out what's in this guy's mind anyway." She sipped more of the soothing elixir Ana had mixed for her. "I could do it for you if you like. I haven't had cause to use the scrying mirror or crystal for weeks. I may be getting stale."

"No." Ana leaned forward and kissed her cousin's cheek. "Thank you. Now, I want you to keep a bag of this with you," she said as she spooned the potpourri into a net bag. "And put the rest in bowls around the house and the shop. You're only working two days a week now, right?"

"Two or three." She smiled at Ana's concern, even as she waved it off. "I'm not overdoing, darling, I promise. Nash won't let me."

With an absent nod, Ana tied the bag securely. "Are you drinking the tea I made up for you?"

"Every day. And, yes, I'm using the oils religiously. I'm carrying rhyolite to alleviate emotional stress, topaz against external stresses, zircon for a positive attitude and amber to lift my spirits." She gave Ana's hand a quick squeeze. "I've got all the bases covered."

"I'm entitled to fuss." She set the bag of potpourri down by Morgana's purse, then changed her mind and opened the purse herself to slip it inside. "It's our first baby."

"Babies," Morgana corrected.

"All the more reason to fuss. Twins come early."

Indulging in a single sigh, Morgana closed her eyes. "I certainly hope these do. It's getting to the point where I can hardly get up and down without a crane."

"More rest," Ana prescribed, "and very gentle exercise. Which does not include hauling around shipping boxes or being on your feet all day waiting on customers."

"Yes, ma'am."

"Now let's have a look." Gently she laid her hands on her cousin's belly, spreading her fingers slowly, opening herself to the miracle of what lay within.

Instantly Morgana felt her fatigue drain away and a physical and emotional well-being take its place. Through her half-closed eyes she saw Ana's darken to the color of pewter and fix on a vision only Ana could see.

As she moved her hands over her cousin's heavy belly and linked with her, Ana felt the weight within her and, for one incredibly vivid moment, the lives that pulsed inside the womb. The draining fatigue, yes, and the nagging discomfort, but she also felt the quiet satisfaction, the burgeoning excitement, and the simple wonder of carrying those lives. Her body ached, her heart swelled. Her lips curved.

Then she *was* those lives—first one, then the other. Swimming dreamlessly in that warm, dark womb, nourished by the mother, held safe and fast until the moment when the outside would be faced. Two healthy hearts beating steady and close, beneath a mother's heart. Tiny fingers flexing, a lazy kick. The rippling of life.

Ana came back to herself, came back alone. "You're well. All of you."

"I know." Morgana twined her fingers with Ana's. "But I feel better when you tell me. Just as I feel safe knowing you'll be there when it's time."

"You know I wouldn't be anywhere else." She brought their joined hands to her cheek. "But is Nash content with me as midwife?"

"He trusts you—as much as I do."

Ana's gaze softened. "You're lucky, Morgana, to have found a man who accepts, understands, even appreciates, what you are."

"I know. To have found love was precious enough. But to have found love with him." Then her smile faded. "Ana, darling, Robert was a long time ago."

"I don't think of him. At least not really of him, but of a wrong turn on a particularly slippery road."

Indignation sharpened Morgana's eyes. "He was a fool, and not in the least worthy of you."

Rather than sadness Ana felt a chuckle bubble out of her. "You never liked him. Not from the first."

"No, I didn't." Frowning, Morgana gestured with her glass. "And neither did Sebastian, if you recall."

"I do. As I recall Sebastian was quite suspicious of Nash, too."

"That was entirely different. It *was*," she insisted as Ana grinned. "With Nash, he was just being protective of me. As for Robert, Sebastian tolerated him with the most insulting sort of politeness."

"I remember." Ana shrugged. "Which, of course, put my back up. Well, I was young," she said with a careless gesture. "And naive enough to believe that if I was in love I must be loved back equally. Foolish enough to be honest. And foolish enough to be devastated when that honesty was rewarded with disbelief, then outright rejection."

"I know you were hurt, but there's little doubt you could do better."

"None at all," Ana agreed, for she wasn't without pride. "But there are some of us that aren't meant to mix with outsiders."

Now there was frustration, as well as indignation. "There have been plenty of men, with elfin blood and without, who've been interested in you, cousin."

"A pity I haven't been interested in them." Ana laughed. "I'm miserably choosy, Morgana. And I like my life just as it is."

"If I didn't know that to be true, I'd be tempted to work up a nice little love spell. Nothing binding, mind," she said with a glint in her eye. "Just something to give you some entertainment."

"I can find my own entertainment, thanks."

"I know that, too. Just as I know you'd be furious if I dared to interfere." She pushed away from the table and rose, regretting for a moment her loss of grace. "Let's take a walk outside before I head home."

"If you promise to put your feet up for an hour when you get there."

"Done."

The sun was warm, the breeze balmy. Both of which, Ana thought, would do her cousin as much good as the long nap she imagined Nash would insist his wife take when she returned home.

They admired the late-blooming larkspur, the starry asters and the big, bold zinnias. Both had a deep love of nature that had come through the blood and through upbringing.

"Do you have any plans for All Hallows' Eve?" Morgana asked.

"Nothing specific."

"We were hoping you'd come by, at least for part of the evening. Nash is going all out for the trick-or-treaters."

With an appreciative laugh, Ana clipped some mums to take inside. "When a man writes horror films for a living, he's duty bound to pull out the stops for Halloween. I wouldn't miss it."

"Good. Perhaps Sebastian will join you and me for a quiet celebration afterward." Morgana was bending awkwardly over the thyme and verbena when she spotted the child and dog skipping through the hedge of roses.

She straightened. "We have company."

"Jessie." Pleased but wary, Ana glanced over to the house beyond. "Does your father know where you are?"

"He said I could come over if I saw you outside and you weren't busy. You aren't busy, are you?"

"No." Unable to resist, Ana bent down to kiss Jessie's cheek. "This is my cousin, Morgana. I've told her you're my brand-new neighbor."

"You have a dog and a cat. Ana told me." Jessie's interest was immediately piqued. Then her gaze focused, fascinated, on the bulge of Morgana's belly. "Do you have a baby in there?"

"I certainly do. In fact, I have two babies in there."

"Two?" Jessie's eyes popped wide. "How do you know?"

"Because Ana told me." With a laugh, she laid a hand on her heavy stomach. "And because they kick and squirm too much to be only one."

"My friend Missy's mommy, Mrs. Lopez, had one baby in her tummy, and she got so fat she could hardly walk." Out of brilliant blue eyes, Jessie shot Morgana a hopeful glance. "She let me feel it kick."

Charmed, Morgana took Jessie's hand and brought it to her while Ana discouraged Daisy from digging in the impatiens. "Feel that?"

Giggling at the movement beneath her hand, Jessie nodded. "Uh-huh! It went pow! Does it hurt?"

"No."

"Do you think they'll come out soon?"

"I'm hoping."

"Daddy says babies know when to come out because an angel whispers in their ear."

Sawyer might be aloof, Morgana thought, but he was also very clever, and very sweet. "That sounds exactly right to me."

"And that's their special angel, forever and ever," she went on, pressing her cheek to Morgana's belly in the hope that she could hear something from inside. "If you turn around really quick, you maybe could get just a tiny glimpse of your angel. I try sometimes, but I'm not fast enough." She peered up at Morgana. "Angels are shy, you know."

"So I've heard."

"I'm not." She pressed a kiss to Morgana's belly before she danced away. "There's not a shy bone in my body. That's what Grandma Sawyer always says."

"An observant woman, Grandma Sawyer," Ana commented while wrestling Daisy into her arms to prevent her from disturbing Quigley's afternoon nap.

Both women enjoyed the energetic company as they walked among the flowers—or rather as they walked and Jessie skipped, hopped, ran and tumbled.

Jessie reached for Ana's hand as they started toward the front of the house and Morgana's car. "I don't have any cousins. Is it nice?"

"Yes, it's very nice. Morgana and Sebastian and I practically grew up together, kind of like brothers and sisters do."

"I know how to get brothers and sisters, 'cause my daddy told me. How do you get cousins?"

"Well, if your mother or father have brothers or sisters, and they have children, those children are your cousins."

Jessie digested this information with a frown of concentration. "Which are you?"

"It's complicated," Morgana said with a laugh, opting to rest against her car for a moment before getting in. "Ana's and Sebastian's and my father are all brothers. And our mothers are sisters. So we're kind of double cousins."

"That's neat. If I can't have cousins, maybe I can have a brother or sister. But my daddy says I'm a handful all by myself."

"I'm sure he's right," Morgana agreed as Ana chuckled. Brushing her hair back, Morgana glanced up. There, framed in one of the wide windows on the second floor of the house next door, was a man. Undoubtedly Jessie's father.

Ana had described him well enough, Morgana mused. Though he was more attractive, and certainly sexier, than her cousin had let on. That very simple omission made her smile. Morgana lifted a hand in a friendly wave. After a moment's hesitation, Boone returned the salute.

"That's my daddy." Jessie pinwheeled her arms in greeting. "He works up there, but we haven't unpacked all the boxes yet."

"What does he do?" Morgana asked, since it was clear Ana wasn't going to.

"Oh, he tells stories. Really good stories, about witches and fairy princesses and dragons and magic fountains. I get to help sometimes. I have to go because tomorrow's my first day of school and he said I wasn't supposed to stay too long. Did I?"

"No." Ana bent down to kiss her cheek. "You can come back anytime."

"Bye!" And she was off, gamboling across the lawn, with the dog racing behind her.

"I've never been more charmed, or more worn out," Morgana said as she climbed into her car. "The girl's a delightful whirlwind." Smiling out at Ana, she jiggled her keys. "And the father is certainly no slouch."

"I imagine it's difficult, a man raising a little girl alone."

"From the one glimpse I had, he looked up to it." She gunned the engine. "Interesting that he writes stories. About witches and dragons and such. Sawyer, you said?"

"Yes." Ana blew tousled hair out of her eyes. "I guess he must be Boone Sawyer."

"It might intrigue him to know you're Bryna Donovan's niece—seeing as they're in the same line of work. That is, if you wanted to intrigue him."

"I don't," Ana said firmly.

"Ah, well, perhaps you already have." Morgana put the car in Reverse. "Blessed be, cousin."

Ana struggled with a frown as Morgana backed out of the drive.

After driving to Sebastian's to give his horses their morning feeding and grooming, Ana spent most of the next morning delivering her potpourris, her scented oils, her medicinal herbs and potions. Others were boxed and packaged for shipping. Though she had several local customers for her wares, including Morgana's shop, Wicca, a great portion of her clientele was outside the area.

Anastasia's was successful enough to suit her. The business she'd started six years before satisfied her needs and ambitions and allowed her the luxury of working at home. It wasn't for money. The Donovan fortune, and the Donovan legacy, kept both her and her family comfortably off. But, like Morgana with her shop and Sebastian with his many businesses, Ana needed to be productive.

She was a healer. But it was impossible to heal everyone. Long ago she had learned it was destructive to attempt to take on the ills and pains of the world. Part of the price of her power was knowing there was pain she could not alleviate. She did not reject her gift. She used it as she thought best.

Herbalism had always fascinated her, and she accepted the fact that she had the touch. Centuries before, she might have been the village wise woman—and that never failed to amuse her. In today's world, she was a businesswoman who could mix a bath oil or an elixir with equal skill.

If she added a touch of magic, it was hers to add.

And she was happy, happy with the destiny that had been thrust on her and with the life she had made from it.

Even if she'd been miserable, she thought, this day would have lifted her spirits. The beckoning sun, the caressing breeze, the faintest taste of rain in the air, rain that would not fall for hours—and then would fall gently.

Wanting to take advantage of the day, she decided to work outside, starting some herbs from seed.

He was watching her again. Bad habit, Boone thought with a grimace as he glanced down at the cigarette between his fingers. He wasn't having much luck with breaking bad habits. Nor was he getting a hell of a lot of work done since he'd looked out of the window and seen her outside.

She always looked so...elegant, he decided. A kind of inner elegance that wasn't the least diminished by the grass-stained cutoffs and short-sleeved T-shirt she wore.

It was in the way she moved, as if the air were wine that she drank lightly from as she passed through it.

Getting lyrical, he mused, and reminded himself to save it for his books.

Maybe it was because she was the fairy-princess type he so often wrote about. There was that ethereal, otherworldly air about her. And the quiet strength in her eyes. Boone had never believed that fairy princesses were pushovers.

But there was still this delicacy about her body—a body he sincerely wished he hadn't begun to dwell upon. Not a frailty, but a serene kind of femininity that he imagined would baffle and allure any male who was still breathing.

Boone Sawyer was definitely breathing.

Now what was she doing? he wondered, crushing out his cigarette impatiently and moving closer to the window. She'd gone into the garden shed and had come out again with her arms piled high with pots.

Wasn't it just like a woman to try to carry more than she should?

Even as he was thinking it, and indulging in a spot of male superiority, he saw Daisy streak across her lawn, chasing the sleek gray cat.

He had a hand on the window, prepared to shoot it up and call off the dog. Before he could make the move, he saw it was already too late.

In slow motion, it might have been an interesting and well-choreographed dance. The cat streaked like gray smoke between Ana's legs. She swayed. The clay pots in her arms teetered. Boone swore, then let out a sigh of relief when she righted them, and herself, again. Before the breath was out, Daisy plowed through, destroying the temporary balance. This time Ana's feet were knocked completely out from under her. She went down, and the pots went up.

Though he was already swearing, Boone heard the crash as he leapt through the terrace doors and down the steps to the lower deck.

She was muttering what sounded to him like exotic curses when he reached her. And he could hardly blame her. Her cat was up a tree, spitting down on the yipping dog. The pots she'd been carrying were little more than shards scattered over the grass and the edge of the patio where the impact had taken place.

Boone winced, cleared his throat. "Ah, are you all right?"

She was on her hands and knees, and her hair was over her

eyes. But she tossed it back and shot him a long look through the blond wisps. "Dandy."

"I was at the window." This certainly wasn't the time to admit he'd been watching her. "Passing by the window," he corrected. "I saw the chase and collision." Crouching down, he began to help her pick up the pieces. "I'm really sorry about Daisy. We've only had her a few days, and we haven't had any luck with training."

"She's a baby yet. No point in blaming a dog for doing what comes naturally."

"I'll replace the pots," he said, feeling miserably awkward.

"I have more." Because the barking and spitting were getting desperate, Ana sat back on her heels. "Daisy!" The command was quiet but firm, and it was answered instantly. Tail wagging furiously, the pup scrambled over to lick at her face and arms. Refusing to be charmed, Ana cupped the dog's face in her hands. "Sit," she ordered, and the puppy plopped her rump down obligingly. "Now behave yourself." With a little whine of repentance, Daisy settled down with her head on her paws.

Almost as impressed as he was baffled, Boone shook his head. "How'd you do that?"

"Magic," she said shortly, then relented with a faint smile. "You could say I've always had a way with animals. She's just happy and excited and roaring to play. You have to make her understand that some activities are inappropriate." Ana patted Daisy's head and earned an adoring canine glance.

"I've been trying bribery."

"That's good, too." She stretched out under a trellis of scarlet clematis, looking for more broken crockery. It was then that Boone noticed the long scratch on her arm.

"You're bleeding."

She glanced down. There were nicks on her thighs, too. "Hard to avoid, with pots raining down on me."

He was on his feet in a blink and hauling Ana to hers. "Damn it, I asked you if you were all right."

"Well, really, I—"

"We'll have to clean it up." He saw there was more blood trickling down her legs, and he reacted exactly as he would if it were Jessie. He panicked. "Oh, Lord." He scooped an amazed Ana into his arms and hurried toward the closest door.

"Honestly, there's absolutely no need—"

"It's going to be fine, baby. We'll take care of it."

Half amused, half annoyed, Ana huffed out a breath as he pushed his way into the kitchen. "In that case, I'll cancel the ambulance. If you'd just put me—" He dropped her into one of the padded ice-cream chairs at her kitchen table. "Down."

Nerves jittering, Boone raced to the sink for a cloth. Efficiency, speed and cheer were the watchwords in such cases, he knew. As he dampened the cloth and squirted it with soap, he took several long breaths to calm himself.

"It won't look so bad when we get it cleaned up. You'll see." After pasting a smile on his face, he walked back to kneel in front of her. "I'm not going to hurt you." Gently he began to dab at the thin line of blood that had dripped down her calf. "We're going to fix it right up. Just close your eyes and relax." He took another long breath. "I knew this man once," he began, improvising a story as he always did for his daughter. "He lived in a place called Briarwood, where there was an enchanted castle behind a high stone wall."

Ana, who had been on the point of firmly telling him she could tend to herself, stopped and did indeed relax.

"Growing over the wall were thick vines with big, razor-sharp thorns. No one had been to the castle in more than a hundred years, because no one was brave enough to climb that wall and risk being scraped and pricked. But the man, who was very poor and lived alone, was curious, and day after day he would walk from his house to the wall and stand on the tips of his toes to see the sun gleam on the topmost towers and turrets of the castle."

Boone turned the cloth over and dabbed at the cuts. "He couldn't explain to anyone what he felt inside his heart whenever he stood there. He wanted desperately to climb over. Sometimes at night in his bed he would imagine it. Fear of those thick, sharp thorns stopped him, until one day in high summer, when the scent of flowers was so strong you couldn't take a breath without drinking it in, that glimpse of the topmost towers wasn't enough. Something in his heart told him that what he wanted most in the world lay just beyond that thorn-covered wall. So he began to climb it. Again and again he fell to the ground, with his hands and arms pricked and bleeding. And again and again he pushed himself up."

His voice was soothing, and his touch—his touch was anything but. As gentle as he was with the cool cloth, an ache began to spread, slow and warm, from the center of her body outward. He was stroking her thighs now, where the sharp edge of a shard had nicked the flesh. Ana closed her hand into a fist, the twin of which clenched in her stomach.

She needed him to stop. She wanted him to go on. And on.

"It took all of that day," Boone continued in that rich, mesmerizing storyteller's voice. "And the heat mixed sweat with the blood, but he didn't give up. Couldn't give up, because he knew, as he'd never known anything before, that his heart's desire, his future and his destiny, lay on the other side. So, with his hands raw and bleeding, he used those thorny vines and dragged himself to the top. Exhausted, filled with pain, he stumbled and fell down and down, to the thick, soft grass that flowed from the wall to the enchanted castle.

"The moon was up when he awoke, dazed and disoriented. With the last of his strength, he limped across the lawn, over the drawbridge and into the great hall of the castle that had haunted his dreams since childhood. When he crossed the threshold, the lights of a thousand torches flared. In that same instant, all his cuts and scrapes and bruises vanished. In that circle of flame that cast shadow and light up the white marble walls stood the most beautiful woman he had ever seen. Her hair was like sunlight, and her eyes like smoke. Even before she spoke, even before her lovely mouth curved in a welcoming smile, he knew that it was she he had risked his life to find. She stepped forward, offered her hand to him, and said only 'I have been waiting for you.'"

As he spoke the last words, Boone lifted his gaze to Ana's. He was as dazed and disoriented as the man in the story he had conjured up. When had his heart begun to pound like this? he wondered. How could he think when the blood was swimming in his head and throbbing in his loins? While he struggled for balance, he stared at her.

Hair like sunlight. Eyes like smoke.

And he realized he was kneeling between her legs, one hand resting intimately high on her thigh, and the other on the verge of reaching out to touch that sunlight hair.

Boone rose so quickly that he nearly overbalanced the table. "I beg your pardon," he said, for lack of anything better. When she only continued to stare at him, the pulse in her throat beating visibly, he tried again. "I got carried away when I saw you were bleeding. I've never been able to take Jessie's cuts and scrapes in stride." Struggling not to babble, he thrust the cloth at her. "I imagine you'd rather handle it yourself."

She accepted the cloth. She needed a moment before she dared speak. How was it possible that a man could stir her so desperately with doctoring and a fairy tale, then leave her fighting to find a slippery hold on her composure when he apologized?

Her own fault, Ana thought as she scrubbed—with more force than was really necessary—at the scrape on her arm. It was her gift and her curse that she would feel too much.

"You look like you should be the one sitting down," she

told him briskly, then rose to go to the cupboard for one of her own medications. "Would you like something cold to drink?"

"No... Yes, actually." Though he doubted that a gallon of ice water would dampen the fire in his gut. "Blood always makes me panic."

"Panicked or not, you were certainly efficient." She poured him a glass of lemonade from the fat pitcher she fetched from the refrigerator. "And it was a very nice story." She was smiling now, more at ease.

"A story usually serves to calm both Jessie and me during a session with iodine and bandages."

"Iodine stings." She expertly dabbed a tobacco-brown liquid from a small apothecary jar onto her cleaned cuts. "I can give you something that won't, if you like. For your next emergency."

"What is it?" Suspicious, he sniffed at the jar. "Smells like flowers." And so did she.

"For the most part it is. Herbs, flowers, a dash of this and that." She set the bottle aside, capped it. "It's what you might call a natural antiseptic. I'm an herbalist."

"Oh."

She laughed at the skeptical look on his face. "That's all right. The majority of people only trust healing aids they can buy at the drugstore. They forget that people healed themselves quite well through nature for hundreds of years."

"They also died of lockjaw from a nick from a rusty nail."

"True enough," she agreed. "If they didn't have access to a reputable healer." Since she had no intention of trying to convert him, Ana changed the subject. "Did Jessie get off for her first day of school?"

"Yeah, she was raring to go. I was the one with the nervous stomach." His smile came and went. "I want to thank you for being so tolerant of her. I know she has a tendency to latch on to people. It doesn't cross her mind that they might not want to entertain her."

"Oh, but she entertains me." In an automatic gesture of courtesy, she took out a plate and lined it with cookies. "She's very welcome here. She's very sweet, unaffected and bright, and she doesn't forget her manners. You're doing a marvelous job raising her."

He accepted a cookie, watching her warily. "Jessie makes it easy."

"As delightful as she is, it can't be easy raising a child on your own. I doubt it's a snap even with two parents when the child is as energetic as Jessie. And as bright." Ana selected a cookie for herself and missed the narrowing of his eyes. "She must get her imagination from you. It must be delightful for her to have a father who writes such lovely stories."

His eyes sharpened. "How do you know what I do?"

The suspicion surprised her, but she smiled again. "I'm a fan—actually, an avid fan—of Boone Sawyer's."

"I don't recall telling you my first name."

"No, I don't believe you did," Ana said agreeably. "Are you always so suspicious of a compliment, Mr. Sawyer?"

"I had my reasons for settling quietly here." He set the half-empty glass down on the counter with a little clink. "I don't care for the idea of my neighbor interrogating my daughter, or digging into my business."

"Interrogating?" She nearly choked on the word. "Interrogating Jessie? Why would I?"

"To get to know a little more about the rich widower in the next house."

For one throbbing moment, she could only gape. "How unbelievably arrogant! Believe me, I enjoy Jessie's company, and I don't find it necessary to bring you into the conversation."

What he considered her painfully transparent astonishment made him sneer. He'd handled her type before, but it was a disappointment, a damned disappointment, for Jessie. "Then it's odd that you'd know my name, that I'm a single parent, and my line of work, isn't it?"

She wasn't often angry. It simply wasn't her nature. But now she fought a short, vicious war with temper. "You know, I doubt very much you're worth an explanation, but I'm going to give you one, just to see how difficult it is for you to talk when you have to shove your other foot in your mouth." She turned. "Come with me."

"I don't want—"

"I said come with me." She strode out of the kitchen, fully certain he would follow.

Though annoyed and reluctant, he did. They moved through an archway and into a sun-drenched great room dotted with the charm of white wicker furniture and chintz. There were clusters of glinting crystals, charming statues of elves and sorcerers and faeries. Through another archway and into a cozy library with a small Adam fireplace and more mystical statuary.

There was a deep cushioned sofa in raspberry that would welcome an afternoon napper, daintily feminine lace curtains dancing in the breeze that teased through an arching window, and the good smell of books mixed with the airy fragrance of flowers.

Ana walked directly to a shelf, rising automatically to her toes to reach the desired volumes. *"The Milkmaid's Wish,"* she recited as she pulled out one book after another. *"The Frog, the Owl and the Fox. A Third Wish for Miranda."* She tossed a look over her shoulder, though tossing one of the books would have been more satisfactory. "It's a shame I have to tell you how much I enjoy your work."

Uncomfortable, he tucked his hands in his pockets. He was already certain he'd taken a wrong turn, and he was wondering if he could find a suitable way to backtrack. "It isn't often grown women read fairy tales for pleasure."

"What a pity. Though you hardly deserve the praise, I'll tell you that your work is lyrical and valuable, on both a child's and an adult's level." Far from mollified, she shoved two of the books back into place. "Then again, perhaps such things are in my blood. I was very often lulled to sleep by one of my aunt's stories. Bryna Donovan," she said, and had the pleasure of seeing his eyes widen. "I imagine you've heard of her."

Thoroughly chastised, Boone let out a long breath. "Your aunt." He flicked his gaze over the shelf and saw several of Bryna's stories of magic and enchanted lands alongside his. "We've actually corresponded a few times. I've admired her work for years."

"So have I. And when Jessie mentioned that her father wrote stories about fairy princesses and dragons, I concluded the Sawyer next door was Boone Sawyer. Grilling a six-year-old wasn't necessary."

"I'm sorry." No, actually, he was much more embarrassed than sorry, but that would have to do. "I had an...uncomfortable experience not long before we moved, and it's made me overly sensitive." He picked up a small, fluidly sculpted statue of an enchantress, turning it in his fingers as he spoke. "Jessie's kindergarten teacher...she pumped all sorts of information out of the kid. Which isn't too hard, really, since Jessie's pump's always primed."

He set the statue down again, all the more embarrassed that he felt this obligation to explain. "But she manipulated Jessie's feelings, her natural need for a mother figure, gave her all sorts of extra attention, requested several conferences to discuss Jessie's unusual potential, even going so far as to arrange a one-on-one with me over dinner where she... Suffice it to say she was more interested in an unattached male with a nice portfolio than she was in Jessie's feelings or her welfare. Jessie was very hurt by it."

Ana tapped a finger on the edge of one of his books before replacing it. "I imagine it was a difficult experience for both of you. But let me assure you, I'm not in the market for a husband. And, if I were, I wouldn't resort to manipulations and maneuvers. I'm afraid happy-ever-after has been too well indoctrinated in me for that."

"I'm sorry. After I get those feet out of my mouth, I'll try to come up with a better apology."

The way she lifted her brow told him he wasn't out of the woods yet. "I think the fact that we understand each other will do. Now I'm sure you want to get back to work, and so do I." She walked past him into a tiled foyer and opened the front door. "Tell Jessie to be sure to drop by and let me know how she likes school."

Here's your hat, what's your hurry, Boone thought as he stepped out. "I will. Take care of those scratches," he added, but she was already closing the door in his face.

## Chapter 3

Good going, Sawyer. Shaking his head, Boone sat down in front of his word processor. First his dog knocks her down in her own yard, then our blundering hero barges into her house uninvited to play with her legs. To cap it, he insults her integrity and insinuates that she's using his daughter to try to trap him.

All in one fun-filled afternoon, he thought in disgust. It was a wonder she hadn't pitched him bodily out of her house rather than simply slamming the door in his face.

And why had he acted so stupidly? Past experience, true. But that wasn't the root of it, and he knew it.

Hormones, he decided with a half laugh. The kind of raging hormones better suited to a teenager than a grown man.

He'd looked up at her face in that sun-washed kitchen, feeling her skin warm under his hand, smelling that serenely seductive scent she exuded, and he'd wanted. He'd craved. For one blinding moment, he'd imagined with perfect clarity what it would be like to drag her off that curvy little chair, to feel that quick jerk-shudder of reaction as he devoured that incredibly soft-looking mouth.

That instant edge of desire had been so sharp, he'd needed to believe there was some outside force, some ploy or plot or plan to jumble his system so thoroughly.

Safest course, he realized with a sigh. Blame her.

Of course, he might have been able to dismiss the whole thing if it hadn't been for the fact that at that moment he'd looked up into her eyes and seen the same dreamy hunger he was feeling. And he'd felt the power, the mystery, the titanic sexuality, of a woman on the point of yielding.

His imagination had a great deal of punch, he knew. But what he'd seen, what he'd felt, had been utterly real.

For a moment, for just a moment, the tensions and needs had had that room humming like a harp string. Then he'd pulled back—as he should. A man had no business seducing his neighbor in her kitchen.

Now he'd very likely destroyed any chance of getting to know her better—just when he'd realized he very much wanted to get to know Miss Anastasia Donovan.

Pulling out a cigarette, Boone ran his fingers over it while he thought through various methods of redemption. When the light dawned, it was so simple he laughed out loud. If he'd been looking for a way into the fair maiden's heart—which he wasn't, exactly—it couldn't have been more perfect.

Pleased with himself, he settled down to work until it was time to pick up Jessie at school.

Conceited jerk. Ana worked off her temper with mortar and pestle. It was very satisfying to grind something—even if it was only some innocent herbs—into a powder. Imagine. *Imagine* him having the idea that she was...on the make, she decided, sneering. As if she'd found him irresistible. As if she'd been pining away behind some glass wall waiting for her prince to come. So that she could snare him.

The gall of the man.

At least she'd had the satisfaction of thumbing her nose at him. And if closing a door in anyone's face was out of character for her, well, it had felt wonderful at the time.

So wonderful, in fact, that she wouldn't mind doing it again.

It was a damn shame he was so talented. And it couldn't be denied that he was a wonderful father. They were traits she couldn't help but admire. There was no denying he was attractive, magnetically sexual, with just a dash of shyness tossed in for sweetness, along with the wild tang of untamed male.

And those eyes, those incredible eyes that just about stopped your breath when they focused on you.

Ana scowled and tightened her grip on the pestle. Not that she was interested in any of that.

There might have been a moment in the kitchen, when he was stroking her flesh so gently and his voice blocked out all other sound, that she found herself drawn to him.

All right, aroused by him, she admitted. It wasn't a crime.

But he'd certainly shut that switch off quickly enough, and that was fine by her.

Beginning this instant, and from now on, she would think of him only as Jessica's father. She would be aloof if it killed her, friendly only to the point where it eased her relationship with the child.

She enjoyed having Jessie in her life, and she wasn't about to sacrifice that pleasure because of a basic and very well justified dislike of Jessie's father.

"Hi!"

There was that pixie face peeping through Ana's screen door. Even the dregs of temper were difficult to hold on to when she was faced with those big smiling eyes.

Ana set the mortar and pestle aside and smiled back. She supposed she had to be grateful that Boone hadn't let the altercation that afternoon influence him to keep Jessie away.

"Well, it looks like you survived your first day of school. Did school survive you?"

"Uh-huh. My teacher's name is Mrs. Farrell. She has gray hair and big feet, but she's nice, too. And I met Marcie and Tod and Lydia and Frankie, and lots of others. In the morning we—"

"Whoa." With a laugh, Ana held up both hands. "Maybe you should come in and sit down before you give me the day's events."

"I can't open the door, 'cause my hands are full."

"Oh." Ana obligingly pushed open the screen. "What have you got there?"

"Presents." On a huff of breath, Jessie dropped a package on the table. Then she held up a large crayon drawing. "We got to draw pictures today, and I made two. One for Daddy and one for you."

"For me?" Touched, Ana accepted the colorful drawing on the thick beige paper that brought back some of her own school memories. "It's beautiful, sunshine."

"See, this is you." Jessie pointed out a figure with yellow hair. "And Quigley." Here a childish, but undeniably clever, depiction of a cat. "And all the flowers. The roses and the daisies and the lark things."

"Larkspur," Ana murmured, misty-eyed.

"Uh-huh. And all the others," Jessie continued. "I couldn't remember all the names. But you said you'd teach me."

"Yes, I will. It's just lovely, Jessie."

"I drew Daddy one of our new house with him standing out on the deck, because he likes to stand there best. He put it on the refrigerator."

"An excellent idea." Ana walked over to center the picture on the refrigerator door, anchoring it with magnets.

"I like to draw. My daddy draws real good, and he said my mommy drew even better. So I come by it naturally." Jessie slipped her hand into Ana's. "Are you mad at me?"

"No, sweetheart. Why would I be?"

"Daddy said Daisy knocked you down and broke your pots, and you got hurt." She studied the scratch on Ana's arm, then kissed it solemnly. "I'm sorry."

"It's all right. Daisy didn't mean it."

"She didn't mean to chew up Daddy's shoes, either, and make him say swear words."

Ana bit her lip. "I'm sure she didn't."

"Daddy yelled, and Daisy got so nervous she peed right on the rug. Then he chased her around and around the house, and it looked so funny that I couldn't stop laughing. And Daddy laughed, too. He said he was going to build a doghouse outside and put Daisy and me in it."

Ana lost any hope of taking it all seriously, and she laughed as she scooped Jessie up. "I think you and Daisy would have a great time in the doghouse. But if you'd like to save your father's shoes, why don't you let me help you work with her?"

"Do you know how? Can you teach her tricks and everything?"

"Oh, I imagine. Watch." She shifted Jessie to her hip and called Quigley out from his nap beneath the kitchen table. The cat rose reluctantly, stretched his front legs, then his back, then padded out. "Okay, sit." Heaving a feline sigh, he did. "Up." Resigned, Quigley rose on his haunches and pawed the air like a circus tiger. "Now, if you do your flip, I might just open a can of tuna fish later, for your dinner."

The cat seemed to be debating with himself. Then—perhaps because the trick was small potatoes compared to tuna—he leapt up, arching his back and flipping over to land lightly on his feet. While Jessie crowed with laughter and applauded, Quigley modestly cleaned his paws.

"I didn't know cats could do tricks."

"Quigley's a very special cat." Ana set Jessie down to give Quigley a stroking. He purred like a freight train, nuzzling his face against her knee. "His family's in Ireland, like most of mine."

"Does he get lonely?"

Smiling, Ana scratched under Quigley's jaw. "We have each other. Now, would you like a snack while you tell me about the rest of your day?"

Jessie hesitated, tempted. "I don't think I can, 'cause it's close to dinner, and Daddy— Oh, I almost forgot." She rushed back to the table to pick up a package wrapped in candy-striped paper. "This is for you, from Daddy."

"From…" Unconsciously Ana linked her hands behind her back. "What is it?"

"I know." Jessie grinned, her eyes snapping with excitement. "But I can't tell. Telling spoils the surprise. You have to open it." Jessie picked it up and thrust it at Ana. "Don't you like presents?" Jessie asked when Ana kept her hands clasped tight behind her back. "I like them best of anything, and Daddy always gives really good ones."

"I'm sure he does, but I—"

"Don't you like Daddy?" Jessie's lower lip poked out. "Are you mad at him because Daisy broke your pots?"

"No, no, I'm not mad at him." Not for the broken pots, anyway. "It wasn't his fault. And, yes, of course I like him— That is, I don't know him very well, and I…" Caught, Ana decided, and she worked up a smile. "I'm just surprised to get a present when it's not my birthday." To please the child, Ana took the gift and shook it. "Doesn't rattle," she said, and Jessie clapped and giggled.

"Guess! Guess what it is!"

"Ah…a trombone?"

"No, no, trombones are too big." Excitement had her bouncing. "Open it. Open it and see."

It was the child's reaction that had her own heart beating a shade too fast, Ana assured herself. To please Jessie, she ripped the paper with a flourish. "Oh."

It was a book, a child's oversize book with a snowy white cover. On the front was a beautiful illustration of a golden-haired woman wearing a sparkling crown and flowing blue robes.

*"The Faerie Queen,"* Ana read. "By Boone Sawyer."

"It's brand-new," Jessie told her. "You can't even buy it yet, but Daddy gets his copies early." She ran a hand gently over the picture. "I told him she looks like you."

"It's a lovely gift," Ana said with a sigh. And a sneaky one. How was she supposed to stay irritated with him now?

"He wrote something inside for you." Too impatient to wait, Jessie opened the cover herself. "See, right there."

*To Anastasia, with hopes that a magic tale works as well as a white flag. Boone.*

Her lips curved. It was impossible to prevent it. How could anyone refuse a truce so charmingly requested?

Which was, of course, what Boone was counting on. As he shoved a packing box out of his way with his foot, he glanced through the window toward the house next door. Not a peep.

He imagined it might take a few days for Ana to calm down, but he thought he'd made a giant stride in the right direction. After all, he didn't want any antagonism between himself and Jessie's new friend.

Turning back to the stove, he lowered the heat on the boneless chicken breasts he had simmering, then deftly began to mash potatoes.

Jessie's number one favorite, he thought, as he sent the beaters whirling. They could have mashed potatoes every night for a year and the kid wouldn't complain. Of course, it was up to him to vary the menu, to make sure she got a healthy meal every night.

Boone poured in more milk and grimaced. He had to admit, if there was one part of parenting he would cheerfully give up, it was the pressure of deciding what they were to eat night after night.

He didn't mind cooking it so much, it was that daily decision between pot roast, baked chicken, pork chops and all the others. Plus what to serve with it. Out of desperation, he'd begun to clip recipes—secretly—in hopes of adding some variety.

At one time he'd seriously considered hiring a housekeeper. Both his mother and his mother-in-law had urged him to, and then they'd gone into one of their competitive huddles on how to choose the proper woman to fit the bill. But the idea of having someone in the house, someone who might gradually take over the rearing of his daughter, had deterred him.

Jessie was his. One hundred percent his. Despite dinner decisions and grocery shopping, that was the way he liked it.

As he added a generous slice of butter to the creamy potatoes, he heard her footsteps racing across the deck.

"Good timing, frog face. I was just about to give you a whistle." He turned, licking potatoes from his finger and saw Ana standing in the doorway, one hand on Jessie's shoulder. The muscles in his stomach tightened so quickly that he nearly winced. "Well, hello."

"I didn't mean to interrupt your cooking," Ana began. "I just wanted to thank you for the book. It was very nice of you to send it over."

"I'm glad you like it." He realized he had a dishcloth tucked in his jeans and hastily tugged it out. "It was the best peace offering I could think of."

"It worked." She smiled, charmed by the sight of him hovering busily over a hot stove. "Thanks for thinking of me. Now, I'd better get out of your way so you can finish cooking your dinner."

"She can come in, can't she?" Jessie was already tugging on Ana's hand. "Can't she, Daddy?"

"Sure. Please." He shoved a box out of her way. "We haven't

finished unpacking yet. It's taking longer than I thought it would."

Out of politeness, and curiosity, Ana stepped inside. There were no curtains on the window as yet, and a few packing boxes littered the stone-colored floor tiles. But ranged along the royal blue countertop there was a glossy ceramic cookie jar in the shape of Alice's white rabbit, a teapot of the mad hatter, and a dormouse sugar bowl. Pot holders, obviously hooked by a child's hand, hung on little brass hooks. The refrigerator's art gallery was crowded with Jessie's drawings, and the puppy was snoozing in the corner.

Unpacked and tidy, no, she thought. But this was already a home.

"It's a great house," she commented. "I wasn't surprised when it sold quickly."

"You want to see my room?" Jessie tugged on Ana's hand again. "I have a bed with a roof on it, and lots of stuffed animals."

"You can take Ana up later," Boone put in. "Now you should go wash your hands."

"Okay." She looked imploringly at Ana. "Don't go."

"How about a glass of wine?" Boone offered when his daughter raced off. "A good way to seal a truce."

"All right." Drawings rustled as he opened the fridge. "Jessie's quite an artist. It was awfully sweet of her to draw a picture for me."

"Careful, or you'll have to start papering the walls with them." He hesitated, the bottle in his hand, wondering where he'd put the wineglasses, or if he'd unpacked them at all. A quick search through cupboards made it clear that he hadn't. "Can you handle chardonnay in a Bugs Bunny glass?"

She laughed. "Absolutely." She waited for him to pour hers, and his—Elmer Fudd. "Welcome to Monterey," she said, raising Bugs in a toast.

"Thanks." When she lifted the glass to her lips and smiled

at him over the rim, he lost his train of thought. "I... Have you lived here long?"

"All my life, on and off." The scent of simmering chicken and the cheerful disarray of the kitchen were so homey that she relaxed. "My parents had a home here, and one in Ireland. They're based in Ireland for the most part now, but my cousins and I settled here. Morgana was born in the house she lives in, on Seventeen Mile Drive. Sebastian and I were born in Ireland, in Castle Donovan."

"Castle Donovan."

She laughed a little. "It sounds pretentious. But it actually is a castle, quite old, quite lovely, and quite remote. It's been in the Donovan family for centuries."

"Born in an Irish castle," he mused. "Maybe that explains why the first time I saw you I thought, well, there's the faerie queen, right next door in the rosebushes." His smiled faded, and he spoke without thinking. "You took my breath away."

The glass stopped halfway to her lips. Those lips parted in surprised confusion. "I..." She drank to give herself a moment to think. "I suppose part of your gift would be imagining faeries under bushes, elves in the garden, wizards in the treetops."

"I suppose." She smelled as lovely as the breeze that brought traces of her garden and hints of the sea through his windows. He stepped closer, surprised and not entirely displeased to see the alarm in her eyes. "How's that scratch? Neighbor." Gently he cupped his hand around her arm, skimmed his thumb up until he felt the pulse inside her elbow skitter. Whatever was affecting him was damn well doing the same to her. His lips curved. "Hurt?"

"No." Her voice thickened, baffling her, arousing him. "No, of course it doesn't."

"You still smell of flowers."

"The salve—"

"No." The knuckles of his free hand skimmed just under

her chin. "You always smell of flowers. Wildflowers and sea foam."

How had she come to be backed against the counter, his body brushing hers, his mouth so close, so temptingly close, that she could all but taste it?

And she wanted that taste, wanted it with a sudden staggering force that wiped every other thought out of her head. Slowly, her eyes on his, she brought her hand to his chest, spread it over his heart where the beat was strong. Strong and wild.

And so would the kiss be, she thought. Strong and wild, from the first instant.

As if to assure her of that, he grabbed a fistful of her hair, tangling his fingers in it. It was warm, as he'd known it would be, warm as the sunlight it took its shade from. For a moment, his entire being was focused on the kiss to come, the reckless pleasure of it. His mouth was a breath from hers, and her sigh was already filling him, when he heard his daughter's feet clattering on the stairs.

Boone jolted back as if she'd burned him. Speechless, they stared at each other, both of them stunned by what had nearly happened and by the force behind it.

What was he doing? Boone asked himself. Grabbing a woman in his kitchen when there was chicken on the stove, potatoes going cold on the counter and his little girl about to skip into the room?

"I should go." Ana set down her glass before it could slip out of her trembling hand. "I really only meant to stay a minute."

"Ana." He shifted, blocking the way in case she sprinted for the door. "I have a feeling what just happened here was out of character for both of us. That's interesting, don't you think?"

She lifted those solemn gray eyes to his. "I don't know your character."

"Well, I don't make a habit of seducing women in the kitchen when my daughter's upstairs. And I certainly don't make a habit out of wanting the hell out of a woman the min-ute I lay eyes on her."

She wished she hadn't set the wine down. Her throat was bone dry. "I suppose you want me to say I'll take your word for it. But I won't."

Both anger and challenge sparkled in his eyes. "Then I'll have to prove it to you, won't I?"

"No, you—"

"My hands are clean, clean, clean." Blissfully unaware of the tension shimmering in the air, Jessie danced into the kitchen, palms held out for inspection. "How come they have to be clean when I don't eat with my fingers anyway?"

Effortfully, he pulled himself back and tweaked his daugh-ter's nose. "Because germs like to sneak off little girls' hands and into their mashed potatoes."

"Yuck." She made a face, then grinned. "Daddy makes the best mashed potatoes in the whole wide world. Don't you want some? She can stay for dinner, can't she, Daddy?"

"Really, I—"

"Of course she can." Mirroring his daughter's grin—but with something a great deal more dangerous in his eyes—Boone studied Ana. "We'd love to have you. We have plenty. And I think it would be a good idea for us to get to know each other. Before."

She didn't have to ask before what. That was crystal-clear. But, no matter how she tried, she couldn't make her temper overtake the quick panicked excitement. "It's very nice of you to ask," she said with admirable calm. "I wish I could, but—" She smiled down at Jessie's sound of disappointment. "I have to drive out to my cousin's and take care of his horses."

"Will you take me with you sometime, so I can see them?"

"If your father says it's all right." She bent down and kissed Jessie's sulky lips. "Thank you for my picture, sunshine. It's beautiful." Taking a cautious step away, she looked at Boone. "And the book. I know I'll enjoy it. Good night."

Ana didn't run out of the house, though she freely admitted she wasn't leaving so much as escaping. Back home, she went through the motions, giving Quigley his promised tuna, then changing into jeans and a denim shirt for the drive to Sebastian's house.

She was going to have to do some thinking, she decided as she pulled on her boots. Some serious thinking. Weigh the pros and cons, consider the consequences. She had to laugh, thinking how Morgana would roll her eyes and accuse her of being impossibly Libran.

Perhaps her birth sign was partially responsible for the fact that Ana could always see and sympathize with both sides of an argument. It complicated matters as often as it solved them. But in this case she was quite certain that a clear head and calm deliberation were the order of the day.

Maybe she was unusually attracted to Boone. And the physical aspect of it was completely unprecedented. Certainly she'd felt desire for a man before, but never this quick, sharp edge of it. And a sharp edge usually meant a deep wound to follow.

That was certainly something to consider. Frowning, she grabbed a jean jacket and started downstairs.

Of course, she was an adult, unattached, unencumbered, and perfectly free to entertain the thought of a relationship with an equally free adult man.

Then again, she knew just how devastating relationships could be when people were unable to accept others for what they were.

Still debating, she swung out of the house. She certainly didn't owe Boone any explanations. She was under no obligation to try to make him understand her heritage, as she had tried to do years before with Robert. Even if they became involved, she wouldn't have to tell him.

Ana got into her car and backed out of the drive, her thoughts shifting back and forth.

It wasn't deception to hold part of yourself back. It was

self-preservation—as she'd learned through hard experience. And it was foolish even to be considering that angle when she hadn't decided if she wanted to be involved.

No, that wasn't quite true. She wanted. It was more a matter of deciding if she could afford to become involved.

He was, after all, her neighbor. A relationship gone sour would make it very uncomfortable when they lived in such close proximity.

And there was Jessie to consider. She was half in love with the girl already. She wouldn't want to risk that friendship and affection by indulging her own needs. Purely physical needs, Ana told herself as she followed the winding road along the coast.

True, Boone would be able to offer her some physical plea-sure. She didn't doubt that for a moment. But the emotional cost would just be too steep for everyone involved.

It would be better, much better, for everyone involved if she remained Jessie's friend while maintaining a wise distance from Jessie's father.

Dinner was over, and the dishes were done. There had been a not-too-successful session with Daisy—though she would sit down if you pushed on her rump. Afterward, there'd been a lot of splashing in the tub, then some horseplay to indulge in with his freshly scrubbed daughter. There was a story to be told, that last glass of water to be fetched.

Once Jessie was asleep and the house was quiet, Boone indulged himself with a brandy out on the deck. There were piles of forms on his desk—a parent's homework—that had to be filled out for Jessie's school files.

He'd do them before he turned in, he decided. But this hour, this dark, quiet hour when the nearly full moon was rising, was his.

He could enjoy the clouds that were drifting overhead, promising rain, the hypnotic sound of the water lapping against rock, the chatter of insects in the grass that he would have to mow very soon, and the scent of night-blooming flowers.

No wonder he had snapped this house up at the very first glimpse. No place he'd ever been had relaxed him more, or given him more of a sense of rightness and peace. And it appealed to his imagination. The mystically shaped cypress, the magical ice plants that covered the banks, those empty and often eerie stretches of night beach.

The ethereally beautiful woman next door.

He smiled to himself. For someone who hadn't felt much more than an occasional twinge for a woman in too long to remember, he was certainly feeling a barrage of them now.

It had taken him a long time to get over Alice. Though he still didn't consider himself part of the dating pool, he hadn't been a monk over the past couple of years. His life wasn't empty, and he'd been able, after a great deal of pain, to accept the fact that he had to live it.

He was sipping his brandy, enjoying it and the simple pleasure of the night, when he heard Ana's car. Not that he'd been waiting for it, Boone assured himself even as he checked his watch. He couldn't quite smother the satisfaction at her being home early, too early to have gone out on a date.

Not that her social life was any of his business.

He couldn't see her driveway, but because the night was calm he heard her shut her car door. Then, a few moments later, he heard her open and close the door to her house.

Propping his bare feet on the rail of the deck, he tried to imagine her progress through the house. Into the kitchen. Yes, the light snapped on, and he could see her move past the window. Brewing tea, perhaps, or pouring herself a glass of wine.

Shortly, the light switched off again, and he let his mind follow her through the house. Up the stairs. More lights, but it looked to Boone like the glow of a candle against the dark glass, rather than a lamp. Moments later, he heard the faint drift of music. Harp strings. Haunting, romantic, and some-how sad.

Briefly, very briefly, she was silhouetted against a window. He could see quite clearly that slim feminine shadow as she stripped out of her shirt.

Hastily he swallowed brandy and looked away. However tempting it might be, he wouldn't lower himself to the level of a Peeping Tom. He did, however, find himself craving a cigarette, and with apologies to his disapproving daughter he pulled one out of his pocket.

Smoke stung the air, soothed his nerves. Boone contented himself with the sound of harpsong.

It was a very long time before he went back into the house and slept, with the sound of a gentle rain falling on the roof and the memory of harpsong drifting across the night breeze.

# Chapter 4

Cannery Row was alive with sounds, the chattering of people as they strolled or rushed, the bright ringing of a bell from one of the tourist bikes, the ubiquitous calling of gulls searching for a handout. Ana enjoyed the crowds and the noise as much as she enjoyed the peace and solitude of her own backyard.

Patiently she chugged along with the stream of weekend traffic. On her first pass by Morgana's shop, Ana resigned herself to the fact that the perfect day had brought tourists and locals out in droves. Parking was going to be at a premium. Rather than frustrate herself searching for a spot on the street, she pulled into a lot three blocks from Wicca.

As she climbed out to open her trunk, she heard the whine of a cranky toddler and the frustrated muttering of weary parents.

"If you don't stop that right this minute, you won't get anything at all. I mean it, Timothy. We've had just about enough. Now get moving."

The child's response to that command was to go limp, sliding in a boneless heap onto the parking lot as his mother tugged uselessly at his watery arms. Ana bit her lip as it curved, but it was obvious the young parents didn't see the humor of it. Their arms were full of packages, and their faces were thunderous.

Timothy, Ana thought, was about to get a tanning—though it was unlikely to make him more cooperative. Daddy shoved his bags at Mommy and, mouth grim, bent down.

It was a small thing, Ana thought. And they all looked so tired and unhappy. She made the link first with the father, felt the love, the anger, and the dark embarrassment. Then with the child—confusion, fatigue, and a deep unhappiness over a big stuffed elephant he'd seen in a shop window and been denied.

Ana closed her eyes. The father's hand swung back as he prepared to administer a sharp slap to the boy's diaper-padded rump. The boy sucked in his breath, ready to emit a piercing wail at the indignity of it.

Suddenly the father sighed, and his hand fell back to his side. Timothy peeked up, his face hot and pink and tear-streaked.

The father crouched down, holding out his arms. "We're tired, aren't we?"

On a hiccuping sob, Timothy bundled into them and rested his heavy head on his daddy's shoulder. "Thirsty."

"Okay, champ." The father's hand went to the child's bottom, but with a soothing pat. He gave his teary-eyed wife an encouraging smile. "Why don't we go have a nice, cold drink? He just needs an n-a-p."

They moved off, tired but relieved.

Smiling to herself, Ana unlocked her trunk. Family vacations, she thought, weren't all fun and frolic. The next time they were ready to snarl at each other, she wouldn't be around to help. She imagined they'd muddle through without her.

After swinging her purse behind her back, she began to unload the boxes she was delivering to Morgana. There were a half dozen of them, filled with sacks of potpourri, bottles of oils and creams, beribboned sachets, satiny sleep pillows and a month's supply of special orders that ran from tonics to personalized perfumes.

Ana considered making two trips, gauged the distance and decided that if she balanced the load carefully she could make it in one.

She stacked, juggled and adjusted, then just managed to shut her trunk with an elbow. She made it across the parking lot and down half a block before she began berating herself.

Why did she always do this? she asked herself. Two comfortable trips were better than one difficult one. It wasn't that the boxes were so heavy—though they were. It was simply that they were awkward and the sidewalk was jammed. And her hair was blowing in her eyes. With a quick, agile dance, she managed, barely, to avoid a collision with a couple of teenage tourists in a surrey.

"Want some help?"

Annoyed with herself and irresponsible drivers, she turned around. There was Boone, looking particularly wonderful in baggy cotton slacks and shirt. Riding atop his shoulders, Jessie was laughing and clapping her hands.

"We had a ride on the carousel and had ice cream and we saw you."

"Looks like you're still overloading," Boone commented.

"They're not heavy."

He patted Jessie's leg and, following the signal, she began to slide down his back. "We'll give you a hand."

"That's all right." She knew it was foolish to reject help when she needed it, but she had managed quite successfully to avoid Boone for the better part of a week. And had managed—almost as successfully—to avoid thinking about him. Wondering about him. "I don't want to take you out of your way."

"We're not going any way in particular, are we, Jessie?"

"Uh-uh. We're just wandering today. It's our day off."

Ana couldn't prevent the smile, any more than she could prevent the wariness from creeping into her eyes when she looked back at Boone. He was certainly looking at her, she realized, in that disconcertingly thorough way of his. The smile creeping around his mouth had less to do with humor than it did with challenge.

"I don't have to go far," she began, grabbing at a package that was beginning to slide. "I can just—"

"Fine." Overriding her objections, Boone shifted boxes from her arms to his. His eyes stayed on hers. "What are neighbors for?"

"I can carry one." Eager to help, Jessie bounced in her sneakers. "I can."

"Thank you." Ana handed Jessie the lightest box. "I'm going a couple of blocks down to my cousin's shop."

"Has she had her babies?" Jessie asked as they started to walk.

"No, not yet."

"I asked Daddy how come she got to have two in there, and he said sometimes there's twice the love."

How could anyone possibly have a defense against a man like this? Ana wondered. Her eyes were warm when they met his. "Yes, sometimes there is. You always seem to have the right answer," she murmured to Boone.

"Not always." He wasn't certain if he was relieved or annoyed that his hands were full of boxes. If they'd been free, he would have been compelled to touch her. "You just try for the best one at the time. Where have you been hiding, Anastasia?"

"Hiding?" The warmth fled from her eyes.

"I haven't seen you out in your yard in days. You didn't strike me as the type to scare that easily."

Because Jessie was skipping just ahead of them, she bit off a more acid response. "I don't know what you mean. I had work. Quite a bit of it, as a matter of fact." She nodded toward the boxes. "You're carrying some of it now."

"Is that so? Then I'm glad I didn't resort to knocking on

your door and pretending I needed to borrow a cup of sugar. I nearly did, but it seemed so obvious."

She slanted him a look. "I appreciate your restraint."

"And so you should."

She merely tossed her hair out of her eyes and called to Jessie. "We'll go down this way, so we can go in the back. Saturdays are usually busy," she explained to Boone. "I don't like going through the shop and distracting the customers."

"What does she sell, anyway?"

"Oh." Ana smiled again. "This and that. I think you'd find her wares particularly interesting. Here we go." She gestured to a little flagstone stoop flanked by pots of bloodred geraniums. "Can you get the door, Jessie?"

"Okay." Anxious as ever to see what was on the other side, Jessie shoved it open, then let out a squeal. "Oh, look. Daddy, look!" Jessie set her package aside on the first available space and made a dive for the big white cat grooming herself on the table.

"Jessica!" Boone's voice was short and firm, stopping his daughter in midstride. "What have I told you about going up to strange animals?"

"But, Daddy, he's so pretty."

"She," Ana corrected as she laid her boxes on the counter. "And your father's quite right. Not all animals like little girls."

Jessie's fingers itched to stroke the thick white fur. "Does she?"

"Sometimes Luna doesn't like anyone." With a laugh, Ana scratched the cat between the ears. "But if you're very polite, and pet her when she gives the royal consent, you'll get along well enough." Ana gave Boone a reassuring smile. "Luna won't scratch her. When she's had enough, she'll just stalk off."

But apparently Luna was in the mood for attention. Walking to the end of the table, she rubbed her head against the hand Jessie had held out. "She likes me!" The smile nearly split her face in two. "See, Daddy, she likes me."

"Yes, I see."

"Morgana usually keeps cold drinks back here." Ana opened the small refrigerator. "Would you like something?"

"Sure." He really wasn't thirsty, but the offer made it easy to linger. He leaned back against the counter of the kitchenette while Ana got out glasses. "The shop through there?"

When he gestured at a door, Ana nodded. "Yes. And through there's the storeroom. A great deal of what Morgana sells is one-of-a-kind, so she doesn't keep a large supply of inventory."

He reached over Ana's shoulder to finger the thin leaves of a rosemary plant on the windowsill. "She into this kind of thing, too?"

Ana tried to ignore the fact that his body was brushing hers. She could smell the sea on him, and imagined he and Jessie had gone down to feed the gulls. "What kind of thing?"

"Herbs and stuff."

"In a manner of speaking." She turned, knowing she'd be entirely too close, and pushed the glass into his chest. "Root beer."

"Terrific." He knew it wasn't particularly fair—and it was probably unwise, as well—but he took the glass and stood precisely where he was. She had to tilt her head back to meet his eyes. "It might be a good hobby for Jessie and me. Maybe you could show us how to grow some."

"It's no different from growing any living thing." It took a great deal of effort to keep her voice even when breathing was so difficult. "Care and attention, and affection. You're very much in my way, Boone."

"I hope so." With his eyes very intense, very focused, he lifted a hand to her cheek. "Anastasia, I really think we need to—"

"A deal's a deal, babe." The smug voice carried through the door as it opened. "Fifteen minutes of sit-down time every two hours."

"You're being ridiculous. For heaven's sake, you act as

though I'm the only pregnant woman in the world." Heaving a sigh, Morgana walked into the back room. Her brows lifted when she saw the trio—and particularly when she saw the way Boone Sawyer was caging her cousin at the rear counter.

"You're the only pregnant woman in my world." Nash stopped short. "Hey, Ana, you're just the woman I need to convince Morgana to take it easy. Now that you're here, I can..." He glanced once at the man beside her, then back again to focus. "Boone? Well, I'll be damned. Boone Sawyer, you son of a—" He caught himself, mostly because Morgana shot an elbow into his ribs. There was a little girl, all eyes, standing at the table. "Gun," he finished, and strode across the room to shake Boone's hand and slap his back in a typical male greeting. "What are you doing here?"

"Delivering stock, I think." He grinned, gripping Nash's hand hard in his. "How about you?"

"Trying to keep my wife in line. Lord, what's it been? Four years?"

"Just about."

Morgana folded her hands on her belly. "I take it you two know each other?"

"Sure we do. Boone and I met at a writers' conference. It has to be ten years ago, doesn't it? I haven't seen you since—" Since Alice's funeral, Nash remembered abruptly. And he remembered, too, the devastation, the despair and the disbelief in Boone's eyes as he'd stood beside his wife's grave. "How are you?"

"Okay." Understanding, Boone smiled. "We're okay."

"Good." Nash put a hand on Boone's shoulder and squeezed before he turned to Jessie. "And you're Jessica."

"Uh-huh." She beamed up at him, always interested in meeting someone new. "Who are you?"

"I'm Nash." He crossed to her, crouched down. Except for the eyes, eyes that were all Boone, she was the image of Alice.

Bright, pretty, pixielike. He offered her a formal handshake. "It's nice to meet you."

She giggled and shook his hand. "Did you put the babies into Morgana?"

To his credit, he was speechless only for a moment. "Guilty." With a laugh, he picked her up. "But I'm leaving it up to Ana to get them out. So, what are the two of you doing in Monterey?"

"We live here now," Jessie told him. "Right next door to Ana's house."

"No kidding?" Nash grinned over at Boone. "When?"

"A little more than a week. I'd heard you'd moved here, and I figured I'd look you up once we got things together. I didn't realize you were married to my neighbor's cousin."

"A small and fascinating world, isn't it?" Morgana commented. She tilted her head at Ana, well aware that her cousin hadn't said a word since they'd come into the room. "Since no one's going to introduce me, I'm Morgana."

"Sorry," Nash said, jiggling Jessie on his hip. "Sit down."

"I'm perfectly—"

"Sit." This from Ana as she pulled out a chair.

"Outnumbered." Sighing, Morgana sat. "Are you enjoying Monterey?"

"Very much," Boone told her, and his gaze shifted to Ana. "More than I anticipated."

"I always enjoy having more than I anticipated." With a light laugh, she patted her belly. "We'll all have to get together very soon, so you can tell me things Nash doesn't want me to know."

"I'd be glad to."

"Babe, you know I'm an open book." He kissed the top of Morgana's head and winked at Ana. "That the stuff Morgana's been waiting for?"

"Yes, all of it." Anxious to keep her hands busy, Ana turned to the pile of boxes. "I'll unpack it for you. Morgana, I want you to try out this new violet body lotion before you put it out, and I brought extra of the soapwort shampoo."

"Good, I'm completely out." She took the bottle of lotion from Ana and unstopped the bottle. "Nice scent." She dabbed a bit on the back of her hand and rubbed it in. "Good texture."

"Sweet violets, and the Irish moss Da sent me." She glanced up from her unpacking. "Nash, why don't you show Jessie and Boone the shop?"

"Good idea. I think you're going to find a lot of this right up your alley," Nash told Boone as he led the way to the door.

Boone shot a look over his shoulder before he passed through. "Anastasia." He waited until she glanced up from the boxes. "Don't run away."

"My, my, my." Morgana settled back and smiled like a cat with a direct line to Bossy. "Want to fill me in?"

With a little more force than necessary, Ana ripped through packing tape. "On what?"

"On you and your gorgeous neighbor, of course."

"There's nothing to fill in."

"Darling, I know you. When I walked into this room, you were so wrapped up in him I could have called out a tornado and you wouldn't have blinked."

Ana busied herself unpacking bottles. "Don't be ridiculous. You haven't called out a tornado since the first time we saw *The Wizard of Oz.*"

"Ana." Morgana's voice was low and firm. "I love you."

"I know. I love you, too."

"You're never nervous. Perhaps that's why it's so fascinating—and concerning—to me that you're so nervous just now."

"I'm not." She rapped two bottles together and winced. "All right, all right, all right. I have to think about it." She whipped around. "He makes me nervous, and it would be ridiculous to deny it's the fact that I'm very attracted to him that's making me so nervous. I just have to think about it."

"Think about what?"

"How to handle it. Him, I mean. I have no intention of making another mistake, particularly since anything I do that involves Boone also involves Jessie."

"Oh, honey, are you falling in love with him?"

"That's absurd." Ana realized too late that the denial was too forceful to be taken at face value. "I'm just jumpy, that's all. I haven't had a man affect me like this, physically, in…" Ever. Never before, and, she was very much afraid, never again. "In a long time. I just need to think," she repeated.

"Ana." Morgana held out both hands. "Sebastian and Mel will be back in a couple of days from their honeymoon. Why don't you ask him to look? It would relieve your mind if you knew."

Resolute, Ana shook her head. "No…not that I haven't considered it. Whatever happens, however it happens, I want it to be on equal terms. Knowing would give me an unfair advantage over Boone. I have a feeling those equal terms would be important, to both of us."

"You know best. Let me tell you something, as a woman." Her lips curved. "As a witch. Knowing, not knowing, makes no difference with a man, once he touches your heart. No difference at all."

Ana nodded. "Then I'll have to make sure he doesn't touch mine until I'm ready."

"This is incredible," Boone was saying as he surveyed Wicca. "Just incredible."

"I thought so, too, the first time I walked in." Nash picked up a crystal wand tipped at the end with a spear of amethyst. "I guess people in our line of work are suckers for this stuff."

"Fairy tales," Boone agreed, accepting the wand before running a finger over a bronze cast of a snarling wolf. "Or the occult. A fine line between the two. Your last movie chilled my blood even when it made me laugh."

Nash grinned. "The humor in horror."

"Nobody does it better." He glanced over at his daughter. She was staring at a miniature silver castle surrounded by a moat of rainbow glass, her eyes huge, her hands behind her back. "I'll never get out of here empty-handed."

"She's beautiful," Nash said, wondering, as he often did, about the children that would be his before much longer.

"Looks like her mother." He saw the question and the concern in his friend's eyes. "Grief passes, Nash, whether you want it to or not. Alice was a wonderful part of my life, and she gave me the best thing in it. I'm grateful for every moment I had with her." He set the wand down. "Now I'd like to know how you—the world's most determined bachelor—came to be married and expecting twins."

"Research." Nash grinned and rocked back on his heels. "I wanted to get out of L.A., and keep within commuting distance. I'd only been here a short time when I needed to do some research on a script. I walked in here, and there she was."

There was more, of course. A great deal more. But it wasn't Nash's place to tell Boone about the Donovan legacy. Not even if Boone would have believed him.

"When you decide to take the plunge, you take it big."

"You, too. Indiana's a long way from here."

"I didn't want to be able to commute," Boone said with a grimace. "My parents, Alice's parents. Jessie and I were becoming their life's work. And I wanted a change, for both of us."

"Next door to Ana, huh?" Nash narrowed his eyes. "The redwood place, with all the glass and decks?"

"That's the one."

"Good choice." He glanced toward Jessie again. She'd wandered around the shop and had worked her way back to the little castle. She hadn't once asked for it, and that made the naked desire in her eyes all the more effective. "If you don't buy her that, I will."

\* \* \*

When Ana came out to restock a few shelves for Morgana, she saw not only the silver castle being rung up on the counter, but the wand, a three-foot sculpture of a winged fairy she'd had her eye on herself, a crystal sun-catcher in the shape of a unicorn, a pewter wizard holding a many-faceted ball, and a baseball-sized geode.

"We're weak," Boone said with a quick, sheepish grin as Ana lifted a brow. "No willpower."

"But excellent taste." She ran a fingertip over the fairy wings. "Lovely, isn't she?"

"One of the best I've seen. I figured I'd put her in my office for inspiration."

"Good idea." She bent over a compartment containing tumbling stones. "Malachite, for clear thinking." Her fingers walked through the smooth stones, testing, rejecting, selecting. "Sodalite to relieve mental confusion, moonstone for sensitivity. Amethyst, of course, for intuition."

"Of course."

She ignored him. "A crystal for all-around good things." Tilting her head, she studied him. "Jessie says you're trying to quit smoking."

He shrugged. "I'm cutting down."

She handed him the crystal. "Keep it in your pocket. Tumbling stones are on the house." When she turned away with her colorful bottles, he picked up the crystal and rubbed it with his fingers.

It couldn't hurt.

He didn't believe in magic crystals or stone power—though he did think they had plot possibilities. Boone also had to admit they looked kind of nice in the little bowl on his desk. Atmosphere, he thought, like the geode he'd bought to use as a paperweight.

All in all, the afternoon had had several benefits. He and

Jessie had enjoyed themselves thoroughly, riding the carousel at the Emporium, playing video games, just walking down Cannery Row and Fisherman's Wharf. Running into Anastasia had been a plus, he mused as he toyed with the creamy moonstone. And seeing Nash again, discovering that they lived in the same area, was gold.

He'd been missing male companionship. Funny, he hadn't realized it, as busy as his life had been over the past few months, with planning the move, executing the move, adjusting to the move. And Nash, though their friendship had primarily been through correspondence over the years, was exactly the kind of companion Boone preferred. Easygoing, loyal, imaginative.

It would be a kick to be able to pass on a few fatherly hints to Nash once his twins were born.

Oh, yeah, he reflected as he held up the moonstone, watching it gleam in the bright wash of moonlight through his office window, it certainly was a small and fascinating world.

One of his oldest friends, married to the cousin of the woman next door. It would certainly be hard for Anastasia to avoid him now.

And, no matter what she said, that was exactly what she'd been doing. He had a very strong feeling—and he couldn't help being a bit smug about it—that he was making the fair maiden nervous.

He'd nearly forgotten what it was like to approach a woman who reacted with faint blushes, confused eyes and rapid pulses. Most of the women he'd escorted over the past couple of years had been sleek and sophisticated—and safe, he added with a little shrug. He'd enjoyed their companionship, and he'd never lost his basic enjoyment of female company. But there'd been no tug, no mystery, no illusion.

He supposed he was still the kind of man attracted to the old-fashioned type. The roses-and-moonlight type, he thought with a half laugh. Then he saw her, and the laugh caught in his throat.

Down in her garden, walking, almost gliding through the silvery light, with the gray cat slipping in and out of the shadows. Her hair loose, sprinkling gold dust down her back and over the sheer shoulders of a pale blue robe. She carried a basket, and he thought he could hear her singing as she cut flowers and slipped them into it.

She was singing an old chant that had been passed down generation to generation. It was well past midnight, and Ana thought herself alone and unobserved. The first night of the full moon in autumn was the time to harvest, just as the first night of the full moon in spring was the time to sow. She had already cast the circle, purifying the area.

She laid the flowers and herbs in the basket as gently as children.

There was magic in her eyes. In her blood.

"Under the moon, through shadow and light, these blooms I chose by touch, by sight. Spells to weave to ease and free. As I will, so mote it be."

She plucked betony and heliotrope, dug mandrake root and selected tansy and balsam. Blood roses for strength, and sage for wisdom. The basket grew heavy and fragrant.

"Tonight to reap, tomorrow to sow. To take only that which I've caused to grow. Remembering always what is begun. To serve, to aid, an' it harm none."

As the charm was cast, she lowered her face to the blooms, drawing in the ripe melody of the fragrance.

"I wondered if you were real."

Her head came up quickly, and she saw him, hardly more than a shadow by the hedge. Then he stepped through, into her garden, and became a man.

The heart that had leapt to her throat gradually settled again. "You startled me."

"I'm sorry." It must be the moonlight, he thought, that made her look so…enchanting. "I was working late, and I looked out and saw you. It seemed late to be picking flowers."

"There's a lot of moonlight." She smiled. He had seen nothing it wasn't safe for him to see. "I would think you'd know that anything picked under the full moon is charmed."

He returned the smile. "Got any rampion?"

The reference to Rapunzel made her laugh. "As a matter of fact, I do. No magic garden is complete without it. I'll pot some for you, if you like."

"I rarely say no to magic." The breeze fluttered her hair. Giving in to the moment, he reached out, took a handful. He watched the smile in her eyes fade. What replaced it had his blood singing.

"You should go in. Jessie's alone."

"She's asleep." He moved closer, as if the hair he'd twined around his finger were a rope and she were drawing him to her. He was within the circle now, within the magic she'd cast. "The windows are open, so I'd hear her if she called for me."

"It's late." Ana gripped the basket so tightly that the wicker dug into her skin. "I need to…"

Gently he took the basket and set it on the ground. "So do I." His other hand moved into her hair, combing it back from her face. "Very much."

As he lowered his mouth toward hers, she shivered and tried one last time to take control. "Boone, starting something like this could complicate things for all of us."

"Maybe I'm tired of things being simple." But he turned his head, just a fraction, so that his lips cruised up her cheek, over her temple. "I'm surprised you don't know that when a man finds a woman picking flowers in the moonlight he has no choice but to kiss her."

She felt her bones melting. Her body was pliant when she slipped into his arms. "And she has no choice but to want him to."

Her head fell back, and she offered. He thought he would

take gently. The night seemed to call for it, with its perfumed breezes and the dreamy music of sea against rock. The woman in his arms was wand-slender, and the thin silk of her robe was cool over the warmth of satin skin.

But as he felt himself sink into that soft, lush mouth, as her fragrance whispered seductively around him, he dragged her hard against him and plundered.

Instantly desperate, instantly greedy. No rational thought could fight its way through the maze of sensations she brought to him. A sharp arrow of hunger pierced him, bringing on a groan that was only part pleasure.

Pain. He felt the aches of a thousand pricks of pain. Yet he couldn't pull himself away from her, couldn't stop his mouth from seeking more of hers. He was afraid, afraid that if he released her she would disappear like smoke—and he would never, never feel this way again.

She couldn't soothe him. Part of her wanted to stroke him and ease him and promise him that it would be all right, for both of them. But she couldn't. He devastated her. Whether it was her own grinding needs, the echo of his need seeping into her, or a mix of both, the result was a complete loss of will.

She had known, yes, she had known that this first meeting would be wild and strong. She'd craved it even as she'd feared it. Now she was beyond fear. Like him, she found the mixture of pain and pleasure irresistible.

Her trembling hands skimmed over his face, into his hair and locked there. Her body, shuddering from the onslaught, pressed urgently to his. When she murmured his name, she was breathless.

But he heard her, heard her through the blood pounding in his head, heard that soft, shaky sound. She was trembling—or he was. The uncertainty about who was more dazed had him slowly, carefully drawing away.

He held her still, his hands on her shoulders, his gaze on her face. In the moonlight, she could see herself there, trapped in that sea of blue. Trapped in him.

"Boone..."

"Not yet." He needed a moment to steady himself. By God, he'd nearly swallowed her whole. "Not just yet." Holding himself back, he touched his lips to hers, lightly, in a long, quiet kiss that wrecked whatever was left of her defenses. "I didn't mean to hurt you."

"You didn't." She pressed her lips together and tried to bring her voice over a whisper. "You didn't hurt me. You staggered me."

"I thought I was ready for this." He ran his hands down her arms before he released her. "I don't know if anyone could be." Because he wasn't sure what would happen if he touched her again, he slipped his hands into his pockets. "Maybe it's the moonlight, maybe it's just you. I have to be straight with you, Anastasia, I don't know quite how to handle this."

"Well." She wrapped her arms tight and cupped her elbows. "That makes two of us."

"If it wasn't for Jessie, you wouldn't go into that house alone tonight. And I don't take intimacy lightly."

Steadier now, she nodded. "If it wasn't for Jessie, I might ask you to stay with me tonight." She took a long breath. She knew it was important to be honest, at least in this. "You would be my first."

"Your—" His hands went limp. Now he felt both a lick of fear and an incredible excitement at the thought of her innocence. "Oh, God."

Her chin came up. "I'm not ashamed of it."

"No, I didn't mean..." Speechless, he dragged a hand through his hair. Innocent. A golden-haired virgin in a thin blue robe with flowers at her feet. And a man was supposed to resist, and walk away alone. "I don't suppose you have any idea what that does to a man."

"Not precisely, since I'm not a man." She bent down for

her basket. "But I do know what realizing that you may soon be giving yourself for the first time does to a woman. So it seems to me we should both give this some clear thinking." She smiled, or tried to. "And it's very difficult to think clearly after midnight, when the moon's full and the flowers are ripe. I'll say good-night, Boone."

"Ana." He touched her arm, but didn't hold on. "Nothing will happen until you're ready."

She shook her head. "Yes, it will. But nothing will happen unless it's meant."

With her robe billowing around her, she raced toward the house.

# Chapter 5

Sleep had been a long time coming. Boone hadn't tossed and turned so much as lain, staring up at the ceiling. He'd watched the moonlight fade into that final deep darkness before dawn.

Now, with the sun streaming in bright ribbons over the bed, he was facedown, spread out, and fast asleep. In the dream floating through his brain, he scooped Ana into his arms and carried her up a long curved staircase of white marble. At the top, suspended above puffy cotton clouds, was an enormous bed pooled in waterfalls of white satin. Hundreds of long, slender candles burned in a drifting light. He could smell them—the soft tang of vanilla, the mystique of jasmine. And her—that quietly sexy scent that went everywhere with her.

She smiled. Hair like sunlight. Eyes like smoke. When he laid her on the bed, they sank deep, as if into the clouds themselves. There was harpsong, romantic as tears, and a whisper that was nothing more than the clouds themselves breathing.

As her arms lifted, wound around him, they were floating, like ghosts in some fantasy, bound together by needs and knowledge and the unbearable sweetness of that first long, lingering kiss. Her mouth moved under his, yielding as she murmured...

"Daddy!"

Boone came awake with a crash as his daughter landed with a thump on his back. His unintelligible grunt had her giggling and scooting down to smack a kiss on his stubbled cheek.

"Daddy, wake up! I fixed you breakfast!"

"Breakfast." He grumbled into the pillow, struggling to clear the sleep from his throat and the dream from his system. "What time is it?"

"The little hand's on the ten, and the big hand's on the three. I made cinnamon toast and poured orange juice in the little glasses."

He grunted again, rolling over to peer through gritty eyes at Jessie. She looked bright as a sunbeam in her pink cotton blouse and shorts. She'd done the buttons up wrong, but she'd brushed the tangles from her hair. "How long have you been up?"

"Hours and hours and hours. I let Daisy outside and gave her breakfast. And I got dressed all by myself and brushed my teeth and watched cartoons. Then I got hungry, so I fixed breakfast."

"You've been busy."

"Uh-huh. And I was real quiet, too, so you didn't have to wake up early on your sleep-in day."

"You were real quiet," Boone agreed, and reached up to fix her buttons. "I guess you deserve a prize."

Her eyes lit. "What? What do I get?"

"How about a pink belly?" He rolled with her on the bed, wrestling while she squealed and wriggled. He let her win, pretending exhaustion and defeat when she bounced on his back. "Too tough for me."

"That's 'cause I eat my vegetables. You don't."

"I eat some."

"Uh-uh, hardly any."

"When you get to be thirty-three, you won't have to eat your brussels sprouts, either."

"But I like them."

He grinned into the pillow. "That's only because I'm such a good cook. My mother was lousy."

"She doesn't ever cook now." Jessie printed her name with a fingertip on her father's bare back. "Her and Grandpa Sawyer always go out to eat."

"That's because Grandpa Sawyer's no fool." She was having trouble with the letter *S*, Boone noted. They'd have to work on it.

"You said we could call Grandma and Grandpa Sawyer and Nana and Pop today. Can we?"

"Sure, in a couple of hours." He turned over again, studying her. "Do you miss them, baby?"

"Yeah." With her tongue between her teeth, she began to print *Sawyer* on his chest. "It seems funny that they're not here. Will they come to visit us?"

"Sure they will." The guilt that was part and parcel of parenthood worked at him. "Do you wish we'd stayed in Indiana?"

"No way!" Her eyes went huge. "We didn't have the beach there, and the seals and stuff, or the big carousel in town, or Ana living next door. This is the best place in the world."

"I like it here, too." He sat up and kissed her brow. "Now beat it, so I can get dressed."

"You'll come right downstairs for breakfast?" she asked as she slid from the bed.

"Absolutely. I'm so hungry I could eat a whole loaf of cinnamon toast."

Delighted, she rushed for the door. "I'm going to make more, right now."

Knowing she would take him at his word and go through an entire loaf of bread, Boone hurried through his shower, opted not to shave, and pulled on cutoffs and a T-shirt that would probably have done better in the rag pile.

He tried not to dwell on the dream. After all, it was simple enough to interpret. He wanted Ana—no big revelation there. And all that white—white on white—was obviously a symbol of her innocence.

It scared the hell out of him.

He found Jessie in the kitchen, busily slathering butter on another piece of toast. There was a plate heaped with them, more than a few of them burnt. The smell of cinnamon was everywhere.

Boone put on the coffee before he snagged a piece. It was cold, hard, and lumped with sugary cinnamon. Obviously, Jessie had inherited her grandmother's culinary talents.

"It's great," he told her, and swallowed gamely. "My favorite Sunday breakfast."

"Do you think Daisy can have some?"

Boone looked at the pile of toast again, glanced down at the pup, whose tongue was lolling out. With any luck he might be able to pawn off half his Sunday breakfast on the dog. "I think she could." Crouching, Boone held out a second piece of toast close enough for Daisy to sniff. "Sit," he ordered, in the firm, no-nonsense voice the training books had suggested.

Daisy continued to loll her tongue and wag her tail.

"Daisy, sit." He gave her rump a nudge. Daisy went down, then bounded back on all fours to jump at him. "Forget it." He held the toast out of reach and repeated the command. After five frustrating minutes—during which he tried not to remember how simple it had been for Ana—he managed to hold the dog's hindquarters down. Daisy gobbled up the bread, pleased with herself.

"She did it, Daddy."

"Sort of." He rose to pour himself some coffee. "We'll take her outside in a little while and have a real lesson."

"Okay." Jessie munched happily on her toast. "Maybe Ana's company will be gone, and she can help."

"Company?" Boone asked as he reached for a mug.

"I saw her outside with a man. She gave him a big hug and a kiss and everything."

"She—" The mug clattered onto the counter.

"Butterfingers," Jessie said, smiling.

"Yeah." Boone kept his back turned as he righted the mug and poured the coffee. "What, ah, sort of a man?" He thought his voice was casual enough—to fool a six-year-old, anyway.

"A really tall man with black hair. They were laughing and holding hands. Maybe it's her boyfriend."

"Boyfriend," Boone repeated between his teeth.

"What's the matter, Daddy?"

"Nothing. Coffee's hot." He sipped it black. Holding hands, he thought. Kissing. He'd get a look at this guy himself. "Why don't we go out on the deck, Jess? See if we can get Daisy to sit again."

"Okay." Singing the new song she'd learned in school, Jessie gathered up toast. "I like to eat outside. It's nice."

"Yeah, it's nice." Boone didn't sit when they were on the deck, but stood at the rail, the mug in his hand. He didn't see anyone in the next yard, and that was worse. Now he could imagine what Ana and her tall, dark-haired boyfriend might be doing inside.

Alone.

He ate three more pieces of toast, washing them down with black coffee while he fantasized about just what he'd say to Miss Anastasia Donovan the next time he saw her.

If she thought she could kiss him to the point of explosion one night, then dally with some strange guy the next morning, she was very much mistaken.

He'd straighten her out, all right. The minute he got ahold of her he'd—

His thoughts broke off when she came out the kitchen door, calling over her shoulder to someone.

"Ana!" Jessie leapt up on the bench, waving and shouting. "Ana, hi!"

While Boone watched through narrowed eyes, Ana looked in their direction. It seemed to him that her hand hesitated on its way up to return the wave, and her smile was strained.

Sure, he thought as he gulped down more coffee. I'd be nervous, too, if I had some strange man in the house.

"Can I go tell her what Daisy did? Can I, Daddy?"

"Yeah." His smile was grim as he set his empty mug on the rail. "Why don't you do that?"

Snatching up some more toast, she darted down the steps, calling for Daisy to follow and for Ana to wait.

Boone waited himself until he saw the man stroll outside to join Ana. He was tall, all right, Boone noted with some resentment. Several inches over six feet. He drew his own shoulders back. His hair was true black, and long enough to curl over his collar and blow—romantically, Boone imagined a woman would think— in the breeze.

He looked tanned, fit and elegant. And the breath hissed out between Boone's teeth when the stranger slipped an arm around Ana's shoulders as if it belonged there.

We'll see about this, Boone decided, and started down the deck stairs with his hands jammed in his pockets. We'll just see about this.

By the time he reached the hedge of roses, Jessie was already chattering a mile a minute about Daisy, and Ana was laughing, her arms tucked intimately around the stranger's waist.

"I'd sit, too, if someone was going to feed me cinnamon toast," the man said, and winked at Ana.

"You'd sit if anyone was going to feed you anything." Ana gave him a little squeeze before she noticed Boone at the hedge. "Oh." It was useless to curse the faint blush she felt heating her cheeks. "Good morning."

"How's it going?" Boone gave her a slow nod. Then his gaze moved suspiciously to the man beside her. "We didn't mean to interrupt while you have...company."

"No, that's all right, I—" She broke off, both confused and disconcerted by the tension humming in the air. "Sebastian, this is Jessie's father, Boone Sawyer. Boone, my cousin, Sebastian Donovan."

"Cousin?" Boone repeated, and Sebastian didn't bother to control the grin that spread over his face.

"Fortunately you made the introductions quickly, Ana," he said. "I like my nose precisely the way it is." He held out a hand. "Nice to meet you. Ana was telling us she had new neighbors."

"He's the one with horses, Daddy."

"I remember." Boone found Sebastian's grip firm and strong. He might have appreciated it if he hadn't seen the gleam of amusement in the man's eyes. "You're recently married?"

"Indeed I am. My..." He turned when the screen door slammed. "Ah, here she is now. Light of my life."

A tall, slim woman with short, tousled hair strode over in dusty boots. "Cut it out, Donovan."

"My blushing bride." It was obvious they were laughing at each other. He took his wife's hand and kissed it. "Ana's neighbors, Boone and Jessie Sawyer. My own true love, Mary Ellen."

"Mel," she corrected quickly. "Donovan's the only one with the nerve to call me Mary Ellen. Great-looking house," she added, with a nod toward the neighboring building.

"I believe Mr. Sawyer writes fairy tales, children's books, much in the manner of Aunt Bryna."

"Oh, yeah? That's cool." Mel smiled down at Jessie. "I bet you like that."

"He writes the best stories in the world. And this is Daisy. We taught her to sit. Can I come see your horses?"

"Sure." Mel crouched down to ruffle the pup's fur. While Mel engaged Jessie in conversation about horses and dogs, Sebastian looked back at Boone.

"It is a lovely house you have," he said. Actually, he'd toyed with buying it himself. Amusement lit his eyes again. "Excellent location."

"We like it." Boone decided it was foolish to pretend not to understand the meaning behind the words. "We like it very much." Very deliberately, he reached out to trail a fingertip down Ana's cheek. "You're looking a little pale this morning, Anastasia."

"I'm fine." It was easy enough to keep her voice even, but she knew very well how simple it would be for Sebastian to see what she was thinking. Already she could feel his gentle probing, and she was quite certain he was poking his nosy mental fingers into Boone's brain. "If you'll excuse me, I promised Sebastian some hawthorn."

"Didn't you pick any last night?"

Her gaze met his, held it. "I have other uses for that."

"We'll get out of your way. Come on, Jess." He reached for his daughter's hand. "Nice meeting both of you. I'll see you soon, Ana."

Sebastian had the tact to wait until Boone was out of earshot. "Well, well… I go away for a couple of weeks, and look at the trouble you get into."

"Don't be ridiculous." Ana turned her back and started toward an herb bed. "I'm not in any sort of trouble."

"Darling, darling Ana, your friend and neighbor was prepared to rip my throat out until you introduced me as your cousin."

"I'd have protected you," Mel said solemnly.

"My hero."

"Besides," Mel went on, "it looked to me as though he was more in the mood to drag Ana off by the hair than tackle you."

"You're both being absurd." Ana snipped hawthorn without looking up. "He's a very nice man."

"I'm sure," Sebastian murmured. "But, you see, men understand this territorial thing—which is, of course, an obscure concept to the female."

"Oh, please." Mel shoved an elbow in his ribs.

"Facts are facts, my dear Mary Ellen. I had intruded on his territory. Or so he thought. Naturally, I would only think less of him if he had made no effort to defend it."

"Naturally," Mel said dryly.

"Tell me, Ana, just how involved are you?"

"That's none of your business." She straightened, deftly wrapping the stems of the hawthorn. "And I'll thank you to keep out of it, cousin. I know very well you were poking in."

"Which is why you blocked me. Your neighbor wasn't so successful."

"It's rude," she muttered, "unconscionably rude, the way you peek into people's heads at the drop of a hat."

"He likes to show off," Mel said sympathetically.

"Unfair." Disgusted, Sebastian shook his head. "I do not poke or peek at the drop of a hat. I always have an excellent reason. In this case, being your only male relative on the continent, I feel it's my duty to survey the situation, and the players."

Mel could only roll her eyes as Ana's spine stiffened. "Really?" Eyes bright, Ana jammed a finger into Sebastian's chest. "Then let me set you straight. Just because I'm a woman doesn't mean I need protection or guidance or anything else from a male—relative or otherwise. I've been handling my own life for twenty-six years."

"Twenty-seven next month," Sebastian added helpfully.

"And I can continue to handle it. What's between Boone and me—"

"Ah." He held up a triumphant finger. "So there is something between you."

"Stuff it, Sebastian."

"She only talks like that when she paints herself into a corner," Sebastian told Mel. "Usually she's extremely mild and well-mannered."

"Careful, or I'll give Mel a potion to put in your soup that'll freeze your vocal cords for a week."

"Oh yeah?" Intrigued by the idea, Mel tilted her head. "Can I have it anyway?"

"A lot of good it would do you, since I do all the cooking," Sebastian pointed out. Then he scooped Ana up in a hug. "Come on, darling, don't be angry. I have to worry about you. It's my job."

"There's nothing to worry about." But she was softening.

"Are you in love with him?"

Instantly she stiffened. "Really, Sebastian, I've only known him for a week."

"What difference does that make?" He gave Mel a long look over Ana's head. "It took me less than that to realize the reason Mel irritated me so much was that I was crazy about her. Of course, it took her longer to understand she was madly in love with me. But she has such a hard head."

"I'm getting that potion," Mel decided.

Ignoring the threat, he drew back to consider Ana at arm's length. "I ask because he definitely has more than a neighborly interest in you. As a matter of fact, he—"

"That's enough. Whatever you dug out of his head, you keep to yourself. I mean it, Sebastian," she said before he could interrupt. "I prefer doing things my own way."

"If you insist," he said with a sigh.

"I do. Now take your hawthorn and go home and be newlyweds."

"Now that's the best idea I've heard all day." Taking a firm grip on her husband's arm, Mel tugged him back. "Leave her alone, Donovan. Ana's perfectly capable of handling her own affairs."

"And if she's going to have one, she should know—"

"Out." On a strangled laugh, Ana gave him a shove. "Out of my yard. I have work to do. If I need a psychic, I'll call you."

He relented and gave her a kiss. "See that you do." A new

smile began to bloom as he walked away with his wife. "I believe we'll stop by and see Morgana and Nash."

"That's fine." She shot a last glance over her shoulder. "I'd like to hear what they have to say about this guy myself."

Sebastian laughed and hugged her close. "You are a woman after my own heart."

"No, I'm not." She kissed him soundly. "I've already got it."

For the next several days, Ana busied herself indoors. It wasn't that she was avoiding Boone—at least not to any great extent. She simply had a lot to do. Her medicinal supplies had become sadly depleted. Just that day, she'd had a call from a client in Carmel who was out of the elixir for her rheumatism. Ana had had just enough to ship, but that meant she had to make more as soon as possible. Even now she had dried primrose simmering with motherwort on the stove.

In the little room adjoining the kitchen through a wide archway, she had her distilling flasks, condensers, burners and bottles, along with vials and silver bowls and candles, set up for the day. To the casual eye, the room resembled a small chemistry lab. But there was a marked difference between chemistry and alchemy. In alchemy there was ritual, and the meticulous use of astrological timing.

All of the flowers and roots and herbs she had harvested by moonlight had been carefully washed in morning dew. Others, plucked under different phases of the moon, had already been prepared for their specific uses.

There was syrup of poppy to be distilled, and there was hyssop to be dried for cough syrup. She needed some oil of clary for a specialty perfume, and she could combine that with some chamomile for a digestive aid. There were infusions and decoctions to be completed, as well as both oils and incense.

Plenty to do, Ana thought, particularly since she had the touch of magic from the flowers picked in moonlight. And she enjoyed her work, the scents that filled her kitchen and workroom, the pretty pink leaves of the flowering marjoram, the deep purple of foxglove, the sunny touch of the practical marigold.

They were lovely, and she could never resist setting some in vases or bowls around the house. She was testing a dilution of gentian, grimacing at the bitter taste, when Boone knocked on her screen door.

"I really do need sugar this time," he told her with a quick, charming grin that had her heart pumping fast. "I'm homeroom mother this week, and I have to make three dozen cookies for tomorrow."

Tilting her head, she studied him. "You could buy them."

"What homeroom mother worth her salt serves the first grade class store-bought? A cup would do it."

The image of him baking made her smile. "I probably have one. Come on in. Just let me finish this up."

"It smells fabulous in here." He leaned over to peek into the pots simmering on the stove. "What are you doing?"

"Don't!" She warned, just as he was about to dip a finger in a black glass pan cooling on the counter. "That's belladonna. Not for internal consumption in that form."

"Belladonna." His brows drew together. "You're making poison?"

"I'm making a lotion—an anodyne—for neuralgia, rheumatism. And it isn't a poison if it's brewed and dispensed properly. It's a sedative."

Frowning, he looked into the room behind, with its chemical equipment and its bubbling brews. "Don't you have to have a license or something?"

"I'm a qualified herbal practitioner, with a degree in pharmacognosy, if that relieves you." She batted his hand away from a pot. "And this is not something for the novice."

"Got anything for insomnia—besides belladonna? No offense."

She was instantly concerned. "Are you having trouble sleeping? Are you feverish?" She lifted a hand to his brow, then went still when he took her wrist.

"Yes, to both questions. You could say you're the cause and the cure." He brought her hand from his brow to his lips. "I may be homeroom mother, but I'm still a man, Ana. I can't stop thinking about you." He turned her hand over, pressing those lips to the inside of her wrist, where the pulse was beginning to jerk. "And I can't stop wanting you."

"I'm sorry if I'm giving you restless nights."

His brow quirked. "Are you?"

She couldn't quite suppress the smile. "I'm trying to be. It's hard not to be flattered that thinking about me is keeping you awake. And it's hard to know what to do." She turned away to switch off the heat on the stove. "I've been feeling a little restless myself." Her eyes closed when his hands came down on her shoulders.

"Make love with me." He brushed a kiss on the back of her neck. "I won't hurt you, Ana."

Not purposely, she thought. Never that. There was so much kindness in him. But would they hurt each other if she gave in to what she wanted, needed, from him, and held back that part of herself that made her what she was?

"It's a big step for me, Boone."

"For me, too." Gently he turned her to face him. "There's been no one for me since Alice died. In the past couple of years there was a woman or two, but nothing that meant any more than filling a physical emptiness. No one I've wanted to spend time with, to be with, to talk to. I care about you." He lowered his mouth to hers, very carefully, very softly. "I don't know how I came to care this much, this quickly, but I do. I hope you believe that."

Even without a true link, she couldn't help but feel it. It made things more complicated somehow. "I do believe you."

"I've been thinking. Seeing as I haven't been sleeping, I've had plenty of time for it." Absently he tapped a loosened pin back into her hair. "The other night, I was rushing you, probably scared you."

"No." Then she shrugged and turned back to filter one of her mixtures into a bottle, already labeled. "Yes, actually, I guess you did."

"If I'd known you were... If I'd realized you'd never..."

With a sigh, she capped the bottle. "My virginity is by choice, Boone, and nothing I'm uncomfortable with."

"I didn't mean—" He let out a hissing breath. "I'm doing a great job with this."

She chose another funnel, another bottle, and poured. "You're nervous."

With some chagrin, he noted that her hands were rock-steady when she capped the next bottle. "I think terrified comes closer. I was rough with you, and I shouldn't have been. For a lot of reasons. The fact that you're inexperienced is only one of them."

"You weren't rough." She continued to work to hide her nerves, which were jumping every bit as much as his. As long as she had to concentrate on what she was doing, she could at least pretend to be calm and confident. "You're a passionate man. That's not something to apologize for."

"I'm apologizing for pressuring you. And for coming over here today fully intending to keep things light and easy, and then pressuring you again."

Her lips curved as she walked to the sink to soak her pans. "Is that what you're doing?"

"I told myself I wasn't going to ask you to go to bed with me—even though I want you to. I was going to ask if you'd spend some time with me. Come to dinner, or go out, or whatever people do when they're trying to get to know each other."

"I'd like to come to dinner, or go out, or whatever."

"Good." That hadn't been so hard, he decided. "Maybe this weekend. Friday night. I should be able to find a sitter." His eyes clouded. "Somebody I can trust."

"I thought you were going to cook for me and Jessie."

A weight lifted. "You wouldn't mind?"

"I think I'd enjoy it."

"Okay, then." He framed her face in his hands. "Okay." The kiss was very sweet, and if it felt as if something inside were going to rip in two, he told himself, he could deal with it. "Friday."

It wasn't difficult to smile, even if her system felt as if it had been rocked by a small earthquake. "I'll bring the wine."

"Good." He wanted to kiss her again, but he was afraid he'd scare her off. "I'll see you then."

"Boone." She stopped him before he'd reached the door. "Don't you want your sugar?"

He grinned. "I lied."

Her eyes narrowed. "You're not homeroom mother, and you're not baking cookies?"

"No, that was true. But I have five pounds in the pantry. Hey, it worked." He was whistling as he walked out the door.

# Chapter 6

"Why isn't Ana here yet? When is she coming?"

"Soon," Boone answered for the tenth time. Too soon, he was afraid. He was behind in everything. The kitchen was a disaster. He'd used too many pans. Then again, he always did. He could never figure out how anyone cooked without using every pot, pan and bowl available.

The chicken cacciatore smelled pretty good, but he was uncertain of the results. Stupid, he supposed, absolutely stupid to try out a new recipe at such a time, but he'd figured Ana was worth more than their usual Friday-night meatloaf.

Jessie was driving him crazy, which was a rarity. She was overexcited at the thought of having Ana over, and she'd been pestering him without pause ever since he'd brought her home from school.

The dog had chosen that afternoon to chew up Boone's bed pillows, so he'd spent a great deal of valuable time chasing dog and feathers. The washing machine had overflowed, flooding the laundry room. He was much too male to consider calling a repairman, so he'd torn the machine apart and put it back together again.

He was pretty sure he'd fixed it.

His agent had called to tell him that *A Third Wish for Miranda* had been optioned for an animated feature by one of the major studios. That would have been good news at any other time, but now he was expected to fit a trip to L.A. into his schedule.

Jessie had decided she wanted to be a Brownie and had generously volunteered him as a Brownie leader.

The thought of having a group of six- and seven-year-old girls looking to him to teach them how to make jewelry boxes out of egg cartons chilled his blood.

With a lot of ingenuity and plenty of cowardice, he thought, he might be able to ease his way out of it.

"Are you sure she's coming, Daddy? Are you sure?"

"Jessica." The warning note in his voice was enough to make her lower lip poke out. "Do you know what happens to little girls who keep asking the same question?"

"Nuh-uh."

"Keep it up and you'll find out. Go make sure Daisy's not eating the furniture."

"Are you awfully mad at Daisy?"

"Yes. Now go on or you're next." He softened the order with a gentle pat on her bottom. "Beat it, brat, or I'll put you in the pot and have you for dinner."

Two minutes later, he heard the mayhem that meant Jessie had located Daisy, and girl and dog were now wrestling. The high-pitched yelps and happy squeals played hell with the headache pulsing behind his eyes.

Just need an aspirin, he thought, an hour or two of quiet, and a vacation on Maui.

He was on the point of giving a roar that would probably pop his head off his shoulders when Ana knocked.

"Hi. Smells good."

He hoped it did. She looked much better than good. He hadn't seen her in a dress before, and the swirl of watercolor silk did wonderful things for her slim body. Things like showing off those soft white shoulders under thin straps. With it she wore an amulet on a long chain that had the square of engraved gold hanging just below her breasts. Crystals glinted in it, drawing the eye, and were echoed by the tear-shaped drops at her ears.

She smiled. "You did say Friday."

"Yeah. Friday."

"Then are you going to ask me in?"

"Sorry." Lord, he felt like a bumbling teenager. No, he decided as he slid the screen open for her, no teenager had ever been this bumbling. "I'm a little distracted."

Ana's brows lifted as she surveyed the chaos of pots and bowls. "So I see. Would you like some help?"

"I think I've got it under control." He took the bottle she offered, noting that the pale green bottle was etched with symbols and that it carried no label. "Homemade?"

"Yes, my father makes it. He has…" Her eyes lit with secrets and humor. "A magic touch."

"Brewed in the dungeons of Castle Donovan."

"As a matter of fact, yes." She left it at that, and wandered to the stove as he took out some glasses. "No Bugs Bunny this time?"

"I'm afraid Bugs met a fatal accident in the dishwasher." He poured the clear golden wine into the crystal glasses. "It wasn't pretty."

She laughed and lifted her glass in a toast. "To neighbors."

"To neighbors," he agreed, clinking crystal against crystal. "If they all looked like you, I'd be a dead man." He sipped, then lifted a brow. "Next time we'll have to drink to your father. This is incredible."

"One of his many hobbies, you might say."

"What's in it?"

"Apples, honeysuckle, starlight. You can give him your compliments, if you like. He and the rest of my family should be here for All Hallows' Eve. Halloween."

"I know what it is. Jessie's torn between being a fairy princess or a rock star. Your parents travel all the way to the States for Halloween?"

"Usually. It's a kind of family tradition." Unable to resist, she took the lid off the pan and sniffed. "Well, well, I'm impressed."

"That was the idea." Equally unable to resist, he lifted a handful of her hair. "You know that story I told you the day Daisy knocked you down? I find myself compelled to write it. So much so that I've put what I was working on aside."

"It was a lovely story."

"Normally I could have made it wait. But I need to know why the woman was bound inside the castle all those years. Was it a spell, one of her own making? What was the enchantment that made the man climb the wall to find her?"

"That's for you to decide."

"No, that's for me to find out."

"Boone..." She lifted a hand to his, then looked down quickly. "What have you done to yourself?"

"Just rapped my knuckles." He flexed his fingers and shrugged. "Fixing the washing machine."

"You should have come over and let me tend to this." She ran her fingers over the scraped skin, wishing she was in a position to heal it. "It's painful."

He started to deny it, then realized his mistake. "I always kiss Jessie's hurts to make them better."

"A kiss works wonders," she agreed, and obliged him by touching her lips to the wound. Briefly, very briefly, she risked a link to be certain there was no real pain and no chance of infection. She found that, while the knuckles were merely sore, he did have real pain from a tension headache working behind his eyes. That, at least, she could help him with.

With a smile, she brushed the hair from his brow. "You've been working too hard, getting the house in order, writing your story, worrying if you made the right decision to move Jessie."

"I didn't realize I was that transparent."

"It isn't so difficult to see." She laid her fingers on either side of his temples, massaging in small circles. "Now you've gone to all this trouble to cook me dinner."

"I wanted—"

"I know." She held steady as she felt the pain flash behind her own eyes. To distract him, she touched her lips to his as she absorbed the ache and let it slowly fade. "Thank you."

"You're very welcome," he murmured, and deepened the kiss.

Her hands slid away from his temples, lay weakly on his shoulders. It was much more difficult to absorb this ache—this ache that spread so insidiously through her. Pulsing, throbbing. Tempting.

Much too tempting.

"Boone." Wary, she slipped out of his arms. "We're rushing this."

"I told you I wouldn't. That's not going to stop me from kissing you whenever I get the chance." He picked up his wine, then hers, offering her glass to her again. "Nothing goes beyond that until you say so."

"I don't know whether to thank you for that or not. I know I should."

"No. There's no more need to thank me for that than there is to thank me for wanting you. It's just the way it is. Sometimes I think about Jessie growing up. It gives me some bad moments. And I know that if there was any man who pushed or pressured her into doing what she wasn't ready to do I'd just have to kill him." He sipped, and grinned. "And, of course, if she thinks she's going to be ready to do anything of the kind before she's, say, forty, I'll just lock her in her room until the feeling passes."

It made her laugh, and she realized as he stood there, with his back to the cluttered, splattered stove, a dishcloth hanging from the waist of his slacks, that she was very, very close to falling in love with him.

Once she had, she would be ready. And nothing would make the feeling pass.

"Spoken like a true paranoid father."

"Paranoia and fatherhood are synonymous. Take my word for it. Wait until Nash has those twins. He'll start thinking about health insurance and dental hygiene. A sneeze in the middle of the night will send him into a panic."

"Morgana will keep him level. A paranoid father only needs a sensible mother to…" Her words trailed off as she cursed herself. "I'm sorry."

"It's all right. It's easier when people don't feel they have to tiptoe around it. Alice has been gone for four years. Wounds heal, especially if you have good memories." There was a thud from the next room, and the sound of racing feet. "And a six-year-old who keeps you on your toes."

At that moment, Jessie ran in and threw herself at Ana.

"You came! I thought you'd never get here."

"Of course I came. I never turn down a dinner invitation from my favorite neighbors."

As Boone watched them, he realized his headache had vanished. Odd, he thought as he switched off the stove and prepared to serve dinner. He'd never gotten around to taking an aspirin.

It wasn't what he would call a quiet, romantic dinner. He had lit candles and clipped flowers in the garden he'd inherited when he'd bought the house. They had the meal in the dining alcove, with its wide, curved window, with music from the sea and birdsong. A perfect setting for romance.

But there were no murmured secrets or whispered promises. Instead, there was laughter and a child's bubbling voice.

The talk was not about what the candlelight did to her skin, or how it deepened the pure gray of her eyes. It centered on first grade, on what Daisy had done that day and on the fairy tale still brewing in Boone's mind.

When dinner was over, and Ana had listened to Jessie's exploits at school, along with those of Jessie's new and very best friend, Lydia, she announced that she and the child were assuming kitchen duty.

"No, I'll take care of it later." He was very comfortable in the sunset-washed dining alcove, and he remembered too vividly the mess he'd left behind in the kitchen. "Dirty dishes don't go anywhere."

"You cooked." Ana was already rising to stack the dishes. "When my father cooks, my mother washes up. And vice versa. Donovan rules. Besides, the kitchen's a good place for girl talk, isn't it, Jessie?"

Jessie didn't have any idea, but she was instantly intrigued by the notion. "I can help. I hardly ever break any dishes."

"And men aren't allowed in the kitchen during girl talk." She leaned conspiratorially toward Jessie. "Because they just get in the way." She sent Boone an arch look. "I think you and Daisy could use a walk on the beach."

"I don't…" A walk on the beach. Alone. With no KP. "Really?"

"Really. Take your time. Jessie, when I was in town the other day, I saw the cutest dress. It was blue, just the color of your eyes, and had a big satin bow." Ana stopped, a pile of dishes in her hands, and stared at Boone. "Still here?"

"Just leaving."

As he walked out in the deepening twilight with Daisy romping around him, he could hear the light music of female laughter coming through his windows.

"Daddy said you were born in a castle," Jessie said as she helped Ana load the dishwasher.

"That's right. In Ireland."

"A for-real castle?"

"A real castle, near the sea. It has towers and turrets, secret passageways, and a drawbridge."

"Just like in Daddy's books."

"Very much like. It's a magic palace." Ana listened to the sound of water as she rinsed dishes and thought of the squabbles and laughing voices in that huge kitchen, with a fire going in the hearth and the good, yeasty smell of fresh bread perfuming the air. "My father and his brothers were born there, and his father, and his, and further back than I can say."

"If I were born in a castle, I would always live there." Jessie stood close to Ana while they worked, enjoying without knowing why, the scent of woman, and the lighter timbre of a female voice. "Why did you move away?"

"Oh, it's still home, but sometimes you have to move away, to make your own place. Your own magic."

"Like Daddy and me did."

"Yes." She closed the dishwasher and began to fill the sink with hot, soapy water for the pots and pans. "You like living here in Monterey?"

"I like it a lot. Nana said I might get homesick when the novelty wears off. What's novelty?"

"The newness." Not a very wise thing to suggest to an impressionable child, Ana mused. But she imagined Nana's nose was out of joint. "If you do get homesick, you should try to remember that the very best place to be is usually where you are."

"I like where Daddy is, even if he took me to Timbuktu."

"Excuse me?"

"Grandma Sawyer said he might as well have moved us to Timbuktu." Jessie accepted the clean pot Ana handed her and began to dry, an expression of deep concentration on her face. "Is that a real place?"

"Um-hmm. But it's also a kind of expression that means far away. Your grandparents are missing you, sunshine. That's all."

"I miss them, too, but I get to talk to them on the phone, and Daddy helped me type a letter on his computer. Do you think you could marry Daddy so Grandma Sawyer would get off his back?"

The pan Ana had been washing plopped into the suds and sent a small tidal wave over the lip of the sink. "I don't think so."

"I heard him telling Grandma Sawyer that she was on his back all the time to find a wife so he wouldn't be lonely and I wouldn't have to grow up without a mother. His voice had that mad sound in it he gets when I do something really wrong, or like when Daisy chewed up his pillow. And he said he'd be damned if he'd tie himself down just to keep the peace."

"I see." Ana pressed her lips hard together to keep the proper seriousness on her face. "I don't think he'd like you to repeat it, Jessie, especially in those words."

"Do you think Daddy's lonely?"

"No. No, I don't. I think he's very happy with you, and with Daisy. If he decided to get married one day, it would be because he found somebody all of you loved very much."

"I love you."

"Oh, sunshine." Soapy hands and all, Ana scooted down to give Jessie a hug and a kiss. "I love you, too."

"Do you love Daddy?"

*I wish I knew.* "It's different," she said. She knew she was navigating on boggy ground. "When you grow up, love means different things. But I'm very happy that you moved here and we can all be friends."

"Daddy never had a lady over to dinner before."

"Well, you've only been here a couple of weeks."

"I mean ever, at all. Not in Indiana, either. So I thought maybe it meant that you were going to get married and live with us here so Grandma Sawyer would get off his back and I wouldn't be a poor motherless child."

"No." Ana did her best to disguise a chuckle. "It meant that we like each other and wanted to have dinner." She checked the window to make certain Boone wasn't on his way back. "Does he always cook like this?"

"He always makes a really big mess, and sometimes he says those words—you know?"

"I know."

"He says them when he has to clean it up. And today he was in a really bad mood 'cause Daisy ate his pillow and there were feathers all over and the washing machine exploded and he maybe has to go on a business trip."

"That's a lot for one day." She bit her lip. Really, she didn't want to pump the child, but she was curious. "He's going to take a trip?"

"Maybe to the place where they make movies, 'cause they want to make one out of his book."

"That's wonderful."

"He has to think about it. That's what he says when he doesn't want to say yes but probably he's going to."

This time Ana didn't bother to smother the chuckle. "You certainly have his number."

By the time they'd finished the kitchen, Jessie was yawning. "Will you come up and see my room? I put everything away like Daddy said to when we have company."

"I'd love to see your room."

The packing boxes were gone, Ana noted as they moved from the kitchen into the high-ceilinged living room, with its open balcony and curving stairs. The furniture there looked comfortably lived-in, bold, bright colors in fabrics that appeared tough enough to stand up under the hands and feet of an active child.

It could have used some flowers at the window, she mused. Some scented candles in brass holders on the mantel. Perhaps a few big, plump pillows scattered here and there. Still, there were homey family touches in the framed photographs, the ticking grandfather clock. And clever, whimsical ones, like the brass dragon's-head andirons standing guard on the stone hearth, and the unicorn rocking horse in the corner.

And if there was a little dust on the banister, that only added to the charm.

"I got to pick out my own bed," Jessie was telling her. "And once everything settles down I can pick out wallpaper if I want to. That's where Daddy sleeps." She pointed to the right, and Ana had a glimpse of a big bed under a jade-colored quilt— sans pillows—a handsome old chest of drawers with a missing pull, and a few stray feathers.

"He has his own bathroom in there, too, with a big tub that has jets and a shower that's all glass and has water coming out of both sides. I get to use the one out here, and it has two sinks and this little thing that isn't a toilet but looks like one."

"A bidet?"

"I guess so. Daddy says it's fancy and mostly for ladies. This is my room."

It was a little girl's fantasy, one provided by a man who obviously understood that childhood was all too short and very precious. All pink and white, the canopy bed sat in the center, a focal point surrounded by shelves of dolls and books and bright toys, a snowy dresser with a curvy mirror, and a child-sized desk littered with colored paper and crayons.

On the walls were lovely framed illustrations from fairy tales. Cinderella rushing down the steps of a silvery castle, a single glass slipper left behind. Rapunzel, her golden hair spilling out of a high tower window while she looked longingly down at her prince. The sly, endearing elf from one of Boone's books, and—a complete surprise to Ana—one of her aunt's prized illustrations.

"This is from *The Golden Ball*."

"The lady who wrote it sent it to Daddy for me when I was just little. Next to Daddy's I like her stories best."

"I had no idea," Ana murmured. As far as she'd known,

her aunt had never parted with one of her drawings except to family.

"Daddy did the elf," Jessie pointed out. "All the rest my mother did."

"They're beautiful." Not just skillful, Ana thought, and perhaps not as clever as Boone's elf or as elegant as her aunt's drawing, but lovely, and as true to the spirit of a fairy tale as magic itself.

"She drew them just for me, when I was a baby. Nana said Daddy should put them away so they wouldn't make me sad. But they don't. I like to look at them."

"You're very lucky to have something so beautiful to remember her by."

Jessie rubbed her sleepy eyes and struggled to hold back a yawn. "I have dolls, too, but I don't play with them much. My grandmothers like to give them to me, but I like the stuffed walrus my daddy got me better. Do you like my room?"

"It's lovely, Jessie."

"I can see the water, and your yard, from the windows." She tucked back the billowing sheer curtains to show off her view. "And that's Daisy's bed, but she likes to sleep with me." Jessie pointed out the wicker dog bed, with its pink cushion.

"Maybe you'd like to lie down until Daisy comes back."

"Maybe." Jessie sent Ana a doubtful look. "But I'm not really tired. Do you know any stories?"

"I could probably think of one." She picked Jessie up to sit her on the bed. "What kind would you like?"

"A magic one."

"The very best kind." She thought for a moment, then smiled. "Ireland is an old country," she began, slipping an arm around the girl. "And it's filled with secret places, dark hills and green fields, water so blue it hurts the eyes to stare at it for long. There's been magic there for so many centuries, and it's still a safe place for fairies and elves and witches."

"Good witches or bad ones?"

"Both, but there's always been more good than bad, not only in witches, but in everything."

"Good witches are pretty," Jessie said, stroking a hand down Ana's arm. "That's how you know. Is this a story about a good witch?"

"It is indeed. A very good and very beautiful witch. And a very good and very handsome one, too."

"Men aren't witches," Jessie informed her, giggling. "They're wizards."

"Who's telling the story?" Ana kissed the top of Jessie's head. "Now, one day, not so many years ago, a beautiful young witch traveled with her two sisters to visit their old grandfather. He was a very powerful witch—wizard—but had grown cranky and bored in his old age. Not far from the manor where he lived was a castle. And there lived three brothers. They were triplets, and very powerful wizards, as well. For as long as anyone could remember, the old wizard and the family of the three brothers had carried on a feud. No one remembered the why of it any longer, but the feud ran on, as they tend to do. So the families spoke not a word to each other for an entire generation."

Ana shifted Jessie to her lap, stroking the child's hair as she told the story. She was smiling to herself, unaware that she'd lapsed into her native brogue.

"But the young witch was headstrong, as well as beautiful. And her curiosity was great. And on a fine day in high summer, she slipped out of the manor house and walked through the fields and the meadows toward the castle of her grandfather's enemy. Along the way was a pond, and she paused there to dangle her bare feet in the water and study the castle in the distance. And while she sat, with her feet wet and her hair down around her shoulders, a frog plopped up on the bank and spoke to her.

"'Fair lady,' he said, 'why do you wander on my land?'

"Well, the young witch was not at all surprised to hear a frog speak. After all, she knew too much of magic, and she sensed a trick. 'Your land?' she said. 'Frogs have only the water, and the marsh. I walk where I choose.'

"'But your feet are in my water. So you must pay a forfeit.'

"So she laughed and told him that she owed a common frog nothing at all.

"Well, needless to say, the frog was puzzled by her attitude. After all, it wasn't every day he plopped down and spoke to a beautiful woman, and he had expected at least a shriek or some fearful respect. He was quite fond of playing tricks, and was sorely disappointed that this one wasn't working as he'd hoped. He explained that he was no ordinary frog, and if she didn't agree to pay the forfeit he would have to punish her. And what forfeit did he expect? His answer was a kiss, which was no more and no less than she had expected, for as I said, she was young, but not foolish.

"She said that she doubted very much if he would turn into a handsome prince if she did so, and that she would save her kisses.

"Now the frog was very frustrated, and he plied more magic, whistling up the wind, shaking the leaves in the trees, but she merely yawned at this. At the end of his tether, the frog jumped right into her lap and began to berate her. To teach him a lesson for his forwardness, she plucked him up and tossed him into the water. When he surfaced, he wasn't a frog at all, but a young man, quite wet and furious to have had his joke turned on him. After he swam to shore, they stood on the bank and shouted at each other, threatening spells and curses, sending lightning walking the sky, and shooting the air with thunder. Though she threatened him with the hounds of hell and worse, he said he would have his forfeit regardless, for it was his land, his water, and his right. So he kissed her soundly.

"And it took only that to turn the heat in her heart to warmth, and the fury in his breast to love. For even witches can fall under that most powerful of spells. There and then they pledged to each other, marrying within the month right there on the banks on the pond. And they were happy, then and after, with lives full of love. Still, every year, on a day in high summer, though she is no longer young, she goes to the pond, dangles her feet and waits for an indignant frog to join her."

Ana lifted the sleeping girl. She had told the end of the story only for herself—or so she thought. But as she drew back the cover, Boone's hand closed over hers.

"That was a pretty good story for an amateur. Must be the Irish."

"It's an old family one," she said, thinking how often she had heard how her mother and father had met.

He expertly unlaced his daughter's shoes. "Be careful. I might steal it from you."

As he tucked the covers around Jessie, Daisy took a running leap and landed on the foot of the bed. "Did you enjoy your walk?"

"After I stopped feeling guilty for leaving you with the dishes—which took about ninety seconds." He brushed Jessie's hair from her brow and bent to kiss her good-night. "One of the most enviable things about childhood is being able to drop off to sleep like that."

"Are you still having trouble?"

"I've got a lot on my mind." Taking Ana's hand, he drew her out of the room, leaving the door open, as he always did. "A lot of it's you, but there are a few other things."

"Honest, but not flattering." She paused at the top of the stairs. "Seriously, Boone, I could give you something—" She flushed and chuckled when she saw the light come into his eyes. "A very mild, very safe herbal remedy."

"I'd rather have sex."

Shaking her head, she continued downstairs. "You don't take me seriously."

"On the contrary."

"I mean as an herbalist."

"I don't know anything about that sort of thing, but I don't discount it." He wasn't about to let her dose him, either. "Why'd you get into it?"

"It's always been an interest. There have been healers in my family for generations."

"Doctors?"

"Not exactly."

Boone picked up the wine and two glasses as they walked through the kitchen and out onto the deck. "You didn't want to be a doctor."

"I didn't feel qualified to go into medicine."

"Now that's a very odd thing for a modern, independent woman to say."

"One has nothing to do with the other." She accepted the glass he offered. "It's not possible to heal everyone. And I... have difficulty being around suffering. What I do is my way of satisfying my needs and protecting myself." It was the most she felt she could give him. "And I like working alone."

"I know the feeling. Both my parents thought I was crazy. The writing was okay, but they figured I'd write the great American novel, at the very least. Fairy tales were hard for them to swallow at first."

"They must be proud of you."

"In their way. They're nice people," he said slowly, realizing he'd never discussed them with anyone but Alice. "They've always loved me. God knows they dote on Jessie. But they have a hard time understanding that I might not want what they want. A house in the suburbs, a decent golf game, and a spouse who's devoted to me."

"None of those things are bad."

"No, and I had it once—except for the golf game. I'd rather not spend the rest of my life convincing them that I'm content with the way things are now." He twined a lock of her hair around his fingers. "Don't you get the same sort of business from yours? Anastasia, when are you going to settle down with some nice young man and raise a family?"

"No." She laughed into her wine. "Absolutely not." The very idea of her mother or father saying, even thinking, such a thing made her laugh again. "I suppose you could say my parents are...eccentric." Comfortable, she laid her head back and looked at the stars. "I think they'd both be appalled if I settled for nice. You didn't tell me you had one of Aunt Bryna's illustrations."

"When you made the family connection, you were ready to chew me up and spit me out. It didn't seem appropriate. Then, I guess, it slipped my mind."

"Obviously she thinks highly of you. She only gave one to Nash after the wedding, and he'd been coveting one for years."

"That so? I'll be sure to rub his nose in it the next time I see him." Tipping up her chin with a finger, he turned her face toward his. "It's been a long time since I sat on a porch and necked. I'm wondering if I still have the hang of it."

He brushed his lips over hers, once, twice, a third time, until hers trembled open in invitation. He took the glass from her fingers, set it aside with his as his mouth moved to accept what was offered.

Sweet, so sweet, the taste of her, warming him, soothing him, exciting him. Soft, so soft, the feel of her, tempting him, luring him, charming him. And quiet, so quiet, that quick, catching sigh that sent a streak of lightning zipping up his spine.

But he was no sweaty, fumbling boy groping in the dark. The volcano of needs simmering inside him could be controlled. If he couldn't give her the fullness of his passion, then he could give her the benefit of his experience.

While he filled himself with her, slowly, degree by painful degree, he gave back a care and a tenderness that had her teetering helplessly on that final brink before love.

To be held like this, she thought dimly, with such compassion mixed with the hunger. In all of her imaginings, she had never reached for this. His tongue danced over hers, bringing her all those dark and dusky male flavors. His hands stroked persuasively while the muscles in his arms went taut. When his mouth left hers to cruise down her jaw and over her throat, she arched back, willing, desperately willing, for him to show her more.

It was surrender he felt from her, as clearly as he felt the night breeze against his skin. Knowing it would drive him nearer to the brink, he gave in to the fevered need to touch.

She was small, gloriously soft. Her heart beat frantically under his hand. He could almost taste it, taste that hot satin skin on his lips, on his tongue, deep within his mouth. It was torture not to sample it now, not to drag her dress down to her waist and feast.

The feel of her hardened nipples pressed against the silk had him groaning as he brought his mouth back to hers.

Her mouth was as avid, as desperate. Her hands moved over him as urgently as his over her. She knew, as she gave herself fully to this one moment, that there would be no turning back. They would not love now. It couldn't be now, on the starlit deck, beneath windows where a child might wake and look for her father in the night.

But there was no turning back from being in love. Not for her. She could not change that tidal wave of feeling any more than she could change the blood that coursed through her veins.

And because of it there would come a time, very soon, when she would give to him what she had given to no other.

Overwhelmed, she turned her head, burying her face in his shoulder. "You have no idea what you do to me."

"Then tell me." He caught the lobe of her ear between his teeth, making her shudder. "I want to hear you tell me."

"You make me ache. And yearn." And hope, she thought,

squeezing her eyes shut. "No one else has." With a long, shuddering sigh, she drew away. "That's what we're both afraid of."

"I can't deny that." His eyes were like cobalt in the dim light. "And I can't deny that the idea of carrying you upstairs now, taking you into my bed, is something I want as much as I want to go on breathing."

The image had her heart thundering. "Do you believe in the inevitable, Boone?"

"I've had to."

She nodded. "So do I. I believe in destiny, the whims of fate, the tricks of what men used to call the gods. When I look at you, I see the inevitable." She rose, pressed a hand to his shoulder to prevent him from standing with her. "Can you accept that I have secrets I can't tell you, parts of myself I won't share?" She saw both puzzlement and denial in his eyes, and shook her head before he could speak. "Don't answer now.... You need to think it through and be sure. Just as I do."

She leaned down to kiss him, and linked quickly, firmly. She felt his jerk of surprise before she backed away. "Sleep well tonight," she said, knowing that he would now. And that she would not.

# *Chapter 7*

The one gift Ana always gave herself on her birthday was a completely free day. She could be as lazy as she chose, or as industrious. She could get up at dawn and gorge on ice cream for breakfast, or she could laze in bed until noon watching old movies on television.

The single best plan for the one day of the year that belonged only to her was no plan at all.

She did rise early, indulging herself in a long bath scented with her favorite oils and a muslin bag filled with dried herbs chosen for their relaxing properties. To pamper herself, she mixed up a toning face pack of elder flowers, yogurt and ka-olin powder, lounging in the tub with harp music and iced juice while it worked its magic.

With her face tingling and her hair silky from its chamo-mile shampoo, she slicked on her personalized body oil and slipped into a silk robe the color of moonbeams.

As she walked back into the bedroom, she considered crawl-ing back into bed and dozing to complete the morning's in-dulgence. But in the center of the room, where there had been nothing but an antique prayer rug when she'd gone in to bathe, stood a large wooden chest.

On a quick cry of pleasure, she dashed over to run her hands over the old carved wood, which had been polished to a mirror gleam. It smelled of beeswax and rosemary and felt like silk under her fingers.

It was old, ages old, for it was something she had admired even as a child living in Donovan Castle. A wizard's chest, it was reputed to have resided once in Camelot, commissioned for Merlin by the young Arthur.

With a laughing sigh, she sat back on her heels. They always managed to surprise her, Ana thought. Her parents, her aunts and uncles...so far away, but never out of her heart.

The combined power of six witches had sent the chest from Ireland, winking through the air, through time, through space, by means that were less, and more, than conventional.

Slowly she lifted the lid, and the scent of old visions, ancient spells, endless charms, rose out to her. The fragrance was dry, aromatic as crusted petals ground to dust, tangy with the smoke of the cold fire a sorcerer calls in the night.

She knelt, lifting her arms out, the silk sliding down to her elbows as she cupped her hands, palms facing.

Here was power, to be respected, accepted. The words she spoke were in the old tongue, the language of the Wise Ones. The wind she called whipped the curtains, sent her hair flying around her face. The air sang, a thousand harp strings crying in the breeze, then was silent.

Lowering her arms, Ana reached into the chest. A bloodstone amulet, the inner red of the stone bleeding through the deep green, had her sitting back on her heels once more. She knew it had belonged to her mother's family for generations, a healing stone of enormous worth and mighty power. Tears stung the backs of her eyes when she realized that it was being passed to her, as it was only every half century, to denote her as a healer of the highest order.

Her gift, she thought, running her fingers over a stone smoothed by other fingers in other times. Her legacy.

She gently set it back in the chest and reached for the next gift. She lifted out a globe of chalcedony, its almost transparent surface offering her a glimpse of the universe if she should choose to look. This from Sebastian's parents, she knew, for she felt them as she cupped the globe in her hands. Next was a sheepskin, inscribed with the writing of the old tongue. A fairy story, she noted as she read and smiled. As old as time, as sweet as tomorrow. Aunt Bryna and Uncle Matthew, she thought as she laid it back inside.

Though the amulet had been from her mother, Ana knew there would always be something special from her father, as well. She found it, and she laughed as she took it out. A frog, as small as her thumbnail, intricately carved in jade.

"Looks just like you, Da," she said, and laughed again. Replacing it, she closed the chest, then rose. It would be afternoon in Ireland, she mused, and there were six people who would be expecting a call to see if she'd enjoyed her gifts.

As she started toward the phone, she heard the knock at her back door. Her heart gave one quick, unsteady leap, then settled calmly. Ireland would have to wait.

Boone held the gift behind his back. There was another package at home, one that he and Jessie had chosen together. But he'd wanted to give Ana this one himself. Alone.

He heard her coming and grinned, the greeting on the tip of his tongue. He was lucky he didn't swallow his tongue, as well as the words, when he saw her.

She was glowing, her hair a rain of pale gold down the back of a robe of silver. Her eyes seemed darker, deeper. How could they be as clear as lake water, he wondered, yet seem to hold a thousand secrets? The gloriously female scent that swirled around her nearly brought him to his knees.

When Quigley rushed against his legs in greeting, Boone jolted as if he'd been shot.

"Boone." With a quiet laugh bubbling in her throat, Ana put her hand on the screen. "Are you all right?"

"Yeah, yeah. I... Did I get you up?"

"No." As calm as he was rattled, she opened the door in invitation. "I've been up quite a while. I'm just being lazy." When he continued to stand on the porch, she tilted her head. "Don't you want to come in?"

"Sure." He stepped inside, but kept a careful distance.

He'd been as restrained as could be over the past couple of weeks, resisting the temptation to be alone with her too often, keeping the mood light when they were alone. He realized now that his control had been as much for his sake as for hers.

She was painful to resist, even when they were standing outside in the sunlight, discussing Jessie or gardening, his work or hers.

But this, standing with her, the house empty and silent around them, the mysterious perfume of a woman's art tormenting his senses, was almost too much to bear.

"Is something wrong?" she asked, but she was smiling, as if she knew.

"No, nothing... Ah, how are you?"

"I'm fine." Her smile widened, softened. "And you?"

"Great." He thought that if he were any more tense he'd turn to stone. "Fine."

"I was going to make some tea. I'm sorry I don't have any coffee, but perhaps you'd like to join me."

"Tea." He let out a quiet breath. "Terrific." He watched her walk to the stove, the cat winding around her legs like gray rope. She put the kettle on, then poured Quigley's breakfast into his bowl. Crouching down, she stroked the cat as he ate. The robe slipped back like water, exposing one creamy leg.

"How's the woodruff coming, and the hyssop?"

"Ah..."

She tossed her hair back as she looked up and smiled. "The herbs I gave you to transplant into your yard."

"Oh, those. They look great."

"I have some basil and some thyme potted in the greenhouse. You might want to take them along, leave them on a windowsill for a while. For cooking." She rose when the kettle began to sputter. "I think you'll find them better than storebought."

"That'd be great." He was almost relaxed again, he thought. Hoped. It was soothing to watch her brew tea, heating the little china pot, spooning aromatic leaves out of a pale blue jar. He hadn't known a woman could be restful and seductive all at once. "Jessie's been watching those marigold seeds you gave her to plant like a hen watches an egg."

"Just don't let her overwater." Setting the tea to steep, she turned. "Well?"

He blinked. "Well?"

"Boone, are you going to show me what's behind your back or not?"

"Can't fool you, can I?" He held out a box wrapped in bright blue paper. "Happy birthday."

"How did you know it was my birthday?"

"Nash told me. Aren't you going to open it?"

"I certainly am." She tore the paper, revealing a box with the logo of Morgana's shop imprinted on the lid. "Excellent choice," she said. "You couldn't possibly go wrong buying me something from Wicca." She lifted the lid and, with a quiet sigh, drew out a delicate statue of a sorceress carved in amber.

Her head was thrown back and exquisite tendrils of the dark gold hair tumbled down her cloak. Slender arms were raised, bent at the elbows, palms cupped and facing—mirroring the age-old position Ana had assumed over the chest that morning. In one elegant hand she held a small gleaming pearl, in the other a slender silver wand.

"She's beautiful," Ana murmured. "Absolutely beautiful."

"I stopped by the shop last week, and Morgana had just gotten it in. It reminded me of you."

"Thank you." Still holding the statue, she lifted her free hand to his cheek. "You couldn't have found anything more perfect."

She leaned in, rising on her toes to touch her lips to his. She knew exactly what she was doing, just as she knew even as he returned the kiss that he was holding himself on a choke chain of control. Power, as fresh and cool as rainwater, washed into her.

This was what she had been waiting for, this was why she had spent the morning in that ancient female ritual of oils and creams and perfumes.

For him. For her. For their first time together.

There were knots of thorny vines ripping through his stomach, an anvil of need ringing frantically in his head. Though their lips were barely touching, her taste was drugging him, making ideas like restraint and control vague, unimportant concepts. He tried to draw back, but her arms wound silkily around him.

"Ana..."

"Shh." She soothed and excited as her mouth played softly over his. "Just kiss me."

How could he not, when her lips were parting so softly beneath his? He brought his hands to her face, framing it with tensed fingers while he fought a vicious internal war to keep the embrace from going too far.

When the phone rang, he let out a groan that was both frustration and relief. "I'd better go."

"No." She wanted to laugh, but only smiled as she drew out of his arms. Never had she sampled a power more delicious than this. "Please stay. Why don't you pour the tea while I answer that?"

Pour tea, he thought. He'd be lucky if he could lift the pot.

System jumbled, he turned blindly to the stove as she took the receiver from the wall phone.

"Mama!" Now she did laugh, and Boone heard the pure joy of it. "Thank you. Thank all of you. Yes, I got it this morning. A wonderful surprise." She laughed again, listening. "Of course. Yes, I'm fine. I'm wonderful. I— Da." She chuckled when her father broke in on the line. "Yes, I know what the frog means. I love it. I love you, too. No, I much prefer it to a real one, thank you." She smiled at Boone when he offered her a cup of tea. "Aunt Bryna? It was a lovely story. Yes, I am. Morgana's very well, so are the twins. Not very much longer now. Yes, you'll be here in time."

Restless, Boone wandered the room, sipping the tea, which was surprisingly good. He wondered what the devil she'd put into it. What the devil she'd put into him. Just listening to her voice was making him ache.

He could handle it, he reminded himself. They'd have a very civilized cup of tea—while he kept his hands off her. Then he'd escape, bury himself in his work for the rest of the day to keep his mind off her, as well.

His story line was all but finished, and he was nearly ready to start on the illustrations. He already knew just what he wanted.

Ana.

With a brisk shake of his head, he gulped more tea. It sounded as if she were going to carry on a conversation with every relative she had. That was fine, that was dandy. It would give him time to calm himself down.

"Yes, I miss you, too. All of you. I'll see you in a couple of weeks. Blessed be."

She was a little teary-eyed when she hung up, but she smiled at Boone. "My family," she explained.

"I gathered."

"They sent me a chest of gifts this morning, and I hadn't gotten a chance to call and thank them."

"That's nice. Look, I really— This morning?" he said with a slight frown. "I didn't see any delivery truck."

"It came early." She looked away to set her cup down. "Special delivery, you could say. They're all looking forward to visiting at the end of the month."

"You'll be glad to see them."

"Always. They were here briefly over the summer, but with all the excitement about Sebastian and Mel getting engaged and married so quickly, there wasn't much time to just be together." She moved to the door to let Quigley out. "Would you like more tea?"

"No, thanks, really. I should go. Get to work." He was edging toward the door himself. "Happy birthday, Ana."

"Boone." She laid a hand on his arm, felt his muscles quiver. "Every year on my birthday I give myself a gift. It's very simple, really. One day to do whatever I choose. Whatever feels right to me." Hardly seeming to move at all, she pulled the door closed and stood between it and him. "I choose you. If you still want me."

Her words seemed to ring in his ears as he stared down at her. She appeared so calm, so utterly serene, she might have been discussing the weather. "You know I want you."

"Yes." She smiled. At that moment she was calm, the eye of the hurricane. "Yes, I do." When she took a step forward, he took one in retreat. Was this seduction? she wondered, keeping her eyes on his. "I see that when I look at you, feel it whenever you touch me. You've been very patient, very kind. You kept your word that nothing would happen between us until I decided it should."

"I'm trying." Unsteady, he took another step back. "It isn't easy."

"Nor for me." She stood where she was, the silver robe shimmering around her in the sunlight. "You've only to accept me, to accept that I'm willing to give you everything I can. Take that, and let it be enough."

"What are you asking me?"

"To be my first," she said simply. "To show me what love can be."

He dared to reach out and touch her hair. "Are you sure?"

"I'm very sure." Offering and asking, she held out both hands. "Will you take me to bed and be my lover?"

How could he answer? There were no words to translate what was churning inside him at that moment. So he wasted no words, only lifted her into his arms.

He carried her as if she were as delicate as the amber enchantress he'd given her. Indeed, he thought of her that way, and he felt a thud of panic at the thought that he wouldn't be careful enough, restrained enough. It was so easy to damage delicacy.

When he reached the base of the stairs and started to climb, his pulse was throbbing in anticipation and fear.

For her sake, he wished it could have been night, a candlelit night filled with soft music and silvery moonglow. Yet somehow it seemed right that he love her, this first time, in the morning, when the sun was growing stronger in a deep blue sky, and music came from the birds that flitted through her garden and the tinkling bells of the wind chimes she had at her windows.

"Where?" he asked her, and she gestured toward her bedroom door.

It smelled of her, a mix of female fragrances and perfumed powders—and something else, something he couldn't quite identify. Like smoke and flowers. The sun streamed gaily through billowing curtains and splashed the huge old bed with the towering carved headboard.

He skirted the trunk, charmed by the rainbow of colors refracted by colored crystals suspended from thin wire in front of each window. Rainbows instead of moonbeams, he thought as he laid her on the bed.

Foolish to be nervous now, she told herself, but her hands

trembled lightly when she reached out to hold him against her. She wanted this. Wanted him. Still, the calm certainty she had felt only moments ago had vanished under a wave of nerves and needs.

He could see the need, the nervousness, in her eyes. Could she possibly understand that they were a mirror of his? She was so fragile and lovely. Fresh and untouched. His for the taking. And he knew it was vital for them both that he take with tenderness.

"Anastasia." Smothering his own fears, he lifted her hand, pressed his lips to the palm. "I won't hurt you. I swear it."

"I know that." She linked her fingers with his, wishing she could be sure if it was fear of the moment a woman experiences only once in her life, or fear of the overwhelming depth of her love for him, that left her shaky and unsure. "Show me."

With rainbows dancing around them, he lowered his mouth to hers. A deep, drugging kiss that both soothed and enticed. Time spun out, drifted. Stopped. Still there was only his mouth against hers.

He touched her hair, his fingers combing through, tangling in the luxurious length of it. To please himself, he spread it over the pillow, where it lay like a pool of gold dust against soft Irish linen.

When his lips left hers, it was to take a slow, lazy journey of her face until he felt her nervous trembling fall away into pliancy. Even as she surrendered her fears to the light, sweet sensations he brought her, he kept the pace slow, so slow that it seemed they had forever just to kiss.

She heard him murmur to her, reassurances, lovely, lovely promises. The low hum of his voice had her mind floating, her lips curving in a quiet smile as they met his again.

She should have known it would be like this with him. Beautiful, achingly beautiful. He made her feel loved, cherished, safe. When he slipped the robe from her shoulders, she wasn't afraid, but welcomed the feel of his mouth on her flesh. Eager now, she tugged on his shirt, and he hesitated only a moment before helping her remove it.

A groan ripped out of him as his body shuddered. God, the feel of her hands on his bare back. He fought back a wave of greed and kept his own hands easy as he parted her robe.

Her skin was like cream. Unbearably soft and fragrant with oils. It drew him like nectar, inviting him to taste. As he closed his mouth over her breast, the quiet, strangled sound she made deep in her throat echoed like thunder in his head.

Gently he used tongue and lips to take her to that next degree of pleasure, while his own passions licked at him, taunting him, demanding that he hurry, hurry, hurry.

Her eyes were so heavy, impossible to open. How could he know just where to touch, just where to taste, to make her heart shudder in her breast? Yet he did, and her breath sighed out between her lips as he showed her more.

Quiet whispers, a gentle caress. The scent of lavender and fairy roses thickening the air. Smooth sheets growing warm, skin dampening with passion. A rainbow of lights playing against her closed lids.

She floated there, lifted by the magic they made together, her breath quickening a little as he eased her higher, just higher.

Then there was heat, searing, torrid. It erupted inside her so quickly, so violently, that she cried out and struggled against him. "No. No, Boone, I—" Then a flash, a lightning spear of pleasure, that left her limp and dazed and trembling.

"Ana." He had to dig his fisted hands into the mattress to keep from plunging into her, driving them both where he knew the rewards were dark and desperately keen. "Sweet." He kissed her, swallowing her gasping breaths. "So sweet. Don't be afraid."

"No." Rocked to the core, she held him close. His heart was thundering against hers, his body taut as wire. "No. Show me. Show me more."

So he slipped the robe away, driving himself mad with the

sight of her naked in a pool of sunlight. Her eyes were open now, dark and steady on his. Beneath the passion just awakened, he saw a trust that humbled him.

He showed her more.

Fears melted away. There was no room for them when her body was vibrating from dozens of more vivid sensations. When he took her to the peak again, she rode out the storm, glorying in the flash of heat, desperate for the next.

He held back, gaining his pleasure from hers, stunned by the way she responded to each touch, to each kiss. Her innocence was his, he knew. With the breath laboring in his lungs, the blood pounding in his head, he entered her, braced for her to stiffen and cry out. Knowing he would have to stop, no matter how his body craved completion, if she asked it of him.

But she didn't stiffen, only gasped out his name as her arms came around him. The brief flash of pain was instantly smothered by a pleasure greater, fuller, than she had ever dreamed possible.

His, she thought. She was his. And she moved against him with an instinct as old as time.

Deeper, he slipped deeper, filling her, rocking her toward that final crest. When she did cry out, her body shuddering, shuddering from the glory of it, he buried his face in her hair and let himself follow.

He watched the dance of light against the wall, listening to her heart calm and slow. She lay beneath him still, her arms around him, her hands stroking his hair.

He hadn't known it could be like this. That was foolish, he thought. He'd had women before. More, he'd loved before, as deeply as anyone could. Yet this union had been more than he'd ever expected or experienced.

He had no way to explain it to her, when he was far from understanding it himself.

After pressing a kiss to her shoulder, he lifted his head to look at her. Her eyes were closed, and her face was flushed and utterly relaxed. He wondered if she had any idea how much had changed, for both of them, that morning.

"Are you all right?"

She shook her head, alarming him. Instantly concerned, he braced on his arms to remove his weight from her. Her lashes fluttered up so that he could see the smoky eyes beneath them.

"I'm not all right." Her voice was low and throaty. "I'm wonderful. You're wonderful." The smile curved beautifully on her lips. "This is wonderful."

"You had me worried." He brushed the hair away from her cheek. "I don't think I've ever been quite so nervous." Her lips were waiting for his when he bent his head to kiss her. "You're not sorry?"

Her brow arched. "Do I look sorry?"

"No." Taking his time, he studied her face, tracing it with a fingertip. "You look kind of smug." And the fact that she did brought him a rush of deep satisfaction.

"I'm feeling very smug. And lazy." She stretched a little, so he shifted to let her head rest on his shoulder.

"Happy birthday."

She chuckled against his throat. "It was the most…unique present I've ever been given."

"The thing about it is, you can use it over and over again."

"Even better." She tipped her head back, and now her eyes were solemn. "You were very good to me, Boone. Very good for me."

"It wasn't what I'd call an act of altruism. I've wanted this since the first time I saw you."

"I know. It frightened me—and excited me, too." She smoothed her palm over his chest, wishing for a moment they could stay like this forever, cocooned together in the sunlight.

"This changes things."

Her hand stilled, tensed. "Only if you want it to."

"Then I want it to." He sat up, bringing her with him so

that they were face-to-face. "I want you to be a part of my life. I want to be with you, as often as possible—and not just like this."

She felt the old, niggling fear trying to surface. Rejection. Rejection now would be devastating. "I am part of your life. I always will be now."

He saw something in her eyes, sensed it in the tension suddenly blooming in the room with them. "But?"

"No buts," she said quickly, and threw her arms around him. "No ands. No anything now. Just this." She kissed him, pouring everything she could into it, knowing she was cheating them both by holding back. Not knowing how to offer it and keep him with her. "I'm here when you want me, as long as you want me. I promise you."

Rushing her again, he berated himself as she clung to him. How could he expect her to be in love just because they had made love? He wasn't even sure what he was feeling himself. It had all happened too fast, and he was riding on the emotion of the moment. He reminded himself, as he held Ana, that he didn't have only his own needs to consider.

There was Jessie.

What happened with Ana would affect his daughter. So there could be no mistaking, no acting on impulse, and no real commitment until he was sure.

"We'll take it slow," he said, but felt a twinge of resentment when Ana immediately relaxed against him. "But if anyone else comes to your door bearing gifts or needing a cup of sugar—"

"I'll boot him out." She squeezed him hard. "There's no one but you." Turning her head, she pressed her lips to his throat. "You make me happy."

"I can make you happier."

She laughed, tilting her head back. "Really?"

"Not like that." Amused, and flattered, he nipped her lower lip. "Not quite yet, anyway. I was thinking more along the lines of going down and fixing you lunch while you lazed around in bed and waited for me. And then making love with you again. And again."

"Well..." It was tempting, but she recalled too well what one of his meals did to a kitchen. And she had too many jars and bottles around that he might use incorrectly. "Why don't we do it this way—you wait for me while I fix lunch?"

"It's your birthday."

"Exactly." She kissed him before she slid out of bed. "Which is why I get to do everything my own way. I won't be long."

It was a pretty stupid man who wouldn't take a deal like that, Boone decided as he leaned back with his arms crossed under his head. He listened to her running water in the adjoining bath, then settled down to imagine what it would be like to spend the afternoon in bed.

Ana belted her robe as she walked downstairs. Love, she thought, did marvelous things for the spirit. Better, far better, than any potion she could brew or conjure. Perhaps in time, perhaps with enough of that love, she could give him the rest.

Boone wasn't Robert, and she was ashamed to have compared them, even for a moment. But the risk was so great, and the day so marvelous.

Humming to herself, she busied herself in the kitchen. Sandwiches would be best, she decided. Not terribly elegant, but practical for eating in bed. Sandwiches, and some of her father's special wine. She all but floated to the refrigerator, which was crowded now with Jessie's artwork.

"Not even dressed yet," Morgana said through the back screen. "I suspected as much."

With a boneless turkey breast in her hand, Ana turned. Not only was Morgana at her kitchen door, but crowded around her were Nash, Sebastian and Mel, too.

"Oh." She felt the flush blooming even as she set the lunch meat aside. "I didn't hear you drive up."

"Obviously too self-involved, with your birthday and all," Sebastian commented.

They piled in, bringing hugs and kisses and pushing ribboned boxes into her hands. Nash was already opening a bottle of champagne. "Find some glasses, Mel. Let's get this party started." He winked at his wife as she collapsed in a chair. "Apple juice for you, babe."

"I'm too fat to argue." She adjusted her weight—or tried to. "So, did you hear from Ireland?"

"Yes, a chest this morning. It's gorgeous. Glasses in the next cupboard," she told Mel. "Gifts inside. I talked to them..." Right before she'd gone upstairs to make love with Boone. Another flush heated her cheeks. "I, ah, I really need to..." Mel shoved a glass into her hand with champagne brimming up to the lip.

"Have the first glass," Sebastian finished for her. He cocked his head to the side. "Anastasia, my love, you look quite radiant. Turning twenty-seven certainly appears to agree with you."

"Keep out of my head," she muttered, and took a sip to give herself a moment to figure out how to explain. "I can't thank you all enough for coming by this way. If you'd just excuse me a minute."

"No need to get dressed for us." Nash poured the rest of the glasses. "Sebastian's right. You look fabulous."

"Yes, but I really need to—"

"Ana, I have a better idea." The sound of Boone's voice from just down the hall had everyone lapsing into silence. "Why don't we—" Shirtless, barefoot and rumpled, he walked into the room, then stopped dead.

"Whoops," Mel said, and grinned into her glass.

"Succinctly put." Her husband studied Boone through narrowed eyes. "Dropping by for a neighborly visit, are we?"

"Shut up, Sebastian." This from Morgana, who rested both

hands on her tummy and smiled. "We seem to have interrupted."

"I think we would have if we'd been any earlier," Nash murmured into Mel's ear, and made her choke back a chuckle.

Ana aimed one withering glance at him before she turned to Boone. "My family's brought along a little party, and they're all quite amused at the idea that I might have a private life—" she looked over her shoulder meaningfully "—that doesn't concern them."

"She always was cranky when you got her out of bed," Sebastian said, resigned to accepting Boone. For now. "Mel, it appears we'll need another glass of champagne."

"Already got it covered." Smiling, she stepped forward and offered it to Boone. "If you can't beat 'em," she said under her breath, and he nodded.

"Well." He took a long sip and sighed. It was obvious that his plans for the rest of the day would have to be adjusted. "Anybody bring cake?"

With a delighted laugh, Morgana gestured toward a large bakery box. "Get Ana a knife, Nash, so she can cut the first piece. I think we'll dispense with candles. She appears to have gotten her wish already."

# Chapter 8

Ana was much too accustomed to her family to be annoyed with or embarrassed by them for long. And she was simply too happy with Boone to hold a grudge. As the days passed, they moved slowly, cautiously, toward cementing their relationship.

If she had come to trust him with her heart, with her body, she had not yet come to trust him with her secrets.

Though his feelings for her had ripened, deepened into a love he had never expected to experience again, he was as wary as she of taking that final step that would join their lives.

At the center was a child neither would have harmed by putting their own needs first.

If they stole a few hours on bright afternoons or rainy mornings, it was theirs to steal. At night Ana would lie alone and wonder how long this magic interlude would last.

As Halloween approached, she and Boone were caught up in their own preparations. Now and again her nerves would jump out at the idea of her lover meeting the whole of her family on the holiday. Then she would laugh at herself for acting like a girl on the point of introducing a first date.

By noon on the thirty-first, she was already at Morgana's, helping her now greatly pregnant cousin with preparations for the Halloween feast.

"I could have made Nash do this." Morgana pressed a hand against the ache in the small of her back before she sat down to knead bread dough from a more comfortable position at the kitchen table.

"You could make Nash do anything simply by asking." Ana cubed lamb for the traditional Irish stew. "But he's having such fun setting up his special effects."

"Just like a layman to think he can outdo the professionals." She winced and moaned and had Ana's immediate attention.

"Honey?"

"No, no, it's not labor, though I damn well wish it was. I'm just so bloody uncomfortable all the time now." Hearing the petulance in her own voice, she winced again. "And I hate whiners."

"You whine all you like. It's just you and me. Here." Always prepared, Ana poured some liquid into a cup. "Drink it down."

"I already feel like I'm going to float away—like Cleopatra's barge. By the goddess, I'm big enough." But she drank, fingering the crystal around her neck.

"And you already have a crew of two."

That did the trick of making her laugh. "Talk to me about something else," she begged, and went back to her kneading. "Anything to take my mind off the fact that I'm fat and grumpy."

"You're not fat, and you're only a little grumpy." But Ana cast her mind around for a distraction. "Did you know that Sebastian and Mel are working on another case together?"

"No, I didn't." And it served to pique her interest. "I'm surprised. Mel's very territorial about her private investigation business."

"Well, she's lowered the gate on this one. A runaway, only twelve years old. The parents are frantic. When I talked to her last night, she said they had a lead, and she was sorry she couldn't take this afternoon off to give you a hand."

"When Mel's in the kitchen, it's more like giving me a foot." There was affection for her new in-law in every syllable. "She's wonderful with Sebastian, isn't she?"

"Yes." Smiling to herself, Ana layered the lamb with potatoes and onions in Morgana's big Dutch oven. "Tough-minded, hardheaded, softhearted. She's exactly what he needs."

"And have you found what you need?"

Saying nothing at first, Ana added herbs. She'd known Morgana would work her way around to it before the day was over. "I'm very happy."

"I like him. I had a good feeling about him from the first."

"I'm glad."

"So does Sebastian—though he has some reservations." Her brows knit, but she kept her voice light. "Particularly after he cornered Boone and picked through his brain."

Ana's lips thinned as she adjusted the heat on the stove. "I haven't forgiven him for that yet."

"Well." Morgana shrugged and set the dough in a bowl to rise. "Boone didn't know, and it soothed Sebastian's feathers. He wasn't exactly pleased to have walked in on your birthday and found you fresh out of bed."

"It's certainly none of his business."

"He loves you." She gave Ana's arm a quick squeeze as she passed the stove. "He'll always worry about you more because you're the youngest—and simply because your gift makes you so vulnerable."

"I'm not without my defenses, Morgana, or common sense."

"I know. Darling, I…" She felt her eyes fill and brushed hastily at the tears. "It was your first time. I didn't want to probe before, but… Lord, I never used to be so sentimental."

"You were just able to hide it better." Abandoning her cooking for the moment, Ana crossed over to take Morgana into her arms. "It was beautiful, and he's so gentle. I knew there was a reason I had to wait, and he was it." She drew back, smiling. "Boone's given me more than I ever imagined I could have."

With a sigh, Morgana lifted her hands to Ana's face. "You're in love with him."

"Yes. Very much in love with him."

"And he with you?"

Her gaze faltered. "I don't know."

"Oh, Ana."

"I won't link with him that way." Her eyes leveled again, her voice firmed. "It would be dishonest when I haven't told him what I am, and haven't the courage to tell him how I feel myself. I know he cares for me. I need no gift to know he cares for me. And that's enough. When there's more, if there's more, he'll tell me."

"It never fails to surprise me how damn stubborn you are."

"I'm a Donovan," Ana countered. "And this is important."

"I agree. You should tell him." She gripped Ana's arms before her cousin could turn away. "Oh, I know. I despise it when someone gives me advice I don't want to hear. But you have to let go of the past and face the future."

"I am facing the future. I'd like Boone to be in it. I need more time." Her voice broke, and she pressed her lips together until she felt she could steady it. "Morgana, I know him. He's a good man. He has compassion and imagination and a capacity for generosity he isn't even aware of. He also has a child."

When Ana turned away this time, Morgana was forced to brace herself on the table. "Is that what you're afraid of? Taking on someone else's child?"

"Oh, no. I love her. Who wouldn't? Even before I loved Boone, I loved Jessie. And she's the center of his world, as it should be. There's nothing, absolutely nothing, I wouldn't do for either of them."

"Then explain."

Stalling, Ana rinsed the hard-cooked eggs she was going

to devil. "Do you have any fresh dill? You know how Uncle Douglas loves his deviled eggs with dill."

On a hiss of breath, Morgana slapped a jar on the counter. "Anastasia, explain."

Emotions humming, Ana jerked off the tap. "Oh, you don't know how fortunate you are with Nash. To have someone love you that way no matter what."

"Of course I know," Morgana said softly. "What does Nash have to do with this?"

"How many other men would accept one of us so completely? How many would want marriage, or take a witch as a mother for his child?"

"In the name of Finn, Anastasia." The impatience in her voice was spoiled a bit by the fact that she was forced to sit again. "You talk as if we're broomstick-riding crones, cackling while we curdle the milk in a mother's breast."

She didn't smile. "Don't most think of us just that way? Robert—"

"A pox on Robert."

"All right, forget him," Ana agreed with a wave of her hand. "How many times through the centuries have we been hunted and persecuted, feared and ostracized, simply for being what we were born to be? I'm not ashamed of my blood. I don't regret my gift or my heritage. But I couldn't bear it if I told him, and he looked at me as if—" she gave a half laugh "—as if I had a smoking cauldron in the basement filled with toads and wolfsbane."

"If he loves you—"

"If," Ana repeated. "We'll see. Now I think you should lie down for an hour."

"You're just changing the subject," Morgana began, then looked up as Nash burst in. There were cobwebs in his hair—simulated, fortunately—and an unholy gleam in his eyes.

"You guys have got to see this. It's incredible. I'm so good,

I scare myself." He snatched a celery stalk from the counter and chomped. "Come on, don't just stand there."

"Amateurs," Morgana sighed, and hauled herself to her feet.

The two women were admiring Nash's hologram ghosts in the foyer when Ana heard a car drive up.

"They're here." Filled with delight at the prospect of seeing her family, she took one bounding leap toward the door. Then stopped dead. She was already whirling around when Morgana sagged against Nash.

Instantly he went as pale as his ghosts. "Babe? Are you—? Oh, boy."

"It's all right." She let out a long breath as Ana took her other arm. "Just a twinge, really." Leaning back against Nash, she smiled at Ana. "I guess having twins on Halloween is pretty appropriate."

"Absolutely nothing to worry about." Douglas Donovan was reassuring Nash. Like his son, he was a tall man, and his mane of raven hair was only lightly silvered. He'd chosen black tie and tails for the occasion, and had set them off with orange neon sneakers that pleased him enormously by glowing in the dark. "Childbirth. Most natural thing in the world. Perfect night for it, too."

"Right." Nash swallowed the lump in his throat. His house was full of people—witches, if you wanted to get technical— and his wife was sitting on the sofa, looking as if she weren't the least bit concerned that she'd been in labor for over three hours. "Maybe it was a false alarm."

Camilla wafted by in a sequined ball gown and tapped Nash on the shoulder with her feather fan. "Leave it to Ana, dear child. She'll take care of everything. Why, when I had Sebastian, I was in labor for thirteen hours. We joked about that, didn't we, Douglas?"

"After you'd stopped shouting curses at me, dear heart."

"Well, naturally." She wandered toward the kitchen, thinking she'd check on the stew. Ana never used quite enough sage.

"Would have turned me into a hedgehog if she hadn't been otherwise occupied," Douglas confided.

"That makes me feel better," Nash muttered. "Heaps."

Delighted to have helped, Douglas slapped him heartily on the back. "That's what we're here for, Dash."

"Nash."

Douglas smiled benignly. "Yes, indeed."

"Mama." Morgana gave her mother's hand a squeeze. "Go rescue poor Nash from Uncle Douglas. He's looking a little queasy."

Bryna obligingly set aside her sketchpad. "Shall I have your father take him out for a walk?"

"Wonderful." She gave a sigh of gratitude as Ana continued to rub her shoulders. "There isn't anything for him to do quite yet."

Ana's father, Padrick, plopped down the moment Bryna vacated the seat. "How's the girl?"

"I'm really fine. It's all very mild as yet, but I'm sure it'll get rolling before too much longer." She leaned over to kiss his plump cheek. "I'm glad you're all here."

"Wouldn't be anywhere else." He put a pudgy hand on her belly to soothe and gave his daughter one of his elvish grins. "And my own little darling. You're pretty as a picture. Take right after your da, don't you?"

"Naturally." Ana felt the next contraction start and kept her hands steady on Morgana's shoulders. "Long, relaxed breaths, love."

"Will you want to give her some blue cohosh?" he asked his daughter.

Ana considered, then shook her head. "Not yet. She's doing well enough. But you could get me my pouch. I'll want some crystals."

"Done." He rose, then flipped his hand over. In the palm

was a sprig of bell heather in full flower. "Now where did this come from?" he said, in the way he had since the laboring woman had been a babe herself. "Take care of this for me. I've business to tend to."

Morgana brushed the heather against her cheek. "He's the dearest man in the world."

"He'll spoil these two if you let him. Da's a pushover for children." With the empathic link, she knew Morgana was in more discomfort than she was letting on. "I'll have to take you upstairs soon, Morgana."

"Not yet, though." She reached over her shoulder for Ana's hand. "It's so nice being here with everyone. Where's Aunt Maureen?"

"Mama's in the kitchen, probably arguing with Aunt Camilla over the stew by now."

On a little groan, Morgana shut her eyes. "Lord, I could eat a gallon of it."

"After," Ana promised, and looked up as the rattle of chains and the moans of the suffering filled the room. "Somebody at the door."

"Poor Nash. He can't relax long enough to appreciate his own handiwork. Is it Sebastian?"

Ana craned her neck. "Uh-huh. He and Mel are critiquing the holograms. Whoops, there goes the smoke machine and the bats."

Sebastian strode in. "Amateurs."

"And Lydia was so scared she screamed and screamed," Jessie said, relating the chills and thrills of the elementary school's haunted house. "Then Frankie ate so much candy he threw up."

"Sounds like a red-letter day." To forestall exactly the same eventuality, he'd already hidden away half of the treats Jessie'd collected in her goodie bag.

"I like my costume best of all." As they got out of the car in

front of Morgana's, Jessie twirled so that the starry pink material floated around her. Rather pleased with himself, Boone
crouched to adjust her wings of aluminum foil. It had taken
him the better part of two days to figure out how to tack and
baste and tie the fairy costume together. But it was worth it.

She tapped her father's shoulder with her cardboard wand.
"Now you're the handsome prince."

"What was I before?"

"The ugly toad." She squealed with laughter as he tweaked
her nose. "Do you think Ana's going to be surprised? Will she
recognize me?"

"Not a chance. I'm not sure I recognize you myself." They'd
opted to dispense with a mask, and Boone had painted her
cheeks with rouge, reddened her lips, and smudged her eye-
lids up to her eyebrows with glittery gold shadow.

"We're going to meet her whole family," she reminded her
father—as if he needed reminding. He'd been worrying about
the event all week. "And I get to see Morgana's cat and dog
again."

"Right." He tried not to be overly concerned about the dog.
Pan might look like a wolf—disconcertingly so—but he'd been
gentle and friendly with Jessie the last time they'd visited.

"This is going to be the best Halloween party in the whole
world." Rising to her tiptoes, she pushed the doorbell. Her
mouth fell open in a soundless gasp when the moans and
clanking chains filled the air.

A husky man with thinning hair and jolly eyes opened the
door. He took one look at Jessie and spoke in his best ghoul's
voice. "Welcome to the haunted castle. Enter at your own risk."

Her eyes were big blue saucers. "Is it really haunted?"

"Come in...if you dare." He squatted down until he was
at eye level with her, then pulled a fluffy stuffed bunny from
up his sleeve.

"Ooh..." Charmed, Jessie pressed it against her cheek. "Are
you a magician?"

"Certainly. Isn't everyone?"

"Uh-uh. I'm a fairy princess."

"That's good enough. And is this your escort for the evening?" he asked, glancing up at Boone.

"No." Jessie laughed gaily. "He's my daddy. I'm really Jessie."

"I'm really Padrick."

He straightened, and though his eyes remained merry, Boone was sure he was being measured. "And you'd be?"

"Sawyer." He offered a hand. "Boone Sawyer. We're Anastasia's neighbors."

"Neighbors, you say? Well, I doubt that's all. But come in, come in." He exchanged Boone's hand for Jessie's. "See what we have in store for you."

"Ghosts!" She nearly bounced out of her Mary Janes. "Daddy, ghosts!"

"Not a bad attempt for a layman," Padrick said kindly enough. "Oh, by the way, Ana's just taken Nash and Morgana upstairs. We've having twins tonight. Maureen, my passion flower, come meet Ana's neighbors." He turned to Boone as a striking amazon in a scarlet turban came striding down the hall.

"I imagine you'd like a drink, boyo," Padrick said to Boone.

"Yes, sir." Boone blew out a long breath. "I believe I would."


Hesitant and uneasy, Mel knocked on the door of Morgana's bedroom, then poked her head in. She wasn't sure whether she'd expected the clinical—and, to her mind, frightening—aura of a delivery room or the mystical glow of a magic circle. Either one she could have done without.

Instead, there was Morgana propped up in a big, cozy-looking bed, flowers and candles all around. Harp and flute music was drifting through the room. Morgana looked a bit flushed, Nash more than a bit pale, but the basic normality of it all reassured Mel enough to have her crossing the threshold when Ana gestured to her.

"Come on in, Mel. You should be an expert at this now. After all, you helped Sebastian and me deliver the foal just a few months ago."

"I feel like a horse," Morgana muttered, "but that doesn't mean I appreciate the comparison."

"I don't want to interrupt, or get in the way or— Oh, boy," she whispered when Morgana threw her head back and began to puff like a steam engine.

"Okay, okay." Nash gripped her hand and fumbled with a stopwatch. "Here comes another one. We're doing fine, just fine."

"We, hell," Morgana said between her teeth. "I'd like to see you—"

"Breathe." Ana's voice was gentle as she placed crystals over Morgana's belly. They hovered in the air, gleaming with an unearthly light that Mel tried to take in stride.

After all, she reminded herself, she'd been married to a witch for two months.

"It's all right, babe." Nash pressed his lips to her hand, wishing desperately for the pain to pass. "It's almost over."

"Don't go." She gripped his hand hard as the contraction began to ease. "Don't go."

"I'm right here. You're wonderful." As Ana had instructed him, he cooled Morgana's face with a damp cloth. "I love you, gorgeous."

"You'd better." She managed a smile and let out a long, cleansing breath. Knowing she had a ways to go, she closed her eyes. "How am I doing, Ana?"

"Great. A couple more hours."

"A couple—" Nash bit off the words and fixed on a smile that was sick around the edges. "Terrific."

Mel cleared her throat, and Ana glanced over. "I'm sorry. We got a little distracted."

"No problem. I just thought you'd want to know Boone's here—with Jessie."

"Oh." Ana mopped her own brow with her shirtsleeve. "I'd forgotten. I'll be right down. Would you send Aunt Bryna up?"

"Sure. Hey, Morgana, we're all with you."

Morgana's smile was just a tad wicked. "Great. Want to change places?"

"I'll pass this time, thanks." She was edging toward the door. "I'll just get out of your way."

"You're not going to be gone long." Struggling against panic, Nash rubbed the small of Morgana's back and looked pleadingly at Ana.

"Only a minute or two. And Aunt Bryna's very skilled. Besides, we need some brandy."

"Brandy? She's not supposed to drink."

"For you," Ana said gently as she slipped out of the room.

The first thing Ana noted when she reached the parlor was that Jessie was being very well entertained. Ana's mother was laughing her lusty, full-bodied laugh as Jessie recounted her class's escapades at the school Halloween party. Since Jessie was already cuddling two stuffed animals, Ana deduced that her father had already been up to his tricks.

She certainly hoped he'd been discreet.

"Things are well upstairs?" Bryna said quietly as they passed in the doorway.

"Perfect. You'll be a grandmother before midnight."

"Bless you, Anastasia." Bryna kissed her cheek. "And I do like your young man."

"He's not—" But her aunt was already hurrying upstairs.

And there was Boone standing by the fireplace, where the flames crackled cheerily, drinking what was surely one of her father's concoctions and listening, with an expression of fascinated bemusement, to one of her uncle Douglas's stories.

"So, naturally, we took the poor soul in for the night. Storm being what it was. And what did he do but go screeching out in the morning, shouting about banshees and ghosts and the like. Touched," Douglas said sadly, tapping a finger to his head, where an orange silk hat now resided. "A sad and sorry tale."

"Perhaps it had something to do with you clanging about in that suit of armor," Matthew Donovan commented, warming a brandy in his long-fingered hands.

"No, no, a suit of armor doesn't resemble a banshee in the least. I imagine it was Maureen's cat screeching that did it."

"My cats do not screech," she said, insulted. "They're quite well behaved."

"I have a dog," Jessie piped up. "But I like cats, too."

"Is that so?" Always willing to oblige, Padrick plucked a yellow-striped stuffed kitten from between her fairy wings. "How about this one?"

"Oh!" Jessie buried her face in its fur, then delighted Padrick by climbing onto his lap and kissing his rosy cheek.

"Da." Ana leaned over the sofa to press her lips to his balding head. "You never change."

"Ana!" Jessie bounced on Padrick's lap and tried to hold up her entire menagerie at once. "Your daddy's the funniest person in the world!"

"I like him myself." She tilted her head curiously. "But who are you?"

"I'm Jessie." Giggling, she climbed down to turn in a circle.

"No, really?"

"Honest. Daddy made me a fairy princess for Halloween."

"You certainly sound like Jessie." Ana crouched down. "Give me a kiss and let's see."

Jessie pressed her painted lips to Ana's, flushing with pleasure at her costume's success. "Didn't you know me? Really?"

"You fooled me completely. I was certain you were a real fairy princess."

"Your daddy said you were his fairy princess 'cause your mama was a queen."

Maureen let out another peal of laughter, and winked at her husband. "My little frog."

"I'm sorry I can't stay and talk," Ana told Jessie.

"I know. You're helping get Morgana's babies out. Do they come out together or one at a time?"

"One at a time, I hope." She laughed, tousling Jessie's hair, and looked over at Boone. "You know you're welcome to stay as long as you like. There's plenty of food."

"Don't worry about us. How's Morgana?"

"Very well. Actually, I came down to get some brandy for Nash. His nerves are about shot."

With an understanding nod, Matthew picked up a decanter and a snifter. "He has my sympathy." When he passed them to her, she felt a jolt of his power and knew that, however calm his exterior, his mind and his heart were upstairs with his daughter.

"Don't worry. I'll take care of her, Uncle Matthew."

"No one better. You are the best I've known, Anastasia." His eyes held hers as he flicked a finger over the bloodstone she wore around her neck. "And I've known many." Then a smile touched his lips. "Boone, perhaps you'd walk Anastasia back up."

"Be glad to." Boone took the decanter from Ana before they started out.

"Your family," Boone began, shaking his head at the foot of the stairs, unaware that she'd stiffened.

"Yes?"

"Incredible. Absolutely incredible. It isn't every day I find myself plopped into the center of a group of strangers, with a woman about to give birth to twins upstairs, a wolf—because I swear that dog is no dog—gnawing what looks like a mastodon bone under the kitchen table, and mechanical bats flying overhead. Oh, I forgot the ghosts in the foyer."

"Well, it is Halloween."

"I don't think that has much to do with it." He stopped at

the top of the stairs. "I can't remember ever being more entertained. They're fabulous, Ana. Your father does these magic
tricks—terrific magic tricks. For the life of me I couldn't figure out how he pulled it off."

"No, you wouldn't. He's, ah...very accomplished."

"He could make a living at it. I've got to tell you, I wouldn't
have missed this party for the world." He cupped his free hand
around her neck. "The only thing missing is you."

"I was worried you'd feel awkward."

"No. Though it does kind of scotch my plans to lure you
into some shadowy corner and make you shiver with some
bloodcurdling story so you'd climb all over me for protection."

"I don't spook easily." Smiling, she twined her arms around
him. "I grew up on bloodcurdling."

"And uncles clanging around in suits of armor," he murmured as he brushed his lips over hers.

"Oh, that's the least of it." She leaned against him, chang-
ing the angle of the kiss. "We used to play in the dungeons.
And I spent an entire night in the haunted tower on one of
Sebastian's dares."

"Courageous."

"No, stubborn. And stupid. I've never been more uncomfortable in my life." She was drifting into the kiss, losing herself. "At least until Morgana conjured up a blanket and pillow."

"Conjured?" he repeated, amused by the term.

"Sent up," she corrected, and poured herself into the embrace so that he would think of nothing but her.

When the door opened beside them, they looked around
like guilty children. Bryna lifted her brows, summed up the
situation and smiled.

"I'm sorry to interrupt, but I think Boone is just what we
need right now."

He took a firmer grip on the brandy bottle. "In there?"

She laughed. "No. If you'd just stay there, and let me send
Nash out for a moment or two. He could use a little man talk."

"Only for a minute," Ana cautioned. "Morgana needs him inside."

Before Boone could agree or refuse, she slipped away. Resigned, he poured a snifter, took a good swallow himself, then refilled it when Nash stepped out.

He pressed the snifter on Nash. "Have a shot."

"I didn't think it would take so long." After a long breath, he sipped the brandy. "Or that it would hurt her so much. If we get through this, I swear, I'm never going to touch her again."

"Yeah, right."

"I mean it." Despite the fact he knew it was an expectant-father cliché, he began to pace.

"Nash, I don't mean to interfere, but wouldn't you feel better—safer—if Morgana was in a hospital, with a doctor and all that handy medical business?"

"A hospital? No." Nash rubbed a hand over his face. "Morgana was born in that same bed. She wouldn't have it any other way with the twins. I guess I wouldn't, either."

"Well, a doctor, then."

"Ana's the best." Remembering that relaxed him slightly. "Believe me, Morgana couldn't be in better hands than hers."

"I know midwives are supposed to be excellent, and more natural, I imagine." He moved his shoulders. If Nash was content with the situation, it wasn't up to him to worry about it. "I guess she's done it before."

"No, this is Morgana's first time."

"I meant Ana," Boone said on a chuckle. "Delivering babies."

"Oh, yeah. Sure. She knows what she's doing. It's not that. In fact, I think I'd go crazy if she wasn't here. But—" He took another swallow, paced a little more. "I mean, this has been going on for hours. I don't know how she can stand it. I don't know why any woman stands it. Just seems to me she could do something about it. Damn it, she's a witch."

Manfully masking another chuckle, Boone gave Nash an

encouraging pat on the back. "Nash, it's not a good time to call her names. Women get a little nasty when they're in labor. They're entitled."

"No, I mean—" He broke off, realizing he was going over the edge. "I've got to pull myself together."

"Yep."

"I know it's going to be all right. Ana wouldn't let anything happen. But it's so hard to watch her hurting."

"When you love someone, it's the hardest thing in the world. But you get through it. And, in this case, you're getting something fantastic out of it."

"I never thought I could feel this way, about anybody. She's everything."

"I know what you mean."

Feeling better, Nash passed the snifter back to Boone. "Is that how it is with Ana?"

"I think it might be. I know she's special."

"Yeah, she is." Nash hesitated, and when he spoke again he chose his words with care. Loyalty, split two ways, was the heaviest of burdens. "You'd be able to understand her, Boone, with your imagination, your way of looking beyond what's considered reality. She is a very special lady, with qualities that make her different from anyone you've ever known. If you love her, and you want her to be a part of your life and Jessie's, don't let those qualities block you."

Boone's brows drew together. "I don't think I'm following you."

"Just remember I said it. Thanks for the drink." He took a steadying breath, then went back in to his wife.

# Chapter 9

"Breathe. Come on, baby, breathe!"

"I am breathing." Morgana grunted out the words between pants and couldn't quite manage to glare at Nash. "What the hell do you call this if it's not breathing?"

Nash figured he was past his own crisis point. She'd already called him every name in the book, and had invented several more. Ana said they were nearly there, and he was clinging to that as desperately as Morgana was clinging to his hand. So he merely smiled at his sweaty wife and mopped her brow with a cool cloth.

"Growling, spitting, snarling." He touched his lips to hers, relieved when she didn't bite him. "You're not going to turn me into a slug or a two-headed newt, are you?"

She laughed, groaned, and let out the last puff of air. "I can come up with something much more inventive. I need to sit up more. Ana?"

"Nash, get in the bed behind her. Support her back. It's going to go quickly now." Arching her own back, which echoed the aches in Morgana's, she checked one last time to see if all was ready. There were blankets warmed by the fire, heated water, the clamps and scissors already sterilized, the glow of crystals pulsing with power.

Bryna stood by her daughter's side, her eyes bright with understanding and concern. Images of her own hours in that same bed fighting to bring life into the world raced through her head. That same bed, she thought blinking at the mists in her eyes, where her child now labored through the last moments, the last pangs.

"No pushing until I tell you. Pant. Pant," Ana repeated as she felt the contraction build within herself—a sweet and terrible pang that brought fresh sweat to her skin. Morgana stiffened, fought off the need to tense, and struggled to do as she was told. "Good, good. Nearly there, darling, I promise. Have you picked out names?"

"I like Curly and Moe," Nash said, panting right along with Morgana until she managed to jab him weakly with an elbow. "Okay, okay, Ozzie and Harriet, but only if we have one of each."

"Don't make me laugh now, you idiot." But she did laugh, and the pain eased back. "I want to push. I have to push."

"If it's two girls," he continued, with an edge of desperation, "we're going with Lucy and Ethel." He pressed his cheek against hers.

"Two boys and it's Boris and Bela." Morgana's laughter took on a slightly hysterical note as she reached back to link her arms around Nash's neck. "God, Ana, I have to—"

"Bear down," Ana snapped out. "Go ahead, push."

Caught between laughter and tears, Morgana threw her head back and fought to bring life into the room. "Oh, God!" Outside, lightning shot across a cloudless sky and thunder cracked its celestial whip.

"Nice going, champ," Nash began, but then his mind seemed to go blank as glass. "Look! Oh, Lord, would you look at that!"

At the foot of the bed, Ana gently, competently turned the

tiny, dark head. "Hold back now, honey. I know it's hard, but hold back just for a minute. Pant. That's it, that's the way. Next time's the charm."

"It's got hair," Nash said weakly. His face was as wet with sweat and tears as Morgana's. "Just look at that. What is it?"

"I haven't got that end out yet." Ana sent a glittering smile to her cousin. "Okay, this is for the grand prize. Bear down, honey, and let's see if we've got Ozzie or Harriet."

With laughter, Morgana delivered her child into Ana's waiting hands. As the first wild, indignant cry of life echoed in the room, Nash buried his face in his wife's tangled hair.

"Morgana. Sweet Lord, Morgana. Ours."

"Ours." The pain was already forgotten. Eyes glowing, Morgana held out her arms so that Ana could place the tiny, wriggling bundle into them. In the language of her blood, she murmured to the babe, as her hands moved gently to welcome.

"What is it?" With a trembling hand, Nash reached down to touch the tiny head. "I forgot to look."

"You have a son," Ana told him.

At the first lusty wail, conversation in the parlor downstairs cut off like a switch. All eyes shifted to the stairs. There was silence, stillness. Touched, Boone looked at his own child, who slept peacefully on the sofa, her head nestled in Padrick's comfortable lap.

He felt a tremor beneath his feet, saw the wine slosh back and forth in his glass. Before he could speak, Douglas was removing his top hat and slapping Matthew on the back.

"A new Donovan," he said, and snatched up a glass to lift in toast. "A new legacy."

A little teary-eyed, Camilla walked over to kiss her brother-in-law's cheek. "Blessed be."

Boone was about to add his congratulations when Sebastian crossed the room. He lit a white candle, then a gold one.

Taking up a bottle of unopened wine, he broke the seal, then poured pale gold liquid into an ornate silver chalice.

"A star dawns in the night. Life from life, blood through blood to shine its light. Through love he was given the gift of birth, and from breath to death will walk the earth. The other gift comes through blood and bone, and is for him to take and own. Charm of the moon, power of the sun. Never forgetting an' it harm none."

Sebastian passed the cup to Matthew, who sipped first. Fascinated, Boone watched the Donovans pass the chalice of wine from one to the other. An Irish tradition? he wondered. It was certainly more moving, more charming, than passing out cigars.

When he was handed the cup, he was both honored and baffled. Even as he began to sip, another wail sounded, announcing another life.

"Two stars," Matthew said in a voice thickened with pride. "Two gifts."

Then the solemn mood was broken as Padrick conjured up a party streamer and a rain of confetti. As he blew a celebratory toot, his wife laughed bawdily.

"Happy New Year," she said, gesturing toward the clock that had just begun to strike twelve. "It's the best All Hallows' Eve since Padrick made the pigs fly." She grinned at Boone. "He's such a prankster."

"Pigs," Boone began, but the group turned as one as Bryna entered the room. She moved directly to her husband, who folded her tightly within his arms.

"They're all well." She brushed at happy tears. "All well and beautiful. We have a grandson and a granddaughter, my love. And our daughter invites us all upstairs to welcome them."

Not wanting to intrude, Boone hung back as the group piled out of the room. Sebastian stopped in the doorway, arched a brow. "Aren't you coming?"

"I think the family…"

"You were accepted," Sebastian said shortly, not certain he agreed with the rest of the Donovans. He hadn't forgotten how deeply Ana had once been hurt.

"An odd way to phrase it." Boone kept his voice mild to counteract a sudden flare of temper. "Particularly since you feel differently."

"Regardless." Sebastian inclined his head in what Boone interpreted as both challenge and warning. But when Sebastian glanced toward the sofa, he softened. "I imagine Jessie would be disappointed if you didn't wake her and bring her up for a look."

"But you'd rather I didn't."

"Ana would rather you did," Sebastian countered. "And that's more to the point." He moved to the doorway again, then stopped. "You'll hurt her. Anastasia sheds no tears, but she'll shed them for you. Because I love her, I'll have to forgive you for that."

"I don't see—"

"No." Sebastian nodded curtly. "But I do. Bring the child, Sawyer, and join us. It's a night for kindness, and small miracles."

Uncertain why Sebastian's words angered him so much, Boone stared at the empty doorway. He damn well didn't have to prove himself to some overprotective, interfering cousin. When Jessie shifted and blinked owlishly, he pushed Sebastian out of his mind.

"Daddy?"

"Right here, frog face." He bent and lifted his child into his arms. "Guess what?"

She rubbed her eyes. "I'm sleepy."

"We'll go home soon, but I think there's something you'd like to see first." While she yawned and dropped her heavy head on his shoulder, he carried her upstairs.

They were all gathered around, making a great deal more noise than Boone imagined was the norm even for a home

delivery room. Nash was sitting on the edge of the bed beside Morgana, holding a tiny bundle and grinning like a fool.

"He looks like me, don't you think?" he was asking of no
one in particular. "The nose. He's got my nose."

"That's Allysia," Morgana informed him, rubbing a cheek
over her son's downy head. "I've got Donovan."

"Right. Well, *she's* got my nose." He peeked over at his son.
"He's got my chin."

"The Donovan chin," Douglas corrected. "Plain as a pike-
staff."

"Hah." Maureen was jockeying for position. "They're both
Corrigans through and through. Our side of the family has always had strong genes."

While they argued over that, Jessie shook off sleep and
stretched forward. "Is it the babies? Did they get born? Can
I see?"

"Let the child in." Padrick elbowed his brother out of the
way. "Let her have a look."

Jessie kept one arm hooked around her father's neck as she
leaned forward. "Oh!" Her tired eyes went bright as Ana took
a babe in each arm to hold them up for Jessie to see. "They
look just like little fairies." Very delicately, she touched a fingertip to one cheek, then the other.

"That's just what they are." Padrick kissed Jessie's nose. "A
brand new fairy prince and princess."

"But they don't have wings," Jessie said, giggling.

"Some fairies don't need wings." Padrick winked at his
daughter. "Because they have wings on their hearts."

"These fairies need some rest and some quiet." Ana turned
to tuck the babies into Morgana's waiting arms. "And so does
their mama."

"I feel wonderful."

"Nevertheless…" Ana shot a warning look over her shoulder that had the Donovans reluctantly filing out.

"Boone," Morgana called out. "Would you wait for Ana, drive her home? She's exhausted."

"I'm perfectly fine. He should—"

"Of course I will." He settled the yawning Jessie on his shoulder. "We'll be downstairs whenever you're ready."

It took another fifteen minutes before Ana was assured that Nash had all her instructions. Morgana was already drifting off to sleep when Ana closed the door and left the new family alone.

She was exhausted, and the powers of the crystals in her pouch were nearly depleted. For almost twelve hours, she had gone through the labor of childbirth with her cousin, as closely linked as it was possible to be. Her body was heavy with fatigue, her mind drugged with it. It was a common result of a strong empathic link.

She staggered once at the top of the stairs, righted herself, then gripped her bloodstone amulet to draw on the last of its strength.

By the time she reached the parlor, she was feeling a little steadier. There was Boone, half dozing in a chair by the fire, with Jessie cuddled against his chest. His eyes opened. His lips curved.

"Hey, champ. I have to admit I thought this whole setup was a little loony, but you did a hell of a job up there."

"It's always stunning to bring life into the world. You didn't have to stay all this time."

"I wanted to." He kissed Jessie's head. "So did she. She'll be the hit of school on Monday with this story."

"It's been a long night for her, and one she won't forget." Ana rubbed her eyes, almost as Jessie had before falling asleep again. "Where is everyone?"

"In the kitchen, raiding the refrigerator and getting drunk. I decided to pass, since I already had more than my share of wine." He offered a sheepish grin. "A little while ago I could

have sworn the house was shaking, so I switched to coffee."
He gestured toward the cup on the table beside him.

"And now you'll be up half the night. I'll just run and tell
them I'm going, if you'd like to go put Jessie in the car."

Outside, Boone took a deep gulp of the cool night air. Ana
was right, he was wide awake. He'd have to work a couple of
hours until the coffee wore off, and he'd more than likely pay
for it tomorrow. But it had been worth it. He glanced over his
shoulder to where the light glowed in Morgana's bedroom. It
had been well worth it.

He slipped Jessie's wings over her shoulders, then laid her
on the back seat.

"Beautiful night," Ana murmured from behind him. "I think
every star must be out."

"Two new stars." Bemused, Boone opened the door for her.
"That's what Matthew said. It was really lovely. Sebastian
made a toast about life and gifts and stars, and they all passed
around a cup of wine. Is that an Irish thing?"

"In a way." She leaned her head back against the seat as he
started the car. Within seconds, she was asleep.

When Boone pulled up in his driveway, he wondered how he
was going to manage to carry both of them to bed. He shifted,
easing his door open, but Ana was already blinking awake.

"Just let me carry her inside, and I'll give you a hand."

"No, I'm fine." Bleary-eyed, Ana stepped out of the car.
"I'll help you with her." She laughed as she gathered up the
store of stuffed animals. "Da always goes overboard. I hope
you don't mind."

"Are you kidding? He was great with her. Come on, baby."
He lifted her and, in the way of children, she remained utterly
lax. "She was taken with your mother, too, and the rest, but
your father was definitely the hero. I expect she'll be bugging
me to go to Ireland now, so she can visit him in his castle."

"He'd love it." She took the silver wings and followed him
into the house.

"Just set those anywhere. Do you want a brandy?"

"No, really." She dropped the animals on the couch, put the wings beside them, then rolled her aching shoulders. "I wouldn't mind some tea. I can brew some while you settle her in."

"Fine. I won't be long."

A low growling emerged from under Jessie's bed when Boone carried her in. "Great watchdog. It's just us, you blockhead."

Desperately relieved, Daisy bounded out, tail wagging. She waited until Boone had removed Jessie's shoes and costume, then leapt onto the bed to settle at Jessie's feet.

"You wake me up at six and I'll staple those doggie lips closed."

Daisy thumped her tail and shut her eyes.

"I don't know why we couldn't have gotten a smart dog while we were at it," Boone was saying as he walked into the kitchen. "It wouldn't have been..." and then his words trailed off.

The kettle was on and beginning to steam. Cups were set out, and the pot was waiting. Ana had her head pillowed on her arms at the kitchen table, and was deep in sleep.

Under the bright light, her lashes cast shadows on her cheeks. Boone hoped it was the harshness of the light that made her look so delicately pale. Her hair spilled over her shoulder. Her lips were soft, just parted.

Looking at her, he thought of the young princess who had been put under a spell by a jealous fairy and made to sleep a hundred years, until wakened by true love's gentle kiss.

"Anastasia. You're so beautiful." He touched her hair, indulging himself. He'd never watched her sleep, and he had a sudden, tearing urge to have her in his bed, to be able to open his eyes in the morning and see her there beside him. "What am I going to do?"

Sighing, he let his hand fall away from her hair and moved

to the stove to shut off the kettle. As gently as he had with Jessie, he lifted her into his arms, and, like Jessie, she remained lax. Gritting his teeth against the knots in his stomach, he carried her upstairs and laid her on his bed.

"You don't know how much I've wanted you here," he said under his breath as he slipped off her shoes. "In my bed, in the night. All night." He spread the covers over her, and she sighed, shifting in sleep and curling into his pillow.

The knots in his stomach loosened as he bent to touch his lips to hers. "Good night, princess."

In her panties and T-shirt, Jessie padded into the bedroom before dawn. She'd had a dream, a bad one about the haunted house at school, and wanted the comfort and warmth of her father.

He always made monsters go away.

She scurried to the bed, and climbed in to burrow against him. It was then that she noted it wasn't her father at all, but Ana.

Fascinated, Jessie curled up. Curious fingers played with Ana's hair. In sleep Ana murmured and tucked Jessie under her arm to snuggle her close. Odd sensations tugged through Jessie's stomach. Different smells, different textures, and yet she felt as loved and safe as she did when her father cuddled her. She rested her head trustingly against Ana's breast and slept.

When Ana woke, she felt arms around her, small, limp arms. Disoriented, she stared down at Jessie, then looked around the room.

Not her room, she realized. And not Jessie's. Boone's.

She kept the child warm against her as she tried to piece together what had happened.

The last thing she remembered was sitting down after she'd put on water for tea. Tired, she'd been so tired. She'd rested her head for a moment and...and obviously had fallen fast asleep.

So where was Boone?

Cautiously she turned her head, unsure whether she was relieved or disappointed to find the bed beside her empty. Impractical, of course, given the circumstances, but it would have been so lovely to be able to cuddle back against him even as the child cuddled to her.

When she looked back, Jessie's eyes were open and on hers.

"I had a bad dream," the girl told her in hushed morning whispers. "About the Headless Horseman. He was laughing and laughing and chasing me."

Ana snuggled down to kiss Jessie's brow. "I bet he didn't catch you."

"Uh-uh. I woke up and came to get Daddy. He always makes the monsters go away. The ones in the closet and under the bed and at the window and everywhere."

"Daddies are good at that." She smiled, remembering how her own had pretended to chase them away with a magic broom every night during her sixth year.

"But you were here, and I wasn't scared with you, either. Are you going to sleep in Daddy's bed at night now?"

"No." She brushed a hand through Jessie's hair. "I think you and I both fell asleep, and your father had to put both of us to bed."

"But it's a big bed," Jessie pointed out. "There'd be room. I have Daisy to sleep with me now, but Daddy has to sleep all alone. Does Quigley sleep with you?"

"Sometimes," Ana said, relieved at the rapid change of topic. "He's probably wondering where I am."

"I think he knows," Boone announced from the doorway. He was wearing only jeans, unsnapped at the waist, and he looked bleary-eyed and harassed, with the gray cat winding between his legs. "He howled and scratched at the back door until I let him in."

"Oh." Ana shoved her tumbled hair back as she sat up. "Sorry. I guess he woke you."

"Right the first time." He tucked his thumbs in his pockets while the cat leapt onto the bed and began to mutter and complain to his mistress. The knots in his stomach were back, doubled. How could he explain what he felt on seeing Ana cuddled with his little girl in the big, soft bed? "Jessie, what are you doing?"

"I had a bad dream." She leaned her head against Ana's arm and stroked the cat's fur. "So I came in to get you, but Ana was here. She made the monsters go away just like you do." Quigley meowed plaintively and made Jessie giggle. "He's hungry. Poor kitty. I can feed him. Can I take him down and feed him?"

"Sure, if you'd like."

Before Ana had finished the sentence, Jessie was bounding off the bed, calling to the cat to follow.

"Sorry she woke you." Boone hesitated, then moved over to sit on the edge of the bed.

"She didn't. Apparently she just climbed right on in and went back to sleep. And I should apologize for putting you to so much trouble. You could have given me a shake and sent me home."

"You were exhausted." He reached out, much as Jessie had, to touch her hair. "Incredibly beautiful, and totally exhausted."

"Having babies is tiring work." She smiled. "Where did you sleep?"

"In the guest room." He winced at the crick in his back. "Which makes getting a decent bed in there a top priority."

Automatically she pressed her hands on his lower back to massage and ease. "You could have dumped me in there. I don't think I would have known the difference between a bed and a sheet of plywood."

"I wanted you in my bed." His gaze met hers and locked. "I very much wanted you in my bed." He tugged on her hair to bring her closer. Much closer. "I still do."

His mouth was on hers, not so patient now, not so gentle.

Ana felt a quick thrill of excitement and alarm as he pressed her back against the pillows. "Boone—"

"Just for a minute." His voice took on an edge of desperation. "I need a minute with you."

He took her breast, searing her flesh through the thin silk of her rumpled blouse. While his hands skimmed over her, his mouth took and took, swallowing her muffled moans. His body ached to cover hers, to press hard against soft, to take quickly, even savagely, what he knew she could bring to him.

"Ana." His teeth scraped down her throat before he gathered her close, just to hold her. He knew he was being unfair, to both of them, and he struggled to back off. "How long does it take to feed that cat?"

"Not long enough." With a shaky laugh, she dropped her head on his shoulder. "Not nearly long enough."

"I was afraid of that." He drew back, running his hands down her arms to take hers. "Jessie's been after me to let her spend the night at Lydia's. If I can work it out, will you stay with me? Here?"

"Yes." She brought his hand to her lips, then pressed it to her cheek. "Whenever you like."

"Tonight." He forced himself to release her, to move away. "Tonight," he repeated. "I'll go call Lydia's mother. Beg if I have to." He steadied himself and slowed down. "I promised Jess we'd go get some ice cream, maybe have lunch on the wharf. Will you come with us? If it all works out, we could drop her off at Lydia's, then go out to dinner."

She pushed off the bed herself, brushing uselessly at the wrinkles in her blouse and slacks. "That sounds nice."

"Great. Sorry about the clothes. I wasn't quite brave enough to undress you."

She felt a quick thrill at the image of him unbuttoning her blouse. Slowly, very slowly, his fingers patient, his eyes hot. She cleared her throat. "They'll press out. I need to change, go check on Morgana and the twins."

"I could drive you."

"That's all right. My father's going to pick me up so I can get my car. What time did you want to leave?"

"About noon, in a couple hours."

"Perfect. I'll meet you back here."

He caught her to him before she reached the doorway, then stopped her heart with another greedy kiss. "Maybe we could pick up some takeout, bring it back and eat here."

"That sounds nice, too," she murmured as she shifted the angle of the kiss. "Or maybe we could just send out for pizza when we get hungry."

"Better. Much better."

By four o'clock, Jessie was standing in Lydia's doorway waving a cheery goodbye. Her pink backpack was bulging with the amazing assortment of necessities a six-year-old girl required for a sleepover. What made the entire matter perfect in her eyes was that Daisy had been invited along for the party.

"Tell me not to feel guilty," Boone asked as he cast one last glance in the rearview mirror.

"About?"

"About wanting my own daughter out of the house tonight."

"Boone." Adoring him, Ana leaned over to kiss his cheek. "You know perfectly well Jessie could hardly wait for us to drive away so she could begin her little adventure at Lydia's."

"Yeah, but... It's not packing her off so much, it's packing her off with ulterior motives."

Knowing what those motives were brought a little knot of heat to Ana's stomach. "She isn't going to have less of a good time because of them—particularly when you promised her she could have a slumber party in a couple of weeks. If you're still feeling guilty think about how you're going to feel riding herd on five or six little girls all night."

He slanted her a look. "I kind of figured you'd help—since you have ulterior motives, too."

"Did you?" The fact that he'd asked pleased her enormously. "Maybe I will." She laid a hand over his. "For a paranoid father riddled with guilt, you're doing a wonderful job."

"Keep it up. I'm feeling better."

"Too much flattery isn't good for you."

"Just for that I won't tell you how many guys gave themselves whiplash craning their necks to get a second look at you when we were walking on the wharf today."

"Oh?" She skimmed back her blowing hair. "Were there many?"

"Depends on how you define many. Besides, too much flattery isn't good for you. I guess I could say I don't know how you could look so good today after the night you put in."

"It could be because I slept like a rock." She stretched luxuriously. A bracelet of agates winked at her wrist. "Morgana's the amazing one. When I got there this morning, she was nursing both of the twins and looking as if she'd just spent a reviving week at an expensive spa."

"The babies okay?"

"The babies are terrific. Healthy and bright-eyed. Nash is already a pro at changing diapers. He claims both of them have smiled at him."

He knew that feeling, too, and had just realized he missed it. "He's a good guy."

"Nash is very special."

"I have to admit, I was stunned when I heard he was married. Nash was always the go-it-on-your-own type."

"Love changes things," Ana murmured, and carefully screened all wistfulness from her voice. "Aunt Bryna calls it the purest form of magic."

"A good description. Once it touches you, you begin to think nothing's impossible anymore. Were you ever in love?"

"Once." She looked away, studying the shimmering ice plants along the banks. "A long time ago. But it turned out the magic wasn't strong enough. Then I learned that my life wasn't over after all, and I could be perfectly happy alone. So I bought my house near the water," she said with a smile. "Planted my garden, and started fresh."

"I suppose it was similar for me." He grew thoughtful as they made the final turn toward home. "Does being happy alone mean you don't think you could be happy with someone?"

Unease and hope ran parallel inside her. "I guess it means I can be happy as things stand, until I find someone who not only brings me the magic, but understands it."

He turned into the drive, shut off the engine. "We have something together, Ana."

"I know."

"I never thought to feel anything this powerful again. It's different from what I had before, and I'm not sure what that means. I don't know if I want to know."

"It doesn't matter." She took his hand again. "Sometimes you just have to accept that today is enough."

"No, it's not." He turned to her then, his eyes dark, intense. "Not with you."

She took a careful breath. "I'm not what you think I am, or what you want me to be. Boone—"

"You're exactly what I want." His hands were rough as he dragged her against him. Her startled gasp was muffled against his hard, seeking mouth.

# Chapter 10

A whip of panicked excitement cracked through her as he tore her free of the seat belt and yanked her across his lap. His hands bruised, his mouth branded. This was not the Boone who had loved her so gently, taking her to that sweet, sweet fulfillment with patient hands and murmured promises. Her lover of quiet mornings and lazy afternoons had become something darker, something dangerous, something she was helpless to resist.

She could feel the blood sizzling under her skin as he took those rough, impatient hands over her. This was the wildness she had tasted that first time, in a moonlit garden with the scent of flowers ripe and heady. This bursting of urgent needs was what he had only hinted at under all that patience and steady control.

In mindless acquiescence she strained against him, willing, eager and ready to race along any path he chose.

Her body shuddered once, violently, as he dragged her over a ragged edge. He heard her muffled cry against his greedy mouth, tasted the ripeness of it as her fingers dug desperately into his shoulders. The thought ran crazily through his mind that he could have her here, right here in the car, before reason caught up with either of them.

He tore at her blouse, craving the taste of flesh. The sound of ripping seams was smothered by her quick gasp as he feasted on her throat. Beneath his hungry mouth, her pulse hammered erratically, erotically. The flavor of her was already hot, already honeyed with passion.

On a vicious oath, he shoved the door open, yanking her out. Leaving it swinging, he half carried, half dragged her across the lawn.

"Boone." Staggered, she tried to gain her feet and lost her shoes. "Boone, the car. You left your keys—"

He caught her hair, pulling her head back. His eyes. Oh, Lord, his eyes, she thought, trembling with something much deeper than fear. The heat in them seared through to her soul.

"The hell with the car." His mouth swooped down, plundered hers until she was dazed and dizzy and fighting to breathe. "Do you know what you do to me?" he said between strangled gasps for air. "Every time I see you." He pulled her up the steps, touching her, always touching her. "Soft, serene, with something smoldering just behind your eyes."

He pushed her back against the door, crushing, conquering, those full, luscious lips with his. There was something more in her eyes now. He could see that she was afraid. And that she was aroused. It was as if they both were fully aware that the animal he'd kept ruthlessly on a choke chain for weeks had broken free.

With the breath coming harsh through his lips, he caught her face in his hands. "Tell me. Ana, tell me you want me. Now. My way."

She was afraid she wouldn't be able to speak, her throat was so dry and this new need so huge. "I want you." The husky sound of her voice had the flames in his gut leaping higher. "Now. Any way."

He hooked his hands in her blouse, watched her eyes go to smoke just before he rent it in two. When he kicked the door open, she staggered back, then was caught up in a torrid embrace. Like her blouse, his control was in shreds. His hands tight at her waist, he lifted her off her feet to take her silk-covered breast in his mouth. As crazed now as he, she arched back, her hands fisted in his hair.

"Boone. Please." The plea sobbed out, though she had no idea what she was asking for. Unless it was more.

He lowered her, only so that he could capture her mouth again. His teeth scraped erotically over her swollen lips, his tongue dived deep. Then his heart seemed to explode in his chest as she began to tug frantically at his clothes.

He stumbled toward the stairs, shedding his shirt as he went. Buttons popped and scattered. But his greedy hands reached for her again, yanking the thin chemise down to her waist as they reached the landing. "Here." He dragged her down with him. "Right here."

At last, he feasted, racing his mouth over her quivering flesh, ruthlessly exploiting her secrets, relentlessly driving her with him where he so desperately needed her to go. No patience here, no rigid control for the sake of her fragility. Indeed, the woman writhing beneath him on the stairs was anything but fragile. There was strength in the hands that gripped him, searing passion in the mouth that tasted him so eagerly, whiplike agility in the body that strained under his.

She felt invincible, immortal, impossibly free. Her body was alive, never more alive, with heat pumping crazily through her blood. The world was spinning around her, a blur of color and blinding lights, whirling faster, faster, until she was forced to grip the pickets of the banister to keep from falling off the edge of the earth.

Her knuckles whitened against the wood as he tore her slacks away, then the thin swatch of lace beneath. His mouth, oh, his mouth, greedy, frantic, fevered. Ana bit back a scream as he sent her flying into hot, airless space.

Her mindless murmurs were in no language he could understand, but he knew he had taken her beyond the boundaries of the sane, of the rational. He wanted her there, right there with him as they catapulted into the madness of vivid, lawless passion.

He'd waited. He'd waited. Now her slim white body bucked. A thoroughbred ready to ride. Quivering like a stallion, he mounted her, driving himself into that wet, waiting heat. She arched to meet him and, hips moving like lightning, raced with him into the roaring dark.

Her hands slid weakly off his damp back. She was too numb to feel the slap of wood against them as they fell against the stairs. She wanted to hold him, but her strength was gone. It wasn't possible to focus her mind on what had happened. All that came were flashes of sensations, bursts of emotions.

If this was the darker side of love, nothing could have prepared her for it. If this terrible need was what had lived inside him, she couldn't comprehend how he could have strapped it back for so long.

For her sake. She turned her damp face into his throat. All for her sake.

Beneath his still-shuddering body, she was as limp as water. Boone struggled to get a grip on reality. He needed to move. After everything else he'd done to her, he was probably crushing her. But when he started to shift, she made a little sound of distress that scraped at his conscience.

"Here, baby, let me help you."

He eased away, picking up a tattered sleeve of her blouse with some idea to cover her. Biting off an oath, he tossed it down again. She'd turned slightly on her side, obviously seeking some kind of comfort. For God's sake, he thought in disgust, he'd taken her like some kind of fiend, and on the stairs. *On the stairs.*

"Ana." He found what was left of his own shirt and tried to wrap it around her shoulders. "Anastasia, I don't know how to explain."

"Explain?" The word was barely audible. Her throat was wild with thirst.

"There's no possible... Let me help you up." Her body slid like wax through his arms. "I'll get you some clothes, or... Oh, hell."

"I don't think I can get up." She moistened her lips, and tasted him. "Not for a day or two. This is fine, though. I'll just stay right here."

Frowning at her, he tried to interpret what he heard in her voice. It wasn't anger. It didn't sound like distress. It sounded like—very much like—satisfaction. "You're not upset?"

"Hmmm? Am I supposed to be?"

"Well, for... I practically attacked you. Hell, I *did* attack you, almost taking you in the front seat of the car, tearing off your clothes, dragging you in here and devouring what was left of you on the stairs."

With her eyes still closed, she drew in a deep breath, then let it out again on a sigh through curved lips. "You certainly did. And it's the first time I've been devoured. I don't think I'll ever go up and down a staircase the same way again."

Gently he tipped a finger under her chin until her eyes opened. "I had intended to at least make it to the bedroom."

"I guess we'll get there eventually." Recognizing concern, she put a hand on his wrist. "Boone, do you think I could be upset because you wanted me that much?"

"I thought you might be upset because this wasn't what you're used to."

Making the effort, she sat up, wincing a little at the aches that would surely be bruises before much longer. "I'm not made of glass. There's no way we could love each other that wouldn't be right. But..." She linked her arms around his neck and her smile was wicked around the edges. "Under the circumstances, I'm glad we made it into the house."

He skimmed his hands down to her hips for the pleasure of bringing her body against his. "My neighbor's very open-minded."

"I've heard that." Experimentally she caught his lower lip between her teeth. Remembering how much pleasure it gave her to feel his lips cruise over her face and throat, she began a lazy journey over his. "Fortunately, my neighbor's very understanding of passions. I doubt anything would shock him. Even if I told him I often fantasize about him at night, when I'm alone, in bed."

It was impossible, but he felt himself stir against her. The deep, dark wanting began to smolder again. "Really? What kind of fantasies?"

"Of having him come to me." Her breath began to quicken as his mouth roamed over her shoulder. "Come to my bed like an incubus in the night, when a storm cracks the air. I can see his eyes, cobalt blue in a flash of lightning, and I know that he wants me the way no one else ever has, or ever will."

Knowing very well that if he didn't take some kind of action now they'd remain sprawled on the stairs, he gathered her up. "I can't give you the lightning."

She smiled as he carried her up. "You already have."

Later, hours later, they knelt on the tumbled bed, feasting on pizza by candlelight. Ana had lost track of time and had no need to know if it was midnight or approaching dawn. They had loved and talked and laughed and loved again. No night in her life had been more perfect. What did time matter here?

"Guinevere was no heroine." Ana licked sauce from her fingers. They had discussed epic poetry, modern animation, ancient legends and folklore and classic horror. She wasn't sure how they had wound their way back to Arthur and Camelot, but on the subject of Arthur's queen, Ana stood firm. "And she certainly wasn't a tragic figure."

"I'd think a woman, especially one with your compassion, would have more sympathy with her situation." Boone debated having a last piece from the cardboard box they'd plopped in the center of the bed.

"Why?" Ana picked it up herself and began to feed it to him. "She betrayed her husband, helped bring down a kingdom, all because she was weak-willed and self-indulgent."

"She was in love."

"Love doesn't excuse all actions." Amused, she tilted her head and studied him in the flickering light. He looked gloriously masculine in nothing but a pair of gym shorts, his hair tousled, his face shadowed with stubble. "Isn't that just like a man? Finding excuses for a woman's infidelity just because it's written about in romantic terms."

He didn't think it was precisely an insult, but it made him squirm a little. "I just don't think she had control of the situation."

"Of course she did. She had a choice, and she chose poorly, just as Lancelot did. All that flowery business about gallantry and chivalry and heroism and loyalty, and the two of them justified betraying a man who loved them both because they couldn't control themselves?" She tossed her hair back. "That's bull."

He laughed before he sipped his wine. "You amaze me. Here I've been thinking you were a romantic. A woman who picks flowers by moonlight, who collects statues of fairies and wizards, and she condemns poor Guinevere because she loved unwisely."

She fired up. "Poor Guinevere—"

"Hold on." He was chuckling, enjoying himself immensely. It didn't occur to either of them that they were debating about people most considered fictional. "Let's not forget some of the other players. Merlin was supposed to be watching over the whole business. Why didn't he do anything about it?"

Fastidiously she brushed crumbs from her bare legs. "It's not a sorcerer's place to interfere with destiny."

"Come on, we're talking about the champ here. One little spell and he could've fixed it up."

"And altered countless lives," she pointed out, gesturing with her glass. "Skewed history. No, he couldn't do it, not even for Arthur. People—witches, kings, mortals—are responsible for their own fates."

"He didn't have any problem abetting adultery by disguising Uther as the duke of Cornwall and taking Tintagel so that Igraine conceived Arthur in the first place."

"Because that was destiny," she said patiently, as she might have to Jessie. "That was the purpose. For all Merlin's power, all his greatness, his single most vital act was bringing Arthur into being."

"Sounds like splitting hairs to me." He swallowed the last bite of pizza. "One spell's okay, but another isn't."

"When you're given a gift, it's your responsibility to know how and when to use it, how and when not to. Can you imagine how he suffered, watching someone he loved destroyed? Knowing, even as Arthur was being conceived, how it would end? Magic doesn't divorce you from emotion or pain. It rarely protects the one who owns it."

"I guess not." He'd certainly had witches and wizards suffering in the stories he wrote. It gave them a human element he found appealing. "When I was a kid, I used to daydream about living back then."

"Rescuing fair maidens from fiery dragons?"

"Sure. Going on quests, challenging the Black Knight and beating the hell out of him."

"Naturally."

"Then I grew up and discovered I could have the best of both worlds, living there up here—" he tapped his head with a fingertip "—when I was writing. And having the creature comforts of the twentieth century."

"Like pizza."

"Like pizza," he agreed. "A computer instead of a quill, cotton underwear. Hot running water. Speaking of which..." he said, fingering the hem of the T-shirt he'd given her to wear. He moved on impulse, and had her shrieking out a laugh as he tossed her over his shoulder and climbed out of bed.

"What are you doing?"

"Hot running water," he repeated. "I think it's time I showed you what I can do in the shower."

"You're going to sing?"

"Maybe later." In the bathroom, he opened the glass shower doors and turned on the taps. "Hope you like it hot."

"Well, I—" She was still over his shoulder when he stepped inside. With the crisscrossing sprays raining, she was immediately drenched, front and back. "Boone." She sputtered. "You're drowning me."

"Sorry." He shifted, reaching for the soap. "You know, this shower really sold me on the house. It's roomy." He slicked the wet bar of soap up her calf. "Pretty great having the twin shower heads."

Despite the heat of the water, Ana shivered when he soaped lazy circles at the back of her knee. "It's a little difficult for me to appreciate it from this position." Then she shoved her dripping hair out of her face and noticed that the floor was mirrored tiles. "Oh, my."

He grinned, and moved slowly up to her thigh. "Check out the ceiling."

She did, tilting her head and staring at their reflections. "Ah, doesn't it just steam up?"

"Treated glass. Does get a little foggy if you're in here long enough." And he intended to be in there just long enough. He began sliding her down his body, inch by dangerous inch. "But that only adds to the atmosphere." Gently he pressed her against the back wall, cupping her breasts through the cling-ing shirt. "Want to hear one of my fantasies?"

"It— Oh." He was rubbing a thumb over an aching nipple. "Seems only fair."

"Better idea." He brushed his lips over hers, teasing, re-treating, until her breath began to hitch. "Why don't I show you? First we get rid of this." He dragged the wet shirt over her head, tossing it aside. It landed with a plop that had another tremor jerking through her system. "And I start here." Toying with her mouth, he rubbed the slick soap over her shoulders. "And I don't stop until I get to your toes."

She had a feeling showers were going to join staircases in the more erotic depths of her imagination. Gripping his hips for balance, she arched back as he circled wet, soapy hands over her breasts.

Steam. It was all around her, it was inside her. The thick, moist air made it all but impossible to breathe. A tropical storm, water pounding, heat rising. The creamy soap had flesh sliding gloriously against flesh when their bodies moved to-gether. Her hands foamed with it as she ran them over his back, over his chest. Even as his mouth raced to possess, his muscles quivered at her touch, and her laugh was low and softly triumphant.

If she burned, so did he. That was power clashing against power. There was no longer any doubt that she could give back the wild, wanton, wicked pleasure he brought to her. A plea-sure so much sweeter, so much richer, because it grew from love, as well as passion.

She wanted to show him. She would show him.

Her hands slid down him, over strong shoulders, the hard chest. She murmured in approval as she traced fingertips over his rib cage and down to the flat plane of his stomach.

He shook his head to try to clear it. He had expected to se-duce her here, yet he was being seduced. The delicate hands flowing over his slick skin were shooting arrows of painful need through his system.

"Wait." His hands groped for hers, held them firm. He knew that if she touched him now he would never be able to hold back. "Let me..."

"No." With the new knowledge brimming inside, her mouth seared over his and conquered. "Let me."

Her fingers closed around him, sliding, stroking, squeezing lightly, while his breath sounded harshly in her ear. A fresh flash of triumph exploded inside her as she felt his quick, helpless shudder. Then greed, to have him, all of him, deep inside her.

"Ana." He felt the last wisps of reality fading. "Ana, I can't—"

"You want me." Delirious with power, she threw her head back. Her eyes were hot with challenge. "Then take me. Now."

She looked like a goddess newly risen from the sea. Wet cables of hair slicked like dark gold over her shoulder. Her skin glowed, shimmered with water. In her eyes were secrets, dark mysteries no man would ever unlock.

She was glorious. She was magnificent. And she was his.

"Hold on to me." Bracing her against the wall, he lifted her hips with his hands. "Hold on to me."

She locked her arms around him, keeping her eyes open. He took her where they stood, plunging into her as the water showered over them. Gasping out his name, she let her head fall back. Through the rising mists, she saw their reflections— a wonderful tangle of limbs that made it impossible to see where he left off and she began.

On a moan of inexpressible pleasure, she dropped her head to his shoulder. She was lost. Lost. Thank God for it. "I love you." She had no idea if the words were in her head or had come through her lips. But she said them again and again until her body convulsed.

He emptied himself into her, then could only stand weakly against the wall as the strength ran out of him. His heart was still roaring in his ears as he closed his hands over her shoulders.

"Tell me now."

Her lips were curved, but she swayed a little and stared up at him through clouded eyes. "Tell you what?"

His fingers tightened, making her eyes clear. "That you love me. Tell me now."

"I... Don't you think we should dry off? We've been in the water quite a while."

With an impatient jerk, he switched off the taps. "I want to look at you when you say it, and have at least some of my wits about me. We're going to stay right here until I hear you say it again."

She hesitated. He could have no idea that he was forcing her to take the next step toward having him—or losing him. Destiny, she thought, and choices. It was time she made hers. "I love you. I wouldn't be here with you, couldn't be here, if I didn't."

His eyes were very dark, very intense. Slowly his grip lightened, his face relaxed. "I feel as though I've waited years to hear you say that."

She brushed the wet hair away from his brow. "You only had to ask."

He caught her hands in his. "You don't." Because she was beginning to shiver, he drew her out of the stall to wrap her in a towel. He caught it close around her, then wrapped his arms tight for more warmth. "Anastasia." Tenderness swelled inside him as he touched his lips to her hair, her cheek, her mouth. "You don't have to ask. I love you. You brought something I thought I'd never have again, never want again, back into my life."

On a broken sigh, she pressed her face to his chest. This was real, she thought. This was hers. She would find a way to keep it. "You're everything I've ever wanted. Don't stop loving me, Boone. Don't stop."

"I couldn't." He drew her away. "Don't cry."

"I don't." The tears shimmered, but didn't spill over. "I don't cry."

*Anastasia sheds no tears, but she'll shed them for you.*

Sebastian's words rang uncomfortably in Boone's head. Resolutely he blocked them out. It was ridiculous. He'd do nothing to hurt her. He opened his mouth, then closed it again. A steamy bathroom was no place for the proposal he wanted to make. And there were things he needed to tell her first.

"Let's get you another shirt. We need to talk."

She was much too happy to pay any heed to the curl of uneasiness. She laughed when he took her back to the bedroom and tugged another of his shirts over her head. Dreamily she poured two more glasses of wine while he pulled on a pair of jeans.

"Will you come with me?" He held out a hand, and she took it willingly.

"Where are we going?"

"I want to show you something." He took her down the shadowy hall, into his office. Delighted, Ana turned a circle.

"This is where you work."

There were wide, uncurtained windows framed with curving cherrywood. A couple of worn, faded scatter rugs had been tossed on the hardwood floor. Starshine sprinkled through the twin skylights. An industrious-looking computer, reams of paper and shelves of books announced that this was a workplace. But he'd added charm with framed illustrations, a collection of dragons and knights that intrigued her. The winged fairy he'd bought from Morgana had a prominent place on a high, carved stool.

"You need some plants," she decided instantly, thinking of the narcissus and daffodils she was forcing in her greenhouse. "I imagine you spend hours in this room every day." She glanced down at the empty ashtray beside his machine.

Following her gaze, he frowned. Odd, he thought, he hadn't

had a cigarette in days—had forgotten about them completely. He'd have to congratulate himself later.

"Sometimes I watch out the window when you're in your garden. It makes it difficult to concentrate."

She laughed and sat on the corner of his desk. "We'll get you some shades."

"Not a chance." He smiled, but his hands went nervously to his pockets. "Ana, I need to tell you about Alice."

"Boone." Compassion had her rising again to reach out. "I understand. I know it's painful. There's no need to explain anything to me."

"There is for me." With her hand in his, he turned to gesture at a sketch on the wall. A lovely young girl was kneeling by a stream, dipping a golden pail into the silver water. "She drew that, before Jessie was born. Gave it to me for our first anniversary."

"It's beautiful. She was very talented."

"Yeah. Very talented, very special." He sipped his wine in an unconscious toast to a lost love. "I knew her most of my life. Pretty Alice Reeder."

He needed to talk, Ana thought. She would listen. "You were high school sweethearts?"

"No." He laughed at that. "Not even close. Alice was a cheerleader, student body president, all-around nice girl who always made the honor roll. We ran in different crowds, and she was a couple of years behind me. I was going through my obligatory rebellious period and kind of hulked around school, looking tough."

She smiled, touched his cheek where the stubble was rough. "I'd like to have seen that."

"I snuck cigarettes in the bathroom, and Alice painted scenery for school plays. We knew each other, but that was about it. I went off to college, ended up in New York. It seemed necessary, since I was going to write, that I get myself a loft and starve a little."

She slipped an arm around him, instinctively offering comfort, waiting while he gathered his thoughts.

"One morning I was in the bakery around the corner from where I was living, and I looked up from the crullers and there she was, buying coffee and a croissant. We started talking. You know...what are you doing here, the old neighborhood, what had happened to whom. That kind of thing. It was comforting, and exciting. Here we were, two small-town kids taking on big bad New York."

And fate had tossed them together, Ana thought, in a city of millions.

"She was in art school," Boone continued, "sharing an apartment only a couple of blocks away with some other girls. I walked her to the subway. We just sort of drifted together, sitting in the park, comparing sketches, talking for hours. Alice was so full of life, energy, ideas. We didn't fall in love so much as we slid into it." His eyes softened as he studied the sketch. "Very slowly, very sweetly. We got married just before I sold my first book. She was still in college."

He had to stop again as the memories swam back in force. Instinctively his hand closed over Ana's. She opened herself, giving what strength and support she could.

"Anyway, everything seemed so perfect. We were young, happy, in love. She'd already been commissioned to do a painting. We found out she was pregnant. So we decided to move back home, raise the child in a nice suburban atmosphere close to family. Then Jessie came, and it seemed as though nothing could ever go wrong. Except that Alice never seemed to really get her energy back after the birth. Everyone said it was natural, she was bound to be tired with a new baby and her work. She lost weight. I used to joke that she was going to fade away." He closed his eyes for a minute. "That's just what she did. She faded away. When it had gone on long enough for us to worry, she had tests, but there was a mess-up in the lab and they didn't detect it soon enough. By the time we found out she had cancer, it was too late to stop it."

"Oh, Boone. I'm sorry. I'm so sorry."

"She suffered. That was the worst. She suffered and there was nothing I could do. I watched her die, degree by degree. And I thought I would die, too. But there was Jessie. Alice was only twenty-five when I buried her. Jessie had just turned two." He took a long breath before he turned to Ana. "I loved Alice. I always will."

"I know. When someone touches your life that way, you never lose it."

"When I lost her, I stopped believing in happy-ever-after, except in books. I didn't want to fall in love again, risk that kind of pain—for myself or for Jessie. But I have fallen in love again. What I feel for you is so strong, it makes me believe again. It's not the same as I felt before. It's not less. It's just...us."

She touched his cheek. She thought she understood. "Boone, did you think I would ask you to forget her? That I could resent or be jealous of what you had with her? It only makes me love you more. She made you happy. She gave you Jessie. I only wish I had known her."

Impossibly moved, he lowered his brow to hers. "Marry me, Ana."

# Chapter 11

She froze. The hands that had reached up to bring him close stopped in midair. Her breath seemed to stall in her lungs. Even as her heart leapt with hope, her mind warned her to wait.

Very slowly, she eased out of his arms. "Boone, I think—"

"Don't tell me I'm rushing things." He was amazingly calm now that he'd taken the step—the step he realized he'd already taken in his head weeks before. "I don't care if I'm moving too fast. I need you in my life, Ana."

"I'm already in your life." She smiled, trying to keep it light. "I told you that."

"It was hard enough when I only wanted you, harder still when I started to care. But it's impossible now that I'm in love with you. I don't want to live next door to you." He took a firm grip on her shoulders to keep her still. "I don't want to have to send my child away so I can spend the night with you. You said you loved me."

"I do." She gave in to desperate need and pressed herself against him. "You know I do, more than I thought I could. More than I wanted to. But marriage is—"

"Right." He stroked a hand down her damp hair. "Right for us. Ana, I told you once I don't take intimacy lightly, and I wasn't just talking about sex." He drew her back, wanting to see her face, wanting her to see his. "I'm talking about what's inside me every time I look at you. Before I met you, I was content to keep my life the way it was. But that's no good anymore. I'm not going to keep running through the hedges to be with you. I want you with me, with us."

"Boone, if it could be so simple." She turned away, struggling to find the right answer.

"It can be." He fought against a quick flutter of panic. "When I walked in this morning and saw you in bed, with your arms around Jessie—I can't tell you what went through me at that moment. I realized that was what I wanted. For you to be there. Just to be there. To know I could share her with you, because you'd love her. That there could be other children. A future."

She shut her eyes, because the image was so sweet, so perfect. And she was denying them both a chance to make the image reality, because she was afraid. "If I said yes now, before you understand me, before you know me, it wouldn't be fair."

"I do know you." He swept her around again. "I know you have passion, and compassion, that you're loyal and generous and openhearted. That you have strong feelings for family, that you like romantic music and apple wine. I know the way your laugh sounds, the way you smell. And I know that I could make you happy, if you'd let me."

"You do make me happy. It's because I don't want to do any less for you that I don't know what to do." She broke away to walk off the tension. "I didn't know this was going to happen so quickly, before I was sure. I swear, if I'd known you were thinking of marriage…"

To be his wife, she thought. Bound to him by handfast. She could think of nothing more precious than that kind of belonging.

She had to tell him, so that he would have the choice of accepting or backing away. "You've been much more honest with me than I with you."

"About?"

"About what you are." Her eyes closed on a sigh. "I'm a coward. So easily devastated by bad feelings, afraid, pathetically afraid, of pain—physical and emotional. So hatefully vulnerable to what others can be indifferent to."

"I don't know what you're talking about, Ana."

"No, you don't." She pressed her lips together. "Can you understand that there are some who are more sensitive than others to strong feelings? Some who have to develop a defense against absorbing too much of the swirl of emotion that goes on around them? Who have to, Boone, because they couldn't survive otherwise?"

He pushed back his impatience and tried to smile. "Are you getting mystical on me?"

She laughed, pressing a hand to her eyes. "You don't know the half of it. I need to explain, and don't know how. If I could—" She started to turn back, determined to tell him everything, and the sketchpad on his desk slid off at the movement. Automatically she bent to pick it up.

Perhaps it was fate that it had fallen faceup, showing a recently completed sketch. An excellent one, Ana thought on a long breath as she studied it. The fierce and wicked lines of the black-caped witch glared up at her. Evil, she thought. He had captured evil perfectly.

"Don't worry about that." He started to take it from her, but she shook her head.

"Is this for your story?"

"*The Silver Castle,* yes. Let's not change the subject."

"Not as much as you think," she murmured. "Indulge me a minute," she said with a careful smile. "Tell me about the sketch."

"Damn it, Ana."

"Please."

Frustrated, he dragged a hand through his hair. "It's just what it looks like. The evil witch who put the spell on the princess and the castle. I had to figure there was a spell that kept anyone from getting in or out."

"So you chose a witch."

"I know it's obvious. But the story seemed to call for it. The vindictive, jealous witch, furious with the princess's goodness and beauty, casts the spell, so the princess stays trapped inside, cut off from love and life and happiness. Then, when true love conquers, the spell's broken and the witch is vanquished. And they live happily ever after."

"I suppose witches are, to you, evil and calculating." Calculating, she remembered. It was one of the words Robert had tossed at her. That, and much, much worse.

"Goes with the territory. Power corrupts, right?"

She set the sketch aside. "There are those who think it." It was only a drawing, she told herself. Only part of a story he'd created. Yet it served to remind her how large a span they needed to cross. "Boone, I'll ask you for something tonight."

"I guess you could ask me for anything tonight."

"Time," she said. "And faith. I love you, Boone, and there's no one else I'd want to spend my life with. But I need time, and so do you. A week," she said before he could protest. "Only a week. Until the full moon. Then there are things I'll tell you. After I do, I hope you'll ask me again to be your wife. If you do, if you can, then I'll say yes."

"Say yes now." He caught her close, capturing her mouth, hoping he could persuade her by his will alone. "What difference will a week make?"

"All," she whispered, clinging tight. "Or none."

He didn't care to wait. It made him nervous and impatient that the days seemed to crawl by. One, then two, finally three.

To comfort himself, he thought about the turn his life would take once the interminable week was over.

No more nights alone. Soon, when he returned restlessly in the dark, she would be there. The house would be full of her, her scent, the fragrances of her herbs and oils. On those long, quiet evenings, they could sit together on the deck and talk about the day, about tomorrows.

Or perhaps she would want them to move into her house. It wouldn't matter. They could walk through her gardens, under her arbors, and she could try to teach him the names of all of her flowers.

They could take a trip to Ireland, and she could show him all the important places of her childhood. There would be stories she could tell him, like the one about the witch and the frog, and he could write about them.

One day there would be more children, and he would see her holding their baby the way she had held Morgana and Nash's.

More children. That thought brought him up short and had him staring at the framed picture of Jessie smiling out at him from his desktop.

His baby. Only his, and his only, for so long now. He did want more children. He'd never realized until now how much he wanted more. How much he enjoyed being a father. It was simply something he was, something he did.

Now as his mind began to play with the idea, he could see himself soothing an infant in the night as he had once soothed Jessie. Holding out his arms as a toddler took those first shaky steps. Tossing a ball in the yard, holding on to the back of an unsteady bike.

A son. Wouldn't it be incredible to have a son? Or another daughter. Brothers and sisters for Jessie. She'd love that, he thought, and found himself grinning like an idiot. He'd love it.

Of course, he hadn't even asked Ana how she felt about adding to the family. That was certainly something they'd have to discuss. Maybe it would be rushing her again to bring it up now.

Then he remembered how she'd looked with her arm cuddling Jessie in his bed. The way her face had glowed when she held two tiny infants up so that his daughter could see and touch.

No, he decided. He knew her. She would be as anxious as he to turn their love into life.

By the end of the week, he thought, they would start making plans for their future together.


For Ana, the days passed much too quickly. She spent hours going over the right way to tell Boone everything. Then she would change her mind and struggle to think of another way.

There was the brash way.

She imagined herself sitting him down in her kitchen with a pot of tea between them. "Boone," she would say, "I'm a witch. If that doesn't bother you, we can start planning the wedding."

There was the subtle way.

They would sit out on her patio, near the arbor of morning glories. While they sipped wine and watched the sunset, they would talk about their childhoods.

"Growing up in Ireland is a little different than growing up in Indiana, I suppose," she would tell him. "But the Irish usually take having witches in the neighborhood pretty much for granted." Then she'd smile. "More wine, love?"

Or the intellectual way.

"I'm sure you'd agree most legends have some basis in fact." This conversation would take place on the beach, with the sound of the surf and the cry of gulls. "Your books show a great depth of understanding and respect for what most consider myth or folklore. Being a witch myself, I appreciate your positive slant on fairies and magic. Particularly the way you handled the enchantress in *A Third Wish for Miranda*."

Ana only wished she had enough humor left to laugh at each

pitiful scenario. She was certainly going to have to think of something, now that she had less than twenty-four hours to go.

Boone had already been more patient than she had a right to ask. There was no excuse for keeping him waiting any longer.

At least she would have some moral support this evening. Morgana and Sebastian and their spouses were on their way over for the monthly Friday-night cookout. If that didn't buck her up for her confrontation with Boone the following day, nothing would. As she stepped onto the patio, she fingered the diamond-clear zircon she wore around her neck.

Obviously Jessie had been keeping an eagle eye out, for she zipped through the hedge, with Daisy yipping behind her. To show his indifference to the pup, Quigley sat down and began to wash his hindquarters.

"We're coming to your house for a cookout," Jessie announced. "The babies are coming, too, and maybe I can hold one. If I'm really, really careful."

"I think that could be arranged." Automatically Ana scanned the neighboring yard for signs of Boone. "How was school today, sunshine?"

"It was pretty neat. I can write my name, and Daddy's and yours. Yours is easiest. I can write Daisy's, but I don't know how to spell Quigley's, so I just wrote *cat*. Then I had my whole family, just like the teacher told us." She stopped, scuffed her shoes, and for the first time since Ana had known her, looked shy. "Was it okay if I said you were my family?"

"It's more than okay." Crouching down, Ana gave Jessie a huge hug. Oh, yes, she thought, squeezing her eyes tight. This is what I want, what I need. I could be a wife to him, a mother to the child. Please, please, let me find the way to have it all. "I love you, Jessie."

"You won't go away, will you?"

Because they were close, because she couldn't prevent it, Ana touched the child's heart and understood that Jessie was thinking of her mother. "No, baby." She drew back, choosing her words with care. "I would never want to go away. But if I had to, if I couldn't help it, I'd still be close."

"How can you go away and still be close?"

"Because I'd keep you in my heart. Here." Ana took the thin braided gold chain with the square of zircon and slipped it over Jessie's neck.

"Ooh! It shines!"

"It's very special. When you feel lonely or sad, you hold on to this and think of me. I'll know, and I'll send you happiness."

Dazzled, Jessie turned the crystal, and it exploded with light and color. "Is it magic?"

"Yes."

Jessie accepted the answer with a child's faith. "I want to show Daddy." She started to dash off, then remembered her manners. "Thank you."

"You're welcome. Is— Ah, is Boone inside?"

"Uh-uh, he's on the roof."

"The roof?"

"'Cause next month is Christmas, and he's starting to put up the lights so we know how many we have to buy. The whole house is going to be lit up. Daddy says this is going to be the most special Christmas ever."

"I hope so." Ana shielded her eyes with the flat of her hand and looked up. There he was, sitting on top of the house, looking back at her. Her heart gave that quick, improbable leap it always did when she saw him. Despite nerves, she smiled, lifting one hand in a wave while the other rested on Jessie's shoulder.

It would be all right, she told herself. It had to be.

Boone ignored the tangle of Christmas lights beside him and pleased himself by watching them until Jessie raced back across the yard and Ana went inside.

It would be all right, he told himself. It had to be.

Sebastian plucked a fat black olive from a tray and popped it into his mouth. "When do we eat?"

"You already are," Mel pointed out.

"I mean real food." He winked down at Jessie. "Hot dogs."

"Herbed chicken," Ana corrected, turning a sizzling thigh on the grill.

They were spread over the patio, with Jessie sitting in a wrought-iron chair carefully cradling a cooing Allysia in her lap. Boone and Nash were deep in a discussion on infant care. Morgana had Donovan at her breast, comfortably nursing, while she listened to Mel relate the happy ending of the runaway she and Sebastian had tracked down.

"Kid was miserable," she was saying. "Sorry as hell he'd taken off, scared to go back. When we found him—cold, broke and hungry—and he realized his parents were scared instead of angry, he couldn't wait to get home. I think he's grounded till he's thirty, but he doesn't seem to care." She waited until Morgana had burped her son. Her hands had been itching to touch. "Want me to put him back down for you?"

"Thanks." Morgana watched Mel's face as she lifted the baby. "Thinking about having one of your own. Or two?"

"Actually." Mel caught the special scent of baby and felt her knees go weak. "I think I might…" She cast a quick look over her shoulder and saw her husband was busy teasing Jessie. "I'm not sure yet, but I think I may have already started."

"Oh, Mel, that's—"

"Shh." She leaned down, using the baby for cover. "I don't want him to know, or even suspect, or I'd never be able to stop him from looking for himself. I want to be able to tell him about this." She grinned. "It'll knock his socks off."

Gently Mel laid the child in his side of the double carriage.

"Allysia's sleeping too," Jessie pointed out, tracing a finger over the baby's cheek.

"Want to put her down with her brother?" Sebastian leaned over to help Jessie stand with the baby. "That's the way." He kept his hands under hers as she laid Allysia down. "You'll be an excellent mother one day."

"Maybe I can have twins, too." She turned when Daisy began to bark. "Hush," she whispered. "You'll wake the babies."

But Daisy was lost in the thrill of the chase. Heading for open ground, Quigley shot through the hedges into the next yard, yowling. Delighted with the game, Daisy dashed after him.

"I'll get him, Daddy." Making as much racket as the animals, Jessie raced after them.

"I don't think obedience school's the answer," Boone commented, tipping back a beer. "I'm thinking along the lines of a mental institution."

Panting a bit, Jessie followed the sounds of barks and hisses, across the yard, over the deck, around the side of the house. When she caught up with Daisy, she put her hands on her hips and scolded.

"You have to be friends. Ana won't like it if you keep teasing Quigley."

Daisy simply thumped her tail on the ground and barked again. Halfway up the ladder Boone had used to climb to the roof, Quigley hissed and spat.

"He doesn't like it, Daisy." On a sigh, she squatted down to pet the dog. "He doesn't know you're just playing and wouldn't really hurt him ever. You made him scared." She looked up the ladder. "Come on, kitty. It's okay. You can come down now."

On a feline growl, Quigley narrowed his eyes, then bounded up the ladder when Daisy responded with another flurry of barks.

"Oh, Daisy, look what you've done." Jessie hesitated at the foot of the ladder. Her father had been very specific about her not going near it. But he hadn't known that Quigley would get so scared. And maybe he'd fall off the roof and get killed. She stepped back, thinking she would go tell her father to come. Then she heard Quigley meow.

Daisy was her responsibility, she remembered. She was supposed to feed him and watch him so he didn't get in trouble. If Quigley got hurt, it would be all her fault.

"I'm coming, kitty. Don't be scared." With her lower lip caught between her teeth, she started up the rungs. She'd seen her father go right on up, and it hadn't looked hard at all. Just like climbing the jungle gyms at school, or up to the top of the big sliding board. "Kitty, kitty," she chanted, climbing higher and giggling when Quigley stuck his head over the roof. "You silly cat, Daisy was only playing. I'll take you down, don't worry."

She was nearly to the top when her sneakered foot missed the next rung.

"Smells wonderful," Boone murmured, but he was sniffing at Ana's neck, not the chicken she'd piled on a platter. "Good enough to eat."

Nash gave him a nudge as he reached for a plate. "If you're going to kiss her, move aside. The rest of us want dinner."

"Fine." Slipping his arms around a flustered Ana, he closed his mouth over hers in a long, lingering kiss. "Time's almost up," he said against her mouth. "You could put me out of my misery now, and—"

The words shut off when he heard Jessie's scream. With his heart in his throat, he raced across the yard, shouting for her. He tore through the hedges, pounded across the grass.

"Oh, God! Oh, my God!"

Every ounce of blood seemed to drain out of him when he saw her crumpled on the ground, her arm bent at an impossible angle, her face as white as linen.

"Baby!" Panicked, he fell beside her. She was too still—even his fevered mind registered that one terrifying fact. And when he reached down to pick her up, there was blood, her blood, on his hands.

"Don't move her!" Ana snapped out the order as she dropped beside them. She was breathing hard, fighting back terror, but her hands clasped firmly over his wrists. "You don't know how or where she's hurt. You can do more harm by moving her."

"She's bleeding." He cupped his hands on his daughter's face. "Jessie. Come on, Jessie." With a trembling finger, he searched for a pulse at her throat. "Don't do this. Dear God, don't do this. We need an ambulance."

"I'll call," Mel said from behind them.

Ana only shook her head. "Boone." The calm settled over her as she understood what she had to do. "Boone, listen to me." She took his shoulders, holding tight when he tried to shake her off. "You have to move back. Let me look at her. Let me help her."

"She's not breathing." He could only stare down at his little girl. "I don't think she's breathing. Her arm. She's broken her arm."

It was more than that. Even without a closer link, Ana knew it was much more than that. And there was no time for an ambulance. "I can help her, but you have to move back."

"She needs a doctor. For God's sake, someone call an ambulance."

"Sebastian," Ana said quietly. Her cousin stepped forward and took Boone's arms.

"Let go of me!" Boone started to swing and found himself pinned by both Sebastian and Nash. "What the hell's wrong with you? We have to get her to a hospital!"

"Let Ana do what she can," Nash said, fighting to hold his friend and his own panic back. "You have to trust her, for Jessie's sake."

"Ana." Pale and shaken, Morgana passed one of her babies into Mel's waiting arms. "It may be too late. You know what could happen to you if—"

"I have to try."

Very gently, oh, so gently, she placed her hands on either side of Jessie's head. She braced, waiting until her own breathing was slow and deep. It was hard, very hard, to block out

Boone's violent and terrified emotions, but she focused on the child, only the child. And opened herself.

Pain. Hot, burning spears of it, radiating through her head. Too much pain for such a small child. Ana drew it out, drew it in, let her own system absorb it. When agony threatened to smother the serenity needed for such deep and delicate work, she waited for it to roll past. Then moved on.

So much damage, she thought as her hands trailed lightly down. Such a long way to fall. A perfect image clicked in her mind. The ground rushing up, the helpless fear, the sudden, numbing jolt of impact.

Her fingers passed over a deep gash in Jessie's shoulder. The mirror image sliced through her own, throbbed, seeped blood. Then both slowly faded.

"My God." Boone stopped struggling. His body was too numb. "What is she doing? How?"

"She needs quiet," Sebastian muttered. Stepping back from Boone, he took Morgana's hand. There was nothing they could do but wait.

The injuries inside were severe. Sweat began to bloom on Ana's skin as she examined, absorbed, mended. She was chanting as she worked, knowing she needed to deepen the trance to save the child, and herself.

Oh, but the pain! It ripped through her like fire, making her shudder. Her breath hitched as she fought the need to pull back. Blindly she clutched a hand over the zircon Jessie still wore and placed the other over the child's quiet heart.

When she threw her head back, her eyes were the color of storm clouds, and as blank as glass.

The light was bright, blindingly bright. She could barely see the child up ahead. She called, shouted, wanting to hurry, knowing that one misstep now would end it for both of them.

She stared into the light and felt Jessie slipping further away.

"This gift is mine to use or scorn." Both pain and power shimmered in her voice. "This choice was mine from the day

I was born. What harms the child bring into me. As I will, so mote it be."

She cried out then, from the tearing price to be paid for cheating death. She felt her own life ebb, teetering, teetering toward the searing light as Jessie's heart began to beat tremulously under her hand.

She fought back, for both of them, calling on every ounce of her strength, every vestige of her power.

Boone saw his daughter stir, watched her lashes flutter as Ana swayed back.

"Jess—Jessie?" He leaped forward to scoop her into his arms. "Baby, are you all right?"

"Daddy?" Her blank, unfocused eyes began to clear. "Did I fall down?"

"Yeah." Weak with relief and gratitude, he buried his face against her throat and rocked her. "Yeah."

"Don't cry, Daddy." She patted his back. "I'm okay."

"Let's see." He took a shaky breath before he ran his hands over her. There was no blood, he discovered. No blood, no bruise, not even the smallest scratch. He held her close again, staring at Ana as Sebastian helped her to her feet. "Do you hurt anywhere, Jessie?"

"Uh-uh." She yawned and nestled her head on his shoulder. "I was going to Mommy. She looked so pretty in all the light. But she looked sad, like she was going to cry, when she saw me coming. Then Ana was there, and she took my hand. Mommy looked happy when she waved goodbye to us. I'm sleepy, Daddy."

His own heart was throbbing in his throat, thickening his voice. "Okay, baby."

"Why don't you let me take her up?" When Boone hesitated, Nash lowered his voice. "She's fine. Ana's not." He took the already dozing child. "Don't let common sense get in the way, pal," he added as he took Jessie inside.

"I want to know what happened here." Afraid he'd babble,

Boone forced himself to speak slowly. "I want to know exactly what happened."

"All right." Ana glanced around at her family. "If you'd leave us alone for just a minute, I'd like to..." She trailed off as the world went gray. Swearing, Boone caught her as she fell, then hoisted her into his arms.

"What the hell is going on?" he demanded. "What did she do to Jessie?" He looked down, alarmed by the translucent pallor of Ana's cheeks. "What did she do to herself?"

"She saved your daughter's life," Sebastian said. "And risked her own."

"Be quiet, Sebastian," Morgana murmured. "He's been through enough."

"He?"

"Yes." She laid a restraining hand on her cousin's arm. "Boone, Ana needs rest, a great deal of rest and quiet. If you'd prefer, you can bring her home. One of us will stay and take care of her."

"She'll stay here." He turned and carried her inside.

She was drifting in and out, in and out of worlds without color. There was no pain now, no feeling at all. She was as insubstantial as a mist. Once or twice she heard Sebastian or Morgana slip inside her deeply sleeping mind to offer reassurance. Others joined them, her parents, her aunts and uncles, and more.

After a long, long journey, she felt herself coming back. Tints and hues seeped back into the colorless world. Sensations began to prickle along her skin. She sighed once—it was the first sound she had made in more than twenty-four hours—then opened her eyes.

Boone watched her come back. He rose automatically from the chair to bring her the medication Morgana had left with him.

"Here." He supported her, holding the cup to her lips. "You're supposed to drink this."

She obeyed, recognizing the scent and the taste. "Jessie?"

"She's fine. Nash and Morgana picked her up this afternoon. She's staying with them tonight."

With a nod, she drank again. "How long have I been asleep?"

"Asleep?" He gave a half laugh at her prosaic term for the comalike state she'd been in. "You've been out for twenty-six hours." He glanced at his watch. "And thirty minutes."

The longest journey she'd ever taken, Ana realized. "I need to call my family and tell them I'm well."

"I'll do it. Are you hungry?"

"No." She tried not to be hurt by his polite, distant tone of voice. "This is all I need for now."

"Then I'll be back in a minute."

When he left her alone, she covered her face with her hands. Her own fault, she berated herself. She hadn't prepared him, had dragged her feet, and fate had taken a hand. On a tired sigh, she got out of bed and began to dress.

"What the hell are you doing?" Boone demanded when he walked in again. "You're supposed to rest."

"I've rested enough." Ana stared down at her hands as she meticulously buttoned her blouse. "And I'd just as soon be on my feet when we talk about this."

His nerves jittered, but he only nodded. "Have it your way."

"Can we go outside? I could use some air."

"Fine." He took her arm and led her downstairs and out on the deck. Once she was seated, he took out a cigarette, struck a match. He'd hardly closed his eyes since he'd carried Ana upstairs, and he'd been subsisting on tobacco and coffee. "If you're feeling up to it, I'd appreciate an explanation."

"I'm going to try to give you one. I'm sorry I didn't tell you before." Ana linked her hands tight in her lap. "I wanted to, but I could never find the right way."

"Straight out," he said as he dragged deeply on smoke.

"I come from a very old bloodline—on both sides. A different culture, if you like. Do you know what wicca is?"

Something cold brushed his skin, but it was only the night air. "Witchcraft."

"Actually, its true meaning is wise. But witch will do." She looked up, and her clear gray eyes met his tired, shadowed ones. "I'm a hereditary witch, born with empathic powers that enable me to link emotionally, and physically, with others. My gift is one of healing."

Boone took another long drag on his cigarette. "You're going to sit there, look me in the face and tell me you're a witch."

"Yes."

Furious, he flung the cigarette away. "What kind of a game is this, Ana? Don't you think after what happened here last night I deserve a reasonable explanation?"

"I think you deserve the truth. You may not think it reasonable." She held up a hand before he could speak. "Tell me how you would explain what happened."

He opened his mouth, closed it again. He'd been working on that single problem for more than twenty-four hours without finding a comfortable solution. "I can't. But that doesn't mean I'm going to buy into this."

"All right." She rose, laid a hand on his chest. "You're tired. You haven't had much sleep. Your head's pounding and your stomach's in knots."

He lifted a brow derisively. "I don't think you have to be a witch to figure that out."

"No." Before he could back away, she touched a hand to his brow, pressed the other to his stomach. "Better?" she asked after a moment.

He needed to sit down, but he was afraid he wouldn't get up again. She'd touched him, barely touched him. And even the shadow of pain was gone. "What is it? Hypnotism?"

"No. Boone, look at me."

He did, and saw a stranger with tangled blond hair billowing out in the wind. The amber enchantress, he thought numbly. Was it any wonder it had reminded him so much of her?

Ana saw both shock and the beginning of belief on his face. "When you asked me to marry you, I asked you to give me time so that I could find the right way to tell you. I was afraid." Her hands dropped away. "Afraid you'd look at me exactly the way you're looking at me now. As if you don't even know me."

"This is bull. Look, I write this stuff for a living, and I know fiction from fact."

"My skill for magic is very limited." Still, she reached into her pocket, where she always carried a few crystals. With her eyes on Boone's, she held them out in her palm. Slowly they began to glow, the purple of the amethyst deepening, the pink of the rose quartz brightening, the green of the malachite shimmering. Then they rose, an inch, two inches, up, circling, spinning in the air and flashing with light. "Morgana is more talented with such things."

He stared at the tumbling crystals, trying to find a logical reason. "Morgana is a witch, too?"

"She's my cousin," Ana said simply.

"Which makes Sebastian—"

"Sebastian's gift is sight."

He didn't want to believe, but it was impossible to discount what he saw with his own eyes. "Your family," he began. "Those magic tricks of your father's."

"Magic in its purest form." She plucked the crystals out of the air and slipped them back in her pocket. "As I told you, he's very accomplished. As are the rest of them, in their own ways. We're witches. All of us." She reached out to him, but he backed away. "I'm sorry."

"You're sorry?" Rocked to the core, he dragged both hands through his hair. It had to be a dream, a nightmare. But he was standing on his own deck, feeling the wind, hearing the sea. "That's good. That's great. You're sorry. For what, Ana?

For being what you are, or for not finding it important enough to mention?"

"I'm not sorry for being what I am." Pride stiffened her spine. "I am sorry for making excuses to myself not to tell you. And I'm sorry, most sorry of all, that you can't look at me now the way you did only a day ago."

"What do you expect? Am I supposed to just shrug this off, pick up where we were before? To accept the fact that the woman I love is something out of one of my own stories, and think nothing of it?"

"I'm exactly what I was yesterday, and what I'll be tomorrow."

"A witch."

"Yes." She folded her hands at her waist. "A witch, born to the craft. I don't make poisoned apples or lure children into houses of gingerbread."

"That's supposed to relieve my mind?"

"Even I don't have the power to do that. As I told you, all of us are responsible for our own destinies." But she knew he held hers in his hands. "You have your choice to make."

He struggled to get a grip on it, and simply couldn't. "You needed time to tell me. Well, by God, I need time to figure out what to do about it." He started to pace, then stopped dead. "Jessie. Jessie's over at Morgana's."

Ana felt the crack in her heart widen. "Oh, yes, with my cousin the witch." A single tear spilled over and ran down her cheek. "What do you think Morgana's going to do? Cast a spell on her? Lock her in a tower?"

"I don't know what to think. For Lord's sake, I've found myself in the middle of a fairy tale! What am I supposed to think?"

"What you will," Ana said wearily. "I can't change what I am, and I wouldn't. Not even for you. And I won't stand here and have you look at me as if I were a freak."

"I'm not—"

"Shall I tell you what you're feeling?" she asked him as another tear fell. "Betrayed, angry, hurt. And suspicious of what I am, what I can do, or will do."

"My feelings are my own business," he shot back, shaken. "I don't want you to get inside me that way."

"I know. And if I were to step forward right now, reach out to you as a woman, you'd only back away. So I'll save us both. Good night, Boone."

When she walked off the deck, into the shadows, he couldn't bring himself to call her back.

# *Chapter 12*

"I guess you're still a little dazed." Nash lounged against the rail of Boone's deck, enjoying a beer and the cool evening breeze.

"I was never a *little* dazed," Boone told him. "Look, maybe I'm just a narrow-minded sort of guy, Nash, but finding out the lady next door is a witch kind of threw me off stride."

"Especially when you're in love with the lady next door."

"Especially. I wouldn't have believed it. Who would? But I saw what she did with Jessie. Then I started piecing other things together." He laughed shortly. "Sometimes I still wake up in the middle of the night and think I dreamed the whole thing." He walked over to the rail, leaning out toward the sound of water. "It shouldn't be real. She shouldn't be real."

"Why not? Come on, Boone, it's our business to stretch the envelope a little."

"This blows the envelope wide open," Boone pointed out. "And what we do, we do for books, for movies. It's entertainment, Nash, it's not life."

"It's mine now."

Boone blew out a breath. "I guess it is. But didn't you... don't you even question it, or worry about it?"

"Sure, I did. I thought she was pulling my leg until she tossed me up in the air and left me hanging there." The memory made him grin, even as Boone shut his eyes. "Morgana's not the subtle type. Once I realized the whole thing was on the level, it was wild, you know?"

"Wild," Boone repeated.

"Yeah. I mean, I've spent most of my life making up stories about this kind of thing, and here I end up marrying an honest-to-goodness witch. Elfin blood and everything."

"Elfin blood." The term had Boone's head reeling. "It doesn't bother you?"

"Why should it bother me? It makes her who she is, and I love her. I have to admit I'm a little dubious about the kids. I mean, once they get going, I'll be outnumbered."

"The twins." Boone had to force his mouth to close. "Are you telling me those babies are...will be..."

"A pretty sure bet. Come on, Boone, they aren't going to grow warts and start to cackle. They just get a little something extra. Mel's expecting, too. She just found out for sure. She's the most down-to-earth lady I know. And she's handling Sebastian as if she's been around a psychic all her life."

"So you're saying, 'Loosen up, Boone. What's your problem?'"

Nash dropped down on the bench. "I know it's not that easy."

"Let me ask you this.... How far into the relationship were you when Morgana told you about her—what do I call it?—her heritage."

"Pretty much right off the bat. I was researching a script, and I'd heard about her. You know how people are always telling me about weird stuff."

"Yeah."

"Not that I believed it, but I thought she'd make a good interview. And—"

"What about Mel and Sebastian?"

"I can't say for sure, but she met him when a client of hers wanted to hire a psychic." Nash frowned into his beer. "I know what you're getting at, and you've got a point. Maybe she should have been straight with you earlier."

He gave a choked laugh. "Maybe?"

"Okay, she should have been. But you don't know the whole story. Morgana told me that Ana was in love with this guy a few years back. She was only about twenty, I think, and really nuts about him. He was an intern at some hospital, and she got the idea that they could work together, that she could help him. So she told him everything and he dumped her. Hard. Apparently he was pretty vicious about it, and with her empathic thing she's really vulnerable to, well...bad vibes, let's say. It left her pretty shaky. She made up her mind she'd go it alone." When Boone said nothing, Nash blundered on. "Look, I can't tell you what to do, or how to feel. I just want to say that she wouldn't have done anything to hurt you or Jessie on purpose. She's just not capable of it."

Boone looked toward the house next door. The windows were blank and dark, as they had been for more than a week. "Where is she?"

"She wanted to get away for a little while. Give everybody some room, I guess."

"I haven't seen her since the night she told me. For the first few days, I figured it was better if I stayed away from her." He felt a quick pang of guilt. "I kept Jessie away from her, too. Then, about a week ago, she took off."

"She went to Ireland. She promised to be back before Christmas."

Because his emotions were still raw, Boone only nodded. "I thought I might take Jessie back to Indiana before the holidays. Just for a day or two. Maybe I'll be able to work all this out in my head by the time we all get back."

"Christmas Eve." Padrick sampled the wassail, smacked his lips and sighed. "No better night in the year." Filling a cup, he handed it to his daughter. "Put color in your cheeks, my darling."

"And fire in my blood, the way you make it." But she smiled and sampled. "Isn't it incredible how the twins have grown?"

"Aye." He wasn't fooled by the bright note in her voice. "I can't stand to see my princess so sad."

"I'm not." She squeezed his hand. "I'm fine, Papa. Really."

"I can turn him into a purple jackass for you, darling. I'd be pleasured to."

"No." Because she knew he was only half joking, she kissed his nose. "And you promised we wouldn't have to talk about it once everyone got here."

"Aye, but—"

"A promise," she reminded him, and moved away to help her mother at the stove.

She was glad her house was filled with the people she loved, with the noise of family. There were the scents she had always associated with this holiday. Cinnamon, nutmeg, pine, bayberry. When she'd arrived home a few days before, she'd thrown herself into a flurry of preparations. Tree trimming, present wrapping, cookie baking. Anything and everything to take her mind off the fact that Boone was gone.

That he hadn't spoken to her in more than a month.

But she would survive it. She had already decided what to do, and she refused to let her own unhappiness ruin the family celebration.

"We'll be pleased to have you home with us back in Ireland, Ana." Maureen bent to kiss her daughter's head. "If it's truly what you want."

"I've missed Ireland," Ana said simply. "I think the goose is nearly ready." After opening the oven and taking a heady sniff, she nodded. "Ten minutes more," she predicted. "I'll just go see if everything's on the table."

"Won't even discuss it," Maureen said to her husband when Ana slipped out.

"Tell you what I'd like, my dove. I'd like to take that young man and send him off to some nice frozen island. Just for a day or two, mind."

"If Ana wasn't so sensitive about such matters, I could brew up a nice potion to bring him around."

Padrick patted his wife's bottom. "You have such a delicate touch, Reenie. The lad would be bound by handfast before he could blink—which would be the best thing to happen to him and that darling child of his." He sighed, nibbling his way up his wife's arm. "But Ana would never forgive us for it. We'll have to let her work this out her own way."

Frustrated by a day of canceled flights and delays, Boone slammed the car door. What he wanted was a long hot bath, and what he had to look forward to was an endless night of dealing with those terrifying words *Some Assembly Required.*

If Santa was going to put in an appearance before morning, Boone Sawyer was going to have to put in some overtime.

"Come on, Jess." He rubbed his tired eyes. He'd been traveling for more than twelve hours, if you counted the six he'd spent twiddling his thumbs in the airport. "Let's get this stuff inside."

"Ana's home." Jessie tugged on his arm and pointed toward the lights. "Look, Daddy. There's Morgana's car, and Sebastian's, and the big black car, too. Everybody's at Ana's house."

"I see that." He felt his heart begin to trip a little faster. Then it all but stopped when he saw the For Sale sign in her front yard.

"Can we go over and say Merry Christmas? Please, Daddy. I miss Ana." She closed her hand around the zircon she wore. "Can we go say Merry Christmas?"

"Yeah." Glaring at the sign, he gripped his daughter's hand. "Yeah, let's go do that. Right now."

Move away, would she? he thought as he strode across the lawn. In a pig's eye. Sell her house when he wasn't looking and just take off? They'd just see about that.

"Daddy, you're walking too fast." Jessie had to trot to keep up. "And you're squeezing my hand."

"Sorry." He drew in a long breath, then let it out again. He scooped her up and took the stairs two at a time. The knock on her door wasn't so much a request as a demand.

It was Padrick who answered, his round face wreathed in a fake white beard, and red stocking cap on his balding head. The minute he saw Boone, the twinkle in his eyes died.

"Well, well, look what the cat dragged in. Brave enough to take us all on at once, are you, boyo? We're not all as polite as my Ana."

"I'd like to see her."

"Oh, would you now? Hold it right there." He gave Jessie his charming smile and lifted her out of Boone's arms. "Looks like I got me a real elf this time. Tell you what, lass, you run right on in and look under that tree. See if there's not something with your name on it."

"Oh, can I?" She hugged Padrick fiercely, then turned back to her father. "Please, can I?"

"Sure." Like Padrick's, his smile faded as soon as Jessie raced inside. "I came to see Ana, Mr. Donovan."

"Well, you're seeing me. What do you think you'd do if someone took your Jessie's heart and squeezed it dry?" Though he was more than a head shorter than Boone, he advanced, fists raised. "I won't use nothing but these on you. You've my word as a witch. Now put 'em up."

Boone didn't know whether to laugh or retreat. "Mr. Donovan..."

"Take the first punch." He stuck his whiskered chin out, looking very much like an indignant Santa. "I'll give you that much, and it's more than you'd be deserving. I've listened to her crying in the night over the likes of you, and it's boiled my blood. Told myself, Padrick, if you get face-to-face with that weasel of a man, you'll have to demolish him. It's a matter of pride." He took a swing that spun him completely around and missed Boone by a foot. "She wouldn't let me go after that other slimy bastard when he broke her poor heart, but I've got you."

"Mr. Donovan," Boone tried again, dodging the peppery blows. "I don't want to hurt you."

"Hurt me! Hurt me!" Padrick was dancing now, fueled by the insult. His Santa cap slipped over his eyes. "Why, I could turn your insides out. I could give you the head of a badger. I could—"

"Papa!" With one sharp word, Ana stopped her father's babbling threats.

"You go on inside, princess. This is man's work."

"I won't have you fighting on my doorstep on Christmas Eve. Now you stop it."

"Just let me send him to the North Pole. Just for an hour or two. It's only fitting."

"You'll do no such thing." She stepped out and put a warning hand on his shoulder. "Now go inside and behave, or I'll have Morgana deal with you."

"Bah! I can handle a witch half my age."

"She's sneaky." Ana pressed a kiss to his cheek. "Please, Papa. Do this for me."

"Could never refuse you anything," he muttered. Then he turned glittering eyes on Boone. "But you watch your step, mister." He jabbed out a plump finger. "You mess with one

Donovan, you mess with them all." With a sniff, he went inside.

"I'm sorry," Ana began, fixing a bright smile on her face. "He's very protective."

"So I gathered." Since he wasn't going to have to defend himself after all, he could think of nothing to do with his hands but shove them in his pockets. "I wanted to—we wanted to say merry Christmas."

"Yes, Jessie just did." They were silent for another awkward moment. "You're welcome to come in, have some wassail."

"I don't want to intrude. Your family..." He offered what almost passed for a grin. "I don't want to risk my life, either."

Even the faint smile faded from her eyes. "He wouldn't really have harmed you. It's not our way."

"I didn't mean..." What the hell was he supposed to say to her? "I don't blame him for being upset, and I don't want to make you or your family uncomfortable. If you'd rather, I could just..." He turned slightly, and the sign on her lawn caught his eye. His temper rose accordingly. "What the hell is that?"

"Isn't it clear enough? I'm selling the house. I've decided to go back to Ireland."

"Ireland? You think you can just pack up and move six thousand miles away?"

"Yes, I do. Boone, I'm sorry, but dinner's nearly ready, and I really have to go in. Of course, you're welcome to join us."

"If you don't stop being so bloody polite, I'm going to—" He cut himself off again. "I don't want dinner," he said between his teeth. "I want to talk to you."

"This isn't the time."

"We'll make it the time."

He backed her through the doorway just as Sebastian came down the hall behind her. Placing a light hand on Ana's shoulder, he sent Boone a warning glance. "Is there a problem here, Anastasia?"

"No. I invited Boone and Jessie for dinner, but he isn't able to join us."

"Pity." Sebastian's smile glittered with malice. "Well, then, if you'll excuse us, Sawyer."

Boone slammed the door behind him, causing all the ruckus inside to switch off like a light. Several pairs of eyes turned their way. He was too furious to note that Sebastian's were now bright with amusement.

"Stay out of my way," Boone said quietly. "Each and every one of you. I don't care who you are, or what you are." More than ready to fight a fleet of dragons, he grabbed Ana's hand. "You come with me."

"My family—"

"Can damn well wait." He yanked her back outside.

From her perch under the Christmas tree, Jessie stared wide-eyed after them. "Is Daddy mad at Ana?"

"No." Happy enough about what she'd seen to burst at the seams, Maureen gave the little girl a squeeze. "I think they've just gone off to take care of another Christmas present for you. One I think you'll like best of all."

Outside, Ana labored to keep up. "Stop dragging me, Boone."

"I'm not dragging you," he said as he dragged her through the side yard.

"I don't want to go with you." She felt the tears she'd thought she was finished with stinging her eyes. "I'm not going through this again."

"You think you can put up a stupid sign in your yard and solve everything?" Guided by moonlight, he tugged her down the rock steps that led to the beach. "Drop a bombshell on my head, then take off for Ireland?"

"I can do exactly as I please."

"Witch or no witch, you'd better think that one over again."

"You wouldn't even talk to me."

"I'm talking to you now."

"Well, now I don't want to talk." She broke away and started to climb back up.

"Then you'll listen." He caught her around the waist and tossed her over his shoulder. "And we're going to do this far enough from the house so that I know your family isn't breathing down my neck." When he reached the bottom, he flipped her over and dropped her to her feet. "One step," he warned. "You take one step away and I'll haul you back."

"I wouldn't give you the satisfaction." She struggled with the tears, preferring temper. "You want to have your say. Fine. Then I'll have mine, as well. I accept your position on our relationship. I deeply regret you feel it necessary to keep Jessie away from me."

"I never—"

"Don't deny it. For days before I left for Ireland you kept her at home." She picked up a handful of pebbles and threw them out to sea. "Wouldn't want your little girl too near the witch, after all." She whirled back to him. "For God's sake, Boone, what did you expect from me? Did you see me rubbing my hands together and croaking out, 'I'll get you, my pretty—and your little dog, too'?"

His lips quirked at that, and he reached out, but she spun away. "Give me some credit, Ana."

"I did. A little later than I should have, but I did. And you turned away. Just as I'd known you would."

"Known?" Though he was getting tired of the choreography, he pulled her around again. "How did you know how I'd react? Did you look in your crystal ball, or just have your psychic cousin take a stroll through my head?"

"Neither," she said, with what control she had left. "I wouldn't let Sebastian look, and I didn't look myself, because it seemed unfair. I knew you'd turn away because…"

"Because someone else had."

"It doesn't matter, the fact is you did turn away."

"I just needed to take it in."

"I saw the way you looked at me that night." She shut her eyes. "I've seen that look before. Oh, you weren't cruel like Robert. There were no names, no accusations, but the result was the same. Stay away from me and mine. I don't accept what you are." She wrapped her arms tight and cupped her elbows for warmth.

"I'm not going to apologize for having what I think was a very normal reaction. And damn it, Ana, I was tired, and half-crazy. Watching you lie there in bed all those hours, and you were so pale, so still. I was afraid you wouldn't come back. When you did, I didn't know how to treat you. Then you were telling me all of this."

She searched for calm, knowing it was the best way. "The timing was bad all around. I wasn't quite strong enough to deal with your feelings."

"If you had told me before—"

"You would have reacted differently?" She glanced toward him. "No, I don't think so. But you're right. I should have. It was unfair, and it was weak of me to let things go as far as they did."

"Don't put words in my mouth, Ana. Unless you're, what do you call it—linked? If you're not linked with me, you don't know what I'm feeling. It hurt that you didn't trust me."

She nodded, brushing a tear from her cheek. "I know. I'm sorry."

"You were afraid?"

"I told you I was a coward."

He frowned, watching the hair blow around her face as she stared out at the moon-kissed sea. "Yes, you did. The night you came across my sketch. The one of the witch. That upset you."

She shrugged. "I'm oversensitive sometimes. It was just the mood. I was…"

"About to tell me, and then I scared you off with my evil witch."

"It seemed a difficult time to tell you."

"Because you're a coward," he said mildly, watching her. "Let me ask you something, Ana. What did you do, exactly, to Jessie that day?"

"I linked. I told you I'm an empath."

"It hurt you. I saw." He took her arm, turning her to face him. "Once you cried out, as if it were unbearable. Afterward, you fainted, then slept like the dead for more than a day."

"That's part of it." She tried to push his hand away. It hurt too much to be touched when her defenses were shattered. "When the injuries are so serious, there's a price."

"Yes, I understand. I asked Morgana. She said you could have died. She said the risk was very great because Jessie…" He could hardly say it. "She was gone, or nearly. And you weren't just fixing some broken bones, but bringing her back from the edge. That the line is very fine, and it's very easy for the healer to become the victim."

"What would you have had me do? Let her die?"

"A coward would have. I think your definition and mine are different. Being afraid doesn't make you a coward. You could have saved yourself and let her go."

"I love her."

"So do I. And you gave her back to me. I didn't even thank you."

"Do you think I want your gratitude?" It was too much, she thought. Next he would offer her pity. "I don't. I don't want it. What I did I did freely, because I couldn't bear to lose her, either. And I couldn't bear for you—"

"For me?" he said gently.

"For you to lose someone else you loved. I don't want to be thanked for it. It's what I am."

"You've done it before? What you did with Jessie?"

"I'm a healer. I heal. She was..." It still hurt to think of it. "She was slipping away. I used what I have to bring her back."

"It's not that simple." His hands were gentle on her arms now, stroking. "Not even for you. You feel more than others. Morgana told me that, too. When you let your defenses down, you're more vulnerable to emotion, to pain, to everything. That's why you don't cry." With his fingertip, he lifted a teardrop from her cheek. "But you're crying now."

"You know everything there is to know. What's the point of this?"

"The point is to take a step back to the night you explained it all to me. The point is for you to take another chance and open yourself up. For me."

"You ask too much." She sobbed the words out, then covered her face. "Oh, leave me alone. Give me some peace. Can't you see how you hurt me?"

"Yes, I can see." He wrapped his arms around her, fighting to soothe while she struggled for release. "You've lost weight, you're pale. When I look into your eyes, I see every ounce of pain I caused you. I don't know how to take it back. I don't know how your father kept himself from cursing me with whatever was in his arsenal."

"We can't use power to harm. It's against everything we are. Please let me go."

"I can't. I almost thought I could. She lied to me, I told myself. She betrayed my trust. She isn't real." He kept a firm grip on her arms as he pulled her away. "It doesn't matter. None of it matters. If it's magic, I don't want to lose it. I can't lose you. I love you, Ana. All that you are. Please." He touched his lips to hers, tasting tears. "Please come back to me."

The shaft of hope was almost painful. She clung to it, to him. "I want to believe."

"So do I." He cupped her face, kissing her again. "And I do. I believe in you. In us. If this is my fairy tale, I want to play it out."

She stared up at him. "You can accept all of this? All of us?"

"I figure I'm pretty well suited to do just that. Of course, it might take a while for me to convince your father not to do something drastic to my anatomy." He traced his fingers over her lips as they curved. "I didn't know if you'd ever smile for me again. Tell me you still love me. Give me that, too."

"Yes, I love you." Her lips trembled under his. "Always."

"I won't hurt you again." He brushed away tears with his thumbs. "I'll make up for everything."

"It's done." She caught his hands. "That's done. We have tomorrow."

"Don't cry anymore."

She smiled, rubbing her fists across her cheeks. "No, I won't. I never cry."

He took those damp fists and kissed them. "You said to ask you again. It's been longer than a week, but I'm hoping you haven't forgotten what you said your answer would be."

"I haven't forgotten."

"Put your hand here." He pressed her palm to his heart. "I want you to feel what I feel." He linked his free hand with hers. "The moon's almost full. The first time I kissed you was in the moonlight. I was charmed, enchanted, spellbound. I always will be. I need you, Ana."

She could feel the strength of that love pouring into her. "You have me."

"I want you to marry me. Share the child you gave back to me. She's yours as much as mine now. Let me make more children with you. I'll take you as you are, Anastasia. I swear I'll cherish you as long as I live."

She lifted her arms to him. Hair like sunlight. Eyes like smoke. Shafts of moonglow shimmered around her like torch-light.

"I've been waiting for you."

Alone Roberts

She lifted her hands to him. Her eyes shimmered, gray as smoke, while her shadow shimmered around her like a night light.

"I've been waiting for you."

# *Epilogue*

Alone on a wild crag facing a stormy sea stood Donovan Castle. This dark night, lightning flashed and shuddered in the black sky, and the wind set the leaded glass to shaking in the diamond panes.

Inside, fires leaped and glowed in the hearths. Those who were witches, and those who were not, gathered close, waiting for the indignant wail that would signal a new life.

"Are you cheating, Grandda?" Jessie asked Padrick as he perused his cards.

"Cheating!" He gave a merry laugh and wiggled his brows. "Certainly I am. Go fish."

She giggled and drew from the pile. "Granny Maureen says you always cheat." She tilted her head. "Were you really a frog?"

"That I was, darling. A fine green one."

She accepted this, just as she accepted the other wonders of her life with the Donovans. She petted the snoring Daisy, who rested her big golden head in Jessie's lap. "Will you be a frog again sometime, so I can see?"

"I might surprise you." He winked and changed her hand of cards into a rainbow of lollipops.

"Oh, Grandda," she said indulgently.

"Sebastian?" Mel hustled down the main stairs and shouted into the parlor, where her husband was sipping brandy and watching the card game. "Shawn and Keely are awake and fussing. I have my hands full helping with Ana."

"Be right there." The proud papa of three months set down his snifter and headed up to change diapers.

Nash bounced one-year-old Allysia on his knee while Donovan sat in Matthew's lap, playing with his pocket watch. "Be careful he doesn't eat it," Nash commented. "Or make it disappear. We're having a little trouble keeping him in line."

"The lad needs to spread his wings a bit."

"If you say so. But when I went to get him out of his crib the other day, it was full of rabbits. Real ones."

"Takes after his mother," Matthew said proudly. "She ran us ragged."

Allysia leaned back against her father and smiled. Instantly Daisy woke and trotted over. Within seconds, every dog and cat in the house was swarming through the room.

"Ally," Nash said with a sigh. "Remember how we said one at a time?"

"Doggies." Squealing, Ally tugged gently on the ears of Matthew's big silver wolf. "Kittycats."

"Next time just one, okay?" Nash plucked a cat off his shoulder, nudged another off the arm of the chair. "A couple of weeks ago she had every hound within ten miles howling in the yard. Come on, monsters." He rose, tucking Allysia, then Donovan, under his arms like footballs. They kicked and giggled. "I think it's time for bed."

"Story," Donovan demanded. "Uncle Boone."

"He's busy. You'll have to settle for one from your old man."

*          *          *

He was indeed busy, watching a miracle. The room was scented with candles and herbs, warmed by the fire glowing in the hearth. He held tight to Ana as she brought their son into the world.

Then their daughter.

Then their second son.

"Three." He kept saying it over and over, even as Bryna settled an infant in his arms. "Three." They'd told him there would be triplets, but he hadn't really believed it.

"Runs in the family." Exhausted, elated, Ana took another bundle from Morgana. She pressed her lips gently to the silky cheek. "Now we have two of each."

He grinned down at his wife as Mel settled the third baby in the crook of Ana's arm. "I think we need a bigger house."

"We'll add on."

"Would you like the others to come up?" Bryna asked gently. "Or would you rather rest awhile?"

"No, please." Ana tilted her head so that it rested against Boone's arm. "Ask them to come up."

They crowded in, making too much noise. Ana made room in the big bed for Jessie to sit beside her, then placed a baby in her arms.

"This is your brother, Trevor. Your sister, Maeve. And your other brother, Kyle."

"I'm going to take good care of them. Always. Look, Grandda, we have a big family now."

"You do indeed, my little lamb." He blew heartily into his checked kerchief. He wiped his runny eyes and looked mistily at Boone. "Just as well I didn't flatten you when I had the chance."

"Here." Boone held out a squealing infant. "Hold your grandson."

"Ah, Maureen, my cheesecake, look at this. He has my eyes."

"No, my frog prince, he has mine."

They argued, with the rest of the Donovans throwing their weight to one side or the other. Boone slipped his arm around his wife, held his family close as his son suckled greedily at his first taste of mother's milk. Lightning flashed against the windows, the wind howled, and the fire leapt high in the grate.

Somewhere deep in the forest, high in the hills, the fairies danced.

And they lived happily ever after.

\* \* \* \* \*

# Enchanted

To the friends I've made in cyberspace,
with gratitude for the hours of fun.

# *Prologue*

Dark as the night and fleet of foot, the wolf raced under a hunter's moon. He ran for the love of it, and he ran alone, through the grand tower of trees, the purple shadows of the forest, the magic of the night.

The wind from across the sea spewed across the pines, sent them singing songs of the ancients and spilling their scent into the air. Small creatures with eyes that gleamed hid and watched the sleek black shape bullet through the lacy layer of mist that shimmered down the beaten path.

He knew they were there, could smell them, hear the rapid beat of their blood. But he hunted nothing that night but the night itself.

He had no pack, no mate but solitude.

A restlessness lived in him that not even speed and freedom could quell. In his quest for peace, he haunted the forest, stalked the cliffs, circled the clearings, but nothing soothed or satisfied.

As the path rose more steeply and the trees began to thin, he slowed to a trot, scenting the air. There was...something in the air, something that had lured him out to the cliffs high above the restless Pacific. With powerful strides he climbed the rocks, his golden eyes scanning, seeking.

There, at the topmost point where the waves crashed like cannon fire and the moon swam white and full, he raised his head and called. To sea, to sky, to night.

To magic.

The howl echoed, spread, filled the night with both demand and question. With power as natural as breath.

And the whispers that flickered back told him only that a change was coming. Endings, beginnings. Destiny.

His fate was waiting for him.

Again the rogue black wolf with gold eyes threw back his head and called. There was more, and he would have it. Now the earth shook, and the water swirled. Far over the sea a single spear of lightning broke the blackness with a blinding white flash. In its afterglow for an instant—a heartbeat only—was the answer.

Love waits.

And the magic trembled on the air, danced over the sea with a sound that might have been laughter. Tiny sparks of light skimmed over the surface, bobbing, twirling to spin into the star-strewn sky in a gilt cloud. The wolf watched, and he listened. Even when he turned back to the forest and its shadows, the answer trailed after him.

Love waits.

As the restlessness in him grew, beat with his heart, he shot down the path, powerful strides tearing the fog to ribbons. Now his blood heated with the speed, and veering left, he broke through the trees toward the soft glow of lights. There the cabin stood sturdy, its windows shining with welcome. The whispers of the night fell quiet.

As he bounded up the steps, white smoke swirled, blue light shimmered. And wolf became man.

# Chapter 1

When Rowan Murray got her first look at the cabin, she was filled with a sense of both relief and fear. Relief that she'd finally come to the end of the long drive from San Francisco to this sheltered spot on the coast of Oregon. And fear for the exact same reason.

She was here. She had done it.

What next?

The practical thing, of course, was to get out of the four-wheel drive, unlock the front door and give herself a tour of the place she intended to make home for the next three months. Unpack what belongings she'd brought with her. Make herself some tea. Take a hot shower.

Yes, those were all practical, reasonable things to do, she told herself. And she sat exactly where she was, in the driver's seat of the two-week-old Range Rover, her long, slender fingers gripping white-knuckled on the wheel.

She was alone. Completely, absolutely alone.

It was what she wanted, what she needed. What she'd pushed herself to accomplish for months so that when the offer of the cabin had come, she'd snatched it as if it were a tree limb and she'd been sinking in quicksand.

Now that she had it, she couldn't even get out of the car.

"You're such a fool, Rowan." She whispered it, leaning back, closing her eyes for just a moment. "Such a coward."

She sat, gathering her energies, a small, slenderly built woman with creamy skin that had lost its sheen of rose. Her hair was straight as rain and the color of polished oak. Now, she wore it pulled back, out of the way, in a thick braid that was coming loose. Her nose was long and sharp, her mouth just slightly overwide for the triangle of her face. Her eyes, tired now from hours of driving, were a deep, dark blue, long lidded and tilted at the corners.

Elf's eyes, her father often said. And thinking of that, she felt tears welling up in them.

She'd disappointed him, and her mother. The guilt of that weighed like a stone on her heart. She hadn't been able to explain, not clearly enough, not well enough, why she hadn't been capable of continuing on the path they'd so carefully cleared for her. Every step she'd taken on it had been a strain, as if every step had taken her farther and farther away from where she needed to be.

What she needed to be.

So in the end she'd run. Oh, not in actuality. She was much too reasonable to have run away like a thief in the night. She'd made specific plans, followed concrete steps, but under it all she'd been fleeing from home, from career, from family. From the love that was smothering her as surely as if its hands had been clamped over her nose and mouth.

Here, she'd promised herself, she'd be able to breathe, to think, to decide. And maybe, just maybe, to understand what it was that kept her from being what everyone seemed to want her to be.

If in the end she discovered she was wrong and everyone

else was right, she was prepared to deal with it. But she would take these three months for herself.

She opened her eyes again, let herself look. And as she did, her muscles slowly relaxed. It was so beautiful, she realized. The grand majesty of trees shooting up into the sky and whistling in the wind, the two-story cabin tucked into a private glen, the silver flash of sun off the busy little stream that snaked to the west.

The cabin itself gleamed dark gold in the sunlight. Its wood was smooth, its windows sparkled. The little covered porch looked perfect for sitting on lazy mornings or quiet evenings. From where she sat, she thought she could see the brave spears of spring bulbs testing the air.

They'd find it chilly yet, she mused. Belinda had warned her to buy flannel, and to expect spring to come late to this little corner of the world.

Well, she knew how to build a fire, she told herself, glancing at the stone chimney. One of her favorite spots in her parents' house had been in the big sprawling living room, beside the hearth, with a fire crackling against the damp chill of the city.

She'd build one as soon as she was settled, she promised herself. To welcome herself to her new home.

Steadier, she opened the door, stepped out. Her heavy boots snapped a thick twig with a sound like a bullet. She pressed a hand to her heart, laughing a little. New boots for the city girl, she thought. Jingling the keys just to make noise, she walked to the cabin, up the two steps to the porch. She slipped the key she'd labeled *front door* into the lock and, taking a slow breath, pushed the door open.

And fell in love.

"Oh, would you look at this!" A smile lit her face as she stepped inside, circled. "Belinda, God bless you."

The walls were the color of warmly toasted bread, framed in dark wood, accented with the magical paintings her friend was renowned for. The hearth was stone, scrubbed clean and laid with kindling and logs in welcome. Colorful rugs were scattered over the polished wood floor. The furnishings were simple, clean lines, with deep cushions that picked up those wonderful tones of emerald, sapphire and ruby.

To complete the fairy-tale aspect, there were statues of dragons, wizards, bowls filled with stones or dried flowers, and sparkling geodes. Charmed, Rowan dashed up the stairs and hugged herself as she toured the two large rooms there.

One, full of light from a ring of windows, was obviously her friend's studio when she used the cabin. Canvases, paints and brushes were neatly stored, an easel stood empty, a smock hung, paint-splattered, on a brass hook.

Even here there were pretty touches—fat white candles in silver holders, glass stars, a globe of smoky crystal.

The bedroom thrilled her with its huge canopy bed draped in white linen, the little fireplace to warm the room, the carved rosewood armoire.

It felt…peaceful, Rowan realized. Settled, content, welcoming. Yes, she could breathe here. She could think here. For some inexplicable reason, she felt she could belong here.

Anxious now to begin settling in, she hurried downstairs, out the door she'd left open to her SUV. She'd grabbed the first box from the cargo area, when the skin on the back of her neck prickled. Suddenly her heart thundered in her chest, and her palms sprang with damp.

She turned quickly, managed only one strangled gasp.

The wolf was pure black, with eyes like gold coins. And it stood at the edge of the trees, still as a statue carved from onyx. Watching her. She could do no more than stare while her pulse beat like fury. Why wasn't she screaming? she asked herself. Why wasn't she running?

Why was she more surprised than afraid?

Had she dreamed of him? Couldn't she just catch the edge

of some misty dream where he'd run through the mist toward her? Is that why he seemed so familiar, almost...expected?

But that was ridiculous. She'd never seen a wolf outside of a zoo in her life. Surely she'd never seen one who stared so patiently at her. Into her.

"Hello." She heard herself speak with a kind of dull shock, and followed it with a nervous laugh. Then she blinked, and he was gone.

For a moment, she swayed, like a woman coming out of a trance. When she shook herself clear, she stared at the edge of the trees, searching for some movement, some shadow, some sign.

But there was only silence.

"Imagining things again," she muttered, shifting the box, turning away. "If there was anything there, it was a dog. Just a dog."

Wolves were nocturnal, weren't they? They didn't approach people in broad daylight, just stand and stare, then vanish.

She'd look it up to be sure, but it had been a dog. She was positive now. Belinda hadn't mentioned anything about neighbors or other cabins. And how odd, Rowan thought now, that she hadn't even asked about it.

Well, there was a neighbor somewhere, and he had a big, beautiful black dog. She imagined they could all keep out of each other's way.


The wolf watched from the shadows of the trees. Who was the woman? he wondered. *Why* was the woman? She moved quickly, a little nervously, tossing glances over her shoulder as she carried things from the car to the cabin.

He'd scented her from half a mile away. Her fears, her excitement, her longings had all come to him. And had brought him to her.

His eyes narrowed with annoyance. His teeth bared in challenge. He'd be damned if he'd take her. Damned if he'd let her change what he was or what he wanted.

Sleek and silent, he turned away and vanished into the thick trees.

Rowan built a fire, delighted when the logs crackled and caught. She unpacked systematically. There wasn't much, really. Clothes, supplies. Most of the boxes she'd hauled in were filled with books. Books she couldn't live without, books she'd promised herself she'd make time to read. Books to study, books for pleasure. She'd grown up with a love of reading, of exploring worlds through words. And because of that great love, she often questioned her own dissatisfaction with teaching.

It should have been the right goal, just as her parents always insisted. She embraced learning and had always learned well and quickly. She'd studied, taken her major and then her master's in education. At twenty-seven, she'd already taught full-time for nearly six years.

She was good at it, she thought now as she sipped tea while standing in front of the blazing fire. She could recognize the strengths and weaknesses of her students, home in on their interests and on how to challenge them.

Yet she dragged her feet on getting her doctorate. She woke each morning vaguely discontented and came home each evening unsatisfied.

Because her heart had never been in it.

When she'd tried to explain that to the people who loved her, they'd been baffled. Her students loved and respected her, the administration at her school valued her. Why wasn't she pursuing her degree, marrying Alan, completing her nice, tidy life as she should?

Why, indeed, she thought. Because the only answer she had for them, and for herself, was in her heart.

And brooding wasn't thinking, she reminded herself. She'd

go for a walk, get a sense of where she was. She wanted to see the cliffs Belinda had told her of.

She locked the door out of habit, then drew in a deep gulp of air that tasted of pine and sea. In her mind she could see the quick sketch Belinda had drawn her of the cabin, the forest, the cliffs. Ignoring her nerves, she stepped onto the path and headed due west.

She'd never lived outside of the city. Growing up in San Francisco hadn't prepared her for the vastness of the Oregon forest, its smells, its sounds. Even so, her nerves began to fade into wonder.

It was like a book, a gorgeously rich story full of color and texture. The giant Douglas firs towered over her, their bushy branches letting the sun splatter into a shifting, luminous, gilded green light nearly the color of the moss that grew so thick and soft on the ground. The trees chilled the air with their shade, scented it with their fragrance.

The forest floor was soft with shed needles and ripe with the tang of sap.

At their bases, ferns grew thick and green, some thin and sharp as swords, others lacy as fans. Like fairies, she thought in a moment's fancy, who only danced at night.

The stream bubbled along, skimming over rocks worn round and smooth, tumbling down a little rise with a sudden rush of white water that looked impossibly pure and cold. She followed the wind of it, relaxed with its music.

There was a bend up ahead, she thought idly, and around the corner there would be a stump of an old tree on the left that looked like an old man's worn face. Foxglove grew there, and in the summer it would grow tall and pale purple. It was a good place to sit, that stump, and watch the forest come to life around you.

She stopped when she came to it, staring blankly at the gnarled bark that did indeed look like an old man's face. How had she known this would be here? she wondered, rubbing the heel of her hand on her suddenly speeding heart. It wasn't on Belinda's sketch, so how had she known?

"Because she mentioned it. She told me about it, that's all. It's just the sort of fanciful thing she'd tell me, and that I'd forget about."

But Rowan didn't sit, didn't wait for the forest to come to life. It already felt alive. Enchanted, she thought, and managed to smile. The enchanted woods every girl dreams of, where the fairies dance and the prince waits to rescue her from the jealous hag or the evil wizard.

There was nothing to fear here. The woods were hers as long as she wanted. There was no one to shake their heads indulgently if her mind wandered toward fairy tales and the foolish. Her dreams were her own as well.

If she had a dream, or a story to tell a young girl, Rowan decided, it would be about the enchanted forest…and the prince who wandered it, searching through the green light and greener shadow for his one true love. He was under a spell, she thought, and trapped in the sleek, handsome form of a black wolf. Until the maiden came and freed him with her courage, her wit, and with her love.

She sighed once, wishing she had a talent for the details of telling stories. She wasn't bad at themes, she mused, but she could never figure out how to turn a theme into an engaging tale.

So she read instead, and admired those who could.

She heard the sea, like an echo of memory, and turned unerringly onto the left fork of the path. What began as a whisper became a roar, and she started to hurry, was nearly running by the time she burst out of the trees and saw the cliffs.

Her boots clattered as she climbed up the rocks. The wind kicked and tore what was left of her braid loose so that her hair flew wild and free. Her laughter rang out, full of delight as she came breathlessly to the top of the rise.

It was, without a doubt, the most magnificent sight she'd

ever seen. Miles of blue ocean, hemmed with fuming white waves that threw themselves in fury against the rocks below. The afternoon sun showered over it, sprinkling jewels onto that undulating mat of blue.

She could see boats in the distance, riding the waves, and a small forested island rising out of the sea like a bunched fist.

Gleaming black mussels clung to the rocks below her, and as she looked closer, she saw the thorny brown sticks of a bird's nest tucked into a crevice. On impulse she got down, bellied out and was rewarded by a glimpse of eggs.

Pillowing her chin on her hands, she watched the water until the boats sailed away, until the sea was empty, and the shadows grew long.

She pushed up, sat back on her heels and lifted her face to the sky. "And that is the first time in too long that I've done nothing at all for an afternoon." She let out a long, contented breath. "It was glorious."

She rose, stretched her arms high, turned. And nearly stumbled over the edge of the cliff.

She would have fallen if he hadn't moved quickly, so quickly she had no sense of him moving at all. But his hands closed firmly over her arms and pulled her to safe ground.

"Steady," he said, and it was more an order than a suggestion.

He might have been the prince of any woman's imaginings. Or the dark angel of her most secret dreams. His hair was black as a moonless night and flew around a face lightly gilded by the sun. A face of strong, sharp bones, of firm, unsmiling mouth, of haunting male beauty.

He was tall. She had only a sense of height as her head reeled. For he had the eyes of the wolf she'd thought she'd seen—tawny and gold, unblinking and intense—under arched brows as black as his hair. They stared directly into hers, making the blood rush hot through her veins. She felt the strength of his hands as he'd yet to release her, thought she saw both impatience and curiosity flicker over that gorgeous face.

But she might have been wrong because he continued to stare, and say nothing.

"I was—you startled me. I didn't hear you. You were just there." She nearly winced as she heard herself babble.

Which was his own fault, he supposed. He could have made her aware of him gradually. But something about the way she'd been lying on the rocks, gazing out at nothing with a half smile on her face had muddled his mind.

"You didn't hear because you were daydreaming." He arched one sweeping black eyebrow. "And talking to yourself."

"Oh. It's a bad habit of mine—talking to myself. Nervous habit."

"Why are you nervous?"

"I'm not—I wasn't." God, she'd tremble in a moment if he didn't let her go. It had been a long, long time since she'd been this close to a man other than Alan. And much too long since she'd felt any kind of response to one. She'd never experienced a reaction this strong, this violent or this disorienting, and put it down to nearly tumbling over a cliff.

"You weren't." He skimmed his hands down to her wrists, felt the jittery bump of her pulse. "Now you are."

"You startled me, as I said." It was an effort, but she glanced over her shoulder and down. "And it's a long drop."

"It is that." He tugged her away another two steps. "Better?"

"Yes, well… I'm Rowan Murray, I'm using Belinda Malone's cabin for a while." She would have offered a hand to shake, but it would have been impossible as he was still cuffing her wrists.

"Donovan. Liam Donovan." He said it quietly, while his thumbs stroked over her pulse beat and somehow steadied it.

"But you're not from around here."

"Aren't I?"

"I mean, your accent. It's beautifully Irish."

When his lips curved and his eyes smiled she very nearly

sighed like a teenager faced with a rock star. "I'm from Mayo, but I've had this place as mine for nearly a year now. My cabin's less than a half-mile from Belinda's."

"You know her, then?"

"Aye, well enough. We're in the way of being relations, distant ones." His smile was gone now. Her eyes were as blue as the wild bellflowers that grew in sunny patches of the forest in high summer. And in them he found no guile at all. "She didn't tell me to expect a neighbor."

"I suppose she didn't think of it. She didn't tell me to expect one, either." Her hands were free now, though she could still feel the warmth of his fingers, like bracelets around her wrists. "What do you do up here?"

"As I choose. You'll be wanting to do the same. It'll be a good change for you."

"Excuse me?"

"You haven't done what you pleased often enough, have you, Rowan Murray?"

She shivered once and slipped her hands into her pockets. The sun was dipping down toward the horizon and was reason enough for the sudden chill. "I guess I'll have to be careful what I talk to myself about with a quiet-footed neighbor around."

"Nearly a half-mile between us should be enough. I like my solitude." He said it firmly, and though it was ridiculous, it seemed to Rowan he wasn't speaking to her, but to someone, something, in the darkening woods beyond. Then his gaze shifted back to her face, held. "I won't infringe on yours."

"I didn't mean to be unfriendly." She tried a smile, wishing she hadn't spoken so abruptly and irritated him. "I've always lived in the city—with so many neighbors I barely notice any of them."

"It doesn't suit you," he said, half to himself.

"What?"

"The city. It doesn't suit you or you wouldn't be here, would you?" And what in bloody hell did it matter to him what suited her? he asked himself. She'd be nothing to him unless he decided differently.

"I'm...just taking a little time."

"Aye, well there's plenty of it here. Do you know your way back?"

"Back? Oh, to the cabin? Yes. I take the path to the right, then follow the stream."

"Don't linger long." He turned and started down, pausing only briefly to glance up at her. "Night comes quickly here this time of year, and it's easy to be lost in the dark. In the unfamiliar."

"No, I'll start back soon. Mr. Donovan—Liam?"

He stopped again, his gaze clear enough that she caught the quick shadow of impatience in it. "Yes?"

"I was wondering...where's your dog?"

His grin was so fast, so bright and amused that she found herself beaming back at him. "I've no dog."

"But I thought—are there other cabins nearby?"

"Not for three miles and more. We're what's here, Rowan. And what lives in the forest between us." He saw her glance uneasily at the verge of trees and softened. "Nothing that's there will harm you. Enjoy your walk, and your evening. And your time."

Before she could think of another way to stop him, he'd stepped into and been swallowed up by the trees. It was then she noticed just how quickly twilight had fallen, just how chilly the air and how brisk the wind. Abandoning pride, she scrambled down the cliff path and called out to him.

"Liam? Wait a minute, would you? I'll walk back with you for a bit."

But her own voice echoed back to her, turning her throat dry. She moved quickly down the path, certain she'd catch a glimpse of him in the trees. There was nothing now but deep shadow.

"Not only quiet," she mumbled, "but fast. Okay, okay." To bolster herself she paused to take three deep breaths. "There's nothing in here that wasn't here when there was more light. Just go back the way you came and stop being an idiot."

But the deeper she went, the thicker the shadows. Like a tide, a thin ground fog slid over the path, white as smoke. She would have sworn she heard music, like bells—or laughter. It harmonized with the sound of the water bubbling over rocks, whispered in counterpoint to the *whoosh* and sigh of the wind in the trees.

A radio, she thought. Or a television. Sounds carried oddly in some places. Liam had turned on music, and for some reason she could hear it playing. It only seemed as if it was just ahead of her, in the direction of her own cabin. The wind played tricks.

The sigh of relief as she came to the last bend of the stream froze in her throat as she saw the glint of gold eyes peering out of the shadows. Then, with a rustle of leaves, they were gone.

Rowan increased her pace to a jog and didn't break stride until she'd reached the door. She didn't start breathing again until she was inside and the door was securely locked behind her.

She moved quickly, switching on lights until the first floor of the cabin blazed with them. Then she poured herself a glass from one of the bottles of wine she'd brought along, lifted it in a toast and swallowed deep.

"To strange beginnings, mysterious neighbors and invisible dogs."

To make herself feel more at home, she heated a can of soup and ate it standing up, dreaming, looking out the kitchen window, as she often did in her apartment in the city.

But the dreams were softer here, and yet more clear. Towering trees and bubbling water, thrashing waves and the last light of the day.

A handsome man with tawny eyes who stood on a wind-swept cliff and smiled at her.

She sighed, wishing she'd been clever and polished, wished she'd known a way to flirt lightly, speak casually so that he might have looked at her with interest rather than annoyance and amusement.

Which was ridiculous, she reminded herself, as Liam Donovan wasn't wasting his time thinking of her at all. So it was pointless to think of him.

Following habit, she tidied up, switching off lights as she moved upstairs. There she indulged herself by filling the wonderfully deep claw-foot tub with hot water and fragrant bubbles, settling into it with a sigh, a book and a second glass of wine.

She immediately decided this was a luxury she hadn't allowed herself nearly often enough.

"That's going to change." She slid back, moaning with pleasure. "So many things are going to change. I just have to think of them all."

When the water turned tepid, she climbed out to change into the cozy flannel pajamas she'd bought. Another indulgence was to light the bedroom fire, then crawl under the cloud-light duvet beneath the canopy and snuggle into her book.

Within ten minutes, she was asleep, with her reading glasses sliding down her nose, the lights on and the last of her wine going warm in her glass.

She dreamed of a sleek black wolf who padded silently into her room, watching her out of curious gold eyes as she slept. It seemed he spoke to her—his mind to her mind.

*I wasn't looking for you. I wasn't waiting for you. I don't want what you're bringing me. Go back to your safe world, Rowan Murray. Mine isn't for you.*

She couldn't answer but to think *I only want time. I'm only looking for time.*

He came close to the bed, so that her hand nearly brushed

his head. *If you take it here, it may trap us both. Is that a risk you're willing to take?*

Oh, she wanted to touch, to feel, and with a sigh slid her hand over the warm fur, let her fingers dive into it. *It's time I took one.*

Under her hand, wolf became man. His breath fluttered over her face as he leaned close, so close. "If I kissed you now, Rowan, what might happen?"

Her body seemed to shimmer with that sudden raw need. She moaned with it, arched, reached out.

Liam only laid a finger on her lips. "Sleep," he told her, and slipped the glasses off, laid them on the table beside her. He switched off the light, closed his hand into a fist as the urge to touch her, to really touch her, lanced through him.

"Damn it. I don't want this. I don't want her."

He flung up his hand and vanished.

Later, much later, she dreamed of a wolf, black as midnight on the cliffs over the sea. With his head thrown back, he called to the swimming moon.

# *Chapter 2*

It became a habit over the next few days for Rowan to look for the wolf. She would see him, most often early in the morning or just before twilight, standing at the edge of the trees.

Watching the house, she thought. Watching her.

She realized, on those mornings when she didn't see him, that she was disappointed. So much so that she began leaving food out in hopes to lure him closer, to keep him a regular visitor in what she was starting to consider her little world.

He was on her mind quite a bit. Nearly every morning she woke with fading snippets of dreams just at the edge of her mind. Dreams where he sat by her bed while she slept, where she sometimes roused just enough to reach out and stroke that soft silky fur or feel the strong ridge of muscle along his back.

Now and then, the wolf became mixed in her dreams with her neighbor. On those mornings, she climbed out of sleep with her system still quivering from an aching sexual frustration that baffled and embarrassed her.

When she was logical, she could remind herself that Liam Donovan was the only human being she'd seen in the best part of a week. As a sample of the species, he was spectacular, and the perfect fodder for erotic dreams.

But all in all she preferred thinking of the wolf, weaving a story about him. She liked pretending he was her guardian, protecting her from any evil spirits that lived in the forest.

She spent most of her time reading or sketching, or taking long walks. And trying not to think that it was nearly time to make her promised weekly call home to her parents.

She often heard music, drifting through the woods or in through her windows. Pipes and flutes, bells and strings. Once there was harpsong so sweet and so pure that it made her throat ache with tears.

While she wallowed in the peace, the solitude, the lack of demand on her time and attention, there were also moments of loneliness so acute it hurt the heart. Even when the need for another voice, for human contact pulled at her, she couldn't quite gather the courage, or find a reasonable excuse, to seek out Liam.

To offer him a cup of coffee, she thought as twilight slipped through the trees and there was no sign of her wolf. Or maybe a hot meal. A little conversation, she mused, absently twisting the tip of her braid around her finger.

"Doesn't he ever get lonely?" she wondered. "What does he do all day, all night?"

The wind rose, and in the distance thunder mumbled. A storm brewing, she thought, moving to the door to fling it open to the fast, cool air. Looking up, she watched dark clouds roll and bump, caught the faint blink of far-off lightning.

She thought it would be lovely to sleep with the sound of rain falling on the roof. Better, to curl up in bed with a book and read half the night while the wind howled and the rain lashed.

Smiling at the idea, she shifted her gaze. And looked directly into the glinting eyes of the wolf.

She stumbled back a step, pressing a hand to her throat

where her heart had leaped. He was halfway across the clearing, closer than he'd ever come. Wiping her nervous hands on her jeans, she cautiously stepped out on the porch.

"Hello." She laughed a little, but kept one hand firmly on the doorknob. Just in case. "You're so beautiful," she murmured while he stood, still as a stone carving. "I look for you every day. You never eat the food I leave out. Nothing else does, either. I'm not a very good cook. I keep wishing you'd come closer."

As her pulse began to level, she lowered slowly into a crouch. "I won't hurt you," she murmured. "I've been reading about wolves. Isn't it odd that I brought a book about you with me? I don't even remember packing it, but I brought so many books. You shouldn't be interested in me," she said with a sigh. "You should be running with a pack, with your mate."

The sadness hit so quickly, so sharply, that she closed her eyes against it. "Wolves mate for life," she said quietly, then jolted when lightning slashed and the bellow of thunder answered by shaking the sky.

The clearing was empty. The black wolf was gone. Rowan walked to the porch rocker, sat and curled up her legs to watch the rain sweep in.

He was thinking about her far too much and far too often. It infuriated him. Liam was a man who prided himself on self-control. When one possessed power, control must walk with it. Power untempered could corrupt. It could destroy.

He'd been taught from birth his responsibilities as well as his advantages. His gifts as well as his curses. Solitude was his way of escaping all of it, at least for short spans of time.

He knew, too well, no one escaped destiny.

The son of princes was expected to accept destiny.

Alone in his cabin, he thought of her. The way she'd looked when he'd come into the clearing. The way fear had danced around her even as she'd stepped outside.

There was such sweetness in her, it pulled at him, even as he struggled to stay away. She thought she was putting him at ease, letting him grow accustomed to her by leaving him food. Speaking to him in that quiet voice that trembled with nerves.

He wondered how many other women, alone in what was essentially wilderness, would have the courage or the desire to talk to a wolf, much less reassure him.

She thought she was a coward—he'd touched her mind gently, but enough to scan her thoughts. She didn't have any concept of what she had inside her, hadn't explored it, or been allowed to.

Strong sense of family, great loyalty and pitifully low self-esteem.

He shook his head as he sipped coffee and watched the storm build. What in Finn's name was he supposed to do about her?

If it had just been a matter of giving her subtle little pushes to discover herself and her own powers, that would have been...interesting, he supposed. He might have enjoyed the task. But he knew it was a great deal more.

He'd been shown just enough to worry him.

If she'd been sent to him and he accepted her, took her, the decision he'd left home and family to make would be made for him.

She was not one of his kind.

Yet already there were needs stirring. She was a lovely woman, after all, vulnerable, a little lost. Those needs would have been natural enough, particularly after his long, self-imposed solitude.

Male required female.

But the needs were deeper, stronger and more demanding than he'd experienced before, or that he cared to experience. When you felt too much, control slipped. Without control, there was no choice. He'd taken this year to himself to make choices.

Yet he couldn't stay away from her. He'd been wise enough,

he considered, to keep his distance in this form—at least when she was awake and aware. Still he was drawn through the forest to watch her, to listen to her mind. Or to sit alone here in this room, cast the fire and study her in the flames.

*Love waits.*

He set his teeth, set his cup down with a snap of china on wood as the whisper floated over him. "Damn it. I'll deal with it, with her. In my own time. In my own way. Leave me be."

In the dark window glass, his own reflection faded, replaced by a woman with tumbling gold hair and eyes of the same rich color, who smiled softly. "Liam," she said. "Stubborn you are, and always were."

He cocked a brow. "Mother, 'tis easy when you learn from the best."

She laughed, eyes sparkling against the night. "That's true enough—if you're speaking of your Da. The storm breaks, and she's alone. Will you leave her that way?"

"It's best for both of us if I do just that. She's not one of us."

"Liam, when you're ready, you'll look into her heart, and into your own. Trust what you find." Then she sighed, knowing her son would follow his own path as always. "I'll give your father your best."

"Do. I love you."

"I know it. Come home soon, Liam of Donovan. We're missing you."

As her image faded, lightning slashed out of the sky, driving down like a lance to stab the ground. It left no mark, no burn, even as thunder roared behind it; Liam understood it was his father's way of echoing his wife's words.

"All right then. Bloody hell. I'll have a look and see how well she's riding out the storm."

He turned, focused, then flicked a wrist, jabbing a finger at the cold hearth. The fire leaped, though there was no log, no kindling to burn.

"Lightning flares and thunder moans. How does the woman fare alone? Chill the fire to let me see. As I will, so mote it be."

He dipped his hands into his pockets as the flames settled, steadied. In the cool gold light, shadows shifted, parted, then opened to him.

He saw her carrying a candle through the dark, her face pale in its flickering light, her eyes wide. She fumbled through drawers in her kitchen, talking to herself, as she was prone to. And jolted like a frightened deer when the next flash of lightning broke the night.

Well, he hadn't thought of that, Liam admitted, and in a rare show of frustration dragged a hand through his hair. Her power was out, and she was alone in the dark, and scared half to death. Hadn't Belinda told her how to work the little generator, or where the flashlight was? The emergency lanterns?

Apparently not.

He could hardly leave her there, could he? Shivering and stumbling around. Which, he supposed with a sour smile, was exactly what his clever, meddling cousin had known.

He'd make sure she had light, and heat, but that would be the end of it. He wouldn't linger.

While he was a witch, he was also a man. And both parts of him wanted her entirely too much for comfort.

"Just a storm, it's just a storm. No big deal." Rowan all but chanted the words as she lit more candles.

She wasn't afraid of the dark, not really. But it was so *damn* dark, and the lightning had struck so close to the cabin. The thunder rattled the windows until she was certain they would just explode.

And if she hadn't been sitting outside, daydreaming while the storm blew in, she'd have had a fire built. She'd have the warmth and light from that *and* the candlelight, and it would be sort of…cozy. If she really worked on believing it.

And now the power was out, the phones were out and the

storm appeared to be at its peak directly over her pretty little cabin.

There were candles, she reminded herself. Dozens and dozens of candles. White ones, blue ones, red ones, green ones. She could only think that Belinda had bought out some candle store. Some were so lovely, with odd and beautiful symbols carved into them, that she held back from lighting them. And after all, she must have fifty flaring away by now, giving adequate light and offering marvelous scents to settle the nerves.

"Okay. All right." She set yet one more candle on the table in front of the sofa and rubbed her chilled hands. "I ought to be able to see enough to get a fire going. Then I'll just curl up right here on the couch and wait it out. It'll be fine."

But even as she crouched in front of the hearth and began to arrange the kindling, the wind howled. Her door banged open like a bullet out of a gun, and half the cheery candles behind her blew out.

She leaped up, whirled around. And screamed.

Liam stood a few paces away, the wind swirling through his hair, the candlelight gleaming in his eyes. She dropped kindling on her stockinged feet, yelped and fell backward into a chair.

"I seem to have startled you again," he said in that mild and beautiful voice. "Sorry."

"I— You. God! The door..."

"It's open." He turned, crossed to it and closed out the wind and rain.

She'd been certain she'd locked it when she'd rushed in out of the storm. Obviously not, she thought now, and did her best to swallow her heart and get it back in its proper place.

"I thought you might have been having some trouble with the storm." He stepped toward her, each movement graceful as a dancer's. Or a stalking wolf. "It seems I was right."

"Power's out," she managed.

"So I see. You're cold." He picked up the scattered kindling and crouched to build a fire with wood and match. He thought she'd had enough surprises for one night, even if it did take quite a bit longer that way.

"I wanted to get some light before I built a fire. Belinda has a lot of candles."

"Naturally." The kindling caught with a quick crackle, and flames licked obligingly at the logs he arranged. "This'll warm the room soon. There's a small generator out back. I can start it for you if you like, but this will pass before long."

He stayed where he was, with the firelight dancing over his face. And looking at him, she forgot about the storm and fears of the dark. She wondered if all that gorgeous hair that fell nearly to his shoulders was as soft as it looked, wondered why it seemed she knew exactly how it would feel under her fingers.

Why she had an image of him leaning over her, leaning close, with his mouth a breath away from hers. Only a breath away.

"You're daydreaming again, Rowan."

"Oh." She blinked, flushed, shook herself clear. "Sorry. The storm's made me jumpy. Would you like some wine?" She pushed herself up, began backing quickly toward the kitchen. "I have a very nice Italian white I tried last night. I'll just... pour some. Won't be a minute."

For Lord's sake, for Lord's sake, she berated herself as she dashed into the kitchen, where a half-dozen candles glowed on the counter. Why did being around him make her so skittish and stupid! She'd been alone with attractive men before. She was a grown woman, wasn't she?

She got the bottle out of the refrigerator by the light of the candles, found glasses and filled them. When she turned, a glass in each hand, he was there just behind her, and she jolted.

Wine sloshed over the rim and onto the back of her hand.

"*Must* you do that!" She snapped it out before she could stop herself, then watched that fast, fabulous grin flash over his face, bright and blinding as the lightning in the storm.

"I suppose not." Ah, the hell with it, he decided. He was entitled to some small pleasures. With his eyes on hers, he lifted her damp hand, bent his head and slowly licked.

The best she could manage was a small, quiet moan.

"You're right. It's very nice wine." He took the glass and when her freed hand fell limply to her side, smiled. Sipped. "You've a lovely face, Rowan Murray. I've thought of it since last I saw you."

"You have?"

"Did you think I wouldn't?"

She was so obviously befuddled it was tempting to press his advantage, to go with the urge grinding in him to take before she knew all he wanted, and what he refused to want. One step closer, he mused, the slow slide of his fingers around the base of her neck where the flesh was warm and smooth. Fragile. His mouth to hers while the taste of her was still mixed with the wine on his tongue.

And he wouldn't be in the mood to leave it at something quite so simple, or quite so innocent.

"Come in by the fire." He stepped back to give her room to pass. "Where it's warmer."

She recognized the ache spreading inside her. The same ache, she thought, as she woke with whenever she dreamed of him. She moved past him, into the living room, praying she could think of something to say that wouldn't sound idiotic.

"If you came here to relax," he began with just a hint of impatience in his voice, "you're doing a preciously poor job of it. Sit down and stop fretting. The storm won't stay long, and neither will I."

"I like the company. I'm not used to being alone for such long stretches of time."

She sat, managing a smile. But he stood by the fire, leaned against the mantel. He watched her. Watched her in a way that reminded her of—

"Isn't that why you came here?" He said it to interrupt her

thoughts before they inched too close to what she wasn't prepared to know. "To have time alone?"

"Yes. And I like it. But it's odd just the same. I was a teacher
for a long time. I'm used to having a lot of people around."

"Do you like them?"

"Them? Students?"

"No, people." He made a vague and oddly dismissive gesture with one elegant hand. "In general."

"Why...yes." She laughed a little, leaning back in her chair
without being aware her shoulders had lost their knots of tension. "Don't you?"

"Not particularly—as a rule." He took a sip of wine, reflect-
ing. "So many of them are demanding, selfish, self-absorbed.
And while that's not so much of a problem, they often hurt
each other quite consciously, quite carelessly. There's no point,
and there should be no pride in causing harm."

"Most people don't mean to." She saw the light in his eye
and shook her head. "Oh, you're cynical. I can't understand
cynics."

"That's because you're a romantic, and a naive one at that.
But it's charming on you."

"Now, should I be flattered or insulted?" she wondered
aloud, smiling with more ease than she'd ever felt with him,
even when he moved to sit at the ottoman in front of her chair.

"Truth can be accepted without either. What do you teach?"

"Literature—or I used to."

"That would explain the books." They were stacked on the
coffee table and in a box beside the couch. He'd seen others
piled on the kitchen table and knew there were still more in
her bedroom upstairs.

"Reading's one of my greatest pleasures. I love sliding into
a story."

"But this..." He leaned back, reached over and plucked up
the top book on the table. "*The Study of Wolves, Their History
and Habits*. That wouldn't be a story, would it?"

"No. I bought that on impulse one day, and didn't even realize I'd packed it. But I'm glad I did." In a habitual gesture, she brushed at the hair that had come loose from her braid. "You must have seen him." She eased forward, the delight in her large, dark eyes nearly irresistible. "The black wolf that comes around."

He continued to look into her eyes, straight in, as he enjoyed his wine. "I can't say I have."

"Oh, but I've seen him nearly every day since I came. He's gorgeous, and doesn't seem as wary of people as you'd expect. He came into the clearing right before the storm tonight. And sometimes I hear him calling, or it seems I do. Haven't you?"

"I'm closer to the sea," he told her. "That's what I listen to. A wolf is a wild thing, Rowan, as I'm sure your book has told you. And a rogue, one who runs alone, the wildest of all."

"I wouldn't want to tame him. I'd say we're just curious about each other at this point." She glanced toward the window, wondered if the wolf had found a warm dry place for the night. "They don't hunt for sport," she added, absently tossing her braid behind her back. "Or out of viciousness. They hunt to feed. Most often they live in packs, families. Protect their young, and—" She broke off, jumping a little when lightning flashed bright and close.

"Nature's a violent thing. It only tolerates the rest of us. Nature can be generous or ruthless." He put the book aside. "You have to have a care how you deal with it, and you'll never understand it."

Their knees were brushing, their bodies close. She caught the scent of him, sharply male, almost animal, and absolutely dangerous. His lips curved in a smile as he nodded. "Exactly so," he murmured, then set his glass aside and rose. "I'll start the generator for you. You'll be happier with some electricity."

"Yes, I suppose you're right." She got to her feet, wondering why her heart was pounding. It had nothing to do with the storm raging outside now, and everything to do with the one so suddenly brewing inside her. "Thank you for helping."

"It's not a problem." He wasn't going to let it be a problem. "It'll only be a moment." Briefly, lightly, his fingers danced over the back of her hand. "It was good wine," he murmured, and walked out to the kitchen.

It took her ten long seconds to get her breath back, to lower the hand she'd pressed to her cheek and follow him. Just as she stepped into the kitchen, the lights flashed on, making her yelp. Even as she laughed at herself, she wondered how the man moved so fast. The kitchen was empty, her lights were on, and it was as if he'd never been there.

She pulled open the back door and winced when the wind and rain lashed at her. Shivering a little, she leaned out. "Liam?" But there was nothing but the rain and the dark. "Don't go," she murmured, leaning on the doorjamb as the rain soaked her shirt. "Please don't leave me alone."

The next burst of lightning shot the forest into bright relief. And gleamed off the coat of the wolf that stood in the driving rain at the foot of the steps.

"God." She fumbled on the wall for the light switch, flicked it and had the floodlights pouring on. He was still there, his coat gleaming with wet, his eyes patiently watching. She moistened her lips, took a slow step back. "You should come in out of the rain."

A thrill sprinted up her spine as he leaped gracefully onto the porch. She didn't realize she was holding her breath until his damp fur brushed her leg as he walked inside, and she released it with a shiver.

"Well." Trembling a little, she turned so they watched each other. "There's a wolf in the house. An incredibly handsome wolf," she murmured, and found herself not thinking twice about shutting the door and closing them inside together. "Um, I'm going to go in…" She gestured vaguely. "There. It's warm. You can—"

She broke off, charmed and baffled when he simply swung around and stalked through the doorway. She followed to see him walk to the fire, settle himself, then look back at her as if waiting.

"Smart, aren't you?" she murmured. "Very smart." As she approached cautiously, his gaze never left her face. She lowered herself to the ottoman. "Do you belong to anyone?" She lifted her hand, her fingers itching to touch. She waited for a growl, a snarl, a warning, and when none came she lightly laid her hand on his head. "No, you wouldn't belong to anyone but yourself. That's how it is for the brave and the beautiful."

When her fingers stroked down to his neck, rubbing gently, his eyes narrowed. She thought she recognized pleasure in them and smiled a little. "You like that? Me, too. Touching's as good as being touched, and no one's really touched me for so long. But you don't want to hear the story of my life. It's not very interesting. Yours would be," she mused. "I bet you'd have fascinating tales to tell."

He smelled of the forest, of the rain. Of animal. And oddly, of something…familiar. She grew bolder, running her hands down his back, over his flanks, back to his head. "You'll dry here by the fire," she began, then her hand paused in midstroke, her brows drew together.

"He wasn't wet," she said quietly. "He came through the rain, but he wasn't wet. Was he?" Puzzled, she stared out the dark window. Liam's hair was as black as the wolf's fur, but it hadn't gleamed with rain or damp. Had it?

"How could that be? Even if he'd driven over, he had to get from a car to the door, and…"

She trailed off when the wolf moved closer, when his handsome head nuzzled her thigh. With a murmur of pleasure, she began to stroke him again, grinning when the rumble in his throat reminded her of a very human, very male sound of approval.

"Maybe you're lonely, too."

And she sat with him while the storm shifted out to sea, the thunder quieted and the whips of rain and wind turned to soft patters.

It didn't surprise her that he walked through the house with her. Somehow it seemed perfectly natural that he would accompany her as she blew out candles, switched off lights. He climbed the stairs with her and sat by her side as she lit the bedroom fire.

"I love it here," she murmured, sitting back on her heels to watch the flames catch. "Even when I'm lonely, like I was tonight, it feels right being here. As if I've always needed to come to this place."

She turned her head, smiled a little. They were eye to eye now, deep blue to dark gold. Reaching out, she skimmed her hand under his powerful jaw, rubbing the silky line of his throat. "No one would believe me. No one I know would believe me if I told them I was in a cabin in Oregon talking to a big, black, gorgeous wolf. And maybe I'm just dreaming. I do a lot of that," she added as she rose. "Maybe everyone's right and I do too much dreaming."

She crossed to the dresser and took a pair of pajamas from the drawer. "I guess it's pretty pitiful when your dreams are the most interesting part of your life. I really want to change that. I don't mean I have to climb mountains or jump out of planes..."

He stopped listening—and he had listened all along. But now, as she spoke, she tugged the navy sweatshirt she wore over her head and began to unbutton the simple plaid shirt beneath.

He stopped hearing the words as she slipped the shirt off, stood folding the sweatshirt wearing only a lacy white bra and jeans.

She was small and slender, her skin milk-pale. Her jeans bagged a bit at the waist, making the man inside the wolf nearly groan as her fingers reached for the button. His blood

warmed, his pulse quickened as she let the denim slide carelessly down her legs.

The swatch of white rode low on her hips. He wanted his
mouth there, just there along that lovely curve. To taste the
flesh, to feel the shape of bone. And to slide his tongue under
the white until she quivered.

She sat, tugging off her socks, shaking her feet free of the
jeans. And nearly drove him mad as she stood to lay them
aside.

The low growl in his throat went unnoticed by both of them
as she unhooked her bra in an innocent striptease. He felt his
control slipping as he imagined cupping his hands there, over
small white breasts, skimming his thumbs over pale pink nipples.

Lowering his head until his mouth was—

The sudden violent slash of lightning had her jumping, muf-
fling a scream. "God! The storm must be coming back. I
thought..." She stopped in midsentence as she glanced over,
saw those gold eyes glinting. In an instinctive gesture, she
crossed her arms over her naked breasts. Beneath them, her
heart bounced like a rabbit.

His eyes looked so...human, she thought with a quick panic.
The expression in them hungry. "Why do I suddenly feel like
Little Red Riding Hood?" She eased out a breath, drew in another. "That's just foolish." But her voice wasn't quite steady
as she made the grab for her pajama top. She made a little
squeak of surprise when he caught the dangling sleeve in his
teeth and dragged it away.

A laugh bubbled up and out. She grabbed the collar of the
flannel, pulled. The quick, unexpected tug-of-war made her
laugh again. "You think it's funny?" she demanded. Damned
if she didn't see amusement in those fascinating eyes. "I just
bought these. They may not be pretty, but they're warm—and
it's cold in here. Now, let go!"

When he did, abruptly, she stumbled back two paces before

she caught her balance. Wonderfully naked but for that triangle at her hips, she narrowed her eyes at him. "A real joker, aren't you?" She held the top up, searching for tears or teeth marks, and found none. "Well, at least you didn't eat it."

He watched her slip it on, button it. There was something erotic even in that, in the way the brightly patterned flannel skimmed her thighs. But before she could pull on the bottoms he pleased himself by shifting his head, running his tongue from her ankle to the back of her knee.

She chuckled, bent down to scratch his ears as though he were the family dog. "I like you, too." After pulling the bottoms on, she reached up to loosen what was left of her braid. As she reached for her brush, the wolf padded over to the bed, leaped up and stretched out at the foot.

"Oh, I don't think so." Amused, she turned, running the brush through her hair. "I really don't. You'll have to get down from there."

He watched her unblinkingly. She would have sworn he smiled. Huffing out a breath, she shook her hair back, set the brush aside, then walked to the side of the bed. In her best teacher's voice, she ordered him down and pointed meaningfully at the floor.

This time she *knew* he smiled.

"You're not sleeping in the bed." She reached out, intended to pull him off. But when he bared his teeth, she cleared her throat. "Well, one night. What could it hurt?"

Watching him cautiously, she climbed up, sliding under the duvet. He simply lay, his head snugged between his front paws. She picked up her glasses, her book, shrugging when the wolf lay still. Satisfied, she piled the pillows behind her and settled in to read.

Only moments later, the mattress shifted, and the wolf moved over to lie at her side, laying his head in her lap. Without a thought, Rowan stroked him and began to read aloud.

She read until her eyes grew heavy, her voice thick, and once more slipped into sleep with a book in her hand.

The air quivered as wolf became man. Liam touched a finger to her forehead. "Dream, Rowan," he murmured, pausing as he felt her slide deeper. He took her book, her glasses, and set them neatly on the bedside table. Then he eased her down, lifting her head so he could spread out the pillows.

"You must be waking every morning stiff as a board," he murmured. "Forever falling asleep sitting up." He skimmed the back of his hand over her cheek, then sighed.

The scent of her, silky and female and subtle, was enough to drive him mad. Each quiet breath through those full and parted lips was a kind of invitation.

"Damn it, Rowan, you lie in bed with me with the rain on the roof and read Yeats aloud in that soft, almost prim voice of yours. How should I resist that? I'll have to have you sooner or later. Later's the better for both of us. But I need something tonight."

He took her hand, pressed palm to palm, linked fingers. And shut his eyes. "Come with me, two minds, one dream. Sleep is not now what it seems. Give what I need, and take what you'll have from me. As I will, so mote it be."

She moaned. And moved. Her free arm flung up over her head, her lips parting on a shuddering breath that seemed to whisper in his blood. His own pulse thickened as he made love to her with his mind. Tasted her, touched her with his thoughts. Gave himself to hers.

Lost in dreams, she arched up, her body shuddering under phantom hands.

She smelled him, that musky, half-animal scent that had already stirred her more than once in dreams. Images, sensations, desires, confused and tangled and arousing beyond belief swarmed through her. Embracing them, she murmured his name and opened to him, body and mind.

The hot wave of his thoughts lifted her up, held her trembling, aching, quivering, then stabbed her with unspeakable pleasure. She heard her name, said quietly, almost desperately. Repeated. Desire drugged the mind, swirled through it, then slid silently away into fulfillment.

He sat, his eyes still closed, his hand still joined with hers. Listened to the rain, her soft and steady breathing. Resisting the urge to lie with her, to touch her now with more than his mind, he threw his head back. And vanished.

# Chapter 3

She woke early, blissfully relaxed. Her body seemed to glow.
Her mind was calm, clear and content. Rowan was out of bed
and in the shower before she remembered anything. Then with
a muttered curse, she jumped out, dripping, grabbed a towel
and dashed back into the bedroom.

The bed was empty. There was no beautiful wolf curled
in front of the cold fire. Ignoring the water sliding down her
legs she dashed downstairs, searching the house and leaving
a trail of damp behind her.

The kitchen door hung open, letting in the chill of the morning. Still she stepped out, her cold toes curling up in protest
as she scanned the line of trees.

How did he get out—and where did he go? she wondered.
Since when do wolves open doors?

She hadn't imagined it. No, she refused to believe that her
imagination could create such clear images, such textures, such
events. That would make her crazy, wouldn't it? she thought
with a half laugh as she backed inside again and closed the door.

The wolf had been in the house. He'd sat with her, stayed

with her. Even slept on the bed. She could remember exactly the feel of his fur, the scent of rain and wild on it, the expressions in his eyes, and the warmth, the simple comfort, when he'd laid his head on her lap.

However...unusual the evening, it had happened. However odd her own actions, letting him in, petting him, she had done so.

And if she'd had a brain cell in her head, she'd have thought to grab her camera and take a few pictures of him.

To prove what? To show to whom? The wolf, she realized, was her personal and private joy. She didn't want to share him.

She went back upstairs, back to the shower, wondering how long it would be before he came back.

She caught herself singing and grinned. She couldn't remember ever waking up happier or with more energy. And wasn't that part of the plan? she thought as she lifted her face to the spray and let the hot water stream. To find out just what made her happy. If it happened to be spending a stormy night with a wolf, so what?

"Try to explain that one, Rowan." Laughing at herself, she toweled off. Humming, she started to wipe the steam from the bathroom mirror, then paused, staring at her own misty reflection.

Did she look different? she wondered, leaning closer to study her face, the glow of her skin, the sleek sheen of wet hair, and most of all the light in her eyes.

What had put that there? She lifted her hand, running her fingers curiously along the ridge of her cheekbones just under her eyes.

Dreams. And her fingers trembled lightly as she dropped them. Hot and shivering dreams. Colors and shapes pulsing through her mind, through her body. So stunning, so...erotic. Hands on her breasts, but not. A mouth crushing down on hers but never really touching.

Closing her eyes, she let the towel fall, skimmed her hands

over her breasts, down, up again, trying to focus on where she had journeyed in sleep.

The taste of male skin, the hot slide of it over her own. Needs rocketing through the mind to be met and met again until the beauty of it brought tears.

She'd never experienced anything like that, not even in life. How could she find it in dreams?

And why should she go to sleep with a wolf and dream of a man?

Of Liam.

She knew it had been Liam. She could all but feel the shape of his mouth on hers. But how could that be? she wondered, tracing a fingertip over her lips. How could she be so sure she knew just what it would be like to meet his mouth with hers?

"Because you want to," she murmured, opening her eyes to meet those in the mirror again. "Because you want him and you've never wanted anyone else like this. And, Rowan, you moron, you don't have the slightest idea how to make it happen, except in dreams. So that's where it happens for you. Psychology 101—real basic stuff."

Not certain if she should be amused or appalled at herself, she dressed, went down to brew her morning coffee. Snug in her sweater, she flung open the windows to the cool, fresh air left behind by the rain.

She thought, without enthusiasm, about cereal or toast or yogurt. She had a yen for chocolate chip cookies, which was absurd at barely eight in the morning, so she told herself. Dutifully she opened the cupboard for cereal, then slammed it shut.

If she wanted cookies, she was having them. And with a grin on her face and a gleam in her eye, began to drag out ingredients. She slopped flour, scattered sugar on the counter. And mixed with abandon. There was no one to see her lick dough from her fingers. No one to gently remind her that she should tidy up between each step of the process.

She made an unholy mess.

Dancing with impatience, she waited for the first batch to bake. "Come on, come on. I've got to have one." The minute the buzzer went off, she grabbed the cookie sheet out, dropped it on the top of the stove, then scooped up the first cookie with a spatula. She blew on it, slipped it off and tossed it from hand to hand. Still she burned her tongue on hot, gleaming chocolate as she bit in. And rolling her eyes dramatically, she swallowed with a hedonistic groan.

"Good job. Really good job. More."

She ate a dozen before the second batch was baked.

It felt decadent, childish. And wonderful.

When the phone rang, she popped the next batch in, and lifted the receiver with doughy fingers. "Hello?"

"Rowan. Good morning."

For a moment the voice meant nothing to her, then, with a guilty start, she realized it was Alan. "Good morning."

"I hope I didn't wake you?"

"No, no. I've been up quite a while. I'm..." She grinned and chose another cookie. "Just having breakfast."

"Glad to hear it. You tend to skip too many meals."

She put the whole cookie into her mouth and talked around it. "Not this time. Maybe the mountain air..." She managed to swallow. "Stimulates my appetite."

"You don't sound like yourself."

"Really?" I'm not myself, she wanted to say. I'm better. And I'm not nearly finished yet.

"You sound a little giddy. Are you all right?"

"I'm fine. I'm wonderful." How could she explain to this solid and serious man with his solid and serious voice that she'd been dancing in the kitchen eating cookies, that she'd spent the evening with a wolf, that she'd had erotic dreams about a man she barely knew?

And that she wouldn't change a moment of any of those experiences.

"I'm getting lots of reading done," she said instead. "Taking long walks. I've been doing some sketching, too. I'd forgotten how much I enjoy it. It's a gorgeous morning. The sky's unbelievably blue."

"I checked the weather for your area last night. There were reports of a severe thunderstorm. I tried to call, but your lines were out."

"Yes, we had a storm. That's probably why it's so spectacular this morning."

"I was worried, Rowan. If I hadn't been able to reach you this morning, I was going to fly to Portland and rent a car."

The thought of it, just the thought of him invading her magical little world filled her with panic. She had to fight to keep it out of her voice. "Oh, Alan, there's absolutely no need to worry. I'm fine. The storm was exciting, actually. And I have a generator, emergency lights."

"I don't like thinking of you up there alone, in some rustic little hut in the middle of nowhere. What if you hurt yourself, or fell ill, got a flat tire?"

Her mood began to deflate, degree by degree. She could actually feel the drop. He'd said the same words to her before, and so had her parents, with the exact same tone of bafflement mixed with concern.

"Alan, it's a lovely, sturdy and very spacious cabin, not a hut. I'm only about five miles outside of a very nice little town, which makes this far from the middle of nowhere. If I hurt myself or get sick, I'll go to a doctor. If I get a flat tire, I suppose I'll figure out how to change it."

"You're still alone, Rowan, and as last night proved, easily cut off."

"The phone's working just fine now," she said between clenched teeth. "And I have a cell phone in the Rover. Added to that, I believe I have a moderately intelligent mind, I'm in perfect health, I'm twenty-seven years old and the entire purpose of my coming here was to be alone."

There was a moment's silence, a moment just long enough

to let her know she'd hurt his feelings. And more than long enough to bring her a swift wash of guilt. "Alan—"

"I'd hoped you'd be ready to come home, but that apparently isn't the case. I miss you, Rowan. Your family misses you. I only wanted to let you know."

"I'm sorry." How many times in her life had she said those words? she wondered as she pressed her fingers to the dull ache forming in her temple. "I didn't mean to snap at you, Alan. I suppose I feel a little defensive. No, I'm not ready to come back. If you speak to my parents, tell them I'll call them later this evening, and that I'm fine."

"I'll be seeing your father later today." His voice was stiff now, his way—she knew—of letting her know he was hurt. "I'll tell him. Please keep in touch."

"I will. Of course, I will. It was nice of you to call. I'll, ah, write you a long letter later this week."

"I'd enjoy that. Goodbye, Rowan."

Her cheerful mood totally evaporated, she hung up, turned and looked at the chaos of the kitchen. As penance, she cleaned every inch of it, then put the cookies in a plastic container, sealing them away.

"No, I am not going to brood. Absolutely not." She banged open a cupboard door, took out a smaller container and transferred half the cookies into it.

Before she could talk herself out of it, she grabbed a light jacket from the hook by the door, and tucking the container under her arm, stepped outside.

She didn't have a clue where Liam's cabin was, but he'd said he was closer to the sea. It only made sense to hunt it out, she decided. In case of...an emergency. She'd take a walk, and if she didn't find it... Well, she thought, shaking the cookies, she wouldn't starve while she was looking.

She walked into the trees, struck again at how much cooler, how much greener it was inside them. There was birdsong, the whisper of the trees and the sweet smell of pine. Where sunlight could dapple through, it danced on the forest floor, sparkled on the water of the stream.

The deeper she walked, the higher her mood rose again. She paused briefly, just to close her eyes, to let the wind ruffle her hair, play against her cheeks. How could she explain this, just this, to a man like Alan? she wondered. Alan, whose every want was logical, whose every step was reasonable and solid.

How could she make him, or anyone else from the world she'd run from, understand what it was like to crave something as intangible as the sound of trees singing, the sharp taste the sea added to the air, the simple peace of standing alone in something so vast and so alive?

"I'm not going back there." The words, more than the sound of her own voice, had her eyes snapping open in surprise. She hadn't realized she'd decided anything, much less something that momentous. The half laugh that escaped was tinged with triumph. "I'm not going back," she repeated. "I don't know where I'm going, but it won't be back."

She laughed again, longer, fuller as she turned a dizzy circle. With a spring to her step, she started to take the curve of the path to the right. Out of the corner of her eye, she saw a flash of white. Turning, she stared with openmouthed wonder at the white doe.

They watched each other with the tumbling stream between them, the doe with serene gold eyes and a hide as white as clouds, and the woman with both shock and awe glowing in her face.

Captivated, Rowan stepped forward. The deer stood, elegant as a sculpture of ice. Then, with a lift of her head, she turned fluidly and leaped into the trees. Without a moment's hesitation, Rowan scrambled across the stream, using polished rocks as stepping stones. She saw the path immediately, then the deer, a bounding blur of white.

She hurried after, taking each twist and turn of the path at a run. But always the deer stayed just ahead, with no more than a quick glimpse of gleaming white, and the thunder of hooves on the packed ground.

Then she was in a clearing. It seemed to open up out of nowhere, a perfect circle of soft earth ringed by majestic trees. And within the circle, another circle, made of dark gray stones, the shortest as high as her shoulder, the tallest just over her head.

Stunned, she reached out, touched her fingertips to the surface of the nearest stone. And would have sworn she felt a vibration, like harp strings being plucked. And heard, in some secret part of her mind, the answering note.

A stone dance in Oregon? That was…certainly improbable, she decided. Yet here it was. It didn't strike her as being new, but surely it couldn't be otherwise. If it was ancient, someone would have written about it, tourists would come to see it, scientists to study.

Curious, she started to step through two stones, then immediately stepped back again. It seemed the air within quivered. The light was different, richer, and the sound of the sea closer than it had seemed only a moment before.

She told herself she was a rational woman, that there was no life in stone, nor any difference between the air where she stood and that one foot inside the circle. But rational or not, she skirted around rather than walking through.

It was as if the deer had waited, halfway around the dance just down a thin, shadowy path through the trees. Just as it seemed she looked at Rowan with understanding, and amusement, before she bounded gracefully ahead.

This time when she followed, Rowan lost all sense of direction. She could hear the sea, but was it ahead, to the left, or to the right? The path twisted, turned and narrowed until it was no more than a track. She climbed over a fallen log, skidded down an incline and wandered through shadows deep as twilight.

When the path ended abruptly, leaving her surrounded

by trees and thick brush, she cursed herself for an idiot. She turned, intending to retrace her steps, and saw that the track veered off in two directions.

For the life of her she couldn't remember which to take.

Then she saw the flash of white again, just a glimmer to the left. Heaving a breath, then holding it, Rowan pushed through the brush, fought her way out of the grasp of a thick, thorny vine. She slipped, righted herself. Cursing vividly now, she tripped and stumbled clear of the trees.

The cabin stood nearly on the cliffs, ringed by trees on three sides and backed by the rocks on the fourth. Smoke billowed from the chimney and was whisked away to nothing in the wind.

She pushed the hair out of her face, smeared a tiny drop of blood from a nick a thorn had given her. It was smaller than Belinda's cabin, and made of stone rather than wood. Sunlight had the mica glittering like diamonds. The porch was wide, but uncovered. On the second floor a small and charming stone balcony jutted out from glass doors.

When she lowered her gaze from it, Liam was standing on the porch. He had his thumbs hooked in the front pockets of his jeans, a black sweatshirt with its arms shoved up to the elbows. And he didn't look particularly happy to see her.

But he nodded. "Come in, Rowan. Have some tea."

He walked back inside without waiting for her response, and left the door open wide behind him. When she came closer, she heard the music, pipes and strings tangled in a weepy melody. She barely stopped her hands from twisting together as she stepped inside.

The living area seemed larger than she'd expected, but thought it was because the furnishings were very spare. A single wide chair, a long sofa, both in warm rust colors. A fire blazed under a mantel of dull gray slate. Gracing it was a jagged green stone as big as a man's fist and a statue of a woman carved in alabaster with her arms uplifted, her head thrown back, her naked body slender as a wand.

She wanted to move closer, to study the face, but it seemed rude. Instead she walked toward the back and found Liam in a small, tidy kitchen with a kettle already on the boil and lovely china cups of sunny yellow set out.

"I wasn't sure I'd find you," she began, then lost the rest of her thought as he turned from the stove, as those intense eyes locked on hers.

"Weren't you?"

"No, I hoped I would, but… I wasn't sure." Nerves reared up and grabbed her by the throat. "I made some cookies. I brought you some to thank you for helping me out last night."

He smiled a little and poured boiling water into a yellow pot. "What kind?" he asked. Though he knew. He'd smelled them, and her before she'd stepped out of the woods.

"Chocolate chip." She managed a smile of her own. "Is there another kind?" She busied her hands by opening the container. "They're pretty good. I've eaten two dozen at least already."

"Then sit. You can wash them back with tea. You'll have gotten chilled wandering about. The wind's brisk today."

"I suppose." She sat at the little kitchen table, just big enough for two. "I don't even know how long I've been out," she began, shoving at her tangled hair as he brought the pot to the table. "I was distracted by—" She broke off as he skimmed his thumb over her cheek.

"You've scratched your face." He said it softly as the tiny drop of blood lay warm and intimate on his thumb.

"Oh, I…got tangled up. Some thorns." She was lost in his eyes, could have drowned in them. Wanted to. "Liam."

He touched her face again, took away the sting she was too befuddled to notice. "You were distracted," he said, shifting back, then sitting across from her. "When you were in the forest."

"Ah…yes. By the white doe."

*Enchanted*

He lifted a brow as he poured out the tea. "A white deer? Were you on a quest, Rowan?"

She smiled self-consciously. "The white deer, or bird, or horse. The traditional symbol of quest in literature. I suppose I was on a mild sort of quest, to find you. But I did see her."

"I don't doubt it," he said mildly. His mother enjoyed traditional symbols.

"Have you?"

"Yes." He lifted his tea. "Though it's been some time."

"She's beautiful, isn't she?"

"Aye, that she is. Warm yourself, Rowan. You've bird bones and you'll take a chill."

"I grew up in San Francisco. I'm used to chills. Anyway, I saw her, and couldn't stop myself from following her. I ended up in this clearing, with a stone circle."

His eyes sharpened, glinted. "She led you there?"

"I suppose you could put it that way. You know the place? I never expected to find something like it here. You think of Ireland or Britain, Wales or Cornwall—not Oregon—when you think of stone dances."

"You find them where they're wanted. Or needed. Did you go in?"

"No. It's silly, but it spooked me a little, so I went around. And got completely lost."

He knew he should have felt relieved, but instead there was a vague sense of disappointment. But of course, he reminded himself, he'd have known if she'd stepped inside. Instantly. "Hardly lost, since you're here."

"It seemed like I was lost. The path disappeared and I couldn't get my sense of direction. I probably have a poor one anyway. The tea's wonderful," she commented. It was warm and strong and smooth, with something lovely and sweet just under it.

"An old family blend," he said with a hint of a smile, then

sampled one of her cookies. "They're good. So you cook, do you, Rowan?"

"I do, but the results are hit-and-miss." All of her early-morning cheer was back and bubbling in her voice. "This morning, I hit. I like your house. It's like something out of a book, standing here with its back to the cliffs and sea and the stones glittering in the sunlight."

"It does for me. For now."

"And the views…" She rose to go to the window over the sink, and caught her breath at the sight of the cliffs. "Spectacular. It must be spellbinding during a storm like the one we had last night."

Spellbinding, he thought, knowing his father's habit of manipulating the weather for his needs, was exactly what the storm had been. "And did you sleep well?"

She felt the heat rise up her throat. She could hardly tell him she'd dreamed he'd made love to her. "I don't remember ever sleeping better."

He laughed, rose. "It's flattering." He watched her shoulders draw in. "To know my company relaxed you."

"Hmm." Struggling to shake off the feeling that he knew exactly where her mind had wandered, she started to turn. She noticed the open door and the little room beyond where he'd left a light burning on a desk, and a sleek black computer running.

"Is that your office?"

"In a manner of speaking."

"I've interrupted your work, then."

"It's not pressing." He shook his head. "Why don't you ask if you want to see?"

"I do," she admitted. "If it's all right."

In answer he simply gestured and waited for her to step into the room ahead of him.

The room was small, but the window was wide enough to let in that stunning view of the cliffs. She wondered how anyone could concentrate on work with that to dream on. Then laughed when she saw what was on the monitor screen.

"So you were playing games? I know this one. My students were wild for it. The Secrets of Myor."

"Don't you play games?"

"I'm terrible at them. Especially this kind, because I tend to get wrapped up in them, and then every step is so vital. I can't take the pressure." Laughing again, she leaned closer, studying the screen with its lightning-stalked castle and glowing fairies. "I've only gotten to the third level where Brinda the witch queen promises to open the Door Of Enchantment if you can find the three stones. I usually find one, then fall into the Pit of Forever."

"There are always traps on the way to enchantment. Or there wouldn't be pleasure in finding it. Do you want to try again?"

"No, my palms get damp and my fingers fumble. It's humiliating."

"Some games you take seriously, some you don't."

"They're all serious to me." She glanced at the CD jacket, admiring the illustration, then blinked at the small lettering: Copyright by the Donovan Legacy. "It's your game?" Delighted, she straightened, turned. "You create computer games? That's so clever."

"It's entertaining."

"To someone who's barely stumbled their way onto the internet, it's genius. Myor's a wonderful story. The graphics are gorgeous, but I really admire the story itself. It's just magical. A challenging fairy tale with rewards and consequences."

Her eyes took on tiny silver flecks of light when she was happy, he noted. And the scent of her warmed with her mood. He knew how to make it warm still more, and how to cause those silver flecks to drown in deep, dark blue.

"All fairy tales have both. I like your hair this way." He stepped closer, skimmed his fingers through it, testing weight and texture. "Tumbled and tangled."

Her throat snapped closed. "I forgot to braid it this morning."

"The wind's had it," he murmured, lifting a handful to his face. "I can smell the wind on it, and the sea." It was reckless, he knew, but he had dreamed as well. And he remembered every rise and fall. "I'd taste both on your skin."

Her knees had jellied. The blood was swimming so fast in her veins that she could hear the roar of it in her head. She couldn't move, could barely breathe. So she only stood, staring into his eyes, waiting.

"Rowan Murray with the fairy eyes. Do you want me to touch you?" He laid a hand on her heart, felt each separate hammer blow pound between the gentle curves of her breasts. "Like this." Then spread his fingers, circled them over one slope, under.

Her bones dissolved, her eyes clouded, and the breath shuddered between her lips in a yielding sigh. His fingers lay lightly on her, but the heat from them seemed to scorch through to flesh. Still, she moved neither toward him nor away.

"You've only to say no," he murmured. "When I ask if you want me to taste you."

But her head fell back, those clouded eyes closed when he lowered his head to graze his teeth along her jawline. "The sea and the wind, and innocence as well." His own needs thickened his voice, but there was an edge on it. "Will you give me that as well, do nothing to stop me taking it?" He eased back, waiting, willing her eyes to open and look into his. "If I kissed you now, Rowan, what might happen?"

Her lips trembled apart as memory of a question once asked in dreams and never answered struggled to surface. Then his mouth was on hers, and every thought willingly died. Lights, a wild swirl of them behind the eyes. Heat, a hot gush of it in the belly. The first sound she made was a whimper that might have been fear, but the next was a moan that was unmistakably pleasure.

He was more gentle than she'd expected, perhaps more than

he'd intended. His lips skimmed, sipped, nipped and nuzzled until hers went pillow-soft and warm under them. She swayed against him in surrender, and request.

*Oh, yes, I want this. Just this.*

A shiver coursed through her as his hand circled the back of her neck, as he urged her head back, took the kiss deeper with a tangle of tongues and tastes, a mingle of breath that grew unsteady and quick. She gripped his shoulders, first for balance, then for the sheer joy of feeling that hard, dangerous strength, the bunch of muscles.

Her hands slid over and into his hair.

She had a flash of the wolf, the rich black pelt and sinewy strength, then of the man, sitting on her bed, gripping her hand as her body shuddered.

The memory of what could be in dreams, the barrage of sensations of what was, battered each other.

And she erupted.

Her mouth went wild under his, tore at his control. Her surrender had been sweet, but her demands were staggering. As his blood leaped, he dragged her closer, let the kiss fly from warm to hungry to something almost savage.

Still she urged him on, pulling him with her until he buried his face in her throat and had to fight not to use his teeth.

"You're not ready for me." He managed to pant it out, then yanked her back, shook her lightly. "By Finn, I'm not ready for you. There might come a time when that won't matter, and we'll take our chances. But it matters now." His grip lightened, his tone gentled. "It matters today. Go home, Rowan, where you'll be safe."

Her head was still spinning, her pulse still roaring. "No one's ever made me feel like that. I never knew anyone could."

Something flashed into his eyes that made her shiver in anticipation. But then he muttered in a language she didn't understand and lowered his brow to hers. "Honesty can be dangerous. I'm not always civilized, Rowan, but I work to be fair. Have a care how much you offer, for I'm likely to take more."

"I'm terrible at lying."

It made him laugh, and his eyes were calm again when he straightened. "Then be quiet, for God's sake. Go home now. Not the way you came. You'll see the path when you head out the front. Follow it and you'll get home right enough."

"Liam, I want—"

"I know what you want." Firmly now, he took her by the arm and led her out. "If it were as simple as going upstairs and rolling around on the bed for an afternoon, we'd already be there." While she sputtered, he continued to pull her to the front door. "But you're not as simple as you've been taught to think. God knows I'm not. Go on home with you, Rowan."

He all but shoved her out the door. Her rare and occasionally awesome temper shot to the surface as the wind slapped her face. "All right, Liam, because I don't want it to be simple." Her eyes flared at him as she dragged her hair back. "I'm tired of settling for simple. So don't put your hands on me again unless you mean to complicate things."

Riding on anger, she spun around, and didn't question the fact that the path was there, wide and clear. She just marched to it and strode into the trees.

From the porch he watched; long after she was out of sight, he continued to watch her, smiling a bit when she finally reached her own home and slammed the door behind her.

"Good for you, Rowan Murray."

# *Chapter 4*

The man had thrown her out of his house, Rowan thought as she stormed into her own. One minute he'd been kissing her brainless, holding her against that marvelously male body—and the next he'd marched her to the door. Given her the boot as if she'd been some pesky saleswoman hawking an inferior product.

Oh, it was mortifying.

With temper still ringing in her ears like bells she strode around the living room, circled it twice. He'd put his hands on her, he'd made the moves. *He'd* kissed her, damn it. She hadn't done anything.

Except stand there like a dolt, she realized as temper sagged miserably into embarrassment. She'd just stood there, she thought as she wandered into the kitchen. And let him put his hands on her, let him kiss her. She'd have let him do anything, that was how dazzled she'd been.

"Oh, you're such a fool, Rowan." She dropped into a chair, and leaning over, lightly beat her head against the kitchen table. "Such a jerk, such a wimp."

She'd gone to him, hadn't she? Stumbling around in the woods like Gretel with a bunch of cookies instead of bread crumbs. Looking for magic, she thought, and rested her cheek on the smooth wood. Always looking for something wonderful, she acknowledged with a sigh. And this time, for just a moment, she'd found it.

It was worse, she realized, when you had that staggering glimpse, then had the door slammed in your face.

God, was she so needy that she'd fall at the feet of a man she'd only met twice before, knew next to nothing about? Was she so weak and wobbly that she'd built fantasies around him because he had a beautiful face?

Not just his face, she admitted. It was the…essence of him, she supposed. The mystery, the romance of him that had very simply bewitched her. There was no other word that fit what he made her feel.

Obviously, quite obviously, it showed.

And when he had touched her because he'd seen through her pitiful ploy of seeking him out to thank him, she'd climbed all over him.

No wonder he'd shown her the door.

But he hadn't had to be so cruel about it, she thought, shoving up again. He'd humiliated her.

"You're not ready for me," she muttered, remembering what he'd said. "How the hell does he know what I'm ready for when I don't know myself? He's not a damn mind reader."

Sulking now, she ripped the top off the container of cookies and snatched one. She ate it with a scowl on her face as she replayed that last scene, and gave herself wonderful, pithy lines to put Liam Donovan in his place.

"So, he didn't want me," she muttered. "Who expected him to? I'll just stay out of his way. Completely. Totally." She shoved another cookie into her mouth. "I came here to figure out myself, not to try to understand some Irish recluse."

Slightly ill from the cookies, she snapped the lid back on.

The first thing she was going to do was drive into town and find a bookstore. She was going to buy some how-to books. Basic home maintenance, she decided, stalking back into the living room for her purse.

She wasn't going to go fumbling around the next time something happened. She'd figure out how to fix it herself. And, she thought darkly as she marched out of the house, if Liam came to her door offering to fix it for her, she'd coolly tell him she could take care of herself.

She slammed the door of the Rover, gunned the engine. An errant thought about flat tires made her think she'd better find a book on car repair while she was at it.

She bumped along the dirt road, clamping down on the urge to work off some of her frustration by stomping on the gas. Just where Belinda's little lane met the main road, she saw the silver bird.

He was huge, magnificent. An eagle, she thought, automatically stepping on the brake to stop and study him. Though she didn't know if any type of eagle was that regal silvery-gray or if they tended to perch on road signs to stare—balefully, she decided—at passing cars.

What wonderfully odd fauna they had in Oregon, she mused, and reminded herself to read more carefully the books on local wildlife she'd brought with her. Unable to resist, she rolled down the window and leaned out.

"You're so handsome." She smiled as the bird ruffled his feathers and seemed to preen. "So regal. I bet you look magnificent in the air. I wonder what it feels like to fly. To just... own the sky. You'd know."

His eyes were green, she realized. A silver-gray eagle with eyes green as a cat's. For an instant, she thought she saw a glint of gold resting in his breast feathers, as if he wore a pendant. Just a trick of the light, she decided, and with some regret leaned back in the window.

"Wolves and deer and eagles. Why would anybody live in the city? Bye, Your Highness."

When the Rover was out of sight, the eagle spread its wings, rose majestically into the sky with a triumphant call that echoed over hill and forest and sea. He soared over the trees, circled, then dived. White smoke swirled, the light shimmered, blue as a lightning flash.

And he touched down on the forest floor softly, on two booted feet.

He stood just over six feet, with a mane of silver hair, eyes of glass green and a face so sharply defined it might have been carved from the marble found in the dark Irish hills. A burnished gold chain hung around his neck, and dangling from it was the amulet of his rank.

"Runs like a rabbit," he muttered. "Then blames herself for the fox."

"She's young, Finn." The woman who stepped out of the green shadows was lovely, with gilded hair flowing down her back, soft tawny eyes, skin white and smooth as alabaster. "And she doesn't know what's inside her, or understand what's inside of Liam."

"A backbone's what she's needing, a bit more of that spirit she showed when she spat in his eye not long ago." His fierce face gentled with a smile. "Never was a lack of spine or spirit a problem of yours, Arianna."

She laughed and cupped her husband's face in her hands. The gold ring of their marriage gleamed on one hand, and the fire of a ruby sparked on the other. "I've needed both with the likes of you, *a stor.* They're on their path, Finn. Now we must let them follow it in their own way."

"And who was it who led the girl to the dance, then to the lad?" he asked with an arrogantly raised eyebrow.

"Well then." Lightly, she trained a fingertip down his cheek. "I never said we couldn't give them a bit of a nudge, now and then. The lass is troubled, and Liam—oh, he's a difficult man, is Liam. Like his da."

"Takes after his mother more." Still smiling, Finn leaned down to kiss his wife. "When the girl comes into her own, the boy will have his hands full. He'll be humbled before he finds the truth of pride. She'll be hurt before she finds the full of her strength."

"Then, if it's meant, they'll find each other. You like her." Arianna linked her hands at the back of Finn's neck. "She appealed to your vanity, sighing over you, calling you handsome."

His silver brows rose again, his grin flashed bright. "I am handsome—and so you've said yourself. We'll leave them to themselves a bit." He slid his arms around her waist. "Let's be home, *a ghra*. I'm already missing Ireland."

With a swirl of white smoke, a shiver of white light, they were home.

By the time Rowan got home, heated up a can of soup and devoured a section on basic plumbing repairs, it was sunset. For the first time since her arrival she didn't stop and stare and wonder at the glorious fire of the dying day. As the light dimmed, she merely leaned closer to the page.

With her elbows propped on the kitchen table, and her tea going cold, she almost wished a pipe would spring a leak so she could test out her new knowledge.

She felt smug and prepared, and decided to tackle the section on electrical work next. But first she'd make the phone call she'd been putting off. She considered fortifying herself with a glass of wine first, but decided that would be weak.

She took off her reading glasses, set them aside. Slipped a bookmark into the pages, closed the book. And stared at the phone.

It was terrible to dread calling people you loved.

She put it off just a little longer by neatly stacking the books she'd bought. There were more than a dozen, and she was still amused at herself for picking up several on myths and legends.

They'd be entertaining, she thought, and wasted a little more time selecting the one she wanted for bedtime reading.

Then there was wood to be brought in for the evening fire, the soup bowl to wash and carefully dry. Her nightly scan of the woods for the wolf she hadn't seen all day.

When she couldn't find anything else to engage her time, she picked up the phone and dialed.

Twenty minutes later, she was sitting on the back steps, the backwash of light from the kitchen spilling over her. And she was weeping.

She'd nearly buckled under the benign pressure, nearly crumbled beneath the puzzled, injured tone of her mother's voice. Yes, yes, of course, she'd come home. She'd go back to teaching, get her doctorate, marry Alan, start a family. She'd live in a pretty house in a safe neighborhood. She'd be anything they wanted her to be as long as it made them happy.

Not saying all of those things, not doing them, was so hard. And so necessary.

Her tears were hot and from the heart. She wished she understood why she was always, always pulled in a different direction, why she needed so desperately to see what was blurred at the edges of her mind.

Something was there, waiting for her. Something she was or needed to be. It was all she was sure of.

When the wolf nudged his head under her hand, she simply wrapped her arms around him and pressed her face to his throat.

"Oh, I hate hurting anyone. I can't bear it, and I can't stop it. What's wrong with me?"

Her tears dampened his neck. And touched his heart. To comfort he nuzzled her cheek, let her cling. Then he slipped a quiet thought into her mind.

*Betray yourself, and you betray all they've given you. Love opens doors. It doesn't close them. When you go through it and find yourself, they'll still be there.*

She let out a shuddering breath, rubbed her face against his fur. "I can't go back, even though part of me wants to. If I did, I know something inside me would just...stop." She leaned back, holding his head in her hands. "If I went back, I'd never find anything like you again. Even if it were there, I wouldn't really see it. I'd never follow a white doe or talk to an eagle."

Sighing, she stroked his head, his powerful shoulders. "I'd never let some gorgeous Irishman with a bad attitude kiss me, or do something as fun and foolish as eat cookies for breakfast."

Comforted, she rested her head against his. "I need to do those things, to be the kind of person who does them. That's what they can't understand, you know? And it hurts and frightens them because they love me."

She sighed again, leaned back, stroking his head absently as she studied the woods with their deep shadows, their whispering secrets. "So I have to make this all work, so they stop being hurt and stop being frightened. Part of me is scared that I will make it work—and part of me is scared I won't." Her lips curved ruefully. "I'm such a coward."

His eyes narrowed, glinted, a low growl sounded in his throat making her blink. Their faces were close, and she could see those strong, deadly white teeth. Swallowing hard, she stroked his head with fingers that trembled.

"There now. Easy. Are you hungry? I have cookies." Heart hammering, she got slowly to her feet as he continued to growl. She kept her eyes on him, walking backward as he came up the steps toward her.

As she reached the door, one part of her mind screamed for her to slam it, lock it. He was a wild thing, feral, not to be trusted. But with her eyes locked on his, all she could think was how he had pressed his muzzle against her, how he had been there when she wept.

She left the door open.

Though her hand shook, she picked up a cookie, held it out. "It's probably bad for you, but so many good things are." She muffled a yelp when he nipped it, with surprising delicacy, from her fingertips.

She'd have sworn his eyes laughed at her.

"Well, okay, now we know sugar's as good as music for soothing savage beasts. One more, but that's it."

When he rose onto his hind legs with surprising speed and grace, set those magnificent front paws on her shoulders, she could only manage a choked gasp. Her eyes, wide and round and shocked, met his glinting ones. Then he licked her, from collarbone to ear, one long, warm stroke, and made her laugh.

"What a pair we are," she murmured, and pressed her lips to the ruff of his neck. "What a pair."

He lowered, just as gracefully, snatching the cookie from her fingers on the way.

"Clever, very clever." Eyeing him, she closed the lid on the cookies and set them on top of the refrigerator. "What I need is a hot bath and a book," she decided. "And that glass of wine I didn't let myself have before. I'm not going to think about what someone else wants," she continued as she turned to open the refrigerator. "I'm not going to think about sexy neighbors with outrageously wonderful mouths. I'm going to think about how lovely it is to have all this time, all this space."

She finished pouring the wine and lifted her glass in toast as he watched her. "And to have you. Why don't you come upstairs and keep me company while I have that bath?"

The wolf ran his tongue around his teeth, let out a low sound that resembled a laugh and thought, *Why don't I?*

She fascinated him. It wasn't a terribly comfortable sensation, but he couldn't shake it. It didn't matter how often he reminded himself she was an ordinary woman, and one with entirely too much baggage to become involved with.

He just couldn't stay away.

He'd been certain he'd tuned her out when she slammed her door behind her. Even though he'd been delighted with that flare of temper, the way it had flashed in her eyes, firmed that lovely soft mouth, he'd wanted to put her out of his mind for a few days.

Smarter, safer that way.

But he'd heard her weeping. Sitting in his little office, toying with a spin-off game for Myor, he'd heard those sounds of heartbreak, and despite the block he'd imposed, he'd felt her guilt and grief ripping at his heart.

He hadn't been able to ignore it. So he'd gone to her, offered a little comfort. Then she'd infuriated him, absolutely infuriated him, by calling herself a coward. By believing it.

And what had the coward done, he thought, when a rogue wolf had snarled at her? Offered him a cookie.

A cookie, for Finn's sake.

She was utterly charming.

Then he had entertained, and tortured, himself by sitting and watching her lazily undress. Sweet God, the woman had a way of sliding out of her clothes that made a man's head spin. Then, in a red robe she hadn't bothered to belt, she'd filled the old-fashioned tub with frothy bubbles that smelled of jasmine.

She'd lit candles. Such a...female thing to do. She ran the water too hot, and turned music on seductively low. As she shrugged out of the robe, she daydreamed. He resisted sliding into her mind to see what put that faraway look in her eyes, that faint smile on her lips.

Her body delighted him. It was so slender, so smooth, with a pearly sheen to the skin and slim, subtle curves. Delicate bones, tiny feet, and breasts tipped a fragile blush-pink.

He wanted to taste there, to run his tongue from white to pink to white.

When she'd leaned over to turn off the taps, it had taken an enormous act of will to prevent himself from nipping at that firm, naked bottom.

It both irritated and charmed him that she seemed to have no vanity, no self-awareness. She piled her hair on top of her head in a gloriously messy mass, and didn't so much as glance at herself in the mirror.

Instead she talked to him, chattering nonsense, then hissed out a breath as she stepped into the tub. Steam billowed as she gingerly lowered herself, until the bubbles played prettily over her breasts.

Until he longed to reform and slip into the tub with her as a man.

She only laughed when he walked forward to sniff at her. Only ran a hand over his head absently while she picked up a book with the other.

*Home Maintenance for the Confused and Inept.*

It made him chuckle, the sound coming out as a soft *woof.* She gave his ears a quick scratch, then reached for her wine.

"It says here," she began, "that I should always have a few basic tools on hand. I think I saw all of these in the utility room, but I'd better make a list and compare. The next time the power goes out, or I blow a fuse—or is it a breaker?—I'm handling it myself. I won't be rescued by anyone, especially Liam Donovan."

She gasped then chuckled when the wolf dipped his tongue into her glass and drank. "Hey, hey! This is a very fine sauvignon blanc, and not for you, pal." She lifted the glass out of reach. "It explains how to do simple rewiring," she continued. "Not that I'm planning on doing any, but it doesn't look terribly complicated. I'm very good at following directions."

A frown marred her brow. "Entirely too good." She sipped wine, slid lower in the tub. "That's the core of the problem. I'm *used* to following directions, so everyone's startled that I've taken a detour."

She set the book aside, idly lifted a leg out of the water, skimmed a fingertip up her calf.

His mind moaned.

"No one's more surprised than I am that I like detours. Adventures," she added, and grinned over at him. "This is really my first adventure." She eased up again, bubbles clinging to her breasts. She scooped up a handful and idly rubbed them up and down her arm.

She only laughed when he ran his tongue slowly from her elbow to her shoulder. "All in all, it's been a hell of an adventure so far."

She lingered in the tub for a half hour, innocently delighting him. The scent of her as she toweled off made him yearn. He found her no less alluring when she slipped into the flannel pajamas.

When she crouched to build up the bedroom fire, he nipped and nuzzled, making her giggle. The next thing she knew she was wrestling playfully with a wolf on the hearth rug. His breath tickled her throat. She rubbed his belly and made him rumble with pleasure. His tongue was warm and wet on her cheek. Breathlessly happy she knelt to throw her arms around his neck, to hug fiercely.

"Oh, I'm so glad you're here. I'm so glad I found you." She pressed her cheek hard against his, locked her fingers in that silky fur. "Or did you find me?" she murmured. "It doesn't matter. It's so good to have a friend who doesn't expect anything but friendship."

She curled up with him to watch the fire, smiling at the pictures she found in the flames. "I've always liked doing this. When I was a little girl I was sure I saw things in the fire. Magic things," she murmured, and settled her head on his neck. "Beautiful things. Castles and clouds and cliffs." Her voice slurred as her eyes grew heavy. "Handsome princes and enchanted hills. I used to think I could go there, through the smoke and into the magic." She sighed, drifted. "Now there are only shapes and light."

And slept.

When she slept, he let himself be Liam, stroking her hair while he watched the fire she'd built. There was a way through the smoke and into the magic, he thought. What would she think if he showed her? If he took her there?

"But you'd have to come back to the other, Rowan. There's no way for me to keep you. I don't want to keep you," he corrected, firmly. "But God, I want to have you."

In sleep she sighed, shifted. Her arm came around him. He closed his eyes. "You'd best hurry," he told her. "Hurry and find out what you want and where you intend to go. Sooner or later I'll send for you."

He rose, lifting her gently to carry her to bed. "If you come to me," he whispered as he lowered her to the bed, spread the cover over her. "If you come to me, Rowan Murray, I'll show you magic." Lightly he touched his lips to hers. "Dream what you will tonight, and dream alone."

He kissed her again, for himself this time. He left her as a man. And prowled the night mists as a wolf.

She spent the next week in the grip of tremendous energy, compelled to fill every minute of every day with something new. She explored the woods, haunted the cliffs and pleased herself by sketching whatever appealed to the eye.

As the weather gradually warmed, the bulbs she'd spotted began to bud. The night still carried a chill, but spring was ready to reign. Delighted, she left the windows open to welcome it in.

For that week she saw no one but the wolf. It was rare for him not to spend at least an hour with her. Walking with her on her hikes through the woods, waiting patiently while she examined the beginnings of a wildflower or a circle of toadstools or stopped to sketch the trees.

Her weekly call home made her heart ache, but she told herself she felt strong. Dutifully she wrote a long letter to Alan, but said nothing about coming back.

Each morning she woke content. Each night she slipped into bed satisfied. Her only frustration was that she'd yet to discover what she needed to do. Unless, she sometimes thought, what she needed was simply to live alone with her books, her drawings and the wolf.

She hoped there was more.

Liam did not wake every morning content. Nor did he go to bed every night satisfied. He blamed her for it, though he knew it was unfair.

Still, if she'd been less innocent, he would have taken what she'd once offered him. The physical need would have been met. And he assured himself this emotional pull would fade.

He refused to accept whatever fate had in store for him, for them, until he was completely in control of his own mind and body.

He stood facing the sea on a clear afternoon when the wind was warm and the air full of rioting spring. He'd come out to clear his head. His work wouldn't quite gel. And though he claimed continually that it was no more than a diversion, an amusement, he took a great deal of pride in the stories he created.

Absently he fingered the small crystal of fluorite he'd slipped into his pocket. It should have calmed him, helped to steady his mind. Instead his mind was as restless as the sea he studied.

He could feel the impatience in the air, mostly his own. But he knew the sense of waiting was from others. Whatever destination he was meant to reach, the steps to it were his own. Those who waited asked when he would take them.

"When I'm damned ready," he muttered. "My life remains

mine. There's always a choice. Even with responsibility, even with fate, there is a choice. Liam, son of Finn, will make his own."

He wasn't surprised to see the white gull soar overhead. Her wing caught the sunlight, tipped gracefully as she flew down. And her eyes glinted, gold as his own, when she perched on a rock.

"Blessed be, Mother."

With only a bit more flourish than necessary, Arianna swirled from bird to woman. She smiled, opened her arms. "Blessed be, my love."

He went to her, enfolded her, pressed his face into her hair. "I've missed you. Oh, you smell of home."

"Where you, too, are missed." She eased back, but framed his face in her hands. "You look tired. You aren't sleeping well."

Now his smile was rueful. "No, not well. Do you expect me to?"

"No." And she laughed, kissed both his cheeks before turning to look out to sea. "This place you've chosen to spend some time is beautiful. You've always chosen well, Liam, and you will always have a choice." She slanted a look up at him. "The woman is lovely, and pure of heart."

"Did you send her to me?"

"The one day? Yes, or I showed her the way." Arianna shrugged and walked back to sit on the rock. "But did I send her here, no. There are powers beyond mine and yours that set events in order. You know that." She crossed her legs and the long white dress she wore whispered. "You find her attractive."

"Why wouldn't I?"

"She's not the usual type you're drawn to, at least to dally with."

He set his teeth. "A grown man doesn't care to have his mother discuss his sex life."

"Oh." She waved a hand dismissively and set her rings

flashing. "Sex, when tempered with respect and affection, is healthy. I want my only child to be healthy, don't I? You won't dally with her because you worry it will involve more than sex, more than affection."

"And what then?" Anger simmered in his voice. "Do I take her, engage her heart only to hurt her? 'An' it harm none.' Does that only apply to magic?"

"No." She spoke gently, held out a hand to him. "It should apply to life. Why assume you'll harm her, Liam?"

"I'm bound to."

"No more than any man hurts any woman when their hearts bump together. You would take the same risks with her." She angled her head as she studied his face. "Do you think your father and I have loved over thirty years without a scratch or bruise?"

"She's not like us." He squeezed the hand he held, then released it. "If I take the steps, if I let us both feel more than we do now, I'd have to let her go or turn my back on my obligations. Obligations you know I came here to sort out." Furious with himself, he turned back to the sea. "I haven't even done that. I know my father wants me to take his place."

"Well, not quite yet," Arianna said with a laugh. "But yes, when the time is right, it's hoped you'll stand as head of the family, as Liam of Donovan, to guide."

"It's a power I can pass to another. That's my right."

"Aye, Liam." Concerned now, she slid from the rock to go to him. "It's your right to step aside, to let another wear the amulet. Is that what you want?"

"I don't know." Frustration rang in his voice. "I'm not my father. I don't have his…way with others. His judgment. His patience or his compassion."

"No. You have your own." She laid a hand on his arm. "If you weren't fit for the responsibility, you would not be given it."

"I've thought of that, tried to come to accept it. And I know that if I commit to a woman not of elfin blood, I abdicate the right to take those responsibilities. If I let myself love her, I turn my back on my obligations to my family."

Arianna's eyes sharpened as she studied his face. "Would you?"

"If I let myself love her, I'd turn my back on anything, on everything but her."

She closed her eyes then, felt the tears welling in them. "Oh, it's proud I am to hear it, Liam." Eyes drenched she lay a hand on his heart. "There is no stronger magic, no truer power than love. This above all I want you to learn, to know, to feel."

Her hand closed into a fist so quickly, her eyes flashed with annoyance so abruptly, he could only gape when she rapped his chest. "And for the love of Finn, why haven't you looked? Your powers are your gifts, your birthright, and more acute than any I know but your father's. What have you been doing?" she demanded, throwing up her hands and whirling with a spin of white silk. "Prowling the woods, calling to the moon, spinning your games. And brooding," she added, jabbing a finger at him as she turned back. "Oh, a champion brooder you ever were, and that's the truth of it. You'll torture yourself with the wanting of her, go keep her company during a storm—"

"Which I know bloody well Da brewed."

"That's beside the point," she snapped, and skewered him with the sharp, daunting look he remembered from childhood. "If you don't spend time with the girl you won't think with anything but your glands, will you? The sex won't answer it all, you horse's ass. It's just like a man to think it will."

"Well, damn it, I *am* a man."

"What you are is a pinhead, and don't you raise your voice to me, Liam Donovan."

He threw up his hands as well, added a short, pithy curse in Gaelic. "I'm not twelve any longer."

"I don't care if you're a hundred and twelve, you'll show your mother proper respect."

He smoldered, seethed and sucked it in. "Yes, ma'am."

"Aye." She nodded once. "That'll do. Now stop tormenting yourself with what may be, and look at what is. And if your lofty principles won't let you look deep enough, ask her about her mother's family."

Arianna let out a huff of breath, smoothed down her hair. "And kiss me goodbye like a good lad. She'll be here any second."

Because he was still scowling, she kissed him instead, then grinned sunnily. "There are times you look so like your Da. Now don't look so fierce, you'll frighten the girl. Blessed be, Liam," she added, then, with a shiver of the light, spread white wings and soared into the sky.

# Chapter 5

He hadn't sensed her, and that irritated him. His temper had been up, blocking his instincts. Now, even as he turned, he caught that scent—female, innocence with a light whiff of jasmine.

He watched her come out of the trees, though she didn't see him—not at first. The sun was behind him, and she looked the other way as she started up the rough path to the apex of the cliffs.

She had her hair tied back, he noted, in a careless tail of gleaming brown the wind caught and whipped. She carried a trim leather bag with its strap crosswise over her body. Her gray slacks showed some wear and her shirt was the color of daffodils.

Her mouth was unpainted, her nails were short, her boots—so obviously new—showed a long, fresh scar across the left toe. The sight of her, muttering to herself as she climbed, both relaxed and annoyed him.

Then both sensations turned to pure amusement as she spotted him, jolted and scowled before she could school her expression to disinterest.

"Good morning to you, Rowan."

She nodded, then clasped both hands on the strap of her bag as if she didn't know what else to do with them. Her eyes were cool, in direct contrast to those nervous hands, and quite deliberately skimmed past him.

"Hello. I'd have gone another way if I'd known you were here. I imagine you want to be alone."

"Not particularly."

Her gaze veered back to his, then away again. "Well, I do," she said very definitely, and began to make her way along the rocks away from him.

"Hold a grudge, do you, Rowan Murray?"

Stiffening with pride, she kept walking. "Apparently."

"You won't be able to for long, you know. It's not natural for you."

She jerked a shoulder, knowing the gesture was bad-tempered and childish. She'd come to sketch the sea, the little boats that bobbed on it, the birds that soared and called above. And damn it, she'd wanted to look at the eggs in the nest to see if they'd hatched.

She hadn't wanted to see him, to be reminded of what had happened between them, what it had stirred inside her. But neither was she going to be chased away like a mouse by a cat. Setting her teeth, she sat on a ledge of rock, opened her bag. With precise movements she pulled out her bottle of water, put it beside her, then her sketchbook, then a pencil.

Ordering herself to focus, she looked out at the water, gave herself time to scan and absorb. She began to sketch, telling herself she would not look over at him. Oh, he was still there, she was sure of it. Why else would every muscle in her body be on alert, why would her heart still be tripping in her chest?

But she would not look.

Of course she looked. And he was still there, a few paces

away, his hands tucked casually in his pockets, his face turned toward the water. It was just bad luck, she supposed, that he was so attractive, that he could stand there with the wind in all that glorious hair, his profile sharp and clean, and remind her of Heathcliff or Byron or some other poetic hero.

A knight before battle, a prince surveying his realm.

Oh, yes, he could be any and all of them—as romantic in jeans and a sweatshirt as any warrior glinting in polished armor.

"I don't mean to do battle with you, Rowan."

She thought she heard him say it, but that was nonsense. He was too far away for those soft words to carry. She'd just imagined that's what he *would* say in response if she'd spoken her thoughts aloud. So she sniffed, glanced back down at her book and, to her disgust, noted that she'd begun to sketch him without realizing it.

With an irritated flick, she turned to a blank page.

"There's no point in being angry with me—or yourself."

This time she knew he'd spoken, and looked up to see that he'd strolled over to her. She had to squint, to shade her eyes with the flat of her hand as the sun streamed behind him and shimmered its light like a nimbus around his head and shoulders.

"There's no point in discussing it."

She huffed out a breath as he sat companionably beside her. When he lapsed into silence, appeared to be settling in for a nice long visit, she tapped her pencil on her pad.

"It's a long coast. Would you mind plopping down on another part of it?"

"I like it here." When she hissed and started to rise, he simply tugged her back down. "Don't be foolish."

"Don't tell me I'm foolish. I'm really, really tired of being told I'm foolish." She jerked her arm free. "And you don't even know me."

He shifted so they were face-to-face. "That could be part of it. What are you drawing there in your book?"

"Nothing apparently." Miffed, she stuffed the book back into her bag. Once again she started to rise. Once again he tugged her easily back.

"All right," she snapped. "We'll discuss it. I admit I stumbled my way through the woods because I wanted to see you. I was attracted—I'm sure you're used to women being attracted to you. I did want to thank you for your help, but that was only part of it. I intruded, no question, but you were the one who kissed me."

"I did indeed," he murmured. He wanted to do so again, right now, when her mouth was in a stubborn pout and there was both distress and temper in her eyes.

"And I overreacted to it." The memory of that still made her blood heat. "You had a perfect right to tell me to go, but you didn't have the right to be so unkind about it. No one has the right to be unkind. Now, obviously, you didn't have the same...response I did and you want to keep your distance."

She pushed at the hair that was coming loose from her ponytail to fly in her face. "So why are you here?"

"Let's take this in order," he decided. "Yes, I'm used to women being attracted to me. As I've a fondness for women, I appreciate that." A smile tugged at his lips as she made a quiet sound of disgust. "You'd think more of me if I lied about that, but I find false modesty inane and deceitful. And though I most often prefer to be alone, your visit wasn't intrusive. I kissed you because I wanted to, because you have a pretty mouth."

He watched it register surprise before it thinned and she angled her face away. No one's told her that before, he realized, and shook his head over the idiocy of the male gender.

"Because you have eyes that remind me of the elves that dance in the hills of my country. Hair like oak that's aged and polished to a gleam. And skin so soft it seems my hand should pass through it as it would with water."

"Don't do that." Her voice shook as she lifted her arms, wrapped them tight to hug her elbows. "Don't. It's not fair."

Perhaps it wasn't, to use words on a woman who so obviously wasn't used to hearing them. But he shrugged. "It's just truth. And my response to you was more...acute than I'd bargained for. So I was unkind. I apologize for that, Rowan, but only for that."

She was over her head with him, and wished the terror of that wasn't quite so enjoyable. "You're sorry for being unkind, or for having a response to me?"

Clever woman, he mused, and gave her the simple truth. "For both if it comes to it. I said I wasn't ready for you, Rowan. I meant it."

It was hearing simple truth that softened her heart—and made it tremble just a little. She didn't speak for a moment, but stared down at the fingers she'd locked together in her lap while waves crashed below and gulls soared overhead.

"Maybe I understand that, a little. I'm at an odd place in my life," she said slowly. "A kind of crossroads, I suppose. I think people are most vulnerable when they come to the end of something and have to decide which beginning they're going to take. I don't know you, Liam." She made herself shift back to face him again. "And I don't know what to say to you, or what to do."

Was there a man alive who could resist that kind of unstudied honesty? he wondered. "Offer me tea."

"What?"

He smiled, took her hand. "Offer me tea. Rain's coming and we should go in."

"Rain? But the sun's—" Even as she said it, the light changed. Dark clouds slipped through the sky without a sound and the first drops, soft as a wish, fell.

His father wasn't the only one who could use the weather for his own purposes.

"Oh, it was supposed to be clear all day." She stuffed the

bottle of water back into her bag, then let out a quick gasp when he pulled her to her feet with casual, effortless strength that left her limbs oddly weak.

"It's just a shower, and a warm one at that." He began to guide her through the rocks, down the path. "Soft weather, we call it at home. Do you mind the rain?"

"No, I like it. It always makes me dreamy." She lifted her face, let a few drops kiss it. "The sun's still shining."

"You'll have a rainbow," he promised, and tugged her into the sheltering trees, where the air was warm and wet and shadows lay in deep green pools. "Will I have tea?"

She slanted him a look, and a smile. "I suppose."

"There, I told you." He gave her hand a little squeeze. "You don't know how to hold a grudge."

"I just need practice," she said, and made him laugh.

"I'm likely to give you plenty of cause for practice before we're done."

"Do you make a habit of annoying people?"

"Oh, aye. I'm a difficult man." They strolled by the stream, where damp ferns and rich moss spread and foxglove waited to bloom. "My mother says I'm a brooder, and my father that I've a head like a rock. They should know."

"Are they in Ireland?"

"Mmm." He couldn't be sure unless he looked—and he damn well didn't want to know if they were lingering nearby, watching him.

"Do you miss them?"

"I do, yes. But we...keep in touch." It was the wistfulness in her voice that had him glancing down as they walked into her clearing. "You're missing your family?"

"I'm feeling guilty because I don't miss them as much as I probably should. I've never been away alone before, and I'm—"

"Enjoying it," he finished.

"Enormously." She laughed a little and fished her keys out of her pocket.

"No shame in that." He cocked his head as she unlocked the door. "Who are you locking out?"

Her smile was a little sheepish as she stepped inside. "Habit. I'll put the tea on. I baked some cinnamon rolls earlier, but they're burned on the bottom. One of my misses."

"I'll take one off your hands." He wandered into the kitchen behind her.

She kept the room neat, he noted, and had added a few touches—the sort he recognized as a kind of nesting. Female making a home. Some pretty twigs speared out of one of Belinda's colorful bottles and stood in the center of the kitchen table beside a white bowl filled with bright green apples.

He remembered when she'd scouted out the twigs. The wolf had walked with her—and had regally ignored her attempts to teach him to fetch.

He sat comfortably at her table, enjoying the quiet patter of rain. And thought of his mother's words. No, he wouldn't look that deeply. He didn't mind a skim through the thoughts, but that deliberate search was something he considered an abuse of power.

A man who demanded privacy had to respect that of others.

But he would pry without a qualm.

"Your family lives in San Francisco."

"Hmm. Yes." She had the kettle on and was choosing from one of Belinda's delightful collection of teapots. "They're both college professors. My father chairs the English department at the university."

"And your mother?" Idly, he slipped the sketchpad out of the bag she tossed on the table.

"She teaches history." After a mild debate, she selected a pot shaped like a fairy, with wings for the handle. "They're brilliant," she continued, carefully measuring out tea. "And really marvelous instructors. My mother was made assistant dean last year and..."

She trailed off, stunned and just a little horrified when she saw Liam studying her sketch of the wolf.

"These are wonderful." He didn't bother to look up, but turned another page and narrowed his eyes in concentration at her drawing of a stand of trees and lacy ferns. Peeking through those airy shapes were the suggestion of wings, of laughing eyes.

She saw the fairies, he thought, and smiled.

"They're just doodles." Her fingers itched to snatch the book, close it away, but manners held her back. "It's just a hobby."

And when his eyes shot to hers, she nearly shivered.

"Why would you say that, and try to believe it, when you have a talent and a love for it?"

"It's only something I do in my spare time—now and again."

He turned the next page. She'd done a study of the cottage, made it look like something out of an old and charming legend with its ring of trees and welcoming porch. "And you're insulted when someone calls you foolish?" he muttered. "It's foolish you are if you don't do what you love instead of wringing your hands about it."

"That's a ridiculous thing to say. I do not wring my hands." She turned back to take the kettle off the bowl and prevent herself from doing exactly that. "It's a hobby. Most people have one."

"It's your gift," he corrected, "and you've been neglecting it."

"You can't make a living off of doodles."

"What does making a living have to do with it?"

His tone was so arrogantly royal, she had to laugh. "Oh, nothing other than food, shelter, responsibility." She came back to set the pot on the table, turned to fetch cups. "Little things like that from the real world."

"Then sell your art if you've a need to make a living."

"Nobody's going to buy pencil sketches from an English teacher."

"I'll buy this one." He rose and held the book open to one of her studies of the wolf. In it, the wolf stood, facing the on-looker with a challenging glint in his eyes exactly like the one in Liam's. "Name your price."

"I'm not selling it, and you're not buying it to make some point." Refusing to take him seriously, she waved him back. "Sit down and have your tea."

"Then give me the sketch." He angled his head as he looked at it again. "I like it. And this one." He flipped the page to the trees and fern fairies. "I could use something like this in the game I'm doing. I've no talent for drawing."

"Then who does the drawings for your graphics?" She asked hoping to change the subject, and as a last resort, got out the burned buns.

"Mmm. Different people for different moods." He sat again, absently took one of the rolls. It was hard and undeniably burned, but if you got past that, it was wonderfully sweet and generously filled with currants.

"So how do you—"

"Do either of your parents draw?" he interrupted.

"No." Even the thought of it made her chuckle. The idea of either of her smart and busy parents settling down to dream with pencil and paper. "They gave me lessons when I was a child and showed an interest. And my mother actually keeps a sketch I made of the bay when I was a teenager framed and in her office at the university."

"So she appreciates your talent."

"She loves her daughter," Rowan corrected, and poured the tea.

"Then she should expect the daughter she loves to pursue

her own gifts, explore her own talents," he said casually, but continued down the path of her family. "Perhaps one of your grandparents was an artist."

"No, my paternal grandfather was a teacher. It seems to come naturally through the family. My grandmother on that side was what I suppose you'd call a typical wife and mother of her time. She still keeps a lovely home."

He struggled against impatience—and against a wince as Rowan added three spoons of sugar to her cup. "And on your mother's side?"

"Oh, my grandfather's retired now. They live in San Diego. My grandmother does beautiful needlework, so I suppose that's a kind of art." Her lips pursed for a moment as she stirred her tea. "Now that I think of it, her mother—my great-grandmother—painted. We have a couple of her oils. I think my grandmother and her brother have the rest. She was... eccentric," Rowan said with a grin.

"Was she now? And how was she eccentric?"

"I never knew her, but children pick up bits and pieces when adults gossip. She read palms and talked to animals—all decidedly against her husband's wishes. He was, as I recall, a very pragmatic Englishman, and she was a dreamy Irishwoman."

"So, she was Irish, was she?" Liam felt a low vibration along his spine. A warning, a frisson of power. "And her family name?"

"Ah..." Rowan searched back through her memory. "O'Meara. I'm named for her," she continued, contentedly drinking tea while everything inside Liam went on alert. "My mother named me for her in what she calls an irresistible flash of sentiment. I suppose that's why she—my great-grandmother—left me her pendant. It's a lovely old piece. An oval moonstone in a hammered silver setting."

In a slow and deliberate move, Liam set aside the tea he could no longer taste. "She was Rowan O'Meara."

"That's right. I think there was some wonderfully romantic

story—or else I've made it up—about how my great-grand-father met her when he was on holiday in Ireland. She was painting on the cliffs—in Clare. That's odd, I don't know why I'm so sure it was Clare."

She puzzled over that for a moment, then shrugged it away. "Anyway, they fell in love on the spot, and she went back to England with him, left her home and her family. Then they emigrated to America, and eventually settled in San Francisco."

Rowan O'Meara from Clare. By the goddess, fate had twisted around and laid one more trap for him. He picked up his tea again to wet his throat. "My mother's family name is O'Meara." He spoke in a voice that was flat and cool. "Your great-grandmother would be a distant cousin of mine."

"You're kidding." Stunned and delighted, Rowan beamed at him.

"In matters such as family, I try not to joke."

"That would be amazing. Absolutely. Well, it's a small world." She laughed and lifted her cup. "Nice to meet you. Cousin Liam."

In the name of the goddess, he thought, and fatalistically tapped his cup to hers. The woman currently smiling at him out of those big, beautiful eyes had elfin blood, and didn't even know it.

"There's your rainbow, Rowan." He continued to look at her, but he knew the colored arch had spread in the sky outside. He hadn't conjured it—but sensed his father had.

"Oh!" She leaped up and, after one quick peek out the window, dashed to the door. "Come out and see. It's wonderful!"

She raced out, clattered down the steps and looked up.

She'd never seen one so clear, so perfectly defined. Against the watery-blue sky, each luminous layer stood out, shimmering at the edges with gold, melting into the next color, from rose to lavender to delicate yellow to candy-pink. It spread high, each tip grazing the tops of the trees.

"I've never seen one so beautiful."

When he joined her, he was both disconcerted and touched when she took his hand. But even as he looked up at the arch, he promised himself he wouldn't fall in love with her unless it was what he wanted.

He wouldn't be maneuvered, cajoled, seduced. He would make his decision with a clear mind.

But that didn't mean he couldn't take some of what he wanted in the meantime.

"This means nothing more, and nothing less, than the other," he said.

"What?"

"This." He cupped her face, bent down and laid his lips on hers.

Soft as silk, gentle as the rain that was still falling through the pearly sunlight. He would keep it that way, for both of them, and lock down on the needs that were fiercer, more keen than was wise or safe.

Just a taste of that innocence, a glimpse of that tender heart she had no idea how to defend, he told himself. He would do what he could to keep that heart from falling too deeply, or he might be forced to break it.

But when her hand came up to rest on his shoulder, when her mouth yielded so utterly under his, he felt those darker needs clawing for freedom.

She couldn't stop herself from giving, could hold nothing back against such tenderness. Even when the fingers on her face tightened, his mouth remained soft, easy, as if teaching hers what there was, what there could be.

Instinctively she soothed her hands over the tension of his shoulders and let herself sink into him.

He eased away before desire could outrace reason. When she only stared up at him with those exotic eyes blurred, those soft lips parted, he let her go.

"I guess it's just, ah, chemistry." Her heart was pounding in great, hammering leaps.

"Chemistry," he said, "can be dangerous."

"You can't make discoveries without some risks." It should have shocked her, a comment like that coming out of her mouth, such an obvious invitation to continue, to finish. But it seemed natural, and right.

"In this case it's best you know all the elements you're dealing with. How much are you willing to find out, I wonder?"

"I came here to find out all sorts of things." She let out a quiet breath. "I didn't expect to find you."

"No. You're looking for Rowan first." He hooked his thumbs in his pockets, rocked back on his heels. "If I took you inside, took you here, for that matter, you'd find a part of her quickly enough. Is that what you want?"

"No." It was another surprise to hear the denial, when every nerve in her body was sizzling. "Because then it would be as you said before. Simple. I'm not looking for simple."

"Still, I'll kiss you again, when I've a mind to."

She angled her head, ignored the quick flutter in her belly. "I'll let you kiss me again, when *I've* a mind to."

He flashed a grin full of power and appreciation. "You've some of that Irishwoman in you, Rowan of the O'Mearas."

"Maybe I do." It pleased her enormously just then to think so. "Maybe I'll have to find more."

"That you will." His grin faded. "When you do, I hope you know what to do about it. Pick a day next week and come over. Bring your sketchbook."

"What for?"

"An idea I have brewing. We'll see if it suits both of us."

It couldn't hurt, she mused. And it would give her some time to think about everything that had happened that morning. "All right, but one day's the same as the next to me. My schedule's open these days."

"You'll know which day when it comes." He reached out to toy with the ends of her hair. "So will I."

"And that, I suppose, is some kind of Irish mysticism."

"You don't know the half of it," he murmured. "A good day to you, Cousin Rowan."

He gave her hair an absent tug, then turned and walked away.

Well, she thought, as days went, it hadn't been half-bad so far.

And when he came to her again in dreams, she welcomed him. When his mind touched hers, seduced it, aroused it, she sighed, yielded, offered.

She shivered in pleasure, breathed his name and sensed somehow that he was as vulnerable as she. For just that moment, just that misty space of time he was tangled with her, helpless not to give what she asked.

If only she knew the question.

Even when her body glowed, her mind soared, part of her fretted.

What should she ask him? What did she need to know?

In the dark, with the half-moon spilling delicate light through her open windows, she woke alone. She burrowed into the pillows and listened with her heart aching at the sound of the wolf calling to the night.

## Chapter 6

Rowan watched spring burst into life. And, watching, it seemed something burst into life inside her as well. Daffodils and windflowers shimmered into bloom. The little pear tree outside the kitchen window opened its delicate white blossoms and danced in the wind.

Deep in the forest, the wild azaleas began to show hints of pink and white, and the foxglove grew fat buds. There were others, so many others; she promised herself a book on local wildflowers on her next trip into town. She wanted to know them, learn their habits and their names.

All the while she felt herself begin to bloom. Was there more color in her face? she wondered, more light in her eyes? She knew she smiled more often, enjoyed the sensation of feeling her own lips curve up for no particular reason as she walked or sketched or simply sat on the porch in the warming air to read for hours.

Nights no longer seemed lonely. When the wolf came, she talked to him about whatever was on her mind. When he didn't, she was content to spend her evening alone.

She wasn't entirely sure what was different, only that something was. And that there were other, bigger changes yet to come.

Maybe it was the decision she'd made not to go back to San Francisco, or to teaching, or the practical apartment minutes from her parents' home.

She'd been cautious with money, she reminded herself. She'd never felt any particular urge to collect things or fill her closet with clothes or take elaborate vacations. Added to that was the small inheritance that had come down to her through her mother's family. One she had cautiously invested and watched grow neatly over the last few years.

There was enough to draw on for a down payment for a little house somewhere.

Somewhere quiet and beautiful, she thought now as she stood on the front porch with a cup of steaming coffee to welcome another morning. It had to be a house, she knew. No more apartment living. And somewhere in the country. She wasn't going to be happy in the bustle and rush of the city ever again. She'd have a garden she planted herself—once she learned how—and maybe a little creek or pond.

It had to be close enough to the sea that she could walk to it, hear its song at night as she drifted toward sleep.

Maybe, just maybe, on that next trip to town she'd visit a realtor. Just to see what was available.

It was such a big step—choosing a spot, buying a house— furnishing it, maintaining it. She caught herself winding the tip of her braid around her finger and deliberately dropped her hand. She was ready to make that step. She *would* make it.

And she'd find work, the kind that satisfied her. She didn't need a great deal of money. She'd be blissfully content puttering around some little cottage of her own, doing the painting, the repairs, watching her garden grow.

If she found something nearby, she wouldn't have to leave the wolf.

*Or Liam.*

With that thought, she shook her head. No, she couldn't add Liam into the equation, or make him part of the reason she was considering settling in the area. He was his own man, and would come and go when and where he pleased.

Just like the wolf, she realized, and sighed. Neither one of them was hers, after all. They were both loners, both beautiful creatures who belonged to no one. And who'd come into her life—helped change it in some ways, she supposed. Though the biggest changes were up to her.

It seemed that after three weeks in the little cabin in the clearing, she was ready to make them. Not just drifting anymore, she thought. Not just wondering. Time to take definite steps.

The subtle tug at her mind had her eyes narrowing, her head angling as if to hear something soft whispered in the distance. It was almost as if she could hear her name, quietly called.

He'd said to come to him, she remembered. That she'd know when the time was right. Well, there was no time like the present, no better time than when she was in such a decisive mood. And after the visit, she'd drive into town and see that Realtor.

He knew she was coming. He'd been careful to keep his contact with her limited over the past several days. Perhaps he hadn't been able to stay away completely. He did worry about her just a bit, thinking of her alone and more out of her element than she knew.

But it was easy enough to check up on her, to walk to her door and have her open it for him. He could hardly deny he enjoyed the way she welcomed him, bending down to stroke his head and back or nuzzle her face against his throat.

She had no fear of the wolf, he mused. He only made her wary when he was a man.

But she was coming to the man, and would have to deal with him. He thought his plan a good one, for both of them.

One that would give her the opportunity to explore her own talents—and would give each of them time to learn more about the other.

He wouldn't touch her again until they did. He'd promised himself that. It was too difficult to sample and not take fully. And on those nights he allowed himself to take her with his mind, he left her glowing and satisfied. And left himself oddly unfulfilled.

Still, it was preparing her for him, for the night when he would make those half dreams full reality. For the night when it was his hands and not his mind on her.

The thought of it had his stomach knotting, his muscles bunching tight. Infuriated with the reaction, he ordered his mind to clear, his body to relax. And was only more infuriated when even his powers didn't calm all the tension.

"The day hasn't come when I can't handle a physical reaction to some pretty half witch," he muttered, and walked back inside his cabin.

Damned if he was going to stand on the porch like some starry-eyed lover and watch for her.

So instead he paced and uttered vile Gaelic curses until he heard the knock on his door.

Mood inexplicably foul, Liam flung open the door. And there she stood, with the sun streaming behind her, a delighted smile on her face, her hair coming loose from her braid and a clutch of tiny purple flowers in her hand.

"Good morning. I think they're wood violets, but I'm not completely sure. I need to buy a book."

She offered them, and Liam felt the heart he was so determined to defend tremble in his breast. Innocence shined in her eyes, lovely color glowed in her cheeks. And there were wildflowers in her hand.

All he could do was stare. And want.

When he didn't respond, she lowered her hand. "Don't you like flowers?"

"I do, yes. Sorry, I was distracted." For the goddess's sake, get a hold of yourself, Donovan. But even with the order, his scowl was in direct contrast to his words. "Come in, Rowan Murray. You're welcome here, as are your flowers."

"If I've come at a bad time," she began, but he was already stepping back, widening the opening of the door in invitation. "I thought I would come by before I drove into town."

"For more books?" He left the door open, as if to give her a route of escape.

"For those, and to talk to someone about property. I'm thinking of buying some in the area."

"Are you now?" His brow winged up. "Is this the place for you?"

"It seems to be. It could be." She moved her shoulders. "Someplace must be."

"And have you decided—how did you put it—what you'll do to make your living?"

"Not exactly." The light in her eyes dimmed a little with worry. "But I will."

He was sorry to have put that doubt on her face. "I have an idea about that. Come back to the kitchen, and we'll find something to put your little flowers in."

"Have you been in the woods? Everything's starting to pop and bloom. It's wonderful. And all these marvelous flowers around Belinda's cottage. I don't recognize half of them, or the ones around yours."

"Most are simple, and useful for one thing or another." He rooted out a tiny blue vase for the violets as she craned up to peer out his kitchen window.

"Oh, you've more back here. Are they herbs?"

"Aye, herbs they are."

"For cooking."

"For that." A smile tugged at his lips as he slipped the delicate stems into the glass. "And all manner of things. Will you hunt up a book on herbs now?"

"Probably." She laughed and dropped back to the flats of her feet. "There's so much I've never paid attention to. Now I can't seem to find out enough."

"And that includes yourself."

She blinked. "I suppose it does."

"So..." He couldn't resist and pleased himself by toying with the ends of her braid. "What have you found out about Rowan?"

"That she's not as inept as she thought."

His gaze swept back up to hers, sharpened. "And why would you have thought that?"

"Oh, I don't mean about everything. I know how to learn, and how to apply what I learn. I'm organized and practical and I have a good mind. It was the little things and the really big ones I never seemed to know what to do about. Anything in between I handled just fine. But the little things I let go, and the big ones... I always felt I should do what others thought I should do about them."

"I'm about to give you a suggestion on what you'd call a big thing. I expect you to do as you like about it."

"What is it?"

"In a bit," he said with a vague wave of his hand. "Come in here and have a look at what I'm doing."

Baffled, she walked into the adjoining office with him. His computer was up and running, the screen saver swimming with moons and stars and symbols she didn't recognize. He tapped a key and had text popping up.

"What do you think?" he asked her, and she bent forward to read. A moment later she was laughing. "I think I can't read what appears to be computer signals and some foreign language."

He glanced down, let out an impatient huff of breath. He'd gotten so involved in the story line he hadn't considered. Well, that could be fixed. He nearly flicked his wrist to have the straight story line brought up, caught himself not a moment too soon, then made a show of tapping keys while the basic spell ran through his mind.

"There." The screen jiggled, then blipped and brought up new text. "Sit down and read it."

Since nothing would have delighted her more, she did as he asked. It only took a few lines for her to understand. "It's a sequel to Myor." Thrilled, she turned her face up to his. "That's wonderful. You've written another. Have you finished it?"

"If you'd read it you'd see for yourself."

"Yes, yes." This time it was she who waved him away as she settled down to be entertained. "Oh! Kidnapped. She's been kidnapped and the evil warlock's put a spell on her to strip her of her powers."

"Witch," he muttered, wincing a little. "A male witch is still a witch."

"Really? Well... He's locked all her gifts up in a magic box. It's because he's in love with her, isn't it?"

"What?"

"It has to be," Rowan insisted. "Brinda's so beautiful and strong and full of light. He'd want her, and this is his way of forcing her to belong to him."

Considering, Liam slipped his hands into his pockets. "Is it now?"

"It must be. Yes, here's the handsome warlock—I mean witch—who'll do battle with the evil one to get the box of power. It's wonderful."

She all but put her nose to the screen, annoyed she hadn't thought to put on her reading glasses. "Just look at all the traps and spells he'll have to fight just to get to her. Then when he frees her, she won't have any magic to help. Just her wits," Rowan murmured, delighted with the story. "They'll face all this together, risk destruction. Wow, the Valley of Storms. Sounds ominous, passionate. This is what was missing from the first one."

More stunned than insulted, he gaped at her. "Excuse me?"

"It had such wonderful magic and adventure, but no romance. I'm so glad you've added it this time. Rilan will fall madly in love with Brinda, and she with him as they work together, face all these dangers."

Her eyes gleamed as she leaned back and refocused them on Liam. "Then when they defeat the evil witch, find the box, it should be their love that breaks the spell, opens it and gives Brinda back her powers. So they'll live happily ever after."

She smiled a bit hesitantly at the shuttered look in his eyes. "Won't they?"

"Aye, they will." With a few adjustments to the story line, he decided. But that was his task, and for later. By Finn, the woman had it right. "What do you think of the magic dragons in the Land of Mirrors?"

"Magic dragons?"

"Here." He bent down, leaning close and manually scrolling to the segment. "Read this," he said, and his breath feathered warm across her cheek. "And tell me your thoughts."

She had to adjust her thoughts to block out the quick jump of her pulse, but dutifully focused on the words and read. "Fabulous. Just fabulous. I can just see them flying away on the back of a dragon, over the red waters of the sea, and the mist-covered hills."

"Can you? Show me how you see it—just that. Draw it for me." He pulled her sketchbook out of her bag. "I haven't got a clear image of it."

"No? I don't know how you could write this without it." She picked up a pencil and began to draw. "The dragon should be magnificent. Fierce and beautiful, with wonderful gold wings and eyes like rubies. Long and sleek and powerful," she murmured as she sketched. "Wild and dangerous."

It was precisely what he'd wanted, Liam noted as the drawing came to life under her hand. No tame pet, no captured oddity. She had it exactly: the proud, fierce head, the long powerful body with its wide sweep of wings, the slashing tail, the feel of great movement.

"Do another now." Impatient, he tore off the first sketch, set it aside. "Of the sea and hills."

"All right." She supposed a rough drawing might help him get a more solid visual for his story. Closing her eyes a moment, she brought the image into her mind, that wide, shimmering sea with cresting waves, the jagged rocks that speared silver out of thick swirling mists, the glint of sunlight gilding the edges, and the dark shadow of mountains beyond.

When she was done with it, he ripped that page away as well, demanded she do another. This time of Yilard, the evil witch.

She had great fun with that, grinning to herself as she worked. He should be handsome, she decided. Cruelly so. No wart-faced gnome with a hunched back, but a tall, dashing man with flowing hair and hard dark eyes. She dressed him in robes, imagined they would be red, like a prince.

"Why didn't you make him ugly?" Liam asked her.

"Because he wouldn't be. And if he were, it might seem as if Brinda refused him just because of his looks. She didn't— it was his heart she rejected. The darkness of it that you'd see in the eyes."

"But the hero, he'd be more handsome."

"Of course. We'd expect, even demand that. But he won't be one of those girlishly pretty men with curly gold hair." Lost in the story, she tore off the page herself to begin another. "He'll be dark, dangerous, too. Brave, certainly, but not without flaws. I like my heroes human. Still, he risked his life for Brinda, first for honor. And then for love."

She laughed a little as she leaned back from the sketch. "He looks a bit like you," she commented. "But why not? It's your story. Everyone wants to be the hero of their own story, after all." She smiled at him. "And it's a wonderful story, Liam. Can I read the rest?"

"Not yet." There were changes to be made now, he thought, and switched off the screen.

"Oh." Disappointment rang in her voice, and fed his ego. "I just want to see what happens after they fly out of the Land of Mirrors."

"If you do, you'll have to accept my proposition."

"Proposition?"

"A business one. Do the drawings for me. All of them. It's a great deal of work, as most of the levels will be complex. I'll need an exacting amount of detail for the graphics, and I'm not easily satisfied."

She held up a hand. She wanted to stop him, to give herself time to find her voice. "You want me to draw the story?"

"It's not a simple matter. I'll require hundreds of sketches, all manner of scenes and angles."

"I don't have any experience."

"No?" He lifted her sketch of the dragon.

"I just tossed those off," she insisted, pushing to her feet with a sense of panic. "I didn't think."

"Is that the way of it?" Interesting. "Fine, then, don't think, just draw."

She couldn't keep up, couldn't quite catch her breath. "You can't be serious."

"I'm very serious," he corrected, and laid the sketch down again. "Were you when you said you wanted to do what made you happy?"

"Yes." She was rubbing a hand over her heart, unaware of the movement.

"Then work with me on this, if it pleases you. You'll make the living you need. The Donovan Legacy will see to that part well enough. It's up to you, Rowan."

"Wait, just wait." She kept her hand up, turned away to walk to the window. The sky was still blue, she noted, the forest still green. And the wind blew with the same steady breath.

It was only her life that was changing. If she let it.

To do something she loved for a living? To use it freely and with pleasure and have it give back everything she needed? Could that be possible? Could it be real?

And it was then she realized it wasn't panic that was hot in her throat, pounding in her blood. It was excitement.

"Do you mean this? Do you think my sketches would suit your story?"

"I wouldn't have said so otherwise. The choice is yours."

"Mine," she said, quietly, like a breath. "Then, yes, it would please me very much." Her voice was slow, thoughtful. But when the full scope of his offer struck, she whirled around, her eyes brilliant. He saw those tiny silver lights in her eyes. "I'd love to work with you on it. When do we start?"

He took the hand she held out, clasped it firmly in his. "We just did."

Later, when Rowan was back in her kitchen celebrating with a glass of wine and a grilled cheese sandwich, she tried to remember if she'd ever been happier.

She didn't think so.

She'd never gotten into town for her books and her house hunting, but that would come. Instead, she mused, she'd found an opening to a new career. One that thrilled her.

She had a chance now, a true and tangible chance for a new direction.

Not that Liam Donovan was going to make it easy. On the contrary, she decided, licking cheese from her thumb. He was demanding, occasionally overbearing and very, very much the perfectionist.

She'd done a full dozen sketches of the gnomes of Firth before he'd approved a single one.

And his approval, as she recalled, had been a grunt and a nod.

Well, that was fine. She didn't need to be patted on the head, didn't require effusive praise. She appreciated the fact that he expected her to be good, that he already assumed they'd make a successful team.

A team. She all but hugged the word to her. That made her part of something. After all these years of quiet wishing, she was telling stories. Not with words; she never had the right words. But with her drawings. The thing she loved most and had convinced herself over the years was an acceptable hobby and no more.

Now it was hers.

Still, she was in many ways a practical woman. She'd cut through her delight to the basics and discussed terms with him. A pity she wasn't clever enough to have masked her sheer astonishment at the amount he'd told her she'd be paid for the work.

She'd have her house now, she thought, and, giggling with glee, poured herself a second glass of wine. She'd buy more art supplies, more books. Plants. She'd scout out wonderful antiques to furnish her new home.

And live happily ever after, she thought, toasting herself. Alone.

She shook off the little pang. She was getting used to alone. Enjoying alone. Maybe she still felt quick pulls and tugs of attraction for Liam, but she understood there would be no acting on them now that they were working together.

He'd certainly demonstrated no sign of wanting a more personal relationship now. If that stung the pride a bit, well, she was used to that, too.

She'd had a terrifying crush on the captain of the debate team her senior year in high school. She could clearly remember those heartbreaking flutters and thrills every time she caught sight of him. And how she'd wished, miserably, she could have been more outgoing, more brightly pretty, more confident, like the girl he'd gone steady with.

Then in college it had been an English major, a poet with soulful eyes and a dark view of life. She'd been sure she could inspire him, lift his soul. When, after nearly a full semester he'd finally turned those tragic eyes her way, she'd fallen like a ripe plum from a branch.

She didn't regret it, even though after two short weeks he'd turned those same tragic eyes to another woman. After all, she'd had two weeks of storybook romance, and had given up her virginity to a man with some sensitivity, if no sense of monogamy.

It hadn't taken her long to realize that she hadn't loved him. She'd loved the idea of him. After that, his careless rejection hadn't stung quite so deeply.

Men simply didn't find her...compelling, she decided. Mysterious or sexy. And unfortunately, the ones she was most attracted to always seemed to be all of that.

With Liam, he was all of that and more.

Of course, there had been Alan, she remembered. Sweet, steady, sensible Alan. Though she loved him, she'd known as soon as they'd become lovers that she'd never feel that wild thrill with him, that grinding need or that rush of longing.

She'd tried. Her parents had settled on him and it seemed logical that she would gradually fall in love, all the way in love, and make a comfortable life with him.

Hadn't it been the thought of that, a comfortable life, that had finally frightened her enough to make her run?

She could say now she'd been right to do so. It would have been wrong to settle for less than...anything, she supposed. For less than what she was finding now. Her place, her wants, her flaws and her talents.

They wouldn't understand—not yet. But in time they would. She was sure of it. After she was established in a home of her own, with a career of her own, they would see. Maybe, just maybe, they'd even be proud of her.

She glanced at the phone, considered, then shook her head. No, not yet. She wouldn't call her parents and tell them what she was doing. Not quite yet. She didn't want to hear the doubt, the concern, the carefully masked impatience in their voices, and spoil the moment.

It was such a lovely moment.

So when she heard the knock on the front door, she sprang up. It was Liam, had to be Liam. And, oh, that was perfect. He'd brought more work, and they could sit in the kitchen and discuss it, toy with it.

She'd make tea, she thought as she hurried through the cabin. A glass and a half of wine was enough if she wanted her mind perfectly clear. She'd had another idea about the Land of Mirrors and how that red sea should reflect when she'd walked home.

Eager to tell him, she opened the door. Her delighted smile of welcome shifted to blank shock.

"Rowan, you shouldn't open the door without seeing who it is first. You're much too trusting for your own good."

With the spring breeze blowing behind him, Alan stepped inside.

# Chapter 7

"Alan, what are you doing here?"

She knew immediately her tone had been short and unwelcoming—and very close to accusatory. She could see it in the surprised hurt on his face.

"It's been over three weeks, Rowan. We thought you might appreciate a little face-to-face. And frankly..." He shoved at the heavy sand-colored hair that fell over his forehead. "The tenor of your last phone call worried your parents."

"The tenor?" She bristled, and struggled to fix on a pleasant smile. "I don't see why. I told them I was fine and well settled in."

"Maybe that's what concerns them."

The worry in his earnest brown eyes brought her the first trickle of guilt. Then he took off his coat, laid it neatly over the banister and made a pocket of resentment open under the guilt. "Why would that be a concern?"

"None of us really knows what you're doing up here—or what you hope to accomplish by cutting yourself off from everyone."

"I've explained all of that." Now there was weariness along with the guilt. It was her cottage, damn it, her life. They were being invaded and questioned. But manners had her gesturing to a chair. "Sit down, please. Do you want anything? Tea, coffee?"

"No, I'm fine, but thanks." He did sit, looking stiffly out of place in his trim gray suit and starched white Oxford shirt. He still wore his conservatively striped, neatly Windsor-knotted tie. It hadn't occurred to him to so much as loosen it for the trip.

He scanned the room now as he settled in a chair by the quiet fire. From his viewpoint the cabin was rustic and entirely too isolated. Where was the culture—the museums, the libraries, the theaters? How could Rowan stand burying herself in the middle of the woods for weeks on end?

All she needed, he was certain, was a subtle nudge and she'd pack up and come back with him. Her parents had assured him of it.

He smiled at her, that crooked, slightly confused smile that always touched her heart. "What in the world do you do here all day?"

"I've told you in my letters, Alan." She sat across from him, leaned forward. This time, she was certain, she could make him understand. "I'm taking some time to think, to try to figure things out. I go for long walks, read, listen to music. I've been doing a lot of sketching. In fact—"

"Rowan, that's all well and good for a few days," he interrupted, the patience so thick in his voice her teeth went instantly on edge. "But this is hardly the place for you. It's easy enough to read between the lines of your letters that you've developed some sort of romantic attachment for solitude, for living in some little cottage in the middle of nowhere. But this is hardly Walden Pond."

He shot her that smile again, but this time it failed to soften her. "And I'm not Thoreau. Granted. But I'm happy here, Alan."

She didn't look happy, he noted. She looked irritable and edgy. Certain he could help her, he patted her hand. "For now, perhaps. For the moment. But what happens after a few more weeks, when you realize it's all just a…" He gestured vaguely. "Just an interlude," he decided. "By then it'll be too late to get your position back at your school, to register for the summer courses you planned to take toward your doctorate. The lease is up for your apartment in two months."

Her hands were locked together in her lap now, to keep them from forming fists and beating in frustration on the arms of the chair. "It's not just an interlude. It's my life."

"Exactly." He beamed at her, as she had often seen him beam at a particularly slow student who suddenly grasped a thorny concept. "And your life is in San Francisco. Sweetheart, you and I both know you need more intellectual stimulation than you can find here. You need your studies, your students. What about your monthly book group? You have to be missing it. And the classes you planned to take? And you haven't mentioned a word about the paper you were writing."

"I haven't mentioned it because I'm not writing it. I'm not going to write it." Because it infuriated her that her fingers were beginning to tremble, she wrenched them apart and sprang up. "And I didn't plan on taking classes, other people planned that for me. The way they've planned every step I've ever taken. I don't want to study, I don't want to teach. I don't want any intellectual stimulation that I don't choose for myself. This is exactly what I've told you before, what I've told my parents before. But you simply refuse to hear."

He blinked, more than a little shocked at her sudden vehemence. "Because we care about you, Rowan. Very much." He rose as well. His voice was soothing now. She rarely lost her temper, but he understood when she did she threw up a wall no amount of logic could crack. You just had to wait her out.

"I know you care." Frustrated, she pressed her fingers to her eyes. "That's why I want you to hear, I want you to understand, or if understanding is too much, to accept. I'm doing what I need to do. And, Alan—" She dropped her hands, looked directly into his eyes. "I'm not coming back."

His face stiffened, and his eyes went cool as they did when he had outlined a logical premise and she disagreed with him. "I certainly hoped you'd had enough of this foolishness by now and would fly back with me tonight. I'm willing to find a hotel in the area for a few days, and wait."

"No, Alan, you misunderstand. I'm not coming back to San Francisco. At all. Not now, not later."

There, she thought, she'd said it. And a huge weight seemed to lift off her heart. It remained light even when she read the irritation in his eyes.

"That's just nonsense, Rowan. It's your home, of course you'll come back."

"It's your home, and it's my parents' home. That doesn't make it mine." She reached out to take his hands, so happy with her own plans she wanted him to be. "Please try to understand. I love it here. I feel so at home, so settled. I've never really felt like this before. I've even got a job sketching. It's art for a computer game. It's so much *fun,* Alan. So exciting. And I'm going to look into buying a house somewhere in the area. A place of my own, near the sea. I'm going to plant a garden and learn how to really cook and—"

"Have you lost your mind?" He turned his hands over to grip hers almost painfully. None of the sheer joy on her face registered. Only the words that were to him the next thing to madness. "Computer games? Gardens? Are you listening to yourself?"

"Yes, for the first time in my life that's just what I'm doing. You're hurting me, Alan."

"I'm hurting you?" He came as close to shouting as she'd ever heard, and transferred his grip from her hands to her shoulders. "What about what I feel, what I want? Damn it, Rowan, I've been patient with you. You're the one who suddenly and for no reason that made sense decided to change our relationship. One night we're lovers, the next day we're not. I didn't press, I didn't push. I tried to understand that you needed more time in that area."

She'd bungled things, she realized. She'd bungled it and hurt him unnecessarily out of her inability to find the right words. Even now, she fumbled with them. "Alan, I'm sorry. I'm so sorry. It wasn't a matter of time. It was—"

"I've circled around this incomprehensible snit of yours," he continued, fired up enough to give her a quick shake. "I've given you more room than anyone could expect, believing you wanted a bit more freedom before we settled down and married. Now it's computer games? *Games?* And cabins in the woods?"

"Yes, it is. Alan—"

She was near tears, very near them, had lifted a hand to his chest, not to push him away, but to try to soothe. With a great feral howl, the wolf leaped through the open window. Fangs gleamed white in the lamplight as he sprang, a vicious snarl erupting from his throat.

His powerful forelegs caught Alan just below the shoulders, knocked him back. A table snapped as the combined weight crashed into it. And before Rowan could draw breath, Alan was lying white-faced on the floor with the black wolf snapping at his throat.

"No, no!" Terror gave her both speed and strength. She jumped to them, dived down to wrap her arms around the wolf's neck. "Don't, don't hurt him. He wasn't hurting me."

She could feel the muscles vibrating beneath her, hear the growls rumble like threatening thunder. The horrible image of ripped flesh, pumping blood, screams raced through her head. Without a thought she shifted, pushed her face between them and looked into the wolf's glowing eyes.

There she saw savagery.

"He wasn't hurting me," she said calmly. "He's a friend. He's upset, but he'd never hurt me. Let him up now, please."

The wolf snarled again, and something flashed in his eyes that was almost…human, she thought. She could smell the wildness around him, in him. Very gently she laid her cheek against his. "It's all right now." Her lips grazed his fur. "Everything's all right."

Slowly he moved back. But his body shoved against hers until he stood between her and Alan. As a precaution, she kept a hand on the ruff of his neck as she got to her feet.

"I'm sorry, Alan. Are you hurt?"

"Name of God, name of God." It was all he could manage in a voice that shook. Sheer terror had his muscles weak as water. Each breath burned his lungs, and his chest was bruised where the beast had attacked him. "Get away from it, Rowan. Get back." Though he trembled all over from shock, he crawled to his feet, grabbed a lamp. "Get away, get upstairs."

"Don't you dare hit him." Indignant, she snatched the lamp out of Alan's unsteady hands. "He was only protecting me. He thought you were hurting me."

"Protecting you? For the love of God, Rowan, that's a wolf."

She jerked back when he tried to grab her, then followed instinct and told perhaps the first outright lie of her life. "Of course it's not. Don't be absurd. It's a dog." She thought she felt the wolf jolt under her hand at the claim. Out of the corner of her eye she saw him angle his head up and…well, glare at her. "My dog," she insisted. "And he did precisely what you would expect from a well-trained dog. He protected me against what he saw as a threat."

"A dog?" Staggered and far from convinced he wasn't about to have his throat torn out, Alan shifted his gaze to her. "You have a dog?"

"Yes." The lie was starting to twist around her tongue. "Um. And as you can see, I couldn't be safer here. With him."

"What kind of dog is that?"

"I don't precisely know." Oh, she was a miserably poor liar, she thought. "He's been wonderful company, though, and as you can see I don't have to worry about being alone. If I hadn't called him off, he'd have bitten you."

"It looks like a damn wolf."

"Really, Alan." She did her best to laugh, but it came out thin and squeaky. "Have you ever heard of a wolf leaping through a window, or taking commands from a woman? He's marvelous." She leaned down to nuzzle her face against his fur. "And as gentle with me as a Labrador."

As if in disgust, the wolf shot her one steely look, then walked over to sit by the fire.

"See?" She didn't let her breath shudder out in relief, but she wanted to.

"You never said anything about wanting a dog. I believe I'm allergic." He dug out a handkerchief to catch the first sneeze.

"I never said a lot of things." She crossed to him again, laying her hands on his arms. "I'm sorry for that, I'm sorry I didn't know what to say or how to say it until now."

Alan's eyes kept sliding back toward the wolf. "Could you put him outside?"

Put him outside? she thought, and felt another shaky laugh tickling her throat. The wolf came and went as he pleased. "He's all right, I promise. Come sit down—you're still shaken up."

"Small wonder," he muttered. He would have asked her for a brandy, but imagined she'd have to leave the room to get it. He wasn't risking being alone with that great black hulk.

As if to show the wisdom of this decision, the wolf bared his teeth.

"Alan." Rowan sat on the couch beside him, took his hands in hers. "I am sorry. For not understanding myself soon enough or clearly enough to make you understand. For not being what you'd hoped I would be. But I can't change any of that, and I can't go back to what was."

Alan pushed his heavy hair back again. "Rowan, be reasonable."

"I'm being as reasonable as I know how. I do care for you, Alan, so much. You've been a wonderful friend to me. Now be a friend and be honest. You're not in love with me. It just seemed you should be."

"Of course I love you, Rowan."

Her smile was just a little wistful as she brushed back his hair herself. "If you were *in* love with me, you couldn't have been so reasonable about not sleeping with me anymore." Her smile warmed with affection when he fidgeted. "Alan, we've been good friends, but we were mediocre lovers. There was no passion between us, no urgency or desperation."

Discussing such a matter quite so frankly embarrassed him. He'd have risen to pace, but the wolf had growled quietly again. "Why should there be?"

"I don't know, I just know there should. There has to be." Thoughtfully she reached up to straighten his tie. "You're the son my parents always wanted. You're kind, and you're smart and so wonderfully steady. They love both of us." She lifted her gaze to his, thought—hoped—she saw the beginnings of understanding there. "So they assumed we'd cooperate and marry each other. And they convinced you that you wanted the same thing. But do you, Alan, do you really?"

He looked down at their joined hands. "I can't imagine you not being part of my life."

"I'll always be part of it." She tilted her head, leaned forward and laid her lips on his. At the gesture, the wolf rose, stalked over and snarled. She put an absent hand on his head as she drew back, and studied Alan. "Did that make your blood swim or your heart flip? Of course not," she murmured before he could answer. "You don't want me, Alan, not the way a man wildly in love wants. You can't make love and passion logical."

"If you came back, we could try." When she only shook her head, he tightened his grip on her hand. "I don't want to lose you, Rowan. You matter to me."

"Then let me be happy. Let me know that at least one person I matter to, and who matters to me, can accept what I want to do."

"I can't stop you." Resigned now, he lifted his shoulders. "You've changed, Rowan. In three short weeks, you've changed. Maybe you are happy, or maybe you're just playing at being happy. Either way, we'll all be there if you change your mind."

"I know."

"I should go. It's a long drive to the airport."

"I—I can fix you a meal. You can stay the night if you like and go back in the morning."

"It's best if I go now." Skimming a cautious glance toward the hovering wolf, he rose. "I don't know what I think, Rowan, and don't honestly know what I'll say to your parents. They were sure you'd be coming back with me."

"Tell them I love them. And I'm happy."

"I'll tell them—and try to convince them. But since I'm not sure I believe it myself..." He sneezed again, backed away. "Don't get up," he told her, certain it was safer if she kept that light hand on her dog's ferocious head. "I'll let myself out. You ought to get a collar for that thing, at least...make sure he's had his shots and—"

The sneezing fit shook his long, lanky frame so that he walked to the door with the handkerchief over his face. It looked as though the dog was grinning at him, which he knew was ridiculous.

"I'll call you," he managed to say, and rushed out into the fresh air.

"I hurt him." Rowan let out a deep sigh and laid her cheek atop the wolf's head as she listened to the sound of the rental car's engine springing to life. "I couldn't find a way not to.

Just like I couldn't find the way to love him." She turned her face, comforting herself with the feel of that warm, soft fur. "You're so brave, you're so strong," she crooned. "And you scared poor Alan half to death."

She laughed a little, but the sound was perilously close to a sob. "Me, too, I guess. You looked magnificent coming through the window. So savage, so fierce. So beautiful. Teeth snapping, eyes gleaming, and that marvelous body fluid as rain."

She slid off the couch to kneel beside him, to burrow against him. "I love you," she murmured, felt him quiver as she caressed him. "It's so easy with you."

They stayed like that for a long, long time, with the wolf staring into the dying fire and listening to her quiet breathing.

Liam kept her busy and kept her close over the next three weeks. She loved the work—and that helped him justify spending so much time with her. It was true enough that most of her sketching could—even should—have been done on her own. But she didn't argue when he insisted she come to him nearly every day to work.

It was only to...keep an eye on her, he told himself. To observe her, to help him decide what to do next. And when to do it. It wasn't as if he wanted her company, particularly. He preferred working alone, and certainly didn't need the distraction of her, the scent and the softness. Or the chatter that was by turns charming and revealing. He certainly didn't need the offerings she so often brought over. Tarts and cookies and little cakes.

As often as not they were soggy or burned—and incredibly sweet.

It wasn't as if he couldn't do without her, very, very easily. That's what he told himself every day as he waited restlessly for her to arrive.

If he went to her nightly in wolf form, it was only because

he understood she was lonely, and that she looked forward to the visits. Perhaps he did enjoy lying beside her on the big canopy bed, listening to her read aloud from one of her books. Watching her fall asleep, invariably with her glasses on and the lamplight shining.

And if he often watched her in sleep, it wasn't because she was so lovely, so fragile. It was only because she was a puzzle that needed to be solved. A problem that required logical handling.

His heart, he continued to assure himself, was well-protected.

He knew the next step was approaching. A time when he would put the choice of what they became to each other in her hands.

Before he did, she would have to know who he was. And what he was.

He could have taken her as a lover without revealing himself. He had done so before, with other women. What business had it been of theirs, after all? His powers, his heritage, his life, were his own.

But that might not be the case with Rowan.

She had a heritage of her own, one she knew nothing of. There would also come a time he would have to tell her of that, and convince her of what ran through her blood.

What she would do about it would be her own choice.

The choice to educate her had been his.

But he guarded his heart still. Desire was acceptable, but love was too big a risk.

On the night of the solstice, when magic was thick and the night came late, he prepared the circle. Deep in the woods, he stood in the center of the stone dance. Around him, the air sang, the sweet song of the ancients, the lively tune of the young, the shimmering strains of those who watched and waited.

And the aching harpstrings of hope.

The candles were white and slender, as were the flowers that lay between them. He wore a robe the color of moon-glow belted with the jewels of his rank.

The wind caught his unbound hair as he lifted his face to the last light of the yielding sun. Beams of it fired the trees, shot lances of glimmering gold through the branches to lie like honed swords at his feet.

"What I do here, I do freely, but I make no vow to the woman or to my blood. No duty binds me, no promises made. Hear my voice before this longest day dies. I will call her, and she will come, but I will not use what I have beyond the call. What she sees, what she remembers and believes is for her to decide."

He watched the silver owl swoop, then perch imperiously on the king stone.

"Father," he said, formally and with a bow. "Your wishes are known, but if I'm ruled by them, would I rule others wisely?"

Knowing that statement would irritate, Liam turned away before the smile could touch his lips. Once more he lifted his face. "I call Earth." He opened his hand to reveal the deep rich soil he held. "And Wind." The breeze rose up high and wild, tossing the earth into a spiral. "And Fire." Two columns of iced blue flame speared up, shivered. "Witness here what fate will conspire. A song in the blood, the power at hand."

His eyes began to glow, twin flames against the glowing dark. "To honor both I've come to this strange land. If she's mine, we both will see. As I will so mote it be."

Then he turned, lighting each of the candles with a flick of his hand until their flames shot up clear gold and straight as arrows. The wind leaped up, howled like a thousand wolves on the hunt, but remained warm and fragrant with sea and pine and wildflowers.

It billowed the sleeves of his robe, streamed through his hair. And he tasted in it the power of the night.

"Moon rise full and Moon rise white, light her path to me

tonight. Guide her here to the circle by the sea. As I will so mote it be."

He lowered the hands he had flung up to the sky, and peered through the night, through the trees and the dark, to where she slept restlessly in her bed.

"Rowan," he said with something like a sigh, "it's time. No harm will come to you. It's the only promise I'll make. You don't need to wake. You know the way in your dreams. I'm waiting for you."

Something...called her. She could hear it, a murmur in the mind, a question. Stirring in sleep, she searched for the answer. But there was only wonder.

She rose, stretching luxuriously, enjoying the feel of the silky new nightshirt against her thighs. It was so nice to be out of flannel. Smiling to herself, she slipped into a robe of the same deep blue as her eyes, tucked her feet into slippers.

Anticipation shivered along her skin.

In that half dream, she walked down the steps, trailing her fingertips along the banister. The light in her eyes, the smile on her lips, were those of a woman going to meet her lover.

She thought of him, of Liam, the lover of her dreams, as she walked out of the house and into the swirling white fog.

The trees were curtained behind it, the path invisible. The air, moist and warm on her skin, seemed to sigh, then to part. She moved through it without fear, into that soft white sea of mist with the full white moon riding the sky above, and the stars glimmering like points of ice.

Trees closed in, like sentinels. Ferns stirred in the damp breeze and shimmered with wet. She heard the long, deep call of an owl and turned without thought or hesitation toward the sound. Once, she saw him, huge and grand and as silver as the mist, with the glint of gold on his breast and the flash of green eyes.

Like walking through a fairy tale. A part of her mind recognized, acknowledged and embraced the magic of it, while another part slept, not yet ready to see, not yet ready to know. But her heart beat strong and steady and her steps were quick and light.

If there were eyes peeking from between the lacy branches of the ferns, if there was joyful laughter tinkling down from the high spreading branches of the firs, she could only enjoy it.

At each step, each turn of the path, the fog shimmered clear to open the way for her.

And the water sang quietly.

She saw the lights glowing, little fires in the night. She smelled sea, candle wax, sweet fragrant flowers. Her soft smile spread as she stepped into the clearing, to the dance of stones.

Fog shivered at the edges, like a foamy hem, but didn't slide between stone and candle and flowers. So he stood in the center, on clear ground, his robe white as the moonshine, the jewels belting it flashing with power and light.

If his heart jerked at the sight of her, if it trembled on the edge of where he'd vowed it would not go, he ignored it.

"Will you come in, Rowan?" he asked, and held out a hand.

Something in her yearned. Something in her shuddered. But her smile remained as she took another step. "Of course I will." And walked through the stones.

Something throbbed on the air, along her skin, in her heart. She heard the stones whisper. The lights of the candles flickered, swayed, then flamed straight up again.

Their fingertips brushed. Her eyes stayed on his, trusting, when those fingers linked firm. "I dream of you, every night." She sighed it, and would have moved into him, but he laid a hand on her shoulder. "And long for you through the days."

"You don't understand, neither the rewards nor the consequences. And you must."

"I know I want you. You've already seduced me, Liam."

A tiny finger of guilt scraped up his spine. "I'm not without needs."

She reached up, cupped his cheek. And her voice was soft where his had been rough. "Do you need me?"

"I want you." Need was too much, too weak, too risky.

"I'm here." She lifted her face to his. "Won't you kiss me?"

"Aye." He leaned down, kept his eyes open and on hers. "Remember this," he murmured when his lips were a breath from hers. "Remember this, Rowan, if you can." And his mouth brushed over hers, once, then again. Testing. Then a gentle nip to make her shiver.

When she sighed, one long quiet breath, he covered her mouth with his, drawing out the moment, the magic, sliding into the taste and texture of her. The warm, slow tangle of tongues thickened his pulse, called to his blood.

On either side of them, the cool blue fire burned bright.

"Hold me. Liam, touch me. I've waited so long."

The sound he made in his throat was caught between growl and groan as he dragged her to him and let his hands roam.

Take her here, take her now, in the circle where we'll be bound. It would be done. That primal urge to cover her, to bury himself in her, warred viciously with his honor. What did it matter what she knew, what she wanted or believed? What did it matter what he gained or lost? There was now, only now, with her hot and eager in his arms and her mouth like a flame against his.

"Lie with me here." Her lips tore from his to race wildly over his face, down his throat. "Make love with me here." She already knew what it would be. Dreams and fantasies danced in her mind, and she knew. Urgent and elemental, fast and potent. And she wanted, wanted, wanted the mad, mindless thrill.

In one rough move, he pushed the robe from her shoulder and set his teeth on that bare flesh. The taste of her swirled through him, drugged wine to cloud the senses. "Do you know who I am?" he demanded.

"Liam." His name was already pounding in her head.

He jerked her back, stared into her dark eyes. "Do you know what I am?"

"Different." It was all she could be sure of, though more, much more hovered at the edge of her senses.

"You're still afraid to know it." And if she feared that, how much more might she fear her own blood? "When you can say it, you'll be ready to give yourself to me. And take what I give you."

Her eyes glowed, deep and blue. Her trembles weren't from fear or cold, but from desire straining for release. "Why isn't this enough?"

He stroked a hand over her hair, soothing her, struggling to soothe himself. "Magic has responsibilities. Tonight, the shortest night, it dances in the forest, sings in the hills of my home, it rides the seas and soars in the air. Tonight it celebrates. But tomorrow, always tomorrow it must remember its purpose. Feel the joy of it."

He kissed her brow, both of her cheeks. "Tonight, Rowan Murray of the O'Mearas, you'll remember what you will. And tomorrow, the choice is yours."

He stepped back, spreading his arms so that the robe whipped around him.

"The night passes, quick and bright, and dawn will break with the softest light. If blood calls to blood come then to me." He paused so that their eyes locked and held. "As you will, so mote it be."

He reached down, took a spray of moonflowers and gave it to her. "Sleep well, Rowan."

The sleeves of his robe fell back, revealing hard muscle. With one flash of power, he sent her from him.

# Chapter 8

The sunlight beamed bright through the windows. With a murmur of complaint, Rowan turned from it, pressed her face into the pillow.

Sleep was what she wanted. Sleep where those wonderful and vivid dreams would come, where she could wrap herself in them. There were tatters of them still waving through her mind.

Fog and flowers. Moonbeams and candleglow. The silver flash of an owl, the quiet roar of the sea. And Liam in a white robe that shimmered with jewels, holding her in the center of a circle of stones.

She could taste that hot male flavor of him on her tongue, feel the ripple of muscle held ruthlessly in check, feel the not-quite-steady thud of his heart against hers.

She had only to slide back into sleep to experience it all again.

But she turned restlessly, unable to find it, or him, again.

It was so real, she thought, rubbing her cheek against the pillow to watch the sunbeams shoot in through the windows.

So real and so...wonderful. She'd often had very odd and textured dreams, particularly during her childhood.

Her mother had said it was imagination, and that she had
a good one. But she needed to learn the difference between
what was real and what was make-believe.

Much too often, Rowan supposed, she'd preferred the make-
believe. Because she'd known that had worried her parents a
little, she'd buried it. She decided it was because she'd chosen to take her own road now that the dreams were coming
back so often.

And it didn't take an expert to understand why her dreams
were so often of Liam—and so romantic and erotic. She supposed the wisest course was to simply enjoy them—and not
to forget what was real and what wasn't.

She stretched, lifting her arms high, linking her hands. And
smiling to herself, replayed what she could remember.

A dream riff on the game they were working on, she
thought. With Liam as hero, she as heroine. Magic and mist,
romance and denial. A circle of stones that whispered, a ring of
candles where the flames rose straight despite the wind. Columns of fire, blue as lake water. Fog that parted as she walked.

Lovely, she mused, then closed her eyes and tried to go
back and remember what he'd said to her. She could remember very well the way he'd kissed her. Gently, then with heat
and hunger. But what had he said? Something about choices
and knowledge and responsibilities.

If she could put it in order she might be able to give him
an idea for a story line for another game. But all that was really clear was the way his hands had moved over her—and
the needs that had pumped inside her.

They were working together now, she reminded herself.
Thinking of him the way she did was both inappropriate and
foolish. The last thing she wanted to do was delude herself
into thinking he could fall in love with her—the way she was
very much aware she could fall in love with him.

So she'd think of the work instead, of the pleasure it gave her. She'd think of the house she meant to buy. It was time to do something about that. But for now, she'd get up, make her coffee, take her morning walk.

She tossed the sheets aside. And there on the bed beside her was a spray of moonflowers.

Her heart took a hard leap into her throat and snapped it shut. Her breath clogged behind it, hot and thick. Impossible, impossible, her mind insisted. But even when she squeezed her eyes tight, she could smell the delicate fragrance.

She must have picked them and forgotten. But she knew there were no such flowers around her cottage or in the woods. Flowers such as she now remembered seeing in her dream, spread like white wishes between the spears of candles.

But it couldn't be. It had been a dream, just another of the dreams that had visited her sleep since she'd come to this place. She hadn't walked through the forest in the night, through the mists. She hadn't gone to that clearing, to Liam, or stepped into the stone dance.

Unless...

Sleepwalking, she thought with a quick lick of panic. Had she been sleepwalking? She scrambled out of bed, her gaze glued to the flowers as she grabbed her robe.

And the hem was damp, as if she'd walked through dew.

She clutched the robe against her, as details of the dream raced much too clearly through her mind.

"It can't be real." But the words echoed hollowly. With a sudden flurry of motion, she began to dress.

She ran all the way, not questioning when temper raced with her fear. He'd caused it, that was all she knew. Maybe there was something in that tea he brewed every day. A hallucinogenic of some kind.

It was the only rational explanation. There had to be a rational explanation.

Her breath was short, her eyes huge when she ran up the

steps to pound on his door. She gripped the flowers in one white-knuckled hand.

"What did you do to me?" she demanded the moment he opened the door.

He watched her steadily as he stepped back. "Come in, Rowan."

"I want to know what you did to me. I want to know what this means." She thrust the flowers at him.

"You gave me flowers once," he said, almost brutally calm. "I know you've a fondness for them."

"Did you drug the tea?"

Now that calm snapped off into insult. "I beg your pardon?"

"It's the only explanation." She whirled away from him to pace the room. "Something in the tea to make me imagine things, to do things. I'd never walk into the woods at night in my right mind."

"I don't deal in potions of that kind." He added a dismissive shrug that had her trembling with fury.

"Oh, really." She spun back to face him. Her hair tumbling over her shoulders, her eyes snapping vivid blue. "What kind, then?"

"Some that ease small hurts of body and soul. But it's not my...specialty."

"And what is your specialty, then?"

He shot her a look of impatience. "If you'd open your mind you'd see you already know the answer to that."

She stared into his eyes. As the image of the wolf flashed into her mind, she shook her head and stepped back. "Who are you?"

"You know who I am. And damn it, I've given you plenty of time to deal with it."

"With what? Deal with *what?*" she repeated, and stabbed a finger into his chest. "I don't understand anything about you." This time she shoved him and had his own temper peaking. "I don't understand anything about what you expect me to know.

I want answers, Liam. I want them now or I want you to leave me alone. I won't be played with this way, or tricked or made a fool of. So you tell me exactly what this means." She ripped the flowers back out of his hand. "Or I'm finished."

"Finished, are you? Want answers, do you?" Anger and insult overpowered reason and he nodded. "Oh aye, then, here's an answer for you."

He threw out his hands. Light, brought on by temper rather than need, flashed cold blue from his fingertips. A thin white mist swirled around his body, leaving only those gold eyes bright and clear.

Then it was the eyes of the wolf, glinting at her as he bared his teeth in what might have been a sneer, his pelt gleaming midnight-black.

The blood drained out of her head, left it light and giddy as the mists faded. She could hear in some dim distance, the harsh, ragged sound of her own breath and the trembling scream that sounded only in her mind.

She stepped back, staggered. Her vision grayed at the edges. Tiny lights danced in front of her eyes.

When her knees buckled, he cursed ripely, and his hands caught her before she could fall.

"Damned if you'll faint and make me feel like a monster." He eased her into a chair and shoved her head between her knees. "Catch your breath, and next time have a care with what you wish for."

There was a hive of bees buzzing in her head, a hundred icy fingers skimming over her skin. She babbled something when he lifted her head. She would have pulled back, but he had his hands firm on her face. "Just look," he murmured, gently now. "Just look at me. Be calm."

Awake and aware this time, she felt his mind touch her. Instinct had her struggling, had her hands lifting to push at him.

"No, don't fight me on this. I won't harm you."

"No... I know you won't." She knew that, was inexplicably certain of it. "Could I—could I have some water?"

She blinked at the glass she hadn't known was in his hand, hesitated and saw that flicker of annoyance in his eyes. "It's only water. You've my word on it."

"Your word." She sipped, let out a shaky breath. "You're a..." It was too ridiculous, but she'd seen. For Lord's sake, she'd seen. "You're a werewolf."

His eyes rounded in what could only be shock, then he shoved himself to his feet to stare at her in baffled fury. "A werewolf? For the love of Finn, where do you come up with these things? A werewolf." He muttered it now as he prowled the room. "You're not stupid, you're just stubborn. It's the broad light of day, isn't it? Do you see a full moon out there? Did I come snapping at your throat?"

He muttered curses in Gaelic as he whirled back around to glare at her. "I'm Liam of Donovan," he said with pride ringing in his voice. "And I'm a witch."

"Oh, well then." Her laugh was quick and lightly hysterical. "That's all right then."

"Don't cringe from me." He snapped it out, cut to the core when she hugged her arms over her chest. "I've given you time to see, to prepare. I'd not have shown you so abruptly if you hadn't pushed me."

"Time to see? To prepare? For *this?*" She ran an unsteady hand through her hair. "Who could? Maybe I'm dreaming again," she murmured, then bolted straight in the chair. "Dreaming. Oh, my God."

He saw her thoughts, jammed his hands into his pockets. "I took nothing you weren't willing to give."

"You made love to me—you came to my bed while I slept and—"

"My mind to your mind," he interrupted. "I kept my hands off you—for the most part."

The blood had come back into her face and flamed there now. "They weren't dreams."

"They were dreams right enough. You'd have given me more than that, Rowan. We both know the truth of it. I won't apologize for dreaming with you."

"Dreaming with me." She ordered herself to her feet, but had to brace a hand on the chair to stay on them. "Am I supposed to believe this?"

"Aye." A smile ghosted around his mouth. "That you are."

"Believe you're a witch. That you can change into a wolf and come into my dreams whenever you like."

"Whenever you like, as well." A different tack, he mused, might be in order. One that would please them both. "You sighed for me, Rowan. Trembled for me." He moved forward to skim his hands up her arms. "And smiled in your sleep when I left you."

"What you're talking about happens in books, in the games you write."

"And in the world, as well. You've been in that world. I've taken you there. You remember last night, I can see it in your mind."

"Don't look in my mind." She jerked back, mortified because she believed he could. "Thoughts are private things."

"And yours are often so clear on your face I don't have to look any further. I won't look further if it upsets you."

"It does." She caught her bottom lip between her teeth. "You're a psychic?"

He blew out a huff of breath. "I've the power to see, if that's your meaning. To brew a spell, to call the thunder." He shrugged negligently, elegantly. "To shift shapes at my will."

Shape-shifter. Good God. She'd read of such things, of course she had. In novels, in books on myths and legends. It couldn't be real. And yet...could she deny what she'd seen with her own eyes? What she knew in her own heart?

"You came to me as the wolf." If she was mad, she thought, she might as well have mad answers.

"You weren't afraid of me then. Others would have been, but not you. You welcomed me in, put your arms around me, wept on my neck."

"I didn't know it was you. If I'd known—" She broke off as other memories crept back. "You watched me undress! You sat there while I was in the tub."

"It's a lovely body you have. Why should you be shamed that I've seen it? Only hours ago you asked me to touch you."

"That's entirely different."

Something that might have been reluctant amusement flickered in his eyes. "Ask me to touch you now, knowing, and it will be even more different."

She swallowed hard. "Why haven't you...touched me already?"

"You needed time to know me, and yourself. I've no right to take innocence, even when it's offered, when no knowledge goes with it."

"I'm not innocent. I've been with men before."

Now there was something dark shimmering in his eyes, something not quite tame. But his voice was even when he spoke. "They didn't touch your innocence, didn't change it. I will. If you lie with me, Rowan, it'll be as the first time. I'll give you pleasure that will make you burn...."

His voice had lowered. When he traced a finger down her throat, she shivered, but didn't step back. Whoever—whatever—he was, he moved her. He called to her. "What will you feel?"

"Delight," he murmured, easing closer to brush his mouth over her cheek. "Demand. Desire. It's the passion you wanted that you didn't find in others. Urgency, you said. And desperation. I feel that for you, whether I will or no. That much power you have over me. Is it enough for you?"

"I don't know. No one's ever felt that for me."

"I do." He brought his hands over, slipped the first two buttons free on her simple cotton shirt. "Let me see you, Rowan. Here, in the light of day."

"Liam." It was insanity. How could it be real? Yet everything she felt was too intense, too immediate to be otherwise. Nothing, she realized with a dull sense of shock, had ever been more real to her. "I believe this." Her breath trembled free. "I want this."

He looked in her eyes, saw both the fear and the acceptance. "So do I."

The skim of his knuckles over her skin left a hot trail down her skin as he unbuttoned her blouse, slipped it off her shoulders. Her heart tumbled in her chest as he smiled. "You were in a hurry this morning," he murmured, noting she hadn't taken the time for a bra.

To please himself he traced a fingertip lightly down the subtle slope, over the tip, and watched her eyes go opaque. "You know I can't stop you," she said, watching him.

"Aye, you can." Through sheer will he kept his touch gentle. "With but a word. I hope you won't, for it'll drive me mad not to have you now. Do you want me to touch you?"

"Yes." More than she wanted to breathe.

"You said once that it shouldn't be simple." With his eyes on hers, he unbuttoned her jeans. "It won't be." Skilled fingertips skimmed under denim to tease, to awaken. "Not for either of us."

It was like a dream, she thought. Just one more glorious dream. "Why do you want this?"

"Because you're in my mind, in my blood." That much was true, but he told himself he could block her out of his heart. Leaning forward, he caught her jaw gently between his teeth. "I'm in yours."

Why should she deny it? Why shouldn't she accept, even embrace, these outrageous sensations, this heat in the belly and flutter in the pulse? He was what she wanted, with a giddy greed she'd felt for no other man.

So take, her mind murmured, and pay whatever price is asked.

Still her fingers shook slightly as she tugged his shirt over his head. Then, with a kind of wonder, she spread her hands over his chest.

Hard, warm. Strength just on the edge of danger, held ruthlessly in check. She knew it, even as her curious fingers traced up, over broad shoulders, down the taut muscles of his arms. She heard the soft feline purr before she realized it had come from her own throat.

Her gaze shot up to his, and in her eyes was a mix of shock and delight. "I've done this before…in my dreams."

"With much the same results." He'd intended his tone to be dry, but there was an edge to it that stunned him. Gently, he ordered himself, she should be treated gently. "Will you move beyond dreams now, Rowan, and lie with me?"

For an answer she stepped to him, rising onto her toes so that her mouth met his. The beauty of that, just that, had his arms coming hard around her. "Hold tight," he murmured.

She felt the air shudder, heard a rustle of wind. There was a sensation of rising, spinning, then tumbling, all in the space of a single heartbeat. Before fear could fully form, before the gasp of it could shudder from her mouth to his, she was lying beneath him, dipped deep into a bed soft as clouds.

Her eyes flew open. She could see the polished beams of a wood ceiling, the stream of sunlight. "But how—"

"I've magic for you, Rowan." His mouth moved to the vulnerable flesh of her throat. "All manner of magic."

They were in his bed, she realized. In the blink of an eye they'd moved from one room to another. And now his hands… oh, sweet Lord, how could the simple touch of flesh to flesh cause such *feeling*?

"Give me your thoughts." His voice was rough, his hands light as air. "Let me touch them, and show you."

She opened her mind to him, gasping when she not only felt the heat of his body, the skim of his hands, but saw, the images forming out of the mists in her mind, the two of them tangled together on a huge, yielding bed in a path of early-summer sunlight.

Every sensation now, every shimmering layer, was reflected back, as if a thousand silver mirrors shone out of her heart. And so, with a kiss only, one long, drugging kiss, he brought her softly to peak.

She moaned out the pleasure of it, the sheer wonder of having her body slide over a velvet edge. Her thoughts scattered, dimmed, reformed in a mixed maze of colors, only to fly apart again as his teeth grazed her shoulder.

She was beyond price. An unexpected treasure in her openness, her utter surrender to him and to her own pleasures. Now, at last now his hands could take, his mouth could feast. Soft, silky flesh, pale as the moon, delicate curves and subtle scents.

The animal that beat in his blood wanted to ravage, to grasp and plunge. She would not deny him. Knowing that, he wrapped the chain tighter around his own pounding throat and offered only tenderness.

She moved beneath him, all quiet sighs and luxurious stretches. Her hands roamed over him freely, building and banking small fires. Dark and heavy, her eyes met his when he lifted his head.

And her lips curved slowly.

"I've waited so long to feel like this." She lifted a hand to slide her fingers through his hair. "I never knew I was waiting."

*Love waits.*

The words came back to him like a drumbeat, a warning, a whisper. Ignoring it, he lowered again to take her breast with his mouth. She arched, gave a little cry, as the movement had been sudden and just a bit rough.

Then she groaned, and the hand that had combed lazily through his hair fisted tight, pressing him urgently against her. Heat flashed, a quick bolt to the center. His tongue tormented, his teeth hinted of pain. She gave herself over to it, to him, trembling again as both mind and body steeped in pleasure.

No one had ever touched her this way, so deep it seemed he knew her needs and secrets better than she herself. Her heart quaked, then soared under his quietly ruthless mouth. And opened wide as love flooded it.

She clung to him now, murmuring mindlessly as they rolled over the bed, as flesh grew damp with desire and minds misted with delight.

She was…glory, he thought dimly while he tumbled to a depth he'd never explored with a woman. His keen senses were barraged with her. Scent like spice on the wind, taste like honeyed wine, texture like heated silk. Whatever he asked for she gave, a rose opening petal by petal.

She rose up when he reached for her, her body impossibly fluid, her lips like a flame on his shoulder, across his chest, against his greedy mouth.

Against his hand she was warm and wet, and her body arched back like a drawn bow when his fingers found her. Eyes sharp on her face, he watched that fresh rush of shock and pleasure and fear flicker over hers as he took her up, urged her over.

Her breath sobbed out, her body shook as that new arrow of sensation pinned her, left her quivering helplessly. Even as her head dropped limply on the shoulder her nails had just bitten into, he sent her spinning up again.

When they tumbled back, he gripped her hands, waited for his vision to clear, waited for her eyes to open and meet his. The air dragged in and out of his lungs. "Now."

The word was nearly an oath as he drove into her.

Held there, held quivering to watch her eyes go wide and

blind. Held there, held gasping while the thrill of filling her burned in his blood.

Then she began to move.

A lift of the hips, a falling away that drew him down. Slow, achingly slow, with a low moan for each long, deep thrust.

It was his eyes, only his eyes, she saw now, brilliantly gold, stunningly intense as they took each other to a secret space where the air fluttered like velvet on the skin. Her fingers clung to his, her eyes stayed open and aware. Every pulse that beat in her body gathered into one steady throb that filled the heart to bursting.

When it burst, and her mind and body with it, she arched high and hard against him, called out his name with a kind of wonder. Saying hers, he buried his face in her hair and dived with her.

He stretched over her, his head between her breasts, his long body lax. She kept her eyes closed, the better to hold on to that sensation of flying, of falling. Never before had she been so aware, so in tune with her own desires or with a man's.

And never, she realized, had she been so willing, even eager, to surrender to both.

A small smile curved her lips as she lazily stroked his hair. In her mind she could see them together there. Wantonly sprawled, naked, damp and tangled.

She wondered how long it would be before he'd want to touch her again.

"I already do." Liam's voice was thick and low. His tongue skimmed carelessly over the side of her breast and made her shiver.

"Thoughts are private."

She was so soft and warm in the afterglow of love, and that lazy sip of her flesh so delightful. He slid a hand up, molded her gently and shifted to nibble. "I've been inside your thoughts." Her nipple hardened against a flick of his tongue and needs stirred again. "I've been inside you, *a ghra*. What's the point of secrets now?"

"Thoughts are private," she repeated, but the last word ended on a moan.

"As you wish." He slipped out of her mind even as he slipped into her.

She must have slept. Though she remembered nothing but curling around him after that second, surprising slide into heaven. She stirred in bed, and found herself alone.

Sunny morning had become rainy afternoon. The sound of its steady patter, the golden haze that seemed to linger inside her body, both urged her to simply snuggle back and sleep again.

But curiosity was stronger. This was his bed, she thought, smiling foolishly. His room. Shoving at her tangled hair, she sat up and looked.

The bed was amazing. A lake of feathers covered in smooth, silky sheets, backed by a headboard of dark polished wood carved with stars and symbols and lettering she couldn't make out. Idly she traced her fingers in the grooves.

He, too, had a fireplace facing the bed. It was fashioned of some kind of rich green stone and topped by a mantel of the same material. Gracing that were colorful crystals. She imagined their facets would catch the sun brilliantly. Fat white candles stood at one end in a triad.

There was a tall chair with its back carved in much the same way as the headboard. A deep blue throw woven with crescent moons was tossed over one of its arms.

The tables by the bed held lamps with bases of bronze mermaids. Charmed, she ran a finger along the curving tails.

He kept the furnishings spare, she noted, but he chose what he kept around him with care.

She rose, stretched, shook back her hair. The rain made her feel beautifully lazy. Instead of looking for her clothes, she walked to his closet hoping she would find a robe to bundle into.

She found a robe, and it made her fingers jerk on the door. A long white robe with wide sleeves.

He'd worn it the night before. In the stone dance. Under the moonlight. A witch's robe.

Closing the door quickly, she spun around, looked around wildly for her clothes. Downstairs, she remembered with a jolt. He'd undressed her downstairs, and then...

What was she doing? What was she thinking of? Was this real or had she gone mad?

Had she just spent hours in bed with him?

And if it was real, if what she'd always thought was fantasy was suddenly truth, had he used it to lure her here?

For lack of anything else, she snatched up the throw, wrapped it around herself. She grasped the ends tight as the door of the bedroom opened.

He lifted a brow when he saw her, draped in the cloth his mother had woven for him when he'd turned twenty-one. She looked tumbled and lovely and outrageously desirable. He took a step toward her before he caught the glint of suspicion in her eyes.

Annoyed, he moved past her to set the tea tray he'd carried up on the bedside table. "What have you thought of that I haven't explained?"

"How can you explain what should be impossible?"

"What is, is," he said simply. "I am a hereditary witch, descended from Finn of the Celts. What powers I have are my birthright."

She had to accept that. She had seen, she had felt. She kept her shoulders straight and her voice even. "Did you use those powers on me, Liam?"

"You ask me not to touch your thoughts. Since I respect your wishes, try to be more specific in your questions." Obviously irritated, he sat on the side of the bed and picked up a cup of tea.

"I was attracted to you, strongly and physically attracted to you, from the first minute. I behaved with you as I've never behaved with a man. I've just gone to bed with you and felt things…" She took a long, steadying breath as he watched her, as she saw a little gleam that had to be triumph light his eyes. "Did you put a spell on me to get me into bed?"

The gleam went dark, and triumph became fury so swiftly she stumbled back a step in instinctive defense. China cracked on wood as he slammed the cup down. From somewhere not so far away, came the irritable grumble of thunder.

But he got to his feet slowly, like a wolf, she thought, stalking prey.

"Love spells, love potions?" He came toward her. She backed away. "I'm a witch, not a charlatan. I'm a man, not a cheat. Do you think I would abuse my gifts, shame my name, for sex?"

He made a dismissive gesture; the window shuddered and cracked, giving her a clue just how dangerous was his temper. "I didn't ask for you, woman. Whatever part fate played in it, you came to this place, and to me, of your own will. And you're free to go in the same manner."

"How can you expect me not to wonder?" she shot back. "I'm just supposed to shrug and accept. Oh, Liam's a witch. He can turn into a wolf and read my mind and blink us from one room to the next whenever he likes. Isn't that handy?"

She whirled away from him, the throw flicking out around her bare legs. "I'm an educated woman who's just been dropped headfirst into some kind of fairy tale. I'll ask whatever questions I damn well please."

"You appeal to me when you're angry," he murmured. "Why is that, I wonder?"

"I have no idea." She spun back. "I don't *get* angry, by the way. And I never shout, but I'm shouting at you. I don't fall naked into bed with men or have arguments wearing nothing but a blanket, so if I ask if you've done something to make me behave this way, I think it's a perfectly logical question."

"Perhaps it is. Insulting, but logical. The answer is no." He said it almost wearily as he went back to sit on the bed and sip his tea. "I cast no spell, wove no magic. I'm wiccan, Rowan. There is one law we live by, one rule that cannot be broken. 'An' it harm none.' I will do nothing to harm you. And my pride alone would prevent me from influencing your response to me. What you feel, you feel."

When she said nothing, he moved his shoulder in a careless jerk, as if there weren't a sharp-clawed fist around his heart. "You'll want your clothes." With no more than those words, her jeans and shirt appeared on the chair.

She let out a short laugh, shook her head. "And you don't think I should be dazzled by something like that. You expect a great deal, Liam."

He looked at her again, thought of what ran in her blood. Not nearly ready to know, he decided, annoyed with his own impatience. "Aye, I suppose I do. You have a great deal, Rowan, if you'd only trust yourself."

"No one's ever really believed in me." Steady now, she walked to him. "That's a kind of magic you offer me that means more than all the flash and wonder. I'll start with trusting this much—I'll believe that what I feel for you is real. Is that enough for now?"

He lifted a hand to lay it over the one that held the ends of the throw. The tenderness that filled him was new, unexplained and too sweet to question. "It's enough. Sit, have some tea."

"I don't want tea." It thrilled her to be so bold, to loosen her grip and let the throw fall away. "And I don't want my clothes. But I do want you."

# *Chapter 9*

She was under a spell. Not one that required incantations, Rowan thought dreamily. Not one that called on mystical powers and forces. She was in love, and that, she supposed, was the oldest and the most natural of magics.

She'd never been as comfortable nor as uneasy with any other man. Never been quite so shy, nor ever so bold as she was with Liam. Looking back, gauging her actions, her reactions, her words and her wishes, she realized she'd fallen under that spell the moment she'd turned and seen him behind her on the cliffs.

The wind in his hair, annoyance in his eyes, Ireland in his voice. That graceful, muscular body with its power held ruthlessly in check.

Love at first sight, she thought. Just one more page of her own personal fairy tale.

And after love, her love, they'd found their way to a friendship she treasured every bit as much. Companionship, an ease of being. She knew he enjoyed having her with him, for work, for talk, for sitting quietly and watching the sky change with evening.

She could tell by the way he smiled at her, or laughed, or absently brushed a hand through her hair.

At times like that she could sense that restlessness that prowled in him shifting into a kind of contentment. The way it had, she remembered, when he'd come to her as a wolf and lain down beside her to listen to her read.

Wasn't it odd, she mused, that in searching for her own peace of mind, she'd given him some?

Life, she decided as she settled down to sketch a line of foxglove on the banks of the stream, was a wonderful thing. And now, finally, she was beginning to live it.

It was lovely to do something she enjoyed, to sit in a place that made her happy and spend time exploring her own talents, to study the way the sun filtered through the treetops, the way the narrow ribbon of water curved and sparkled.

All these shades of green to explore, the shapes of things, the marvelously complicated bark of a Douglas fir, the charming fancy of a lush fern.

There was time for them now, time for herself.

No longer was she required to get up in the morning and put on a neat, conservative suit, to wade through morning traffic, drive through the rain with a briefcase full of papers and plans and projects in the seat beside her. And to stand at the front of the classroom, knowing that she wasn't quite good enough, certainly not dedicated enough an instructor, as each one of her students deserved.

She would never again have to come home every evening to an apartment that had never really felt like home, to eat her solitary dinner, grade her papers, go to bed. Except for every Wednesday and Sunday, when she would be expected for dinner by her parents. They would discuss their respective weeks, and she would listen to their advice on the direction of her career.

Week after week, month after month, year after year. It was hardly any wonder they'd been so shocked and hurt when she'd broken that sacred routine. What would they say if she told them she'd gone way beyond the scope of any imaginings and fallen headlong in love with a witch? A shape-shifter, a magician. A wonder.

The idea made her laugh, shake her head in delighted amusement. No, she thought, it was best to keep certain areas of her new life all to herself.

Her much-loved and decidedly earthbound parents would never believe, much less understand it.

She couldn't understand it herself. It was real, it was true, there was no way to deny it. Yet how could he be what he claimed to be? How could he do what she had seen him do?

Her pencil faltered, and she reached up to toy nervously with the end of her braid. She *had* seen it, less than a week ago. And since then there had been a dozen small, baffling moments.

She'd seen him light candles with a thought, pluck a white rose out of the air, and once—in one of his rare foolish moods—he'd whisked her clothes away with no more than a grin.

It amazed and delighted her. Thrilled her. But she could admit here, alone, in her deepest thoughts, that part of her feared it as well.

He had such powers. Over the elements, and over her.

*He'll never use them to harm you.*

The voice in her head made her jolt so that her sketchpad slapped facedown on the forest floor. Even as she pressed a hand to her jumping heart she saw the silver owl swoop down. He watched her from the low branch of a tree out of unblinking eyes of sharp green. Gold glinted against the silver of his breast.

Another page from the fairy tale, she thought giddily, and managed to get to her feet. "Hello." It came out as a croak, forcing her to clear her throat. "I'm Rowan."

She bit back a shriek as the owl spread his regal wings,

soared down from the tree and with a ripple of silver light, became a man.

"I know well enough who you are, girl." There was music and magic in his voice, and the echo of green hills and misty valleys.

Her nerves were forgotten in sheer pleasure. "You're Liam's father."

"So I am." The stern expression on his face softened into a smile. He moved toward her, footsteps silent in soft brown boots. And, taking her hand, lifted it gallantly to kiss. "It is a pleasure to be meeting you, young Rowan. Why do you sit here alone, worrying?"

"I like to sit alone sometimes. And worrying's one of my best things."

He shook his head, gave a quick snap of his fingers and had her sketchpad fluttering up into his hand. "No, this is." He sat comfortably on the fallen tree, cocking his head so that his hair flowed like liquid silver to his shoulders. "You've a gift here, and a charming one." He gave the space beside him an absent pat. "Sit yourself," he said when she didn't move. "I'll not eat you."

"It's all so...dumbfounding."

His gaze shifted to hers with honest puzzlement lighting the green. "Why?"

"Why?" She was sitting on a tree in the woods beside a witch, the second she'd met so far. "You'd be used to it, but it's just a little surprising to a mere mortal."

His eyes narrowed, and if Rowan had been able to read his mind she'd have been stunned to read his quick and annoyed thoughts aimed at his son. *The stubborn whelp hasn't told her yet. What is he waiting for?*

Finn had to remind himself it was Liam's place and not his own, and smiled at Rowan again.

"You've read stories, haven't you? Heard legends and songs that speak of us?"

"Yes, of course, but—"

"And where, young Rowan, do you think stories and legends and songs come from if not from grains of truth?" He gave her hand a fatherly pat. "Not that truth doesn't all too often become stretched and twisted. There you have witches tormenting innocent young children, popping them into ovens for dinner. Do you think we're after baking you up for a feast?"

The amusement in his voice was contagious. "No, of course not."

"Well then, stop your fretting." Dismissing her concerns he paged through her sketches. "You'll do well here. You do well here." His grin flashed as he came to one with fairy eyes peeking through a thick flood of flowers. "Well and fine here, girl. Why is it you don't use colors?"

"I'm no good with paints," she began. "But I thought I might get some chalks. I haven't done much with pastels and thought it might be fun."

He made a sound of approval and continued to flip pages. When he came to one of Liam standing spread-legged and arrogant on the cliffs, he grinned like a boy. And there was pride in his eyes, in his voice. "Oh, this is like him, isn't it? You've got him."

"Have I?" she murmured, then flushed when that green gaze rested on her face again.

"Every woman has power, Rowan. She's only to learn to use it. Ask him for something."

"For what?"

"What pleases you." Then he tapped a finger on the page. "Will you give me this? For his mother."

"Yes, of course." But when she started to tear the page out, it vanished.

"She misses him," Finn said simply. "Good day to you, Rowan of the O'Mearas."

"Oh, but won't you—" He was gone before she could ask

him to walk to Liam's with her. "'There are more things on heaven and earth, Horatio,'" she murmured, and, rising, walked to Liam's alone.

He wasn't waiting for her. That's what he told himself. He had a great deal to occupy his mind and fill his time. He certainly wasn't roaming aimlessly around the house waiting for a woman. Wishing for her.

Hadn't he told her he didn't intend to work that day? Hadn't he said that specifically, so they'd each have a little time apart? They both required their little pieces of solitude, didn't they?

So where the devil was she? he wondered as he roamed aimlessly around the house.

He could have looked, but it would be too undeniable an admission that he wanted her there. And she had been very clear about her expectations of privacy. No one knew or respected the need for privacy more.

And he was giving it to her, wasn't he? He didn't follow the urge just to take a quick glance into the glass and see, or skim lightly into her thoughts.

Damn it.

He could call her. He stopped his restless pacing and considered. A quiet murmur of her name on the air. It was hardly an intrusion, and she was free to ignore it if she wished. Tempted, sorely tempted, he moved to the door, opened it to step out into the balmy air.

But she wouldn't ignore it, he thought. She was too generous, too giving. If he asked, she'd come. And if he asked, it would be like an admission of weakness for her.

It was only a physical need yet, he assured himself. Just a longing for the taste of her, the shape, the scent. If it was sharper than was comfortable, it was likely due to his own restraint.

He'd been gentle with her, always. No matter how his blood

burned, he'd treated her carefully. When every instinct clawed at him to take more, he'd held back.

She was tender, he reminded himself. It was his responsibility to control the tone of their lovemaking, to yank back the fury of it lest he frighten her.

But he wanted more, craved it.

Why shouldn't he have it? Liam jammed his hands into his pockets and strode up and down the porch. Why the devil shouldn't he do as he pleased with her? If he decided—and it was still his decision to make—to accept her as a mate, she would have to accept him as well. All aspects of him.

He'd had enough of waiting around while she was off somewhere ignoring him. As he paced, his temper and the passion stirring to life beneath grew more fierce and more restless. And he'd had enough of minding his step with her.

It was time she knew what she was dealing with—in him and in herself.

"Rowan Murray," he muttered, and his eyes seared the air. "You'd best be ready for the likes of me."

He flung up his arms. The flash of light that snapped out simmered to a glow as he reformed on her porch.

And knew immediately she wasn't there.

He snarled, cursed, furious with himself, not only for the act that had demonstrated his need for her, but with her for not being exactly where he expected her to be.

By the goddess, he could fix that, couldn't he?

Rowan smiled as she stepped out of the trees. She could hardly wait to tell Liam she'd met his father. She imagined they would settle down in the kitchen where he would tell her stories about his family. He had such a marvelous way of telling stories. She could listen to that musical rise and fall of his voice for hours.

And now that she'd met his father, there might be a way to

ask him if she could meet other members of his family. He'd
mentioned cousins from time to time, so...

She stopped, staggered by the sudden realization. Belinda.
For heaven's sake, he'd told her that first day that he and Belinda were related. Didn't that mean Belinda was...

"Oh!" With a laugh, Rowan turned in a circle. "Life is just
astonishing."

As she said it, as her laughter rose up, the air shook. The
pad fell out of her hands for the second time that day as she
raised her hands to her throat. Earthquake? she thought with
a dim, dizzy panic.

She felt herself spin, the wind gallop. Light, bright and
blinding, flashed in front of her eyes. She tried to call out for
Liam, but the words stuck in her throat.

Then she was crushed against him, lights still whirling,
wind still rushing, as his mouth ravaged hers.

She couldn't get her breath, couldn't find a single coherent
thought. Her heart boomed in her chest, in her head, as she
struggled for both. Suddenly her feet were dangling in the air
as he yanked her off them with a strength that was both casual and terrifying.

His mouth was brutal on hers, hard and greedy, as it swallowed her gasps. He was in her mind as well, tangled in her
thoughts, ruthlessly seducing it as he ruthlessly seduced her
body. Unable to separate the two, she began to shake.

"Liam, wait—"

"Take what I give you." He dragged her head back by the
hair so that she had one terrifying glimpse of the fire in his
eyes. "Want what I am."

He savaged her throat, spurred on by each helpless whimper. And with his mind drove her violently to peak. When she
cried out, he fell with her onto the bed. Her hair tumbled free
as he liked it best, spread out around her head like a gleaming lake. Her eyes were wide, the passion that rode with the
fear turning them midnight-dark.

"Give me what I need."

When her mind whispered yes, he took it.

Heat came in floods, sensations struck like fists. All was a confused mass of wrenching feelings as he drove her beyond the civilized. He was the wolf now, she thought, as he tore at her clothes. If not in form, in temperament. Savage and wild. She heard the growl sound in his throat as he bared her breast to his mouth.

Then she heard her own scream. And it was one of glory.

No time to float or to sigh. Only to race and to moan with every nerve inside her scraped raw and sparking. Her breath heaved out of tortured lungs, her body arched and twisted, energized by every new, outrageous demand.

His hands bruised her, his teeth nipped and each separate, small pain was the darkest of pleasures.

And somewhere inside her came the answering call for more.

He yanked her up so that they knelt on the bed, torso to torso, and his hands could find more. Take more. Freed, the animal inside him devoured, and it ravaged. And still it hunted.

Hands slipped over flesh slick with sex. Mouths met like thunder. They rolled over the bed, locked and lost together. Desire had fangs, and a voice that howled like a beast.

He drove her up again, hard and fast so that she wept out his name, so that her body shuddered and her nails clawed at him. She gasped for air, felt it sear her throat, and struggled to find some steady ground.

Then he found her with his mouth.

She went wild beneath him, bucking, arching. Her head whipped from side to side as she clawed at the bedclothes, his hair, his back. With tongue and teeth he drove both of them mad, shuddering himself when the orgasm ripped through her, when her body rose up with it like a flame, then melted, slow and soft as candle wax.

"You'll come with me." He panted it out as he moved up her

body with hot, greedy kisses over still-quivering flesh. With one jerk, he lifted her hips, opened her to him.

Then plunged.

Hot, hard, fast, their bodies and minds climbed together. He buried himself deep, locking his teeth on her shoulder as he drove into her with savage thrusts. Mindlessly she locked around him, hungering for each dark and dangerous thrill. Energy pumped through her, wild and sweet, so her movements and demands were as fierce as his.

Blood called to blood and heart to heart. With one last violent stroke, with one low, feral cry, he emptied into her. And she willingly let herself come apart.

He was too appalled to speak, too stunned to move. He knew he weighed heavily on her, could feel the quick, hard trembles that shook her beneath him. Her breath sounded short and harsh in his ear and shamed him.

He'd used her without control.

Deliberately, purposefully, selfishly.

It was perfectly clear that he'd allowed himself to rationalize it for his own needs and, giving her no choice, taken her like a beast rutting in the woods.

He'd sacrificed compassion for passion, kindness for a momentary physical release.

Now he had to face the consequences: her fear of him and his own discarding of his most sacred vow.

He rolled aside, not quite ready to look at her face. He imagined it would be pale, her eyes glazed with fright.

"Rowan..." He cursed himself again. Every apology he could think of had less substance than air.

"Liam." She sighed it. When she shifted to curl against him, he pulled away abruptly, then rose to go to the window.

"Do you want water?"

"No." Her body continued to glow as she sat up. She didn't think to pull the sheets up as she usually did, but sat with them tangled around her legs. As she studied his stiff back, the glow began to fade. Doubts moved in.

"What did I do wrong?"

"What?" He glanced back. Her hair was a tangled mass of rich and gleaming brown around her shoulders, her body, so smooth and white, showed the marks of his hands, of the stubble he'd neglected to shave.

"I thought—well, but obviously I wasn't… I don't have any experience with what just happened here," she said with a faint edge to her voice. "If I did something wrong, or didn't do something you were expecting, the least you can do is tell me."

He could only stare. "Are you out of your mind?"

"I'm perfectly rational." So much so she wanted to bury her head in the pillow, pound her fists on the bed and weep. And scream. "Maybe I don't know a great deal about sex in practice, but I do know that without communication and honesty, that aspect of a relationship, as any other, is bound to fail."

"The woman's giving me a lecture," he murmured, dragging both hands through his hair. "At such a time she's giving me a lecture."

"Fine. Don't listen." Insulted, mortally wounded, she climbed out of bed. "You just stay there brooding out the window and I'll go home."

"You are home." He was nearly amused. "It's your cabin, your bedroom and your bed I just savaged you in."

"But—" Confused, and with the tattered remains of her shirt dangling from her hand, she focused. It was her bedroom, she realized. The big canopy bed stood between them, her lace curtains fluttered at the window where Liam stood, naked and irritable.

"Well then." She clutched her shirt and what was left of her dignity. "You can go."

"You've a right to be angry."

"I certainly do." And she wasn't about to stand there having a crisis without any clothes on. She marched to the armoir and dragged out a robe.

"I'll apologize, Rowan, but it seems weightless after what I did to you. You had my word I wouldn't hurt you, and I broke it."

Unsure, she turned back, lifting the robe to her breasts instead of slipping it on. "Hurt me?"

"I wanted you, and I didn't think beyond that. Deliberately didn't think beyond it. I took what I pleased and I hurt you."

It wasn't annoyance in his eyes, she realized. It was guilt. And just one more wonder. "You didn't hurt me, Liam."

"There are marks on you I put there. You've tender flesh, Rowan, and I bruised it with carelessness. That I can fix easily enough, but—"

"Wait a minute, just a minute." She held up a hand as he started forward. He stopped immediately, winced before he could prevent it.

"I don't mean to touch you but to take the bruises away."

"Just leave my bruises where they are." To give herself time to sort it out, she turned away and slipped on the robe. "You're upset because you wanted me."

"Because I wanted you enough to forget myself."

"Really?" She was smiling when she turned back, and was thrilled to see his eyes narrow in what had to be confusion. "Well, I'm delighted. No one's ever wanted me enough for that. In my life no one's ever wanted me like that. I never imagined they could. My imagination isn't that...expansive," she decided.

It was she who stepped to him. "Now I don't have to imagine, because I know."

He combed his fingers through her hair before he realized he wanted to. Needed to. "I took your thoughts after you asked me not to."

"And gave me yours. Under these particular circumstances, I'm not complaining." She cupped her elbows, refused to be shy now. "What happened just now was thrilling. It was wonderful. You made me feel desired. Outrageously desired. The only thing that would hurt me is if you're sorry for it."

She was more than he'd understood, he realized. And her needs perhaps less...delicate. "Then I'm not a bit sorry." Still, he took her hand, slid up the sleeve of her robe. "Let me take the bruises away. I don't want marks on you, Rowan. It matters to me."

He kissed her fingers, sending her heart into a long, slow flip. Then her lips, making it settle. As his lips rubbed gently on hers, she felt the cool slide of something over her skin. The tiny aches she'd hardly noticed faded away.

"Will I get used to it, do you think?"

"To what?"

"Magic."

He wound a lock of her hair around his finger. "I don't know." *You would know,* a voice murmured in his head, *if you looked.*

"I've had a very magical day." She smiled. "I was going to see you when you...changed venues. I wanted to tell you that I met your father."

The finger in her hair stilled as his eyes whipped to hers. "My father?"

"I was sketching in the woods, and there he was. Well, the owl first, but I think I realized almost at once. I've seen him before," she added. "Once as an eagle. He wears a gold pendant always around his neck."

"Aye, he does." One that Liam had to accept or refuse.

"Then he—well, changed, and we talked. He's very handsome and very kind."

More than a little uneasy, Liam turned away to dress. "What did you speak of?"

"My sketches, for the most part. He wanted one I'd done of you for your mother. I hope she likes it."

"That she will. She's partial to me."

She heard the affection in his voice and smiled. "He says she misses you—but I think he was speaking as much of himself. Actually, I thought he might come to see you." Bottom lip caught between her teeth, she glanced at the tangled sheets of the bed. "It's a good thing he didn't, ah, drop in."

"He wouldn't be slipping into your bedroom for a visit," Liam said, and relieved now, grinned wickedly. "That's for me to do."

"But you'd like to see him, just the same."

"We keep in touch," he said, and found himself both amused and charmed as she walked over to tidy the bed. Wasting your time, Rowan Murray, for I'll be having you back in it before long.

"He's proud of you, and I think he liked me. He said—I probably shouldn't tell you."

"But you will." Liam tossed back his hair, moving to her as she plumped the pillows. "You've no guile at all."

"That's not such a bad thing." She nearly sulked, but felt too happy to bother. "He said I should ask you for something."

"Did he?" With a laugh, Liam sat on the bed. "And what will you, Rowan Murray? What should I conjure for you? A sapphire to go with your eyes? Diamonds to sparkle at your feet? If you want a boon from me, you've only to ask."

He grinned, fully amused now as she caught her bottom lip between her teeth once more. Women enjoyed baubles, he thought, and began to wonder what sort he would give her.

"I'd like to meet more of your family." She blurted it out before she could change her mind.

He blinked twice. "My family?"

"Yes, well, I've met your father now, and Belinda—you said she was a relative, but I didn't know she was... Is she?"

"Aye." He said it absently, trying to realign his thoughts. "You'd rather that than diamonds?"

"What would I do with diamonds? I suppose you think it's silly, but I'd just like to see how your family...lives."

He considered, began to see the advantages and the path. "It would make it easier for you to understand the magic, the life."

"Yes, at least it seems it might. And I'm curious," she admitted. "But if you'd rather not—"

He waved off her words. "I've some cousins I haven't seen in some time."

"In Ireland?"

"No, in California." He was too involved planning to note her quickly masked disappointment.

She had a craving to see Ireland.

"We'll pay them a visit," he decided, and, rising, held out a hand.

"Now?"

"Why not now?"

"Because I..." She'd never expected him to agree or to move so quickly, and could only look down helplessly at her robe and bare feet. "Well, I need to dress, for one thing."

With a delighted laugh, he grabbed her hand. "Don't be foolish," he said, and vanished them both.

# *Chapter 10*

The next thing Rowan was absolutely sure of was standing with her arms locked like iron around Liam and her face pressed into his shoulder. Her heart was sprinting, her stomach jumping, and there was the echo of rushing wind in her head.

"Beam me up, Scotty" was the best she could manage. And it made him roar with laughter.

"This is much simpler, and more enjoyable," he decided as he nudged her face up and indulged himself in a long, mind-numbing kiss.

"It has its points." Her voice had thickened, the way it did when she was stirred. It made Liam wonder if this impulsive trip might have been put off just a little while longer. As she loosened her grip, he kept his arms snug around her waist. "Where are we?"

"My cousin Morgana's garden. She kept one of the old family homes, raises her family here."

She jerked back, looked down and with a mixture of shock and relief noted her robe had been replaced by simple slacks and a shirt the color of ripening peaches.

She lifted a hand to her hair, found it still tousled. "I don't suppose I could have a brush."

"I like your hair this way" was his answer, as he drew her back so he could sniff it. "It's easier to get my hands into it."

"Hmm." As her system began to level, she could smell the flowers. Wild roses, heliotrope, lilies. She shifted and scanned the beams of sunlight, the cool pockets of shade. Arbors buried under triumphant blooms, sweeps of color, spears of shape with little stone paths winding through, seemingly at will.

"It's beautiful. Wonderful. Oh, I wish I knew how to make something as magical as this." She drew away to turn, to take in the trees sculpted by wind into bent, eerie shapes. Then she beamed as a gray wolf walked majestically down the path toward them. "Oh, is that—"

"A wolf," Liam said, anticipating her. "Not a relative. He's Morgana's." A child with dark hair and eyes as blue as lapis darted over the stones, then stopped with a keen and curious look in those striking eyes. "And so is he. Blessed be, cousin."

Liam felt the tug on his mind, stronger than he'd have expected from a boy no more than five, and lifted a brow. "It's rude to look so deep, or attempt to, without permission."

"You're in my garden," the boy said simply, but his lips curved in a sweet smile. "You're cousin Liam."

"And you're Donovan. Blessed be, cousin." Liam stepped forward and offered a hand with great formality. "I've brought a friend. This is Rowan. And she prefers to keep her thoughts to herself."

Young Donovan Kirkland tilted his head, but minding his manners did no more than study her face. "She has good eyes. You can come in. Mama's in the kitchen."

Then the intense look faded from his face and he was just a normal little boy skipping ahead of them on the path with a dog prancing beside him, rushing to tell his mother they had company.

"He's a—he's a witch?" The full force of it struck her then.

He was a child, astonishingly pretty even with a missing front tooth, but he had power.

"Yes, of course. His father isn't, but blood runs strong in my family."

"I bet." Rowan let out a long breath. Witches or not, she thought, this was still a home and Liam hadn't bothered to, well, call ahead. "We shouldn't just...drop in like this on your cousin. She might be busy."

"We'll be welcome."

"It's just like a man to assume—" Then every thought ran out of her head as she caught her first glimpse of the house. It was tall, rambling, glinting in the sunlight. Towers and turrets speared up to that blue bowl that was the sky over Monterey. "Oh! It's like something out of a book. What a marvelous place to live."

Then the back door opened and Rowan was struck dumb with a combination of awe and pure female envy.

It was obvious where the boy got his looks. She'd never seen a more beautiful woman. Black hair cascaded over slim, strong shoulders, eyes of cobalt were heavily fringed by inky lashes. Her skin was creamy and smooth, her features fine and graceful. She stood, one hand on her son's shoulder, the other on the fierce head of the wolf, while a large white cat ribboned between her legs.

And she smiled.

"Blessed be, cousin. You're welcome here." She moved to them, kissed Liam on both cheeks. "It's so good to see you. And you, Rowan."

"I hope we're not disturbing you," Rowan began.

"Family is always welcome. Come in, we'll have something cool to drink. Donovan, run up and tell your father we have company." As she spoke, she turned and gave her son a narrow glance. "Don't be lazy now. Go upstairs and tell him properly."

With a weary shrug of his shoulders, the boy dashed back in, shouting for his father.

"Well, close enough," Morgana murmured.

"He has a strong gift of sight."

"And he'll learn to use it well." Her voice took on the edge
of an experienced and somewhat exasperated mother. "We'll
have some iced tea," she said as they went into the large, airy
kitchen. "Pan, sit."

"I don't mind him," Rowan said quickly, rubbing his ears
as he sniffed at her. "He's gorgeous."

"I suppose you'd be used to handsome wolves, wouldn't
you?" Sending Liam an amused look, she took out a clear
pitcher filled with golden tea. "It's still your favorite form,
isn't it, Liam?"

"It suits me."

"That it does." She glanced over as Donovan rushed in, side
by side with his double.

"He's coming," Donovan said. "He has to kill somebody
first."

"With a really big, sharp knife," said the twin, with relish.

"That's nice." After the absent comment, Morgana caught
the look of shock on Rowan's face and laughed. "Nash writes
screenplays," she explained. "He often murders gruesomely
on paper."

"Oh, yes." She accepted the glass of tea. "Of course."

"Can we have cookies?" the twins wanted to know in uni-
son.

"Yes. But sit down and behave." She only sighed as a tall
glass jar filled with frosted cookies soared off the counter and
landed on the table with a small crash and a wild wobble. "Allysia, you'll wait until I serve our company."

"Yes, ma'am." But she grinned mischievously as her brother
giggled.

"I'll just sit, too...if you don't mind." Her legs had gone
weak and Rowan dropped into a chair. "I'm sorry, I just can't—
I'm not really used to all this."

"You're not..." Morgana cut herself off, re-evaluating, and

offered an easy smile. "My children definitely take some getting used to."

She reached for plates and opened her mind to her cousin. *You haven't told her yet, you dolt?*

*It's my business. She's not ready.*

*Omission is kin to deceit.*

*I know what I'm doing. Serve your tea and cookies, Morgana, and let me handle this in my own way.*

*Stubborn mule.*

Liam smiled a little, remembering she'd threatened to turn him into one during some scrap during their childhood. She might have managed it, he mused. She had a great deal of power in that particular area.

"I'm Ally, who are you?"

"I'm Rowan." Steadier, she smiled at the girl. A girl, she realized, she'd initially taken for a boy because of the scrappy little body and scraped knees. "I'm a friend of your cousin."

"You wouldn't remember me." Liam walked over to take a seat at the table. "But I remember you, young Allysia, and your brother, and the night you were born. In a storm it was, here in this house, as your mother had been born in a storm in that same room. And in the hills of home there was starlight and singing to celebrate it."

"Sometimes we go to Ireland to visit Granda and Grandmama in our castle," Donovan told him. "One day I'll have a castle of my own on a high cliff by the sea."

"I hope you manage to figure out how to clean up your room first." This came from a man who stepped in with a rosy-cheeked girl tucked into each arm.

"My husband, Nash, and our daughters, Eryn and Moira. This is my cousin Liam, Nash, and his friend Rowan."

"Nice to meet you. The girls woke up from their naps smelling cookies."

He set the girls down. One toddled to the wolf who was sitting by the table hoping for crumbs. She fell adoringly on his neck. The other went directly to Rowan, crawled into her lap and kissed both of her cheeks much as her mother had kissed Liam in greeting.

Charmed, Rowan hugged her and rubbed a cheek on the soft golden hair. "Oh, you have such beautiful children."

Like, Liam thought as Moira settled cozily on Rowan's lap, often recognizes like.

"We've decided to keep them." Nash reached out to tickle the ribs of the older twins. "Until something better comes along."

"Daddy." Allysia sent him an adoring look, then nimbly snatched up her cookie before he could make the grab.

"You're quick." Nash tickled her again, and nipped the cookie out of her fingers. "But I'm smarter."

"Greedier," Morgana corrected. "Mind your cookies, Rowan, he's not to be trusted around sweets."

"What man is?" Liam stole one from Rowan's plate and had Donovan snickering. "How are Anastasia and Sebastian, their families?"

"You can judge for yourself." Morgana decided on the spot to invite her two cousins and their spouses and families over. "We'll have a family cookout tonight to welcome you—and your friend."

Magic could be confusing, and it could be casual, Rowan discovered. It could be stunning or as natural as rain. Surrounded by the Donovans, flooded by the scents from Morgana's garden, she began to believe there could be little in this world that was more natural or more normal.

Morgana's husband, Nash, her cousin Sebastian and Anastasia's husband, Boone, bickered over the proper way to fire the grill. Ana sat comfortably in a wicker chair nursing her infant son while her three toddlers raced around the yard with the other children and the dogs, all to the clashing sympathy of laughter, shouts and wild barks.

At ease, Morgana nibbled on canapés and talked lazily with Sebastian's wife, Mel—about children, work, men, the weather, all the usual sorts of subjects friends and family speak of on summer afternoons.

Rowan thought Liam held himself a bit aloof, and wondered why. But when Ana's little sunshine-haired daughter held up her arms to him, she saw him smile, pluck her up and fit her with casual skill on his hip.

She watched with some surprise as he walked with her and apparently listened with great interest as she babbled on to him.

He likes children, she realized, and the inner flutter of longing nearly made her sigh.

This was a home, she thought. Whatever power lived here, it was a home where children laughed and squabbled, where they tumbled and whined just like children everywhere. And men argued and talked of sports, women sat and spoke of babies.

And they were all so striking, she mused. Physically stunning. Morgana with her dazzling dark beauty, Anastasia so delicate and lovely, Mel sharp and sexy, her long body made only more compelling with its belly swollen with child.

Then the men. Just look at them, she thought. Gorgeous. Nash was dashing, golden, movie-star handsome; Sebastian as romantic as a storybook prince with just an edge of wicked. And Boone tall and rugged.

And Liam, of course. Always Liam, dark and brooding with those wonderful flashes of amusement that glinted in his gold eyes.

Could she have stopped herself from falling in love with him? she wondered. No, not in a million years, not with all the power in heaven and earth in her hands.

"Ladies." Sebastian strolled over. Though he smiled at Rowan there was an intense look in his eyes that had her nerves dancing lightly. "The men require beer in order to accomplish such manly work."

Mel snorted. "Then you should be man enough to get it out of the cooler yourself."

"It's so much more fun being served." He stroked a hand over the slope of her belly. "She's restless," he murmured. "Do you want to lie down?"

"We're fine." She patted his hand. "Don't hover."

But when he leaned down, murmured something soft in her ear, her smile turned into a quiet glow. "Get your beer, Donovan, and go play with your little friends."

"You know how excited I get when you insult me." He nipped her ear, making her laugh, before he plucked four bottles from the cooler and strolled off.

"The man gets mushy around babies," Mel commented, shifting herself so that she could reach the platter of finger food. "When Aiden was born, Sebastian walked around as if he'd accomplished the whole deal by himself."

She watched their son wrap his arms around Sebastian's leg, then observed her elegant husband's limping, playful progress back to the men with Aiden in tow.

"He's a wonderful father." Ana lifted the heavy-eyed baby to her shoulder, gently rubbed his back. She smiled when her stepdaughter hurried over, glossy brown hair bouncing.

"Can I hold him now? I'll walk him until he's asleep, then put him in the daybed in the shade. Please, Mama, I'll be careful."

"I know you will, Jessie. Here, take your brother."

Rowan watched, studying the girl of ten. Since she was Ana's stepdaughter and Boone wasn't...then neither was Jessie. Yet the girl didn't appear to feel out of place among her cousins. In fact, Rowan had seen her speak with the sharp impatience an older child often had for a younger one when Donovan had beaned her with a rubber ball.

"Would you like some wine, Rowan?" Without waiting for an answer, Morgana poured delicate straw-colored liquid into a glass.

"Thanks. It's so nice of you to have us here, to go to all this trouble without a bit of notice."

"It's our pleasure. Liam so rarely visits." Her eyes were warm and friendly as they met Rowan's. "Now why don't you tell us how you managed to get him here?"

"I just asked to meet some of his family."

"Just asked." Morgana exchanged a meaningful look with Ana. "Isn't that...interesting?"

"I hope you'll stay for a few days." Ana gave her cousin a warning pinch under the table. "I've kept my old house next door to where we live for family and friends when they visit. You're welcome to stay there."

"Thank you, but I didn't bring anything with me." She glanced down at the trim cotton blouse and slacks, reminding herself she'd left Oregon in nothing but a robe and popped into Monterey neatly outfitted. "I suppose that doesn't matter, does it?"

"You'll get used to it." Mel laughed and bit into a carrot stick. "Mostly."

Rowan wasn't sure about that, but she did know she was comfortable here, with these people. Sipping her wine, she glanced over to where Liam stood with Sebastian. It was so nice for him, she thought, to have family to talk with, who understood and supported him.

"You're a moron," Sebastian said coolly.

"It's my business."

"So you always say." Tipping back his beer, Sebastian eyed his cousin out of amused gray eyes. "You don't change, Liam."

"Why should I?" He knew it was a childish response, but Sebastian often made him feel defensive and annoyed.

"What are you trying to accomplish? What do you need to prove? She's meant for you."

A chilly line he refused to recognize as fear snaked up Liam's spine. "It's still my decision."

Sebastian would have laughed, but he caught the flicker of unease in Liam's eyes, felt the shimmer of it in his mind. "More fool you," he murmured, but with some sympathy. "And if you feel that way, cousin, why haven't you told her?"

"I told her who I am." Liam spoke evenly, determined not to sound defensive. "Shown her. She nearly fainted." He remembered that moment, and the fury, the guilt, he'd felt. "She's been raised not to believe."

"But she does believe. What she is has always been there. Until you tell her, she has no choice. And isn't choice your most prized possession?"

Liam studied Sebastian's smug smile with the active dislike only family could feel. When they'd been boys, Liam had competed ruthlessly against his older cousin, determined to be as fast, as clever, as smart. Under that competitive streak had been a secret layer of hero worship.

Even now, as a grown man, he wanted Sebastian's respect.

"When she's ready, she'll have the choice. And she'll make it."

"When *you're* ready," Sebastian corrected. "Is it arrogance, Liam, or fear?"

"It's sense," Liam shot back, and fought not to let his teeth go on edge. "She's barely had time to absorb what I've told her already, much less to fully understand. Her own heritage is buried so deep there's hardly a glimmer of it in her mind. She's just begun to discover herself as a woman, how can I ask her to accept her gifts?"

*Or me.* But he didn't say that, infuriated himself that he would even think it.

He's in love with her, Sebastian realized as Liam turned to scowl down at the beach. In love and too hardheaded to admit it. For a second time, a smile trembled on his lips, with laughter just beneath. So the mighty fall, he mused, fighting all the way.

"It may be, Liam, you don't give the woman enough credit."

He glanced back to where Rowan sat with his wife at the table. "She's lovely."

"She sees herself as plain, as simple. As ordinary. She's none of those things." Liam didn't look around. He could see her in his mind's eye clearly enough if he chose. "But she is tender. I may end up asking her for a great deal more than she's prepared to give."

Lovesick, Sebastian thought, though not without sympathy. He'd been similarly afflicted when he'd met Mel. And had very likely made similar stupid mistakes because of it.

"Living with you's more than any woman could be prepared for." He grinned when Liam turned his head and shot him a look with those hard gold eyes. "I pity her at the thought of seeing that ugly, scowling face of yours day after day."

Liam's smile was sharp as a blade. "And how does your wife tolerate yours, cousin?"

"She's crazy about me."

"She strikes me as a smart woman."

"Her mind's like a dagger," Sebastian said, with a grinning glance at his wife.

"So how much time did it take you to weave the spell into her mind for that?"

This time Sebastian did laugh and, in a quick move grabbed Liam in a snug headlock. "A much shorter time than it'll take you to make your pretty lady believe you're a prize to look at."

"Kiss my—" He could only curse, struggle against laughter, as Sebastian kissed him full on the mouth. "I'll have to kill you for that," he began, then lifted a brow as little Aiden dashed over to throw his arms around his father's legs. "Later," Liam decided, and plucked the child up himself.

It was late when Liam left Rowan sleeping in the house Ana kept by the sea. He was restless, unsettled, and baffled by the ache around his heart that refused to ease.

He thought of running along the water, or flying over it. Racing until he was settled again.

And he thought of Rowan, sweetly sleeping in the quiet house.

He walked through the shadows and scents of Ana's garden, searching for peace of mind. He stepped through the hedge of fairy roses, crossed the lawn and stepped up on the deck of the house where Ana lived with her family.

He'd known she was there.

"You should be asleep."

Ana simply held out a hand. "I thought you'd want to talk."

But, taking her hand, he sat beside her and contented himself with silence. He knew of no one more comfortable to sit with, to be with, than Anastasia.

Overhead the moon winked in and out of clouds, the stars glimmered. The house where Rowan slept was dark and full of dreams.

"I didn't know how much I missed you, all of you, until I saw you again."

Ana gave his hand a supportive squeeze. "You needed to be alone for a while."

"Aye. It wasn't because you didn't matter that I blocked you all out for a time." He touched her hair. "It was because you did."

"I know that, Liam." She brushed her fingers over his cheek, felt his conflict in her own heart. "Your mind's so troubled." Her quiet gray eyes looked into his, her lips curved gently. "Must you always think so hard?"

"It's the only way I know." Still, he felt the strain ease as he sat with her, sliding away knot by knot. That was Ana's gift. "You've a lovely family, Ana, and have made a lovely home here. Your mate is your match. Your children your joy. I can see how happy you are."

"Just as I can see how unhappy you are. Isn't a family and a home what you want, Liam? What would make you happy?"

He studied their linked fingers, knowing he could and would say things to her he wouldn't to another. "I might not be good at it."

Ah, she realized, of course. Liam's standards for himself were always higher than anyone else's could be. "What makes you think that?"

"I'm used to thinking for and of myself. Used to doing as I please. And I like it." He lifted his gaze to hers, smiled. "I'm a selfish man, and fate's asking me to take the responsibility my father's borne so well, to take a woman who'll understand only pieces of what that means."

"You're not giving either of you credit for who you are." There was impatience in her voice now, all the more effective as it was so rare. "You've been stubborn, and you've been proud, but you've never been selfish, Liam. What you are is too bloody serious about too many things. And so you too often miss the joy of them." She sighed, shook her head. "And Rowan can and will understand a great deal more than you seem to think."

"I like going my own way."

"And your own way led you straight to her, didn't it?" This time Ana laughed. He looked so irritated that logic had turned back and nipped him. "Do you know one of the things I've always admired most about you? Your instinct to question and pick apart everything. It's a fascinating and annoying trait. And you do it because you care so much. You'd rather not, but you care."

"What would you do, Ana, if you were standing where I am?"

"Oh, that's easy for me." Her smoky eyes were soft, her smile gentle. "I'd listen to my heart. I always do. You'll do the same when you're ready."

"Not everyone's heart speaks as clearly as yours." Restless again, he drummed his fingers against the bench. "I've shown her who I am, but I haven't told her what that might mean to her. I've made her my lover, but I haven't given her love. I've shown her my family without telling her about her own. So yes, it troubles me."

"You can change it. It's in your hands."

He nodded, stared into the night. "I'm taking her back in the morning, when she wakes. And I'll show her what's sleeping inside her. As for the rest, I don't know yet."

"Don't only show her the obligations, Liam, the duties. Show her the joys, too." She rose, keeping her hand in his. "The baby's stirring. He'll be hungry. I'll make your good-byes in the morning if you like."

"I'd appreciate it." He got to his feet, gathered her close. "Blessed be, cousin."

"Don't stay away so long." She kissed his cheeks before she drew away, and at the door paused, looked back. He stood in a shower of moonlight. Alone. "Love waits," she murmured.

It waited, Liam thought when he slipped into bed beside Rowan. Here, in dreams. Would it wait in the morning, when he awakened her to all she was?

Like the princess in the fairy tale, he thought, stirred to life by a kiss. The fact that he was, in his way, a prince made him smile humorlessly into the dark.

Fate, he supposed, enjoyed its ironies.

Those thoughts, and others, kept him awake and waiting for dawn. At first light he slipped a hand over hers, linked fingers and took them back to Rowan's own bed.

She murmured, shifted, then settled again. Rising, he dressed, studying her as she slept. Then he went quietly downstairs to make very strong coffee.

He thought both of them would need it.

With his mind tuned to hers, he knew the moment she stirred. He stepped outside, carrying his coffee. She would come to him, questioning.

Upstairs, Rowan blinked in puzzlement. Had she dreamed

it all? It didn't seem possible when she could remember every-thing so clearly. The aching blue sky of Monterey, the bright music of children's laughter. The warmth of welcome.

It had to be real.

Then she let out a weak chuckle, resting her brow on her updrawn knees. Nothing had to be real, not anymore.

She rose, and prepared to experience yet another magi-cal day.

# Chapter 11

When she saw him standing on the porch, it struck her all
over again. The wild thrill, the rush of love, the wonder. That
this stunning, extraordinary man should want her left her
speechless with delight.

Moving on pure emotion, she rushed through the door to
throw her arms around him, press her cheek against that strong
back.

It staggered him, those sweet, fresh feelings that poured out
of her so freely, the quick rise of his own that tangled with
them. He wanted to whirl around, to sweep her up and away
to someplace where there was no one and nothing to think
of but her.

Instead, he laid his free hand over hers lightly.

"You brought us back before I had a chance to say goodbye to your family."

"You'll see them again…if you like."

"I would. I'd love to see Morgana's shop. It sounds wonderful. And Sebastian and Mel's horses. I loved meeting all
of your cousins." She rubbed her cheek over his shirt. "You're

so lucky to have such a big family. I have some cousins on my father's side, but they live back east. I haven't seen them since I was a child."

His eyes narrowed. Could there have been a more perfect opening for what he meant to tell her? "Go inside and get your coffee, Rowan. I need to talk to you."

Her mood teetered as she loosened her grip, stepped back. She'd been so sure he'd turn and hold her. Instead, he hadn't even looked at her, and his tone was cool.

What had she done wrong? she asked herself as she went inside to stare blindly at the line of cheerfully colored mugs. Had she said something? Not said something? Had she—

She squeezed her eyes shut, disgusted with herself. Why did she do that? she demanded. Why did she always, always assume she'd done something? Or lacked something?

Well, she wasn't going to do that anymore. Not with Liam. Not with anyone. A little grim, she got a mug and poured hot, black coffee to the rim.

When she turned, he was inside watching her. Ignoring the sudden dread in her stomach, she struggled to keep her voice impassive. "What do you want to talk to me about?"

"Sit down."

"I'm fine standing." She pushed at her tumbled hair, sipped coffee hot enough to scorch her tongue. "If you're angry with me, tell me. I don't like having to guess."

"I'm not angry with you. Why should I be?"

"I have no idea." To keep herself busy, she took out a loaf of bread to make toast she imagined would stick in her throat. "Why else would you be scowling at me?"

"I'm not scowling."

She glanced back at his face, sniffed in derision. "You certainly are, and I don't care for it."

His eyebrow shot up. Her mood had certainly shifted from soft and cuddly to cold and snappy quickly. "Well, I beg your pardon then." In an irritable move, he yanked out a chair, straddled it.

Get on with it, he ordered himself.

"I took you to meet my family, and it's family I want to speak of. I'd prefer it if you'd sit the bloody hell down instead of prowling about the room."

Her shoulders wanted to hitch up in defense at the angry tone and she forced them to stay straight. "I'm making break-fast, if you don't mind."

He muttered something, then flung out his hands. A plate of lightly browned toast appeared on the counter. "There. Though how you can call that breakfast is beyond me. Now sit down with it."

"I'm perfectly capable of making my own." But she carried the plate to the table before deliberately going to the refrigerator and taking her own sweet time choosing jam.

"Rowan, you're trying my patience. I'm only asking you to sit down and talk to me."

"Asking is exactly what you didn't do, but now that you have, I will." Surprised at just how smug she felt over that small victory, she came back to the table and sat down. "Do you want some toast?"

"No, I don't." And hearing the snap in his voice, sighed. "Thank you."

She smiled at him with such sudden, such open sweetness, his heart stumbled. "I hardly ever win arguments," she told him as she spread jam on the toast. "Especially when I don't know what the argument's about."

"Well, you won that one, didn't you?"

Her eyes danced as she bit into the toast. "I like winning."

He had to laugh. "So do I." He laid a hand on her wrist as she lifted her mug. "You didn't add your cream and all that sugar. You know you don't like your coffee black."

"Only because I make lousy coffee. Yours is good. You said you wanted to talk about your family."

"About family." He moved his hand so he was no longer touching her. "You understand what runs through mine."

"Yes." He was watching her so closely, his eyes so focused on hers, she had to fight the urge to squirm. "Your gift. The Donovan Legacy." She smiled. "That's what you named your company."

"Aye, that's right. Because I'm proud of where I come from. Power has obligations, responsibilities. It's not a toy, but it's not something to fear."

"I'm not afraid of you, Liam, if that's what worries you."

"Maybe, in part."

"I'm not, I couldn't be." She wanted to reach out to him, to tell him she loved him, but he pushed back from the table and began to prowl about the room just as he'd asked her not to.

"You're seeing it as a storybook. Magic and romance and happy-ever-after. But it's just life, Rowan, with all its messes and mistakes. Its needs and demands. Life," he repeated, turning back to her, "that has to be lived."

"You're only half right," she told him. "I can't help but see it as magical, as romantic, but I understand the rest. How could I not understand after meeting your cousins, seeing their families? That's what I met yesterday, a family. Not a picture in a book."

"And you were...comfortable with them?"

"Very much." Her heart began to trip in her throat. It mattered to him, she could see it. Mattered that she accepted his family, and him. Because...was it possible it was because he loved her, too? That he wanted her to be part of his life?

Joy spurted through her in one long liquid gush.

"Rowan." He came back to sit, so that she hid her trembling hands under the table. "My cousins are many. Here, in Ireland. In Wales, Cornwall. Some are Donovans, some Malones, some Rileys. And some are O'Mearas."

Her heart had bounded into her head to spin dreamily. "Yes, you said your mother was an O'Meara. We might even be distant relatives. Wouldn't that be nice? Then in some convoluted way I might be connected to Morgana and the rest."

He bit back a sigh, then, reaching for her hands, he took them firmly in his and leaned closer. "Rowan, I didn't say we might be cousins, but that we *are* cousins. Distant, it's true, but we share blood. A legacy."

Puzzled by the sudden intensity she frowned at him. "I suppose we might be. Tenth cousins or something, however many times removed. I'm not entirely clear how that works. It's interesting, but..."

This time her heart seemed to stop. "What do you mean?" she said slowly. "We share a legacy?"

"Your great-grandmother, Rowan O'Meara, was a witch. As I am. As you are."

"That's absurd." She started to jerk her hands free, but he held them fast. "That's absurd, Liam. I didn't even know her, and you certainly didn't."

"I know of her." He spoke calmly now. "Of Rowan O'Meara from Clare, who fell in love and married, and left her homeland, and abjured her gifts. She did this because the man she loved asked it of her. She did this freely, as was her right. And when she birthed her children, she said nothing of their heritage until they were grown."

"You're thinking of someone else" was all she could say.

"So they thought her eccentric, and perhaps a bit fey, but they didn't believe. When they birthed children of their own, they only said Rowan O'Meara was odd. Kind and loving, but odd. And when the daughter of her daughter birthed a daughter, that child was raised not knowing what ran in her blood."

"A person would have to know. How could you not know?" This time he released her hands so she could pull back, spring to her feet. "You'd feel it. You'd sense it."

"And haven't you?" He got to his feet as well, wishing he'd found a way to tell her without frightening her. "Haven't you felt it, from time to time? Felt that stirring, that burn in the blood, wondered at it?"

"No." That was a lie, she thought and backed away. "I don't know. But you're wrong, Liam. I'm just ordinary."

"You saw pictures in the flames, dreamed your dreams as a child. Felt the tingle of power under your skin, in your mind."

"Imagination," she insisted. "Children have wonderful ones." But she felt a tingle now, and part of it was fear.

"You said you weren't afraid of me." He said it softly, as he might to a deer startled in the woods. "Why would you be afraid of yourself?"

"I'm not afraid. I just know it's not true."

"Then you'd be willing to test it, to see which of us is right?"

"Test what? How?"

"The first skill learned and the last to leave is the making of fire. What's inside you already knows how it's done. I'll just remind you." He stepped to her, taking her hand before she could evade. "And you have my word that I won't do it myself, just as I want your word that you won't block what comes."

It seemed even her soul was trembling now. "I don't have to block anything because there isn't anything."

"Then come with me."

"Where?" she demanded as he pulled her outside. But she already knew.

"The dance," he said simply. "You won't have control just yet, and it's protected."

"Liam, this is ridiculous. I'm just a normal woman, and in order to make a fire I need kindling and a match."

He paused just long enough to glare at her. "You think I'm lying to you?"

"I think you're mistaken." She had to scramble to keep up with his ground-eating strides. "There probably was a Rowan O'Meara who was a witch. There probably was, Liam, but she wasn't my great-grandmother. My great-grandmother was a sweet, slightly dotty old woman who painted beautifully and told fairy stories."

"Dotty?" The insult of that brought him up short. "Who told you that?"

"My mother...that is..."

"So." He nodded as if she'd just confirmed everything he'd said. "Dotty," he muttered as he began to stride along again. "The woman gives up everything for love and they call her dotty. Aye, maybe she was at that. She'd have been better off staying in Ireland and mating with one of her own."

Then he wouldn't be stalking down this path with Rowan's trembling hand in his, he thought.

He wasn't entirely sure if he was pleased or annoyed with that particular twist of fate.

When he reached the stone circle, he pulled her directly to the center. She was out of breath, from the quick walk and from what she could feel swimming in the air.

"The circle's cast and so it begins. I ask that all be safe within. This woman comes that she may see. As I will, so mote it be."

As the chant ended, the wind swept through the stones, wrapped like a warm caress around Rowan's body. Startled, she crossed her arms over her breasts, gripped her own shoulders. "Liam—"

"You should be calm, but that will be hard for you. Nothing here will harm you, Rowan, I swear to you." He laid his hands over hers and kissed her, gently but deeply, until the stiffness of her body softened. "If you won't trust yourself, trust me."

"I do trust you, but this—I'm afraid of this."

He stroked a hand down her hair, and realized that in many ways what he was doing was like initiating a virgin to love. It should be done sweetly, patiently, and with thoughts only on her.

"Think of it as a game." He smiled at her as he stepped back. "A more basic one than you imagine just now." He drew her down to her knees. "Breathe deep and slow until you hear your heartbeat in your head. Close your eyes if it helps, until you're steady."

"You tell me I'm going to make fire out of nothing, and then ask me to be steady." But she closed her eyes. The sooner she could prove to him he was mistaken, the sooner it would be over.

"A game," she said on the first long breath. "All right, just a game, and when you see I'm no good at it, we'll go home and finish breakfast."

*Remember what you weren't told, but knew.* Liam's voice was a quiet murmur inside her mind. *Feel what you always felt but never understood. Listen to your heart. Trust your blood.*

"Open your eyes, Rowan."

She wondered if this was like being hypnotized. To be so fully, almost painfully aware, yet to be somehow outside yourself. She opened her eyes, looked into his as sunlight streamed between them. "I don't know what to do."

"Don't you?" There was the faintest lilt of amusement in his voice now. "Open yourself, Rowan. Believe in yourself, accept the gift that's been waiting for you."

A game, she thought again. Just a game. In it she was a hereditary witch, with power sleeping just under the surface. Waking it was only a matter of believing, of wanting, of accepting.

She stretched out her hands, stared at them as if they belonged to someone else who watched them tremble lightly. They were narrow hands, with long slender fingers. Ringless, strangely elegant. They cast twin shadows on the ground.

She heard her own heartbeat, just as he'd told her. And she heard the slow, deep sound of her own breathing, as if she were awake listening to herself sleep.

Fire, she thought. For light, for heat. For comfort. She could see it in her mind, pale gold flames just touched with deep red at the edges. Glowing low and simmering, rising up like torches to the sky. Smokeless and beautiful.

Fire, she thought again, for heat, for light. Fire that burns both day and night.

Dizzy, she swayed a little. Liam had to fight every instinct to keep from reaching out to her.

Then her head fell back, her eyes went violently blue. The air hushed. Waited. He watched as she lost a kind of innocence.

Power whipped through her like the wind that suddenly rose to send her hair flying. The sudden heat of it made her gasp, made her shudder. Then it streaked like a rocket down her arms, seemed to shoot from her fingers into a pool of light.

She saw with dazzled eyes, the fire she'd made.

It sizzled on the ground, tiny dancing flames of gold edged with red. The heat of it warmed her knees, then her hands as she hesitantly stretched them over it. As she drew them back, the flames shot high.

"Oh. Oh, no!"

"Ease back, Rowan. You need a bit of control yet."

He brought the thin column of fire down as she stared and stuttered.

"How did I— How could I—" She snapped her gaze to his. "You."

"You know it wasn't me. It's your heritage, Rowan, and your choice whether you accept it or not."

"It came from me." She closed her eyes, inhaling, exhaling slowly until she could do so without her breath shuddering out. "It came from me," she repeated, and looked at him. She couldn't deny it now, what some part of her knew. Perhaps had always known.

"I felt it, I saw it. There were words in my head, like a chant. I don't know what to think, or what to do."

"What do you feel?"

"Amazed." She let out a dazed laugh and stared at her own hands. "Thrilled. Terrified and delighted and wonderful.

There's magic in me." It shimmered in her eyes, glowed on her face. This time her laugh was full and free as she sprang up to turn circles inside the ring of stones.

Grinning widely, Liam sat with his legs crossed and watched her embrace self-discovery. It made her beautiful, he realized. This sense of sheer joy gave her a rich and textured beauty.

"All my life I've been average. Pathetically ordinary, tediously normal." She spun another circle then collapsed on the ground beside him to throw her arms around his neck. "Now there's magic in me."

"There always was."

She felt like a child with hundreds and hundreds of brightly wrapped presents waiting to be opened and explored. "You can teach me more."

"Aye." Understanding something of what was racing through her, he flicked a finger down her cheek. "I can. I will. But not just now. We've been here more than an hour, and I want my breakfast."

"An hour." She blinked as he rose and hauled her to her feet. "It seems like just a few minutes."

"It took you a while to get down to things. It won't take you so long the next time." With a thought, he put out the fire. "We'll see if we can find where your talents lie once I've had my meal."

"Liam." She turned into him for a moment, pressed her lips to his throat. "Thank you."

She learned fast. Liam had never considered himself a good teacher, but he supposed it had something to do with the student.

This one was open and eager and quick.

It didn't take long to determine that her talents channeled into magic, as Morgana's did. Within a day or two, they determined she had no real gift for seeing. She could give him her thoughts, but could only read his clearly if he put them into her head.

And while she couldn't, even after more than an hour of sweaty concentration, transform herself, she turned a footstool into a rosebush with laughing delight.

Show her the joy, Ana had told him. But he understood that she was showing *him* as she danced around the clearing, turning the early-summer flowers into a maze of color and shape. Rocks became jewel-colored crystals, infant blooms exploded into huge fireworks of brilliant hues. The little stream rose into an elegant waterfall of luminous blue.

He didn't rein her in. She deserved to ride on the wonder of it. Responsibilities, choices, he knew, would come soon enough.

She was creating her own fairy tale. It was so easy all at once to see it perfectly in her mind. And, in seeing it, to make it real. Here was her little cottage in the forest, with the stunning witch garden spread out, the sweep of water rising, the whip of the wind blowing free.

And the man.

She turned, unaware how devastating she looked just then with her hair streaming, glossy and wild, her arms flung out and the light of young power in her eyes.

"Just for today. I know it can't stay like this, but just for today. I used to dream of being in a place just like this, with water and wind rushing, and flowers so huge and bright they dazzled your eyes. And the scent of them..."

She trailed off, realizing she had dreamed of this, exactly this. And of him, of Liam Donovan stepping off the porch of a pretty cottage and moving to her, walking under an arbor of flowers that rained pretty pink petals onto the ground.

He would pluck a rose, white as a snowflake, from a bush as tall as he. And offer it to her.

"I dreamed," she said again. "When I was a little girl."

He plucked a rose, white as a snowflake from a bush as

tall as he. And offered it to her. "What did you dream, Rowan Murray?"

"Of this." Of you. So often of you.

"Just for today, you can have your dream."

She sighed as she traced the rose down her cheek. Just for today, she thought, would be enough. "I was wearing a long blue dress. A robe, really. And yours was black, with gold edgings." She laughed, enchanted, as she felt the thin silk caress her skin. "Did I do that, or did you?"

"Does it matter? It's your dream, Rowan, but I'm hoping I kissed you in it."

"Yes." She sighed again as she moved into his arms. "The kind of kiss dreams are made on."

He touched his lips to hers, softly at first. Warming them, softening them, until they parted on a quiet breath. Then deeper, slowly deeper, while her arms came up to circle him, while her fingers slipped lazily into his hair.

As he did, something trembled in his memory, as well. Something once seen or once wished for. When he gave himself to it, he began to float in dreams with her. And so drew her closer.

Together they circled, a graceful dance with hearts keeping the beat.

Her feet no longer touched the ground as they spun. The dreams of a romantic young girl shimmered and shaped into the needs of a woman. Warmth skimmed over her skin as she held him tighter, drew him into her heart. As she offered him more. Offered him everything.

There were candles in her dream. Dozens of them, fragrant and white and burning in tall silver stands with gilded leaves winding around them. And a bed, lit by them, draped in white and gold.

When he carried her to it, she was dizzy with love, washed in wonder.

"How could I have known?" She drew him down to her. "How could I have forgotten?"

He wondered the same of himself, but couldn't question it now, not now when she was so soft, so giving, when her lips were parting for his and her sigh of pleasure slipped into him like wine from a golden cup.

The sun dipped down behind the trees, edging them with fire, shooting color into the deepening sky. In the trees, the birds sang to those last lights.

"You're beautiful."

She wouldn't have believed it. But here, now, she felt beautiful. She felt powerful. She felt loved. Just for today, she thought, and met his mouth with hers.

He drank from her, with thirst but without greed. Held her close but without desperation. Here, they both knew, time could spin out. Time could be taken.

Tongues met and tangled in a slow, intimate dance. Breath mixed. Murmurs melded.

She stroked her hands along the silk of his robe, then beneath to flesh. So warm. So smooth. His mouth on her throat, urging her to tip her head to give him more, and the light nip of teeth where her pulse beat. The erratic bump of it tempted him to slick his tongue over her skin, to fill himself with the flavor that was only her.

He parted her robe, lightly as air. When his hands, his mouth took possession of her, she arched gently.

Enjoy me, she seemed to say. Enchant me.

She sighed with him, moved with him, while the air swam with scent and the warm, soft wind caressed her naked skin. Sensations glimmered, tangled with delights both bright and dark. Lost in them, steeped in them, she rolled with him, rose languidly over him.

Her body was wand slim, white as marble in the delicate light. Her hair was lifted by the wind, her eyes full of secrets.

Captivated, he ran his hands up her thighs, over her hips, her torso, closed them over her breasts.

And there her heart beat in the same hammer blows as his own.

"Rowan," he murmured, as those secrets, as that power glinted in her eyes. "You are all manner of witch."

Her laugh was quick and triumphant. She leaned down, took his mouth hungrily with hers. Heat, sudden and brutal, slammed into him, leaped into his blood like the fire she'd made only hours before.

She felt it, too, the quick change, and that she had made it. That, she thought wildly, that was power. Riding on it, she took him into her, bowing back to revel in the shock of it, watching stars wheel in the black sky overhead.

His hands gripped her hips, his breath exploded from his lungs. Instinctively he struggled for control, but his already slippery grasp broke as she took him.

She took. Her hips moved like lightning, her body soared with a wild whip of energy that pushed him, raced ahead, dragged him with her.

She rocked herself to madness, then beyond, and still she drove him on. He said her name. She heard the sound break from him as his body plunged with hers. And she saw as they flew up, how his eyes flashed, then went dark and blind.

She all but wept with triumph as she grabbed hold and fell over with him.

He'd never allowed a woman to take control. Now, as Rowan lay sprawled over him, he realized he hadn't been able to stop it. Not with her. There were a great many things he hadn't been able to stop with her.

He turned his face into her hair and wondered what would come next. Only seconds later, when she spoke, he knew.

"I love you, Liam." She said it quietly, with her lips over his heart. "I love you."

He called the panic that sprang up inside him sense, responsibility. "Rowan—"

"You don't have to love me back. I just can't stand not telling you anymore. I was afraid to tell you before." She shifted, looked at him. "I don't think I'll be afraid of anything ever again. So I love you, Liam."

He sat up beside her. "You don't know all there is to know, so you can't know what you think or what you feel. Or what you'll want," he added on a huff of breath. "I have things to explain, things to show you. We'll do better at my cabin."

"All right." She made her smile easy, even as a dread filled her heart that the magic of that day was over.

# Chapter 12

What else could he tell her that would shock or surprise? Rowan asked herself. He'd told her he was a witch, then proved it and somehow made her accept it. He'd wiped out twenty-seven years of her simple beliefs about herself by telling her she was a witch as well. Had proved it. She had not only accepted it, but had embraced it.

How much more could there be?

She wished he would speak. But he said nothing as they walked through moonlight from her cabin to his. She'd known him long enough to understand that when he fell into this kind of silence he would tell her nothing until he was ready.

By the time they reached his cabin and stepped inside, her nerves were strung tight.

What she didn't think about, refused to consider, was the fact that he'd withdrawn into that silence after she'd told him she loved him.

"Is it so serious?" She tried for a light tone, but the words came out uneven, and very close to a plea.

"For me, yes. You'll decide what it means to you."

He moved into the bedroom and, running his fingers over the wall beside the fireplace, opened a door she hadn't known was there into a room she'd have sworn didn't exist.

A soft light glowed from it, as pale and cool as the moonlight.

"A secret room?"

"Not secret," he corrected. "Private. Come in, Rowan."

It was a measure of her trust in him that she stepped forward into that light. The floor was stone, smooth as a mirror, the walls and ceiling of wood, highly polished. Light and the shadow she cast reflected back off those surfaces and shimmered like water.

There was a table, richly carved and inlaid, and on it a bowl of thick blue glass, a stemmed cup of pewter, a small mirror with a silver back ornately scrolled and a slim, smooth handle of amethyst. Another bowl held small, colorful crystals. A round globe of smoky quartz stood on the silver backs of a trio of winged dragons.

What did he see when he looked into it? she wondered. What would she see?

But she turned and watched Liam light candles, watched their flames rise into air already perfumed with fragrant smoke.

She saw another table then, a small round surface on a simple pedestal. Liam opened the box resting there, took out a silver amulet on a chain. He held it a moment, as if testing its weight, then set it down with a quiet jingle of metal on wood.

"Is this...a ceremony?"

He glanced over, those tawny eyes distracted as if he'd forgotten she was there. But he hadn't forgotten her. He'd forgotten nothing.

"No. You've had a lot to deal with, haven't you, Rowan? You've asked me not to touch your thoughts, so I can't know what's in your mind, how you're thinking of all this."

He hadn't meant to touch her, but found his fingers grazing her cheek. "A lot of it I can read in your eyes."

"I've told you what I think and what I feel."

"So you have."

*But you haven't told me,* she thought, and because it hurt her, she turned away. "Will you explain to me what everything is for?" she asked, and traced a fingertip over the scrolling on the little mirror.

"Tools. Just pretty tools," he told her. "You'll need some of your own."

"Do you see things in the glass?"

"Aye."

"Are you ever afraid to look?" She smiled a little and looked back at him. "I think I might be."

"What's seen is...possibility."

She wandered, avoiding him. There was change coming. Whether it was her woman's instincts or her newly discovered gifts that told her, she was sure of it. In a glass case were more stones, stunning clusters with spears rising, smooth towers, jewel-tone globes.

He waited her out, not with patience but because for once he didn't know how to begin. When she turned back to him, her hands linked nervously, her eyes full of doubts, he had no choice but to choose.

"I knew you were coming here."

He didn't mean here, to this room, tonight. He saw her acknowledge this. "Did you know...what would happen?"

"Possibilities. There are always choices. We each made ours, and have more to make yet. You know something of your heritage and of mine, but not all. In my country, in my family, there is a tradition. It's simplest, I suppose, to compare it to rank, though it's not precisely that. But one takes a place as head of the family. To guide, and counsel. To help in settling disputes should they arise."

Once again he picked up the silver amulet, once again he set it down.

"Your father wears one of those in gold."

"Aye, he does."

"Because he's head of the family?"

She was quick, Liam thought. Foolish of him to have forgotten that. "He is, until he chooses to pass on the duty."

"To you."

"It's traditional for the amulet to be passed down to the oldest child. But there are choices, on both sides, and there are... stipulations. To inherit, one must be worthy of it."

"Of course you are."

"One must want it."

Her smile faded into a look of puzzlement. "Don't you?"

"I haven't decided." He slipped his hands into his pockets before he could pick up the amulet again. "I came here to take time, to think and consider. It must be my choice. I won't be bullied by fate."

The regal tone of his voice made her smile again. "No, you wouldn't be. That's another reason you'd be good at it." She started to go to him, but he held up a hand.

"There are other requirements. If there is marriage, it must be to a mate with elfin blood, and the marriage must be for love, not for duty. Both must enter into it freely."

"That seems only right," she began, then stopped. As Liam had said, she was quick. "I have elfin blood, and I've just told you I'm in love with you."

"And if I take you, my choices diminish."

This time it took her a moment. It had been said so coolly it was like an iced sword to the heart. "Your choices. I see." She nodded slowly while inside she fought to save the scattered pieces of her heart, the pitiful tatters of her pride. "And your choices include accepting this aspect of your heritage or abjuring it. You'd take that very, very seriously, wouldn't you, Liam?"

"How could I not?"

"And I'm more or less like a weight for the scale. You just have to decide which bowl to set me in. How...awkward for you."

"It's not as simple as that," he shot back, knocked off balance by her sudden sharp tones. "It's my life."

"And mine," she added. "You said you knew I was coming here, but I didn't know about you. So I had no choice there. I fell in love with you the minute I saw you, but you were prepared and you had your own agenda. You *knew* I would love you."

It was hurled at him, a bitter accusation that had him staring at her. "You're mistaken."

"Oh, really? How many times did you slip into my mind to see? Or come into my house as a wolf and listen to me babble? Without giving me the choice you're so damn fond of. You knew I met the requirements, so you studied and measured and considered."

"I didn't know!" He shouted it at her, furious to have his actions tilted toward deceit. "I didn't know until you told me about your great-grandmother."

"I see. So up to that point you were either playing with me or deciding if you could use me as your out should you decide to refuse your position."

"That's ridiculous."

"Then suddenly you've got a witch on your hands. You wanted her—I don't doubt you wanted me, and I was pathetically easy. I took whatever you chose to give me, and was grateful."

It humiliated her to think of it now, to remember how she had rushed into his arms, trusting her heart. Trusting him.

"I cared for you, Rowan. I care for you."

Her cheeks were ghost pale in the flickering light, her eyes dark and deep. "Do you know how insulting that is? Do you know how humiliating it is to understand that you knew I was in love with you while you figured the angles and made your choices? What choice did I have, what choice did you give me?"

"All I could."

She shook her head fiercely. "No, all you *would*," she tossed back. "You knew exactly how vulnerable I was when I came here, how lost."

"I did, yes. That's why I—"

"So you offer me a chance to work with you," she interrupted. "Knowing I was already dazzled by you, knowing how desperately I needed something. Then, in your own good time, you told me who you were, who I was. At your pace, Liam, always at your pace. And each time I moved exactly as you expected I would. It's all been just another game."

"That's not true." Incensed, he took her arms. "I thought of you, too damn much of you. And did what I thought was right, what was best."

The jolt shot through his fingertips, up his arms, with such heat and power, it knocked him back a full two steps. This time he could only gape at her, shocked to the core that she'd caught him so completely unaware.

"Damn it, Rowan." His hands still stung from the slap of her will.

"I won't be bullied, either." Her knees were jellied at the realization she'd had not only the ability but the fury to shove him back with her mind. "This isn't what you expected, this isn't one of your possibilities. I was supposed to come in here with you tonight, listen to you, then fold my hands, bow my head like the quiet little mouse I am, and leave it all up to you."

Her eyes were vividly blue, her face was no longer pale but flushed with anger and, to his annoyance was outrageously beautiful. "Not precisely," he said with dignity. "But it is up to me."

"The hell it is. You have to decide what you want, true enough, but don't expect me to sit meekly while you choose or discard me. Always, always, people have made decisions for me, chosen the way my life should go. What have you done but the same?"

"I'm not your parents," he shot back. "Or your Alan. These were different circumstances entirely."

"Whatever the circumstances, you held the controls and guided me along. I won't tolerate that. I've been ordinary." The words ripped out of her, straight from the belly. "You wouldn't understand that, you've never been ordinary. But I have, all my life. I won't be ordinary again."

"Rowan." He would try calm, he told himself. He would try reason. "All I wanted for you was what you wanted for yourself."

"And what I wanted most, was for you to love me. Just me, Liam, whatever and however I am. I didn't let myself expect it, but I wanted it. My mistake was in still not thinking enough of myself."

Tears shone in her eyes now, unmanning him. "Don't weep. Rowan, I never meant to hurt you." He took her hand now, and she let it lie limply in his.

"No, I'm sure you didn't," she said quietly. The force of her fury had passed. Now she was only tired. "That only makes it sadder. And me more pathetic. I told you I loved you." Tears still trembled on the edge of her voice. "And you know I do. But you can't tell me, you can't decide if it…suits you."

She swallowed the tears, reached deep for the pride she'd used too rarely. "From here, I decide my own fate." She drew her hand from him, stood back. "And you yours."

She turned to the door, bringing him a fresh and baffling wave of panic. "Where are you going?"

"Where I please." She glanced back. "I was your lover, Liam, but never your partner. I won't settle for that, not even for you." She let out a quiet breath, studying him in the shifting light. "You had my heart in your hands," she murmured. "And you didn't know what to do with it. I can tell you, without the crystal ball, without the gift, you'll never have another like it."

As she slipped away from him, he knew it was not only prophecy, it was truth.

It took her a week to deal with the practicalities. San Francisco hadn't changed in the months she'd been gone, nor in the days she'd been back. But she had.

She could look out her window now, at the city, and realize it hadn't been the place that had dissatisfied her, but her place in it. It was doubtful she'd ever live there again, but she thought she could look back and find memories—good and bad. Life was made up of both.

"Are you sure you're doing the right thing, Rowan?" Belinda asked. She was a graceful woman, with dark hair, short as a pixie's, and eyes of misty green.

Rowan glanced up from her packing and looked into Belinda's concerned face. "No, but I'm doing it just the same."

Rowan had changed, Belinda mused. She was certainly stronger, more than a little wounded. Guilt nagged at her. "I feel some responsibility in this."

"No." Rowan said it firmly, and smoothed a sweater into her suitcase. "You're not responsible."

Restless, Belinda wandered to the window. The bedroom was nearly empty now. She knew Rowan had given many of her things away, stored others. In the morning, she would be gone. "I sent you there."

"No, I asked if I could use your cabin."

Belinda turned. "There were things I could have told you."

"You weren't meant to—I understand that, Belinda."

"If I'd known Liam would be such a jackass, I—" She broke off, scowled. "I should have, I've known him all my life. A more stubborn, thickheaded, irritating man has yet to be born." Then she sighed. "But he's kind with it, and most of his stubbornness comes from caring so much."

"You don't have to explain him to me. If he'd trusted me, believed in me, things might be different." She took the last of her clothes from the closet, laid them on the bed. "If he'd loved me, everything would be different."

"Are you so sure he doesn't?"

"I've decided the only thing I can be sure of is myself. It was the hardest and most valuable thing I learned while I was away. Do you want this blouse? It never flattered me."

"It's more my color than yours." Belinda wandered over, laid a hand on Rowan's shoulder. "Did you speak with your parents?"

"Yes. Well, I tried." Thoughtfully Rowan folded trousers, packed them. "On one level it went better than I ever expected. They were upset at first, and baffled, that I'm going away, that I'm giving up teaching. Naturally, they tried to point out the flaws, the consequences."

"Naturally," Belinda repeated, just dryly enough to make Rowan smile.

"They can't help it. But we talked a long time. You know, I don't think we've actually talked like that before. I explained why I was going, what I wanted to do and why—well not all the why."

"You didn't ask your mother about what you are?"

"In the end, I couldn't. I mentioned my grandmother, and legacies, and how being named after her had turned out to be so...appropriate. My mother waved it off. No," Rowan corrected with a sigh, "closed it off. It's as if she'd blocked it off—if she ever even really knew or suspected. What runs through my blood, and even through her own, simply doesn't exist in her world."

"So you left it at that?"

"Why should I push her on something that makes her uncomfortable or unhappy?" Rowan lifted her hands. "I'm content with it, so that's enough. If I'd insisted on stripping away whatever barrier she'd put up, what purpose would it serve?"

"None. You did the right thing, for yourself and your mother."

"What matters is, in the end, my parents understood as much as they're able about the decisions I've made. Because in the end all they want is for me to be happy."

"They love you."

"Yes, maybe more than I ever gave them credit for." And she smiled. "It helps some that Alan's been seeing someone else—a math instructor. My mother finally broke down and told me she's had them over for dinner and they're charming together."

"We'll wish them well."

"I wish them very well. He's a nice man and deserves to be happy."

"So do you."

"Yes, you're right." Giving it one last look, Rowan closed the last suitcase. "I intend to be. I'm excited, Belinda, nervous but excited. Going to Ireland like this. One-way ticket." She pressed a hand to her uneasy stomach. "Not knowing if I'll stay or where I'll go or what I'll do. It's thrilling."

"You'll go first to Castle Donovan in Clare? See Morgan's and Sebastian's and Ana's parents?"

"Yes. I appreciate you contacting them, and their asking me to stay."

"You'll enjoy them, and they you."

"I hope so. And I want to learn more." Rowan stared into the middle distance. "I very much want to learn."

"Then you will. Oh, I'll miss you. Cousin." With this, Belinda caught Rowan in a hard embrace. "I have to go, before I start blubbering. Call me," she ordered, scooping up the blouse as she hurried out of the room. "Write, whistle in the wind, but keep in touch."

"I will." Rowan walked her to the door of the empty apartment, exchanged one last fierce hug. "Wish me luck."

"That and more. Blessed be, Rowan." Already sniffling, she dashed out.

Weepy herself, Rowan closed the door, turned and looked. There was nothing left here, she thought. Nothing left to do. She'd be moving on in the morning. Moving in a way she'd never imagined. She had family in Ireland, and roots. It was time to explore them, and in doing so, to explore herself.

What she'd already learned gave her the foundation to build more.

And if she thought of Liam, if she pined for him, so be it. She could live with heartache, but she couldn't—wouldn't—live with distrust.

The knock on the door surprised her, then she smiled. Belinda, she imagined, not quite ready to say goodbye.

But the woman at the door was a stranger. Beautiful, elegant in a simple dress of mossy green. "Hello, Rowan, I hope I'm not disturbing you."

The voice, that lilt of Irish hills. The eyes, warm, deep gold. "No, not at all. Please come in, Mrs. Donovan."

"I wasn't sure I'd be welcome." She stepped inside, smiled. "Since my son's made such a fool of himself."

"I'm glad to meet you. I'm sorry—I can't even offer you a chair."

"You're leaving, then. Well, I'll give you this as a going-away present." She held out a box of carved apple wood. "And as a thank-you for the drawing of Liam. They're chalks, the pastels you wanted."

"Thank you." Rowan took the box, grateful to have something to do with her hands. "I'm surprised you'd want to see me since Liam and I...since we argued."

"Ah." The woman waved a hand in dismissal and wandered the room. "I've argued with him enough myself to know it's impossible not to. He's a head like a brick. But his heart isn't hard."

When Rowan looked away, she sighed. "I don't mean to make you uncomfortable."

"It's all right." Rowan carried the box to the narrow counter that separated the living area from the kitchen. "He's your son and you love him."

"I do, very much. Flaws and all." She laid a gentle hand on Rowan's arm. "He's hurt you, and I'm sorry for it. Oh, I could box his ears for it," she snapped in a lightning change of mood that had Rowan smiling uncertainly.

"Have you ever?"

"Boxed his ears?" This time Arianna laughed, light and free. "Oh, with Liam what choice do you have? He was never an easy one. Girl, the stories I could tell you would curl your hair. Takes after his father, he does, and can go royal on you in a blink. Now Finn would say it's my temper running through him, and he'd be right. But if a woman doesn't have spine and temper, men like that will march right over you."

She paused, studying Rowan's face and her own eyes filled abruptly with tears. "Oh, you love him still. I didn't want to look and offend you. But I can see it."

"It doesn't matter."

But before she could turn away, Arianna gripped her hands, gave them an impatient squeeze. "Love is all that matters, and you're smart enough to know it. I've come to you as a mother only, with no more than a mother's right, and a mother's heart. He suffers, Rowan."

"Mrs. Donovan—"

"Arianna. It's your decision to make, but you need to know. He's hurt as well, and missing you."

"He doesn't love me."

"If he didn't he wouldn't have made so many foolish mistakes. I know his heart, Rowan." She said it softly and with such simple faith, Rowan felt a flutter in her stomach. "It's yours if you'll have it. I don't say it because I want him to step into his father's place. Whoever he loved would have been welcome with joy. Don't turn your back on your own happiness just to hug your pride. One's cold without the other."

"You're asking me to go to him."

"I'm asking you to listen to your heart. Nothing more or less."

Rowan crossed her arms over her breasts, rubbed her own shoulders as she paced the bare room. "I still love him. I always will. Maybe part of me recognized him in that first instant. And my heart just fell at his feet."

"And he didn't treasure it as he should have, because he was afraid of it."

"He didn't trust me."

"No, Rowan, he didn't trust himself."

"If he loves me..." Even the thought of it weakened her, so she shook her head, turned back with her eyes level, her hands steady. "He'll have to say it. And he'll have to accept me on equal grounds. I'll take nothing less."

Arianna's smile was slow, and it was sweet. "Oh, you'll do, Rowan Murray, for yourself and for him. Will you go back and see?"

"Yes." She let out the breath she hadn't known she was holding. "Will you help me?"


The wolf raced through the woods, as if trying to outrun the night. The thin crescent of the moon offered little light, but his eyes were keen.

His heart was burdened.

He rarely sought sleep now, for the dreams would come no matter how he willed them away. They were always of her.

When he reached the cliffs, he threw back his head and called out for his mate. Even as the sound swept away the silence, he grieved for what he'd so carelessly lost.

He tried to blame her, and did. Often. Whatever form he took, his mind worked coolly, finding dozens of ways, small and large, to shift the burden to her.

She'd been too impulsive, too rash. She'd twisted his motives, his logic. Deliberately. She'd refused to see the clear-cut sense in everything he'd done.

But tonight that line of thinking did nothing to ease his heart. He turned away from the cliffs, outraged that he couldn't stop yearning for her. When the voice whispered, *Love waits* in his head, he snarled viciously and blocked it out.

He prowled the shadows. He sniffed the air, snarled again. It was Rowan he scented, some trick of the mind, he thought, infuriated with his own weakness. She'd left him, and that was the end of it.

Then he saw the light, a gold glimmer through the trees. Tawny eyes narrowed as he moved toward the circle of stones. He stepped through them, saw her standing in the center. And went very still.

She wore a long dress the color of moondust that foamed around her ankles. Her hair was loose, flowing over her shoulders, with hints of silver shining in it from the jewels wound through. There was silver at her wrists, as well, at her ears.

And on the bodice of her dress lay a pendant, an oval of moonstone in a setting of hammered silver.

She stood slim and straight behind the fire she'd made. Then she smiled at him.

"Waiting for me to scratch your ears, Liam?" She caught the quick flash of temper in his eyes, and only continued to smile.

The wolf stepped forward, became a man. "You left without a word."

"I thought we had plenty of words."

"Now you've come back."

"So it seems." She arched a brow with a studied coolness even as her stomach jumped with raw nerves. "You're wearing your amulet. So you've decided."

"Aye. I'll take my duty when it comes. And you wear yours."

"My great-grandmother's legacy to me." Rowan closed her

fingers around the stone, felt it calm her nerves. "I've accepted it, and myself."

His hands burned to touch her. He kept them lightly fisted at his sides. "I'll be going back to Ireland."

"Really?" She said it lightly, as if it meant nothing to her. "I'm planning on leaving for Ireland myself in the morning. That's why I thought I should come back and finish this."

"Ireland?" His brows drew together. Who was this woman? was all he could think, so cool, so self-possessed.

"I want to see where I came from. It's a small country," she said with a careless shrug, "but large enough for us to stay out of each other's way. If that's what you want."

"I want you back." The words were out before he could stop them. He hissed out a curse, jammed his fisted hands into his pockets. So he'd said it, he thought, humbled himself with the words and the needs. And the hell with it. "I want you back," he repeated.

"For what?"

"For—" She baffled him. He dragged his hands free to rake them through his hair. "For what do you think? I'll take my place in the family, and I want you with me."

"It's hardly that simple."

He started to speak, something ill-advised and much too heated, he realized, and pulled himself back. Control might be shaky—*In the name of Finn, just look at her*—but it was still there. "All right, I hurt you. I'm sorry for it. It was never my intention, and I apologize."

"Well then, you're sorry. Let me just jump into your arms."

He blinked, deeply shocked at the biting tone. "What do you want me to say? I made a mistake—more than one. I don't like admitting it."

"You'll have to, straight out. You took your time deciding if I'd suit you—and your purposes. Once you decided what those purposes would be. When you didn't know about my bloodline, you considered if you should take me and get out of the duty you weren't sure you wanted. And when you did know, then it was a matter of deciding if I'd suit you if you did accept it."

"It wasn't that black-and-white." He let out a breath, admitting that sometimes the gray areas didn't matter. "But yes, more or less. It would have been a big step either way."

"For me, as well," she tossed back, eyes firing. "But how much did you consider that?"

She whirled away, and had him rushing after her before he'd realized he'd moved. "Don't go."

She hadn't intended to, just to pace off her temper, but the quick desperation in the two words had her turning slowly.

"For pity's sake, Rowan, don't leave me again. Do you know what it was for me to come for you that morning and see you were gone? Just gone." He turned away, scrubbing his hands over his face as he struggled with the pain. "The house empty of you, and still full of you. I was going to go after you, right then and there, drag you back where I wanted you. Where I needed you."

"But you didn't."

"No." He turned to face her. "Because you were right. All the choices had been mine. This was yours and I had to live with it. I'm asking you now not to leave me again, not to make me live with it. You matter to me."

Everything inside her cried out to go to him. Instead she lifted her brows again. "Matter to you? Those are small words for such a big request."

"I care for you."

"I care for the puppy the little girl next door has. I'm not content with that from you. So if that's all—"

"I love you. Damn it, you know very well I love you." He snatched her hand to keep her from leaving. Both the gesture and the tone were anything but loverlike.

Somehow she kept her voice steady. "We've established I

don't have the gift to see, so how do I know very well what you don't tell me?"

"I am telling you. Damn it, woman, can't you hear, either?" His control slipped enough to have sparks snapping in the air around them. "It's been you, all along, right from the start of it. I told myself I didn't—that I wouldn't until I decided. I made myself believe it, but there was no one ever but you."

The thrill of it—the words, the passion behind them driven by as much anger as heart—spun through her like rainbows. Even as she started to speak, he released her hand to prowl the circle much as the wolf he favored.

"And I don't like it." He flung the words over his shoulder at her. "I'm not required to like it."

"No." She wondered why she should feel delighted rather than insulted. And it came to her that it gave her an unexpected, and desperately sweet power over him. "No, you're not. Neither am I."

He whirled back, glaring at her. "I was content in my life as it was."

"No, you weren't." The answer surprised both of them. "You were restless, dissatisfied and just a little bored. And so was I."

"You were unhappy. And the way you're thinking now, it's that I should have taken advantage of that. Plucked you up straight away, told you things you couldn't have been prepared to hear and carried you off to Ireland. Well, I didn't and I won't be sorry for that much. I couldn't. You think I deceived you, and maybe I did."

He shrugged now, a regal motion that made her lips want to curve into a smile. "You needed time, and so did I. When I came to you as a wolf it was to comfort. It was as a friend. And so I saw you naked—and enjoyed it. Why shouldn't I?"

"Why indeed?" she murmured.

"When I loved you in dreams, we both enjoyed it."

Since that was issued as a challenge, she merely inclined

her head. "I don't think I ever said otherwise. But still, that choice was yours."

"Aye, it was, and I'd make it again if only to touch you with my mind. It's not easy for me to admit that I want you as I do. To tell you that I've suffered being without you. Or to ask you to forgive me for doing what I thought was right."

"You've yet to tell me what it is you expect from me now."

"I've been clear enough on it." Frustration shimmered around him. "Do you want me to beg?"

"Yes," she said after a very cool, very thoughtful moment.

His eyes went bright gold with shock, then dark with what she thought was temper. When he started toward her, her knees began to tremble. Then, eyes narrowed, he was down on his.

"Then I will." He took her hands that had gone numb. "I'll beg for you, Rowan, if that's what it takes to have you."

"Liam—"

"If I'm to humble myself, at least let me get on with it," he snapped. "I don't think you were ordinary ever. Weak is something I don't believe you could be. What I see in you is a woman with a tender heart—too tender at times to think of herself. You're the woman I want. I've wanted before, but I've never needed. I need you. You're who I care for. I've cared before, but never loved. I love you. I'm asking that it be enough for you, Rowan."

She'd been struck speechless, but found her voice as she laid a hand on his shoulder. "Why did you never ask before?"

"Asking's not easy for me. If it's arrogance, that's how I am. Damn it, I'm asking you to take me as I am. You love me. I know you do."

So much for begging, she thought, and had to fight back a smile. He managed to look arrogant and not a little fierce even on his knees. "I never said I didn't. Are you asking me for more?"

"For everything. I'm asking you to take me on—what I am and what I'll do. To be my wife, leave your home for mine and understand that it's forever. Forever, Rowan." The faintest of smiles touched his mouth. "For wolves mate for life, and so do I. I'm asking you to share that life, to let me share yours. I'm asking you here, in the heart of this sacred place, to belong to me."

He pressed his lips to her hands, held them there until she felt his words turn to feelings and the feelings rush through her like magic.

"I'll have no other but you," he murmured. "You said to me that I held your heart in my hands, and that I'd never have another like it. I'm telling you now you have mine in yours, and I swear to you, Rowan, you'll never have another like it. No one will ever love you more. The choice is yours."

She studied him, the way his face lifted to hers, how the light from the fire he'd taught her to make danced over it. She didn't need his thoughts to see now. All she wanted was there, in his eyes.

She made her choice, and lowered to her knees so their eyes were on level. "I'll take you on, Liam, as you'll take me. And I'll take nothing less than forever. I'll share the life we make together. I'll belong to you, as you belong to me. That's my choice, and my promise."

Swamped with emotion, he lowered his brow to hers. "God, I missed you. Every hour of every day. There's no magic without you. No heart in it."

He found her mouth with his, pulling her close, swaying as the force of feeling rocked him. She wrapped her arms around him, gave him every answer to every question.

"I could drown in you." He rose to his feet, lifting her high, and her laughter rang out pure and bright as she threw her arms up.

Starlight dazzled her eyes. She watched one shoot across the sky as he spun with her. A trail of gold, a shower of silver. "Tell me again!" she demanded. "Tell me now. Right now!"

"I love you. Now..." He lowered her until their mouths met again. "And ever."

She held him close, heartbeat to heartbeat. "Liam of Donovan." Leaning back, she smiled at him. Her prince, her witch. Her mate. "Will you grant me a boon?"

"Rowan of O'Meara, you have only to ask what you will."

"Take me to Ireland. Take me home."

Pleasure swirled into his eyes. "Now, *a ghra?*" My love.

"In the morning." She drew him back to her. "It's soon enough."

And when they kissed with the firelight glowing, the stars shimmering, the fairies danced in the forest. In the hills far away, pipes played in celebration, and songs of joy were sung.

Love no longer waited, but found its mark.

\* \* \* \* \*

# BRAND NEW RELEASE

Don't miss the next instalment of the Powder River series by bestselling author B.J. Daniels! For lovers of sexy Western heroes, small-town settings and suspense with your romance.

## RIVER WILD

—R—
**A POWDER RIVER NOVEL**

**PERFECT FOR FANS OF YELLOWSTONE!**

In-store and online January 2025

## Previous titles in the Powder River series

September 2023     January 2024     August 2024

# Subscribe and fall in love with a Mills & Boon series today!

You'll be among the first to read stories delivered to your door monthly and enjoy great savings.

WE SIMPLY LOVE ROMANCE